THE LION IN GLORY

THE LION IN GLORY

SHANNON DRAKE

ZEBRA BOOKS
KENSINGTON PUBLISHING CORP.

ZEBRA BOOKS are published by

Kensington Publishing Corp.
850 Third Avenue
New York, NY 10022

ISBN: 0-7394-3115-3

PROLOGUE

The king is dead.
Long live the king!
And thus it had been for centuries.

On July 11, 1307, having determined in his fury that he would take to his horse himself and lead his troops against the wayward Robert Bruce of Scotland, Edward I expired. And despite the ravages of age that had begun to tear at the mighty monarch, a very great king, indeed, had died. Known as Longshanks, Edward I had been the epitome of the image of royalty: tall, a warrior king, a gleaming Plantagenet, a man who had earned respect and admiration through his strength and prowess, and the determination of his will. Wise, wily, and cunning, brutal to his enemies, a man who had brought England to law and power, he had reigned long and given England a position of prominence in Europe that could not be disputed by any man.

The king is dead.

His people mourned.

His enemies rejoiced.

Long live the king.

The father was not the son, though he was his father's namesake.

Edward II began his rule by ignoring his father's deathbed request that his bones be carried with the vanguard marching against the Scots, and that they be carried into the war with the Scots until those unruly barbarians were brought to heel, completely subjugated, ready to bow to their overlord, the English monarch. Edward the father was delivered into Waltham Abbey to await a more regal burial, and the new king immediately called his favorite back to his side, a man greatly disliked by his nobles, Piers Gaveston. He rode against the Scots, but at his own pace. He rode to the borders of Ayrshire, and then retreated for want of supplies, never striking a single blow against the Scots.

Whereas England had just lost one of her mightiest monarchs ever, to be replaced by a frivolous mind with personal pleasures of a far greater import than the power of his realm, Scotland had been nurturing a very different man.

Upon claiming the throne of Scotland, Robert Bruce had fought for the right to be recognized as king. He had been reduced to running through the forests of Scotland with no more than a few men, while many of the great barons of the land remained against him, and he would have forever as an enemy the family of John Comyn, the Red, dead due to the king, whether it had been Robert Bruce to strike the fatal blow, or whether the deed had been done by his followers. But in his desperate days, he learned. He had known the nobility and peerage of his land, and that of England. In his early days of penury and desperation, he learned the mettle of the common man of Scotland, and he grew in the wisdom of his most simple folk.

There were lessons to be had in those days which he would never forget. Power did not always come with strength of arms; it was in the hearts and souls of his countrymen, and it was for a glory greater than gold, power, property or prestige that they would fight. It was for the more elusive glories of freedom and nationality. He proved himself before his people, risking his own life, waging his own mighty battles—as the old English king had once done—and with each passing day, became the warrior king so desperately needed by a country too long forced to her knees. The price he paid for his crown was heavy: family members executed, his wife and child taken by the English to be held through many long years.

Despite the cruelties done to him and the strengths that he had gained, he remained throughout his days of hardship and beyond an exceptionally merciful man for his day. He gained his power slowly. Step by step. And just as he quickly decided on a path of benevolence, so, as well, he never forgot those who supported him, especially in the early days, and in time, those who rode by his side throughout were richly rewarded.

The Scottish king had another policy. Well aware that even with a weak leader now at the head of the great English force, the power of the English far outweighed his own. He made it a point never to engage in a pitched battle with the English. The Scotsmen, accustomed to a fight in which they must constantly attack and disappear, were experts at strike and run assaults. They knew their land as no others could— the forests, waterways, valleys, mountains and hills.

The death of Edward I bought the Scots something they dearly needed.

Time.

And time became the greatest ally of Robert Bruce. At the death of the great Plantagenet king, he was still the leader of little more than outlaw bands. His first order of business was to subdue the great barons of Scotland who stood against him. He proved not only his courage, but that he was a brilliant strategist, capable of using any weapon at hand, be that weapon tact and diplomacy, or an onslaught of arms. In a matter of years, he had begun to rally his kingdom around him.

Edward II, reputed to be large and as fine in appearance as his family name would warrant, was busily engaged in keeping his dear companion, Piers Gaveston, at his side—and keeping those who heartily resented Gaveston at bay. Matters came to a head and Gaveston was banished to Ireland.

At this time, Edward called for an army to invade Scotland. He came with all the fantastic trappings of war with which his father had ridden. He trampled the lowlands, and planned to wage battle for the heart of the country.

But Bruce would not bring his army for a pitched battle. He watched the English—and then swept down upon the northern counties of his enemies.

Edward II did nothing to support his desperate barons. And so it was that the English lords of those northern counties turned to a desperate measure—they sent forth envoys to pay the Scottish king to leave them in peace. And thus began a period in which Robert Bruce, so lately no more than an outlaw king with a forest bed, began to turn the tide against his enemies.

Matters in England deteriorated further, for Edward's great barons were determined that the king would sign the Articles of Ordinance laid before him, and he would not do so when the banishment of Piers Gaveston remained among them. So desperate was Edward that he offered a peace and truce to Robert Bruce, but the Scottish king, aware that Edward lied to and deceived his own barons in his crusade to save his companion, turned down the request. Edward's country was torn in two as an army of his own Englishmen rose against him. Gaveston, who had returned secretly to England, was captured and executed.

Bitterness, and a great divide took place in England.

Robert Bruce used it to his great advantage, once again invading the enemy. His knights rode forth with great relish, for it had been their lands continually ravaged in the years gone by, their livestock destroyed, their homes reduced to earth. Still, only those in direct resistance to the Bruce and his men were slain, and English lands were looted with a minimum of bloodshed and slaughter.

The king of France, whose daughter had been wed to Edward II in 1308, stepped in to try to make peace within his son-in-law's realm. And thus, though the breach continued, Edward II began to regain the power of his station.

With little help to his people. He failed to give the support needed, and furiously berated his people who paid tribute to the Scots. He listened to men of poor judgment who stood with him in his fury against the murderers of Piers Gaveston.

Edward II was bitter and angry. Without his father's wisdom, he was reclaiming his place as the leader of his father's people, for after all, he was the rightful king.

He had not given up his claim over Scotland.

Robert Bruce was determined to be the king of a free and sovereign nation.

In the borderlands, life became hell and not only for those who had been trampled and laid low for many years.

New lands, previously untouched by the ravages of invading armies, now lay vulnerable to a king who had learned the lessons of leadership through dire hardships of his own, now coolly proficient in the art of a war of plunder.

Yet now, it was not the Scots who paid so dearly in the yearslong struggle for power and freedom.

It was the English of the region who suddenly found themselves living in deadly peril.

Robert Bruce was known as the lion of Scotland.

And the lion was beginning to come into his glory.

CHAPTER 1

"They're coming, my lady!"

Despite the many preparations they had made, Christina felt a chill sweep through her, and for a moment, she felt as if she had been frozen in a sheet of winter ice, paralyzed at the mere prospect of action.

But she couldn't freeze, and she couldn't fail, and she knew it. Their course of action had been discussed at length, debated and argued, and she and the men of Hamstead Heath had agreed on what they must do.

So many things were at stake, she reminded herself.

And so she replied with a cool and calm control, no matter how her heart was racing. "Ralph has seen them?" she asked Sir Alfred Cheney, the white-bearded bearer of the news.

"Aye, down at the stream in the forest."

"How many?"

"Forty . . . fifty, perhaps."

"Well armed and armored?"

"Glittering in the sun."

She nodded. "Still, with so small a party, they expect compliance. And, of course, it will appear that we will give it. See that everyone is warned."

Sir Alfred nodded gravely, but then paused. "Perhaps we should just pay the tribute."

"It is too late to change a course of action now. We don't have the amount demanded. The matter has been decided, and we would never get the word out, and far too many would die if we were suddenly to falter from within. And . . . well, we know what may well happen to Steven."

"Many have paid the tribute; the king cannot punish all of the north of his country."

"The king hasn't been fed lies about the whole of the north of his country—only about Steven," Christina reminded him. Not long ago, the King of England had been in no position to bear such a hatred toward one of his subjects. But that was before civil war raged in England, before the king himself had torn up half of Yorkshire—and before his favorite, Piers Gaveston, had been captured by the Earl of Pembroke, then seized by the Earl of Warwick, and then beheaded by order of the Earl of Lancaster.

Since then, the King of France had stepped in, desperately trying to bring about a peace between his son-in-law and his great barons. As yet, no true apologies or pardons had been given. And the king bitterly longed to punish those he could easily reach. No matter what peace was being attempted, the king hadn't forgotten, and he hadn't forgiven.

And it was his belief that Lord Steven Steel of Hamstead Heath had been aligned with his enemies. The great upheaval that had come at that time had abated, and the king was gaining power again, held in check only so far by his ministers. It was far easier to claim a man guilty of treason than to find a different revenge for his part in the death of Gaveston.

"Steven is in grave danger," she said. "We can't do anything to further that danger."

Her last reminder touched Sir Alfred deeply, and he straightened his aging shoulders. "Then we take aim against the devil," he said, and turned, ready to walk out of the once grand manor of Hamstead Heath. There, he would ride to the low stone wall that dated back to the Romans, and welcome the heathens who had come to collect from the village for the privilege of living.

But still, just when he reached the door, he hesitated. "You are certain? You'll see that all is handled in the kitchen?"

"Personally," Christina assured him.

"You will be the one at great risk. If Steven knew—"

"But he does not know, and when he does, it will be because we have demanded his release in exchange for the men we will present to the king."

Sir Alfred turned without another word. As he went out, Lauren came rushing into the hall. "My God! It's time. They're coming!"

"All is in readiness."

But Lauren paused, studying Christina, and shaking her head. "That is the best gown you have? We will look like paupers."

"Unless Steven is freed and collects the payments due us, we *are* paupers."

"Yes, but we are to greet them, feast with them, impress them with the affluence of the manor, and our ability to pay their tribute as long as they leave us be. You must be completely serene. Haughty, as well, knowing exactly who you are . . . My gown. You'll have to wear my gown."

"The one you had made for your wedding? No."

Lauren stared at the wall. "How sad . . . the nicest piece we have left is the tapestry. It's a pity we can't put you in it . . . Never mind. The wedding gown must do."

"I will not wear your wedding gown."

"I will not have a wedding if we are not successful," Lauren said.

She was right.

"Place the gown on my bed. I must hurry to the kitchen. They are here already, Lauren, riding down upon us."

Lauren froze for a moment. "Christina . . . we could take the coins from beneath the kitchen floor."

"They're not enough. And even if the place were ever leveled, or burned to the ground, they would be there . . . to be found. Should one of us, or Steven, ever need them . . ."

"They could be a payment in part—"

"Lauren! We can't make the payment that they want, no matter what. Please . . . get the gown, put it on my bed. And take care yourself. Whatever should come, they mustn't know who you are."

Lauren immediately turned to do as she was bidden. Christina sped for the kitchen. Plans had been laid, instructions given, but they must be repeated once again, because there was no room for chance or error.

None at all.

They came in glory. Riders on the wind. Armed, and bearing the colors of the king, and of the clans who had fought so to set him upon his throne.

As they had now ridden for several years. Not that true freedom had been completely won, but Robert Bruce's hold on Scotland was now far greater than that held by Edward II of England.

And the neighboring northern lands of England had

learned the fear that the lowlands of Scotland had endured for so many years.

But even in the worst of the vengeance visited upon the English, years ago, when Sir William Wallace, fresh from his victory at Stirling Bridge, had invaded England, Hamstead Heath had not been attacked. There was no fine castle here, just the manor. And in those days, it had been a cruel revenge that the Scots had visited upon the English.

Now, they did not come for revenge, but in the name of a strangely humane and wily man who was proving to be a careful king.

Hamstead Heath was not a walled town or a fortress, just a manor in the center of a thriving village. It did not offer a military stronghold, caches of arms, or the jewels of an immensely affluent noble. But then again, the house was a fine enough manor, and, in its way, the village offered riches aplenty, even if they weren't the gold and silver and precious gems so usually sought.

Hamstead Heath raised some of the finest and fastest horses in all England. Her cattle and sheep were renowned. The wool produced here was comparable to the best in Scotland or Flanders.

"Remember the king's command!" Jamie shouted. Then he let his hand fall.

His men, only forty-eight in all, let out a battle cry brought from the Highlands, and started down the hill in a gallop.

Though their numbers were not great, their cry, along with the heavy thunder of their approach, was meant to strike terror into the hearts of the enemy.

Jamie expected no resistance and, as he rode, feeling the powerful beat of his horse's hooves beneath him, seeing the well-armed and armored knights of his own command glisten in the sun as they rode with menacing purpose, he allowed himself a moment's elation.

The tide had turned.

And it was good.

For far too many years they had been outlaws in the forests, when they had been dangerously outnumbered, when they had starved, when even kinsmen might be enemies. But the years of tenacious struggle were now proving their merit. Though the English still held lands and castles in Scotland, the Scots steadily gained ground.

Edward II of England was no man to match his father. And now, it was the English who shivered at the approach of the Scots.

And must pay tribute.

Robert Bruce, warrior king that he might be, had never acquired a taste for senseless blood and senseless slaughter. Yet the wages of gaining a kingdom were high, and he had learned to improve his kingdom with his slowly gained might.

Dirt spat up from the ground beneath the thunderous gait of his black steed, and the air was cool, crisp, and fresh. On the rolling hills, sheep grazed and bleated and gave awkward flight. Cows, on a distant hill, gave little notice.

They rode down upon the farmstead manor and scattered houses of a small village known as Hamstead Heath.

In the years since Robert Bruce had claimed the crown and proclaimed the sovereignty of Scotland, they had gone from being a pathetic band of outlaws in the forest to the law of the land. *All* of the land, nearly. Though Edward II still claimed his right as overlord, his armies had failed against the Bruce. And bit by bit, the tenacious king had claimed his homeland, to a point where, now, they, the Scots, could well afford to be on the attack.

The seeming eons of struggle and loss had taught the king well. What revenge he would take, on those who had slain members of his own family, had long been slaked. Now, the king had learned that governing a country required not just the loyalty of his subjects, but something more tangible as well. Gold, money, currency. And so, over the last years, he had taken to raiding into England, a just satisfaction in itself, stripping the northern lands of his enemy as they had stripped the southern lands of Scotland for years. But he didn't send his men to kill and destroy. He sent them to demand payment for his peace. And for Jamie, as well, it seemed a sweet justice.

Nearing the manor of Hamstead Heath, he slowed his gait, and the men behind did as well. There were no armed men to meet them, no mounted knights, no foot soldiers.

The manor stood alone upon a mound within a small village of thatched-roof houses, keeping a distance between the gentry and the tenants and servants who worked the land and within the house. A low, crumbling Roman wall surrounded a scene both picturesque and peaceful. They had not come to Hamstead Heath before, nor had any of the Bruce's men: the year before, the lord of the manor had come to the King of Scots, and offered a payment before his village could feel the brunt of Scottish power.

A few people milled about in the expanse of stone and dirt that served as a courtyard for the manor: a woman carrying rushes on her shoulder, a milkmaid with pails, a blacksmith carrying a yoke with buckets balanced at either end.

"The king's command!" he said, the tone of his voice low, but strong enough to carry to the men around him. "Only those who resist are to be taught the cost of violence against the King of the Scots."

"It doesn't look like much resistance," Liam O'Connell, riding at his side, said to him.

"Aye, no resistance," Jamie said. The wooden fence at the center of the wall stood open. Still, the years had taught him caution, and he reined up, surveying the scene before him as they approached. There were vast stables to the left of the manor, and more storage and farm buildings to the right. More of the villagers were in evidence there, men hauling bales of hay up to a loft, a lad in unbleached cotton shoveling droppings, two young women feeding the chickens that flocked around the front of the building.

"Be on guard," Jamie said. "George, you will remain with most of the men in the yard; Liam, we'll approach the manor with a party of ten. Ragnor, you'll come inside with us, and be ready to quickly relay any words to the men beyond."

"Aye, Jamie," Ragnor said.

"Do you think they've any number of men with any kind of weapons within?" George asked, his eyes on the scene before them.

"We began our battle for freedom with peasants, farmers, and craftsmen fighting with no more than pitchforks and sticks," Jamie said quietly. "We'll expect no less from any enemy."

He nudged his horse's flanks, passing through the open gate. As he did so, the door of the manor opened, and a tall, dignified man with snow white hair and beard to match walked out upon the broad stone step that led to the double wooden doors of the manor. Another five steps brought him to the ground, and he walked out alone to meet the riders. He was not clad in armor or mail, but he wore a sword at the belt around his hips. His tunic and shirt appeared fine, clean and well cut, and his boots were softly worked leather while his hose gave the appearance of excellent wool.

He lifted a hand in greeting. "You're from the Bruce?" he said.

"Aye, that we are," Jamie said, moving forward on his horse. He then dismounted, watching the elderly fellow. He had perfect, proud posture, and was a tall man with brilliant blue and intelligent eyes.

"Sir James Graham," he said, introducing himself. "Messenger for the King of Scots, Robert Bruce."

"We have expected you."

Jamie raised a brow. "If you have expected us, why has it been necessary for us to come?"

"I'm afraid the Lord Steven has been absent on business for several months now. We keep no standing army, so there was no escort for his lady sister to come north, into what may well have been dangerous territory for such a young woman. But she is within, sir, and ready to greet you. You've ridden long and hard. Though we are a small village, naturally, beyond the tribute, we offer you every hospitality. The barn will accommodate many of your men, while you and your close retainers are welcome to the shelter of the manor."

"Have you the tribute ready?"

"We are in process of gathering the sum required. The Lady Christina will negotiate the arrangements. If you will join me? The kitchen is preparing food and drink for you and all your men. We will be pleased if you will honor us with your presence in the hall. The servants will be out quickly to tend to your men."

Jamie lowered his head in agreement and turned to his men. Liam quickly dismounted behind him, calling out orders. Then Liam and Ragnor fell in step behind him, with five other of their number in their wake.

They walked up the steps to the manor. The great double doors opened. A woman stood ready to greet them.

She was tall and slender with wheat blond hair falling freely around her shoulders and down her back. She was dressed elegantly in a soft blue, fur trimmed and embroidered tunic over a silken underdress. He didn't pay much heed to her costume, however, for as soon as his eyes adjusted to the shadow against the streaking gold and crimson of the dying day, his vision was riveted to her eyes. They were the deepest, brightest green he had ever seen, and set in a face of perfect and delicate proportion. She was a completely stunning sight, her beauty as grand as her stance and composure.

"Sir James Graham, my lady," the old man said. "The emissary of the king of the Scots."

She inclined her head with the slightest, most regal, movement. "Enter, gentlemen," she said, her voice low and well modulated. And she turned her back on them, walking through a long entry and to her right, where most of the manor's lower level was one great hall.

A large hearth filled half the far wall with a wondrous marble mantel surrounding it. The floors were strewn with fresh rushes. Fine, large hounds sniffed and whined as the visitors entered, then, at a word from their mistress, settled again before the hearth.

Tapestries lined the wall, rich with intricate needlework. A table, easily accommodating twenty to thirty guests, created a U-shape in the center of the hall. The table was already set with elaborate servings, trays bearing whole fish, a boar's head, sides of veal, and more. Each place setting was complete with thrown pottery plates and glass goblets. There was a scent of fresh flowers about the hall, and the sense that this was, indeed, far more of a home than any kind of fortress.

It also appeared as if they had prepared to greet a king or much honored nobility, rather than foreigners come to demand tribute.

Once, the area might have been protected by the knights in such fortresses as those at York or other large castled towns in the north.

Now, with the upheaval between the English aristocracy and the ever-present fear of the Scots, such places as this were often left to their own devices. Jamie might have felt pity for the occupants, had he not suffered so much during the years when the old king of England lived—and taken such a brutal toll among so many of his friends, kin, and people. The English left their own to battle it out with the Scots or pay tribute. But once the tribute was paid, the aristocracy that did not fight held a bitter grudge against those who'd had little choice. Pay the tribute, or be robbed of every cow and pig in sight, every serviceable horse, and every bit of value within the scope of buildings and land. Robert Bruce had often torn down his own castles and fortifications, determined never to leave the enemy a place to hide, gather force, or ride out the winter—or plan battle strategy against him.

The woman was watching him as he surveyed the hall. Her chin was high; vast green eyes were shrewd and cool. She had prepared all this, but she despised the men who had come. She meant to show every courtesy, but her contempt was complete. She apparently knew just what orders Robert Bruce gave his men, and knew that she was safe in person and place as long as she complied with payment of the demanded tribute.

She lifted a hand elegantly, indicating a place in the center of the U-shaped table. "Please, if you will . . . I assume you have ridden a distance to reach us."

"And I am impressed that you are so prepared."

"A shepherd saw your approach when you and your men paused at the stream by the forest."

A simple enough explanation. He didn't believe her.

"How kind that you have looked to our needs, when payment of the tribute was all that was necessary."

"We wish to continue to prosper," she said lightly, then added, "And live, as well, of course."

"The king of Scots isn't a cold-blooded murderer, as you are aware."

"Well, with all men, it depends on the circumstances, does it not?" she inquired. "Please, be seated. We couldn't be certain exactly when you would arrive, and I hope that the meal has not grown cold. Sir Alfred will be joining us in the manor. Some of my retainers will be joining your men outside."

Jamie bowed to her, and took her hand, startling her for a moment. Despite her cool demeanor, her flesh felt like fire. She longed to jerk her hand away, he thought, and yet she did not. The smile that came to her lips was forced.

"I meant only to escort you to your chair, Lady Christina, not chop off your fingers."

"Of course," she said, and allowed him to escort her. As he walked by her side, he felt the tension in her body, as if she emitted sparks of heat.

As he seated her in one of the large chairs at the head of the table, he saw that Sir Alfred was seating his men. Servants came from the kitchen. All were male. Mostly large men, and those who were not still appeared to be heavily muscled. The only one to serve wine was a comely young woman with round blue eyes and delicate features. As she reached to fill his glass, Jamie noted that her hands were smooth, her nails neatly trimmed. No callouses from long labors touched her tender flesh.

She moved to his left, serving his men, rather than the lady of the manor.

"You had no difficulty riding?" Sir Alfred, just at the curve of the table, asked. His words were jovial, as if he were welcoming kin from afar.

"Aye, the roads were fine," Jamie said. "Despite the

season, the roads remain passable. The winter has been mild
for our journey here.'' He pointed out one of the tapestries
and asked, ''What battle is depicted there?'' Both Sir Alfred
and the lady looked at the tapestry. He took the moment to
give a sign to Liam.

Then, in a heartbeat, both the lady and Sir Alfred were
looking at him. They seemed to share a certain discomfort.
He arched a brow to the woman. ''Ah . . . it's a fairly new
piece, is it not? The battle of Falkirk. I see the colors now.
Edward the First, there, in all his glory and splendor. And
all the Scots there—dead and in pools of blood. It's quite
a use of color. Did you create the piece, Lady Christina?''

She appeared pale. ''No, sir, I did not.''

''Now there would be a fine piece to bring the king,''
Liam commented to Jamie.

''Hm. Perhaps not,'' Jamie said. A man stood at his left
shoulder, ready to serve one of the trays of meat. He sat
back, watching the woman at his side. Then he turned from
her and addressed George. ''I had forgotten. How remiss.
George, tell Grayson that I believe Satan has picked up a
stone. I'd not have my horse go lame.''

''Aye, Jamie,'' George said, excusing himself and rising.
He bowed to the lady and Sir Alfred before leaving the hall.

The serving woman with the soft hands was back. She
poured for the lady and Sir Alfred, and seemed to find that
her pitcher was empty.

''So, tell me, how will the tribute be paid?'' Jamie said,
addressing the woman.

''I've ten excellent warhorses for you to take now,'' she
said.

He shrugged. ''A good warhorse is a hefty payment,
indeed. But I believe the king was expecting a certain amount
of gold.''

She nodded, sipping her wine, and not looking his way.

"I'm afraid that you've come before we've been entirely able to prepare. My brother has gone to collect the revenue from some of the stock we've recently sold. At his return, the remainder of the payment will be made in gold."

"Ah, so that is why you are here to deal with this business," he said.

"Sir, it doesn't take a scholar or a well-schooled knight to pay off men who hold innocent people under ransom, does it?" she asked pleasantly.

He smiled, picked up his glass, an unusual and elegant piece, and drank deeply from it. "An excellent wine," he told her.

"I am glad you approve. Please, you must drink your fill."

"Innocent people," he repeated softly.

"I've certainly done you no harm," she said.

He sipped more wine, smiling politely in return. "I believe, my lady, that your father was Sir Adam Steel."

"He was."

His smile deepened. "I believe he was with a group under Edward the First who agreed to meet with a number of Scottish nobles to negotiate years ago . . . twelve-ninety-six, I think it was."

Again, he saw the color leaving her face.

"They all met in peace. The Scots deposited their weapons as agreed. They died with their throats slit."

"I was an infant, sir, and have no idea where my father was at the time. But I might point out that not far from here, your William Wallace cornered a number of English knights, herded them into a barn, and stood and smelled the air as they all burned to death."

"But I don't believe that he would have come south— had the English not come north."

She turned on him suddenly. "You should take care. There are still many English in Scotland."

"Oh, we are aware of that. But then again . . . here we are in England."

"Demanding payment."

"Aye."

She wanted to say more; she refrained. "We've entertainment for you," she said, rising. She strode to the kitchen. Sir Alfred remarked on the quality of their horses.

"I admit, Sir Alfred, they were taken from the English at a castle we recently restored to the king's domain," he said.

A moment later the lady returned with a small man in a jester's costume and another who carried a lute. The one stood with his instrument while the other performed acrobatic feats, then sang an innocuous ballad about pirates at sea. The lady had taken her chair again. He watched as the jester sat with his men, accepted wine, and encouraged the Scots to drink. Jamie watched Liam next to the jester. His men appeared amused and entertained, as they were intended to be.

They lifted their glasses, raised a toast to Hamstead Heath and its beautiful lady.

She smiled, and graciously accepted the compliment.

A moment later, when another song had begun, he turned to her.

"You don't have, nor will you have, the tribute, Lady Christina," he said.

She lifted her glass and eyed him over it, a challenge in her eyes.

"And if we do not?"

"Well, then, we take all the livestock, everything of value in the manor, burn it and the outbuildings to the ground, and depart. Oh, and I'm afraid we have to kill anyone who tries to prevent us from doing so.''

''How merciful,'' she said, her tone dry, and not at all frightened.

''You don't have the payment.'' He leaned closer to her. ''You really should be alarmed.''

She looked at him with her cool, green eyes calm and assessing. ''I'm afraid, sir, that you will not be able to bring harm and destruction to Hamstead Heath.''

''And why is that?''

She set down her glass, watched him for a moment, and smiled with little humor. ''Because soon, you will not be able to move at all. Your wine has been drugged.''

He digested that information, allowing his fingers to knot around the glass on the table, and his voice to deepen as if with fear and fury.

''So you have meant to murder us all.''

She shook her head. ''Murder you? Such fine prisoners for ransom? No, dear sir. Your eyes will shortly close, and you will sleep the sleep of the dead for a good many hours. You will awaken within English prisons in the very best of health.''

He looked at her gravely. ''I am glad you did not intend murder.''

''Why is that?'' she inquired. Then her eyes fell for a moment and she shook her head. ''It would be easier for you to die here beneath the spell of a strong opiate than to face the death that will be intended by the decree of the king.''

''How courteous of you to consider a lesser death for my men and me,'' he said. Her eyes once again met his. They seemed impassive. She might not wish extreme violence upon any man, but then again, it didn't seem that his fate meant much to her one way or the other.

"You've no right on English land," she said and shrugged. "Even if the English king is now little more than a . . . well, even if he is not a *hammer* of the Scots. You have brought about your own doom."

"But I haven't fallen flat quite yet," he told her. "What makes you think that, in my fury, I will not draw my sword, and slice out your heart for such treachery?"

"I doubt if you will have the strength to do so."

He smiled. "I've the strength, but not the need."

"And why is that?" she inquired, and still she seemed little interested. She expected that he would fall face first into his plate any minute. Her work would be done, men would be summoned to take them away, shackle them, drive them onward to whatever dungeon was intended.

He leaned back in his chair, watching her, fascinated by the green cat eyes that returned his stare with cool apathy.

"Because, my lady, *you* have been drinking the opiate."

At last, a response. Those beautiful eyes went wide with alarm. Then they narrowed in disbelief.

"You are a liar, sir. There was no reason to expect any treachery here."

He leaned forward. "There is always a reason to expect treachery among the English," he said, and he couldn't keep the bitterness and anger out of his voice. "Trust me, my lady, the cups were long ago switched, and the alarm was given to my men. You will find your people sleeping the sleep of the dead very soon."

She started to rise. And it was at that moment she realized that he was telling the truth. She sat back down quickly, her fingers shaking on the table where they lay, fighting what she must surely know was to come.

"You will have no power here. Your men—"

"I'm afraid that you'll find the floor beneath the table

quite wet with the fruit of the vine. Ah! Look! There goes Sir Alfred!''

As he spoke, the white-bearded fellow's face fell flat into his plate.

''Your men outside—''

''Were warned.''

She shook her head. ''You can't . . .''

''Can't what? I told you what will happen.''

''No . . . all these people. They will starve come winter.''

''Alas, you should have thought of that.''

He was startled when her fingers suddenly curled around his wrist with a surprising and desperate strength. And he was even more surprised when she spoke.

''You can't leave me here!''

''What?''

''You can't leave me here.''

''My lady, Robert Bruce is one of the most humane men I have ever seen. We do not slay the populace, nor do we even seize prisoners and bring them back to Scotland. Not unless they're of incredible value, which you are not. You've really nothing to fear.''

She shook her head. ''No! You must take me with you.''

''As what?'' he inquired, eyes narrowing.

This was definitely a strange form of treachery.

''As . . . anything,'' she said. ''Anything!'' she repeated.

''You know what you're saying?'' he demanded.

''Indeed, exactly.'' Her voice seemed to quaver slightly. He wondered if it was the drug doing its work, or if she was speaking boldly to hide another kind of fear.

Truly puzzled, he stared at her.

''You wish to become a camp follower? Or far worse? There are other names for what you're suggesting, of course . . .''

''You can't leave me here!'' she insisted again.

"Why?" he demanded. "You are the child of a respected English knight. A murderer to those of us who are Scots, but a hero in the days of the old king of England."

She moistened her lips, seeking an answer that wouldn't come. He lowered his head and leaned closer, his mouth nearly against her own.

"Why?" he demanded again.

He was not to have his answer.

The lady fell forward into his arms.

CHAPTER 2

Her throat was dry. Christina's first sense upon beginning to awaken was that her mouth felt like a fur pelt. She then became aware that her temples were pounding, and all that before she opened her eyes.

When she did so at last, it seemed that the sun poured into them like a stream of knives. She closed them quickly, then more carefully slitted them open. It was day. She was alive, and lying . . . somewhere.

In her own bed, in her own room, she realized quickly, seeing the worn tapestries that bordered the windows. She was very careful to make no movement. The memory that she had failed came sweeping upon her. She had failed, and then . . .

She had pitched into a world of blackness. As had the other inhabitants of Hamstead Heath seated at the table with her.

And now . . .

She was, at least, alive. That had to be a good sign. Or was it? Were they all alive, only to face a far worse fate?

She lay atop the tapestry coverlet, still completely clad in her borrowed finery from the night before.

The night before . . .

She bolted to an upright position on the bed, panic flooding through her. She was alive, yes, but what now? They had failed. Abysmally. With no hint or notice, the Scots had surmised their deception, and turned the tables—or rather the wine—on them. So . . .

Some slight sound or movement drew her attention to the mantel.

And he was there, leaning against the mantel, warming his hands at the fire.

The Scotsman who had come the night before. Sir James Graham. Apparently relaxed, at ease, as if he hadn't a care in the world, little to do, and all the time in the world to wait. As she had noted the night before, he was a tall man, his height given a greater edge by the breadth of his shoulders. Like many Scotsmen, he had most probably been wielding a sword since he had begun to walk. No manner of clothing would disguise the mass of tight and sinewed power within those muscles strengthened by constant warfare. His eyes were a strange and curious blue-gray, the kind that seemed to have a natural shield, and a piercing quality all in one. His stare seemed quite capable of ripping through any defense, while in turn, he gave nothing away.

"Good morning, my lady. Well, of course, I still assume you are my lady. Any deception here might be expected, but none of the servants suggest that you are anyone else other than Christina, lady of the household, sister of Count Steven. And the title . . . I understand it was something your father acquired under the command of the late King Edward—a simple knighthood would not do for a man who had scored so many victories over the king's enemies, the Scots. Your father died with quite a respectable title—and a fair fortune, I imagine.''

He was dressed in no armor, but the lack of steel about him did nothing to assure her that the man was any less formidable.

Or any less her enemy. His tone held a dagger twist within it as sharp as any blade.

And yet, in her present state of misery, she wasn't certain he could cause her any further harm. Even the absolute horror of what could now follow her defeat—not for herself, but for others—was kept in the back of her mind by the dull, thudding pain in her head. She wanted to speak, but the effort seemed too great. She groaned, praying that her head and throat would clear, and fell back upon the bed, twisting to her side, away from him. She kept her eyes open, staring at the windows where the heavy draperies had been pulled back purposely to let in the cruel light of the brilliant morning sun.

''My lady, it's excessively rude to turn your back upon someone speaking directly to you.''

The deep, rich, disdainful tone of his voice managed what the brilliance of the morning sun could not. An answer flew to her lips, and both her tongue and lips seemed to work just fine.

''I consider it rude, sir, that you should be here without an invitation.''

''Well, I could hardly leave you face down upon the supper table.''

''Would it matter, since you surely intend to burn the manor to the ground?''

''I should, of course. Considering your father.''

''My father fought for his king, as he was commanded. If I'm not mistaken, there was a time when your king fought for Edward the First as well. Actually, come to think of it, sir, many of your most noble knights have felt compelled to change their loyalties time and time again throughout these past many years. One might even be given to refer to the mass of your fine, brave people as opportunists.''

With her back to him, she winced, gritting her teeth, and wondering what was forcing her tongue when her fate, and that of the village, lay in his hands. She reminded herself that her head was hammering, and that a swift blow into the realm of unconsciousness might be a mercy at this time. And yet, though she was dismayed and deeply afraid of what her failure would mean, and though she wasn't sure her own life had much value at the moment, the manor and village held farmers, craftsmen, servants, artisans and more. And their lives, which they might well cherish, were equally at risk.

Still, she felt as if hackles rose at her nape as he moved with a fluid and alarming quiet, coming around the bed to take a seat at her side.

''You're either truly brave,'' he said softly, then shrugged, ''or the most pathetic creature on earth.''

''I'm neither,'' she snapped, sitting up again and edging toward the headboard, wanting to put distance between them. ''I'm in agony.''

He arched a well-defined brow with a certain amusement. ''And I should feel sympathy for your plight?''

''At least you do know that we weren't intent upon murder,'' she murmured, her lashes falling as she found herself fighting a bitter battle to keep from trembling. She knew he was staring at her, seeing far too deeply into what she feared might be a naked and terrified soul.

''Hm. We know it—and you aren't dead by your own fool hand. So shake off the stupor in your mind, my lady. Be glad. It is a rare beautiful day. And you will be left to live in its glorious sunshine. Since my king is a benign and compassionate man, we'll refrain from burning the roof over your heads, though were he here himself, the king might not be inclined to such a great measure of compassion after facing such treachery.''

She still didn't look at him. His words reminded her not of any kindness or mercy they might receive, but what horror would befall them if Edward II believed that they had done anything at all to merit Scottish benevolence.

"Compassion, sir, would have been to leave us all the hell alone.''

"Ah, there the gentle speech of a true lady born," he murmured. "It's a great pity that, years ago, your present king's father did not see fit to leave the Scots the hell alone. But then, we—none of us—can change history, so here we are.''

Christina didn't reply. The thudding at her temples increased with his every word. She brought her fingers to her forehead, pressing against her skull, longing to relieve the pressure.

He awaited her reply. When she gave none, he said, "Well, now that I see you are alive and well, we will be on our way. I'm afraid that you will be missing a good number of horses, and of course, we are taking the cattle. And I must say, the men have done an excellent job of ferreting out the lovely little hiding places where you had hidden such fine pieces of gold and silver. I daresay, someone in your illustrious family did a fine job of pillaging during a crusade to the Holy Land, since you had some remarkable jeweled chalices tucked away. The Bruce will enjoy them, I know.''

Her lashes flew open—she wasn't the least concerned about the chalices—but she was very concerned that the Scots should leave with no appearance of real vengeance taken against them for what should have been a strong and stalwart—*even suicidal*—stand against the Scottish king. She knew that she should be exceedingly grateful that the Scots didn't intend to raze the village. It would have been well within the customary retaliation in these many years of bloodshed and war.

But any concessions would damn her family even further. She couldn't afford kindness from the enemy. There was only one way to leave the village standing, the people able to survive—and to prove the loyalty of the family to a man she had to admit was not an honorable king.

He rose. "Good day, my lady. And good life."

He had already made it across the room and toward the door as her feet hit the floor. No matter. Desperately, she went flying after him, catching hold of his arm. The heat and pulse of him through fabric caused her to quickly draw back, flushing, but she held her ground as he looked down at her expectantly.

"You can't—go," she said.

He arched a brow. "Are English troops racing now toward Hamstead Heath? Is this another of your lures? If you're hoping that a contingent of English knights will arrive to save your horses, treasures, and livestock, I'm afraid that my spies—practiced, seasoned fellows—will assure you that no such assistance is on the way."

She couldn't quite prevent the note of disdain that came to her voice with her reply, "I'm well aware that no help is on its way."

"Then, my lady . . . why on earth would you want to keep us here?"

"I don't want to keep you here."

"Ah. Then we are agreed. Good day."

He turned to the door. Once again, she grabbed his arm. "You can't just . . . leave."

"You *want* me to burn the manor to the ground?"

"No . . . yes . . . no," she said, as he stared at her. If the manor were burned to the ground, yes, it would appear that they had given good fight, and that the Scots had retaliated. It would also destroy the livelihood of several hundred people, and leave them to starvation and freezing in the winter close ahead.

"You have to take me with you. As a hostage," she said quickly.

A slow, then broad, smile split his features, lightening the steely gray of his eyes. "You? My lady? So that we all might wake with knives in our backs?"

"Do I really strike fear into such a formidable warrior of the great Scottish king?" she inquired.

He leaned toward her, a smile still twitching his lips. "Indeed, my lady, you do. I have been at war many, many years. And in those years I've learned that it isn't always the strength of a warrior's arm, but the muscle within his mind that matters most. And you, lass, are, in that respect, terrifying."

"That's not at all true, not at all fair, I didn't set out to poison you, merely to . . ."

"Rob us blind, inflict insult and injury, and capture scores of prisoners."

"There could be much worse."

"Hm, let's see, imprisonment for a Scotsman with the English? A mock trial, a death sentence, beaten, tortured, disemboweled, chopped to bits, burned to ash, thrown to the wind . . ."

Christina felt the blood draining from her face as she spoke.

"You must take a hostage," she told him.

"I don't want a hostage."

"But you must!"

He shook his head, apparently tiring of their verbal exchange. Again, he started out the door. She clung to him, and he turned to disengage himself.

"Fine! I'll take a hostage."

"I'll get some things together."

"My lady, I said that I'd take a hostage. I did not say that I'd take you."

"What?"

She was so startled that she released her hold on him, stepping back.

"There was a comely and soft-spoken wench serving the wine last night. Her hands were soft as silk, without the least sign of any form of labor upon them. Therefore I presume she is a young woman of some noble standing . . . a friend, a cousin, some poor relation, or a visitor simply in the wrong place at the wrong time. But in an accent decidedly English I heard her called Lauren. We might well discover that she is the daughter of an even greater butcher—excuse me, knight—than your father."

She must have been as white as the new snow that came in winter; it felt as if every ounce of blood had drained from her body.

"No!"

"Ah, so have I a duchess on my hands?" he inquired.

She shook her head vehemently. "No . . . Lauren is no great jewel in the English aristocracy, I swear it."

"Still, she is pleasant and mild mannered. I believe that we'll take her."

He started down the hall. Christina found strength and came flying after him, practically catapulting against his back.

"You mustn't, truly, you mustn't!"

"But that's my will."

"Please, you cannot take Lauren!"

"Why? She's an extremely beautiful young lass. And her manner! So very gentle, the tone of her voice, so soft. She'll make an excellent hostage."

"I'll make a better hostage, I swear it."

"Really? And why is that?"

Christina stared at him, eyes wide, at a total loss. Not even when she had wakened, her plan a total loss, her home filled with pillaging invaders, had she imagined being in so humiliating a position. The lowlands of Scotland and the north of England had paid bitterly throughout endless years of conflict, but pride could still be maintained when sheer power of force made hell of the world. Most women had feared the coming of the enemy, feared slaughter and rape, and the possibility of being taken.

At the back of her mind, she knew that Steven would be furious. That he would never consider his honor, even his life, as fair payment for her casting her own soul into the flames. But Steven was not here. She was.

And she couldn't help but believe that her own humiliation was well worth his life.

And the life he might share with Lauren.

And yet . . .

She didn't seem able to force this man to take her as a hostage!

He was waiting, she realized, for her to explain. She thought quickly, knew she had no time left, and let out the first lie that came to her lips.

"She's promised to a nunnery. You would be damned before the eyes of God, if you were to touch her."

"Is that so?" he inquired.

"She has already gone before the altar . . . at Westminster Abbey, and vowed herself to God's service. And surely, sir, you are a good Christian—laying waste to England in your desire to serve your good and godly king. You could spend eternity burning in hell, were you to take Lauren.''

"So you don't think that I shall burn in hell already?''

"Not if you leave Lauren. In fact, if you leave her safe, I myself will pray for your soul daily.''

"From your lips, my lady, to God's ears?''

"I will pray for you, I swear it.''

"And what of you?''

"Pardon?''

"Do you think that you will burn in hell forever, my lady?''

"Why should I burn in hell? I don't ride about the country-side killing men and creating havoc and ruin.''

"But you lie with such astonishing sincerity. One might presume that you lie even in your conversations with God, my lady. I'm not so certain that I would want you to be my representative before the Almighty!''

His mockery made her so furious that she was tempted to clench a hand into a fist and send it flying across his cheek. She nearly bit through her lower lip in her effort to remain still.

"Good day, Christina,'' he said, turning once again.

She watched him for a moment, growing ever more desperate. Then she flew after him again, catching his arm, spinning him around, and falling on her knees before him.

He seemed an incredible height from her position, but she couldn't allow that fact to daunt her. "I am begging you, sir, in all truth and sincerity, begging you, before God, to take me as a hostage, and to leave the Lady Lauren be.''

She was afraid that he might well have grown impatient enough to simply kick her aside. But he sighed deeply, hands on his hips. "Once again, Christina, I require no hostage at all. If I were to take one, I'd prefer someone docile and sweet. So—''

"She's *too* sweet," Christina said quickly.

He frowned, staring down at her.

Christina moistened her lips. "Too . . . genteel, if you will. Um . . . frigid. And the physicians say that she will be barren. She is all but . . . sexless."

Gray-blue eyes hid the depths of his thoughts as he suddenly hunkered down, closer to her position upon her knees. "Sexless? But you're mistaken. She's an incredibly beautiful young woman."

"She has no interest in men whatsoever. She would be . . . you wouldn't be . . . sir, you would simply not enjoy her company."

"And I would enjoy yours?"

Despite the direction of the conversation which she had created herself, his question took her a bit off guard. She was stumbling badly, groping her way through the tangle of lies she created with every sentence. But at least, it seemed, she had his attention. Too much of it. The pounding in her head was increasing its beat once again. His eyes seemed to penetrate her mind, and cause that vicious tempo within her mind to increase.

She lowered her lashes for a moment, then stared at him with her eyes wide and frank, her tone as low and seductive as she could manage.

"You cannot begin to imagine, sir, the heights of pleasure and enjoyment to be found in time spent within my company."

He lowered his head. She longed again to kick him, convinced that he was laughing at her.

He looked at her again.

"You are that . . . talented."

"There would be no way to tell you."

"Jamie!"

They were both startled by the arrival of a third party in

the hall. Jamie came to his feet. He reached to assist her up, absently, she was certain. He had been bred to certain courtesies, despite the fact that he apparently spent his days slaying the English.

She was startled by the firmness of the grasp. And the fact that he did not release her as she came to her feet.

They were approached by the man he had called Liam the night before, another great hulk of a fellow, tall, broad-shouldered, with almost white-blond hair and blue eyes.

"We've gathered most of the cattle and sheep. Did you wish to leave behind any of the horses? There are some fine draft animals in the fields, and my God, some of the crossbreeds are magnificent. You'll want to see what we've selected, since you said we'd not leave the desperate bastards here to starve." As the man spoke, he noted Christina at Jamie's side, and gave her a nod of acknowledgment, his eyes as wary and stern as those of an owl. Apparently, it was known among these men that the lady of Hamstead Heath was a treacherous spider, and she would be held in distrust and aversion by all.

And yet, despite the circumstances, she felt a little shudder in her heart. The horses. Naturally, they would be robbed blind of their horses. The breeding, nurturing, and training of some of the finest warhorses ever to ride to battle had been accomplished here, at Hamstead Heath. It had been her great-grandfather who had returned from the Crusades with a herd of twenty exquisite and legendary Arab horses. Throughout the years, those original acquisitions had been parlayed into a stable of unrivaled quality. There were riding horses, warhorses, and work horses, all unequaled for their purpose in life. If there were riches to be found here, they were to be found in the animals that remained—both Edwards had helped themselves to many an animal for a war campaign.

"You can't take all the horses," she said quickly.

"I can take whatever I choose," Jamie said. A flat and absolute quality in his voice brought chills racing down her spine. He could be courteous, he could laugh, smile, perhaps mock and tease, and seem to offer no terrible vengeance. And yet, in that moment, she knew that she would indeed risk her life if she were to cross him again.

"The cattle have been herded for the journey?" Jamie inquired.

Liam nodded, his eyes upon Christina.

"I'll see to the horses then," Jamie said. "Lady Christina, if you'd be good enough to return to your room."

"But . . ."

"Now," he said quietly.

"Actually, sir, I cannot do so. It's imperative that I see just exactly what you and your men are doing."

"Actually, my lady, it's imperative that you return to your room."

"Surely, sir," she said, her tone level, struggling to remember her circumstances and yet maintain some control over the situation, "I can tell you a great deal about our livestock. And since you've been telling me about the great benevolence of King Robert Bruce, I'm certain that you don't want to see the people here starve come the winter. Beyond the moral point of this, and your king's largesse, it makes sound intelligence to leave the people living and working with some manner of hope—therefore, you can return and rob us blind once again."

The last had not been at all necessary, and she didn't know what it was about the man that made her temper flare so that she dared far too many barbs and risks. The last had apparently been too much. He inclined his head slightly toward her. "Liam, will you see the Lady Christina to her room, please? I've a tremendous fear that my fingers would slip around her throat were I to be her escort at this time.''

He walked past Liam.

''Wait!'' Christina cried, unwilling to let him go, frustrated—and feeling ever more desperate. She had all but offered to dance naked on a table, and hadn't drawn the least interest. She was insulted as well as humiliated. She was willing to do anything to keep them from leaving with the impression that she and her people had taken no action against the Scots, but rather had done nothing but strip themselves bare to pay the tribute.

A heavy hand fell on her arm. She turned back to the man they called Liam. He seemed a giant. A long-healed scar, presumably acquired in a sword battle, ran down the side of his cheek.

''He doesn't understand, I need—''

''You don't understand,'' he interrupted flatly. ''You will return to your room, my lady.''

She jerked from his hold. Well aware that it would do no good to try to rush past him, she squared her shoulders and walked, with her head high, to her room, slamming the heavy wooden door shut with all the power she could muster.

In her room, she walked to the narrow window. The sun was still streaming in. She winced as the light once again hit her eyes, but her determination was now at a reckless stage. There was a masonry gutter just beyond the window, and below that, the overhang of the first floor of the manor. She bit her lip, remembering the last time she had crawled out the window. They had been children, and Steven had said that men were meant to be agile, adventurous, and courageous, to stand against any adversity. Women were allowed to be cowards.

Naturally, she had followed her brother out the window. But that, of course, was a very long time ago. And she had suffered severely when the two of them were caught, and her father profoundly agreed with what had been her brother's challenge to her. To his credit, Steven had admitted baiting her. She could still remember the way her brother had stood in the hall, straight as an arrow, announcing himself as guilty as she. Steven's greatest virtue—which had brought about his downfall—was his honor. And his lack of fear, and sometimes sense, when it came to speaking his mind.

And still . . .

She really didn't have much time.

Christina slipped out the window, held her breath, then let herself fall the few feet to grasp the gutter. There, with her hands clasped firmly around the protrusion, she dangled precariously for several seconds, got her bearings and her balance, and leaped to the roof below. From there, she rolled, as Steven had taught her, allowing for an agile impetus to spring safely to the ground. She caught herself on bended knees, but then fell backward. Chickens that had idly dallied and pecked at the side of the house gave off loud squawks; they panicked, flapping their wings, rousing the dust.

It settled over her face, and her mouth and eyes.

Swearing softly, she came to her feet, ruefully remembering that she was wearing Lauren's wedding gown. To the best of her ability, she dusted off her face and clothing, reminding herself that there could be no wedding if Steven was executed.

She walked softly around to the rear of the house and leaned against the wall, watching the activity around the outbuildings and stables. Fury filled her; her fists tightened at her sides, and she swallowed a taste of bile. There weren't really so many of them, but it seemed as if her home had suddenly been blazoned with the colors of the Bruce, the king of the Scots, and the tartans and crests of the clan of the leader who had brought this horde against her people.

The shaggy cattle had been amassed, and the dogs seemed to be working for the invaders, holding the animals in formation for the journey about to commence. Some of the men were already mounted, and some, apparently the mathematicians of the group, were counting animals, making notes. A number of the most beautiful horses had been led from the fields and stables, and in the midst of it all, Jamie Graham stood with a number of his men, commenting on a certain exquisite Arabian mare.

She had long been warned about her temper. And upon occasion, complimented on her intelligence, even by her father. The latter deserted her completely now; the former took control, tearing into her with a force that all but rendered her a lunatic.

She left her hiding place against the wall, striding firmly across the yard, hands on her hips, fury spouting from her lips.

"How dare you, wretched barbarians! You will not take her anywhere! That is *my* horse!"

She went striding through the milling men, all of them apparently quite surprised to see her there. Jamie stared at Liam, frowning.

"I thought the lady had been escorted to her room."

"She was in her room," Liam replied, perplexed. "I'll see that she is returned immediately."

He turned, ready to accost Christina.

She realized the sheer idiocy of making such an announcement—and striding against nearly fifty men, as if she could have her way against so many. But the big brute of a fellow had turned to her now; he didn't intend to escort her anywhere, she would be dragged, or lifted and thrown.

Just before he reached her, she ducked beneath the outstretch of the arm coming toward her. With no other recourse, she made a beeline for the horse. *Her* horse. Crystal. She had seen the filly born, she had trained her, she had been the first to ride her, she had raced the wind upon that mare.

None of the men made a move to stop her. Perhaps they were all too startled by her sudden appearance. She measured her mark carefully, making a flying leap as she approached the animal. She easily sailed up on her mare's back, and though one of the men had been holding Crystal's lead, the mare reared up, jerking free. Christina needed no reins to guide Crystal. She leaned against her, urging her with soft whispers and the tightening of her thighs. Crystal hit the ground, reared again, hooves pawing the air. Men fell back, lest they risk the steel of her shoes against the bones of their faces. When Crystal landed again, earth churned, dust blew, a path had cleared, and they were ready to ride.

Hamstead Heath horses were among the best in the world, and Christina had probably been riding longer than she had been walking. When the mounted Scots rallied to prevent her exit as she raced toward the valley, she faced the old Roman wall still surrounding the village, and much of the house area. Crystal seemed to fly over the low barrier. And yet, once she had sailed over the wall, it occurred to Christina that she was escaping when she had nowhere to go, when her flight would achieve nothing. The Scots hadn't wanted any part of her.

But apparently, they did want her horse.

Despite the pounding of Crystal's hooves, she could hear the pursuers following quickly in her wake. Glancing back, she saw their steel-eyed leader close behind her. Crystal was a magnificent animal, but somewhere in time and place, though the Scots claimed years of starvation and penury in their great fight for freedom against the English, Graham had managed to buy, beg, or steal an incredible animal of his own. His horse was black, as black as night, with a facial dish that clearly delineated Arabic blood, but a greater size and muscle tone that indicated the animal was the result of studied and careful breeding. A perfect warhorse, capable of tremendous speed while bearing the weight of man, armor, and weaponry.

Her perusal and assessment of her enemy proved to be her downfall. She had ridden with a total reckless abandon at breakneck speed. But, like Lot's wife, she had looked back.

She wasn't about to turn into a pillar of salt, but when she looked forward again, she saw that they had cleared the length of the valley and were heading straight into the trees.

And a low branch.

Too late, she urged Crystal to slow her galloping gait. She threw herself as low as she could against the horse's neck. Her hair, however, tossed into a mass of disarray by the wicked wind brought on by the sheer speed of her flight, tangled within the branch. The sudden jerk should have rendered her bald, but instead, the horse went on—she did not. She grabbed desperately at the branch; her effort brought it disengaging from the tree, and with the limb, leaves and what seemed like a ridiculous pile of foliage, she fell hard to the earth, covered in a wealth of cascading autumn.

CHAPTER 3

Steven woke with abrupt suddenness, feeling as if he'd been struck. Eyes open, he stared around the room.

A room, yes. Not a prison, a cage, or a cold damp chamber within the crypts of a castle. Yet there was no mistaking his position. He was a prisoner, and one at the mercy and whim of an unprincipled man who behaved like a boy let free from the restraining hands of parents or mentors, set upon the world with far too much power, and far too much money.

Edward II, King of England, God bless the fool! He'd be the death of them all, and of England herself with his excesses and foolishness.

Looking around the room, though, Steven was puzzled. He was alone in his solitary chamber, just as he was most often. He lay on a soft enough bed—not a particularly good one, but damned decent to have one at all, since he wouldn't have been surprised if the king's anger had sent him to a dungeon of rough stone and chains. He was in a tower rather than in the bowels of the castle, not at York, but at Thistle-on-Downs, the family holding of the DeClabert family. He wasn't termed a prisoner at all—he was a guest. A guest who was not allowed to leave. He was not to have a servant with him, he was not to leave the room at all, unless Edward or one of his key administrators were to arrive and *invite* him to a *discussion* on affairs in the north of the country—and the Scottish *situation.*

Steven rose, looking around the room, stretching to ease the tension that had seized him on waking.

Beyond a doubt, the room was empty. He walked over to the small marble table holding a pitcher of water and a bowl, poured a substantial pool into the bowl, and doused his face with the chilly water. He saw his own features then in the mirror above the bowl. Green eyes, light hair, lean face, pale and somewhat haggard from his months here now, but ... he grinned at his reflection, still something of a handsome face after all. Then the grin he offered his reflection faded, and a certain churning began in his stomach. He was fine—in good health at the very least, though his political situation was certainly precarious—and so ...

Christina must be in trouble.

He lowered his head, teeth gritting with impotent fury. His honesty had caused his incarceration.

Lying, however, might have already brought him to the block.

Beyond a doubt, a man with property in northern England lay between the devil and the deep. Though King Edward expressed rage at the English landholders who paid a tribute to Robert Bruce, he did nothing to protect the properties that the Scots could now ravage so easily. Determined never to accept the fact that he was not a tenth of the warrior king his father had been, he blamed those around him for any failing. A sly, weak man, he doted upon those sycophants who held his favor, Lord Rowan DeClabert—Steven's host, and a man to pretend well that he rued this sad task set to him—among them.

But while Steven sat here day after day, slyly promised the death penalty should he so much as attempt to disdain the *hospitality* offered here, Christina was left to tend Hamstead Heath. And the time for the Scots to demand tribute was coming near . . .

Or had come.

He sank back on his bed, heedless of the cold water dripping down his face. He lowered his head, certain that Christina had been hurt. And he was worse than useless to fight for or save his sister. Or Lauren.

The agony he suffered then was not a physical pain, but a fierce rise of rage and helplessness. He should let them lop off his head and be done with all this! Perhaps he should have forced Christina's hand—he was, after all, lord of the manor, and her elder as well. And yet, the vows they had made to one another as children had stayed in his heart, and the horror in her face when she assured him she'd rather wed a decaying boar than Rowan DeClabert was something he would not forget. He and Christina had grown up together; they had shared a frightening legacy. While there was breath in his body, he would keep those promises he had made.

He prayed that she was not paying in a way she had not imagined for her determination to live her own life. And still, he felt that knotting in his stomach. Something had happened, and if Christina was in trouble, then Lauren was in distress as well. He fought the rage and pain engulfing him. Trying to break through the stone wall of the castle in which he was kept was not possible. As he had always argued with Christina, thought and reason could be wielded as the world's greatest weapons.

He heard a tapping at his door and the sound of the bolt

sliding. He expected the dour old fellow who usually brought his morning meal—his host *did* see that he ate well. But it was not the gaunt, almost skeletal fellow Lambert who appeared as he bid his visitor enter. He was startled to see his good friend, Sir Ralph Miller.

"Ralph!" His surprise brought him to his feet; pleasure let him forget his worries for a moment. "My God, what a pleasure, man. I hadn't thought I was allowed so much as a glimpse of a friendly face. I had heard you'd been commanded to gather forces and ride north to the king's stronghold at Berwick." About Steven's own age, Ralph was a friend of long standing. Though Ralph was from the south of the country and Steven from the north, they had both been sent to apprentice as pages to the same man, a baron with great property just beyond London. Ralph had sandy hair, a clean-shaven face, and green eyes that still carried a sense of honor, despite the battles he had fought and the civil conflict that had shaken the whole country.

"That's the truth. But as I had heard you were here, I brought my forces in a short detour along the road." Ralph tried to smile as he spoke, but his effort was in vain. He shook his head in bewilderment. "Steven, what have you done, what have you said? The king's displeasure with you is enormous. They call you a guest of the Crown, though at what time Rowan's family became part of the *Crown* I do not know. Apparently, he has sworn to the king to lie down and die before allowing you to leave this place, while frankly, your place is at home. The word has gone throughout the north that the Scottish king's men are on their missions over the countryside, demanding payment for peace."

"Yes, well, you see, I made one of those payments last year. I personally thought it rather magnanimous of the Bruce to allow us to buy life when so much butchery was done to his family and to so many Scots in the years gone by.''

Ralph's frown warned Steven that he might have gone too far—in days gone by, Scottish raiders had also brutalized northern England, pillaging, raping, ransacking, and doing murder with a vengeance close to madness. "Ralph, this was my very point to the king—lords of manors such as Hamstead Heath, with little or no standing army, have no recourse. Edward refuses to defend what is his, and therefore, rather than see my people slain or starving, I paid a tribute. I believe my choice was to pay the tribute, or watch the Scots take everything, and then burn the manor and village to the ground. No matter. At the moment, since the Bruce now has quite an army of truly hardened warriors and I had, at most disposal, children, old women, milkmaids, and craftsmen, it made sense to pay. Others have done the same. But then the king requested that I come here for an audience with him, which I did most willingly. Unfortunately, I had forgotten that he had thought I had supported Lancaster's execution of Piers Gaveston, when, actually, that hadn't been my position at all.''

''What had been your position?''

Steven shrugged. "I didn't care if the king chose to sleep with sheep, as long as he kept such sheep out of the government. Apparently, such words did not translate well. Needless to say, I had no concept of his anger when I rode to tell him about the position in which we found ourselves. When I tried to explain the situation to Edward, he was enraged. I was condemned, I believe, before I arrived. Although others have paid a tribute, I—apparently—should have died on the spot and allowed the Scots to ravage my sister and fiancée and then walk away with whatever they chose. Reason did not bear weight with the king. The next thing I knew . . . I was a *guest* of DeClabert, and Edward was *assessing* my situation, and my sister was informed that I had been imprisoned for giving in to the threats of barbarians.''

Ralph nodded gravely. ''There are few men who are not in complete sympathy with you, Steven. But though he may be a wretched king—'' Ralph broke off as if the walls themselves might be listening.

''It's all right. I have been through this room dozens of times. There are no nooks or crannies for the enemy to hide within,'' Steven said.

''He's a wretched king, but he *is* king,'' Ralph said. ''I can't believe, though, that he would dare to execute you as a traitor.''

''Is that it, then? The king has suggested that I am a traitor?'' Steven asked, his tone dry and weary.

''There are those who say such things.''

''I imagine those who say such things are friends of my host, DeClabert?''

Ralph nodded glumly. ''We haven't the power, I'm afraid, to go against the king. Many who loathe him still feel that he is the king, and therefore, before God, our rightful ruler. But if any man were to attempt your execution . . . .''

Steven nodded an acceptance of the brave words Ralph could not quite bring himself to say. ''I know that you would defend me at the risk of your own life, Ralph, and I am grateful. But in truth, for now, I'm deeply concerned about my sister and Lauren. If the Scots are again marauding through the countryside, Christina will be in a truly wretched position, unable to defend the manor, and yet, I'm afraid, she will refuse to offer a tribute, assuming that the king's anger against me would then be great enough to bring about an execution. Ralph, though you are on your way to war, you must travel by Hamstead Heath as you ride. I beg you, get to my sister, and Lauren, for me.'' There were no quills or any manner of writing material in the room; he had not been permitted to correspond with anyone. His only communication with anyone outside the castle had been confession to a surly priest and attendance at mass.

Steven pulled his family signet ring from his finger and pressed it into Ralph's hand. "If you give this to my sister, she'll believe that you've seen me, and that what you say is my will. And I beg of you, Ralph, get word back to me somehow that my sister is well. That she and Lauren are safe. This morning . . . I woke with a feeling of pain and dread that I could not begin to explain. Please, help me in this, old friend."

Ralph solemnly placed his hand over his heart. "Before God, I'll find Christina and Lauren, and I would lay down my life for either."

"Let us hope it will not come to that."

"I'd best go, before DeClabert knows that I'm here."

"He doesn't know?"

Ralph grinned. "I have a note from the king, demanding hospitality from his nobility on my way to strengthen the defenses at Berwick. No one would dare forbid me to visit a guest in this castle."

Steven grinned. Bless Ralph. He was a good man. Not a noble, not a man richly endowed with the material objects of life, but a fine warrior from a decent family. An oddly slim fellow for one so competent at arms, but as he had seen many times, agility and grace could outweigh the heft of muscle in the midst of charged battle.

He was about to sincerely thank his old friend again, but Ralph spoke before he could, hurriedly, and once again, looking over his shoulder. "Do you think this is entirely the king's wrath? Or might it have to do with Rowan DeClabert's anger with you for your refusal when it came to his suit regarding Christina?"

"My family was not in any way legally or morally beholden to the whims of Rowan DeClabert," Steven said tightly.

As he spoke, he brought a finger to his lips. From his months of incarceration, he had come to hear the lightest sound against the floor beyond, or the touch of a hand on the door.

A brief knock sounded, but there was no pause to await a bid to enter. The door opened, and Rowan DeClabert appeared in the entry.

He was a tall, well-appointed man with ebony-dark hair, and handsomely trimmed mustache and beard. His face was an aesthetically pleasing arrangement that should have rendered him a striking man, and certainly, in his own mind, he was so. Frankly, Steven wasn't certain just what it was that made the man so distasteful to his sister, and to Lauren as well. He was well educated, had proven himself on the battlefield, and spoke well. Yet . . .

There always seemed to be something underneath. He was not a man others trusted; they feared him rather than respected him.

"Sir Ralph!" Rowan announced, and there it was, that tone which sounded truly welcoming, and yet . . . held something beneath. "What a pleasure. I heard of your arrival, and was delighted. I'm afraid that it's a difficult and bitter task to which the king has ordered my compliance, forcefully entertaining a guest as distinguished as Lord Steven. I know that your visit must be breaking the monotony of long and lonely days. Will you be staying? I know that you come with a large contingent of men, but the castle and outbuildings here are spacious; we can accommodate so many with ease."

"To my great regret, my lord, I'm afraid that I am called to duty myself. I came only to assure Steven that he has many friends who will gladly plead his case before the king. I know, Lord Rowan, how distressed you must be, charged with the imprisonment of such a good friend.''

''It's a sorry lot, indeed,'' Rowan agreed. ''There is little I can do but honor the king's command, and of course, see that Steven is as comfortable as possible while being true to a royal order. I'm so sorry you must leave so quickly. We might have spent an evening by the fire, reliving old times, old haunts, old glories, though it's true that I, too, am expecting a summons to arms at any time.''

''Well, I will bid my leave from you both, then. Steven, God be with you. Lord Rowan, my deepest thanks for your hospitality, and indeed, I wish that I could remain to enjoy more.''

With a low bow, Ralph departed the tower room, leaving them both.

''I beg pardon for arriving while you're still clad in no more than night clothes,'' Rowan said. ''But then, you already had a visitor.''

''You need beg pardon for nothing, Rowan,'' Steven said pleasantly. ''You're kind enough to give what comfort you can while I am your—guest.''

''Steven, surely, were you just to go to the king, beg his pardon, and perhaps align yourself with a greater power, this sad state of affairs could be corrected.''

''Until the Scottish matter is settled, I am prey to every manner of bandit out there—royal or other,'' Steven said. ''But, Rowan, as always, I am deeply reassured by your concern for my affairs, and of course, your sorrow at your station in this sad travesty.''

He was as capable of guile as his host, and yet, in his tone as well, there was surely a hint of his disdain, for Rowan's eyes narrowed and the facial features that should have been so pleasing seemed to tense into a mask that hinted of a penchant for cruelty that might well lie deep within the man's soul. If certain rumors were at all true, Rowan was not a friend at all, but an enemy never to be underestimated.

"Well, then, Steven, I'll leave you to your thoughts and your great morality, as I have business, preparing to ride for king and country."

With a curt bow, Rowan left the tower room. Steven doubled over again, startled by a thudding pain that seemed to encompass the whole of him.

Lord, but she landed hard!

The breath was knocked from Christina so completely that there were long moments when she looked up at the sun filtering its brilliant light through the canopy of leaves and trees, her thoughts, fears, and ever more desperate machinations swept cleanly from her mind. Then she winced, aware that she had fallen on pebbles and rocks, sticks and more. She closed her eyes, trying to clear her head. When she opened them again, he was there, a foot upon the boulder she had barely missed, his elbow upon his knee.

"You're alive," he observed. "You don't deserve to be."

If she expected a hand to help her to her feet, she wasn't about to receive it. As she started to struggle up on her own, he warned, "Lie still a moment."

To her surprise, he hunkered down at her side. "Make sure you haven't any broken bones."

She shook her head. "Nothing is broken."

"Are you trying to kill yourself?"

"No!"

"Then just what are you doing?"

"Crystal is my horse."

"Nothing is yours, if I choose to take it."

"Then you should cease extolling the magnificent kindness and mercy of your king."

"My lady, in the years gone by, being left alive has been considered a tremendous mercy. And you, lass, seem to have the strangest desires one could imagine—the king's emissary would be cruel to take your horse, but kind to take you."

She lay back, again watching as the sun played through the branches and leaves, creating dazzling patterns of light and shadow when she closed her eyes.

"Are you in pain?"

"I've broken nothing," she said dully.

She opened her eyes. He was gazing thoughtfully into the shadowy forest trail into which Crystal had now disappeared.

"She is an amazing mare," he murmured.

"Amazing—when I ride her," Christina informed him.

"Ah—so, if I take the horse, I must take you?"

"You must take me!" she whispered, surprising herself at the depth of desperation in her simple words.

"I must—ah. So, let me see, I should take a hostage prone to tainting the wine. I'd be hesitant to indulge in a sip of water from a skin!" he said. "And now, I'd know as well that my hostage could probably outride half my men, and might disappear at any time she thought that my enemies might be about in greater number or force."

"I—have no intention of tainting water, ale, or wine again," she said, rising to a sitting position and wincing only slightly at her bruised flesh and sore muscles.

"And I should believe you. Oh, my lady, a man would be a fool to trust you for an instant. Your plan might well be to accompany me, only to find out the location of various groups of men, and report back to the troops of Edward the Second."

For a moment, she felt so exhausted, pained, and worn that it didn't seem to matter. But it had to matter.

She found the strength to leap to her feet, her action so sudden that he was caught off guard, nearly falling backward himself but catching his balance in time to rise and face her as she challenged, "You idiot. You truly must be illiterate barbarians up in your rocky cairns and highlands. Is there no simple sense you can comprehend? No, Edward the Second is not half the man his father was, and not a third the king! Whereas the father could be brutal, he was far more capable of being so with a sense of rhyme, reason, and destiny. The son is little more than a bitter boy, ruthless and punitive when he feels the slightest tug against his authority, a slur against his power, the least sense of humiliation. If you don't take me, it will appear that we handed our riches to you upon a silver platter, and as you ride away with all that would sustain several hundred people through winter, it might matter little since the king's retaliation could take all worry of survival off their shoulders!"

She had no idea what went through his mind then, for the sharp blue-gray eyes upon her never wavered, never flickered in the least, nor did he move in any manner; he did nothing to indicate anger, amusement, or deadly intent.

He turned away, causing her to cry out again. "Please, don't you understand?"

"Perfectly," he called over his shoulder.

"Where are you going?" she called out after him, fists knotted at her sides.

"To see to the cattle."

She ran after him as he headed for his massive black horse. "But—"

He stopped, turning back to her. "What, my lady? Are you going to try to jump on a cow and run her into the woods as well?"

"No, no . . . but I—"

"You're sorely in need of a bath and brush, my lady," he informed her.

She stopped herself, feeling a rush of blood to her face, and finding it absurd that she should be standing there realizing that she was certainly far less than attractive and appealing at the moment. But then, at her best, he hadn't seemed to find her worth the effort of imprisonment.

"You heard me, you said that you understood!" she reminded him.

"Don't worry, we'll take prisoners."

He swung on to his huge black charger. She raced to the horse's side. "Please, not Lauren."

"Aye, lady, Lauren."

"But—"

"If I don't take her, there will be no way to assure your good behavior, Christina."

She inhaled, feeling the breeze touch her cheeks, enter her lungs, sweet as the promise of life, and a spring to come.

"Give me your hand."

"What?"

"Your hand. I'm assuming your Crystal will run back to the manor soon."

She nodded blankly, so relieved that she couldn't move. He let out an oath of impatience, dismounted, caught her by the waist, and seemed to toss her up on the horse. A second later, he had mounted behind her. Now, it seemed that every muscle and bone in her body ached and pulsed along with the beat that continued to thud within her temples. His horse's gait was amazingly smooth for so large and muscled an animal, but each hoofbeat seemed to send new streaks of pain to radiate throughout her. The wool tartan he wore brooched at his shoulder felt rough against her cheek when she turned her head as they rode. She wasn't sure that he was actually made of flesh and blood himself at all, since it seemed like she was hitting solid rock each time she slammed against him. He needed to shave, she decided. Her hair was tangling in her face, and catching against the roughness of his skin. She deplored her position, and was yet afraid, even when they returned to the yard of the manor, to be set down on the ground. *She couldn't let him take Lauren, and leave her behind. She would be powerless to protect Lauren, to stand in any way as a symbol that could keep Steven alive . . .*

Of course, there was little choice to any of it. There was no way to stop him when he leaped down, reached for her, and set her less than gently on the ground as well. "Good fellows," he announced pleasantly to his men, "I believe we'll take another hour before departing—the Arab mare should return by then, and since the good lady of Hamstead Heath will be accompanying us along with her young friend, we'll give them time to prepare. Liam, I'll go over the counts in a moment while we wait," he said, and Christina assumed herself dismissed, and yet he had announced to his men that she would be accompanying them, so surely he meant to bring her with him.

And Lauren as well.

She wasn't actually dismissed, she realized, as he suddenly turned back to her. "Perhaps you'd like to use your time wisely, my lady. Not to add greater insult to injury, but you're quite a fright. Filthy, and I do believe there's a full young oak tree sticking out of your head."

"How courteous you are, sir," she murmured, "to take such full note of a woman's appearance."

"I'm afraid that yours is currently rather difficult not to note. I really do prefer my hostages to appear far more genteel."

As he spoke, she noted the cattle waiting to be herded

along, the creatures oddly oblivious to whomever led them. So many of them!

"You're taking too many of the cattle," she said.

A flicker of anger at last touched the steel gray of his eyes. "As I have informed you many times now, my lady, I'm afraid the smallest cow is of a far greater value than you are yourself. And if you don't make a few improvements and make them quickly, you will be left behind."

He strode by her then, intent on a conversation with Liam. Christina held still, hating her position with such a sudden fury that she couldn't move. Then words poured from her mouth again, despite her sure knowledge that she was doing nothing but making matters worse.

"Sir, you are taking too many cattle!" she repeated.

He stopped, stopped dead, and turned to her. And in the steel of his eyes she knew that she had indeed made a serious mistake. If he were to grant the smallest request to her now, his actions would appear weak. And if he were to speak again, it would be to order her hog-tied and locked in a dungeon until he and his men were long gone.

On impulse she went flying across to where he stood, well aware of her audience. She fell upon her knees, and implored him in sure, solid tones that could certainly be heard, and yet were filled with the deepest pathos and respect, "Dear Sir, I beg of you, please, if you find new cattle and sheep to bring to the great glory of your king, Robert Bruce of Scotland, I beg that you leave behind just a few more beasts, assuring that the people here survive the harshness of winter, and allow for a greater bounty to be paid your overlord come the next season."

Silence greeted her words.

Yet mercy came from an unexpected direction. The great hulking Liam stepped forward and spoke lightly. "Surely, Jamie, such a fervent and pretty plea is worthy of a cow or two! And the lady makes sound sense, for these people do well here, raising such animals and indeed, God knows, we can return, and Hamstead Heath will have flourished once again to provide for us.''

She dared to look up then. Jamie's eyes were narrowed. He wasn't in the least fooled by her performance, and his anger was as great as it had been. Icy fingers seemed to close around her throat as he looked down at her, and yet she knew that she would have to play every moment as it came, and that there was nothing else she could do, or would do, because as long as there was breath in her body, she would do whatever it took for the hope of keeping her brother alive, Lauren safe, and the people of Hamstead Heath surviving.

''Get up,'' he said to her, so quietly that no one else would hear. ''Get up, now.'' He reached down. It would appear that his move was a courtesy. The hand that held her, drawing her to her feet, was rigid, and as hot as molten steel. The words he spoke and his tone belied his tension. ''Liam, by God, you're right! We must extend all courtesy to a woman who intended merely our great embarrassment, defeat, and incarceration—and not our agonized deaths at her hands. By all means, we must take greater care, and make better selections of the livestock—leaving behind a legacy for the years to come.'' He was smiling. He drew her closer. ''If you do not go now, I swear I will have you bound and gagged and locked in the lowest dungeon until we are long gone from this place. Do you understand?''

So close, so afraid, her heart pounding furiously, she was aware of his hold, of his position, and the warm touch of his breath against her cheek. The world seemed to be spinning, and for a minute she was afraid she was going to faint, which would be an incredible humiliation for her, since she never gave way to such weakness or wiles.

"Do you understand?" he repeated, and she winced, feeling the pressure of his hand upon her.

She nodded, and still, it suddenly seemed that she couldn't move. If she did at all, she would pitch forward. Black spots were appearing before her eyes. Her bones were sore, her flesh was bruised, all from her fall, but she hadn't thought that she had struck her head particularly hard, and still, it came to her that she was about to pitch to the earth.

"I'm going . . . I . . ."

"If this is another act," he warned, "I swear I'll let you fall face first into the dirt!"

She shook her head desperately, and yet, was ready to taste dirt again.

He didn't let her fall. At least, she didn't think that he did so. The black spots seemed to cover the canopy of the day, and she had the sensation of sinking downward . . . but no pain came to her, only a feel of being swept gently into the air, and somehow, securely embraced. She vaguely heard shouts, and then no more.

As he stood in the hall, surveying the decoration and architecture, Jamie mused that he liked Hamstead Heath very much. It was no great castle. And for that very reason, it had a great deal to offer. The wood paneling made the hall, certainly as large as that found in many a castle, warm and inviting, where the stone walls of many fortresses were cold and stern, no matter how many tapestries might be hung to dispel the cold. The furnishings were finely carved, with the styles of many different artisans, with touches of so many different nationalities. Woven rugs that were attractively cast over various chairs, and in the front window seats, appeared to be of fine Flemish design. Draperies spoke of a Gaelic influence, while the great table and surrounding seats had the lines of French woodworking. There had actually been quite a great deal here to which he might have helped himself—in the king's name, of course. And yet, though it might have greatly surprised the lady of the house, he had taken great pains not to rob the place blind. It had appealed to him far too greatly. He had also grown up watching the devastation of warfare.

The years gone by had bred an inherent bitterness into many Scots, and he would have to admit that he had acquired a natural enmity toward the English. It was equally true that he had seen many of his own people change sides time and time again in this war for the sovereign grace of Scotland. Though deep hatreds that could last decades, if not longer, were often formed, it wasn't without understanding—too many of the great landholders in Scotland had owned great properties in England as well, thus a dual loyalty had been forced from the beginning. Yet it had been a common man who had created the army that had become the guiding light of Scotland herself. William Wallace had turned to the people, and men had fought with hoes and scythes against the great weaponry and trained knights of the English. Robert Bruce, with all his wealth and power, had learned from Wallace, sadly coming to grips with the true strength of his country only after the brutal execution of his country's great hero, Wallace. Robert Bruce, too, had paid a great price. For years, he had led his followers as little more than a bandit in the forests. He had seen his own brothers captured in the war against the English and cruelly executed, lost his wife to English imprisonment, her incarceration kept from cruelty only by the fact that her father was a great English baron. He had fought long and hard to gain the respect and support of his own people. Jamie had learned from both Wallace, who had believed in the country and the people, and from Robert Bruce—who had determined to keep his personal losses and agony as a cross he must bear himself. As his power had increased, his sense of vengeance had often been suppressed for the good of the country. He meant to lead Scotland from devastation. He never hesitated when a military stance was necessary, but when possible, he preferred diplomacy over murder. There would always be a border with England, though the line itself might change in the years to come. And one day, there would be peace between the two countries. Edward I was dead. He had earned his sobriquet; he had indeed been the *hammer* of the Scots. His son was a poor substitute. Bruce was by far the superior man, and king.

As he silently contemplated the flames burning in the hearth, Jamie heard soft footsteps falling on the stone floor. The woman, Lauren, who had served the wine the night before was moving slowly across the room, unaware of his presence there. She was carrying a woman's gown, frowning as she smoothed out a wrinkle in the cloth. She paused by the light of the front window, shaking her head over her task. He found himself once again intrigued by the quiet and mysterious young beauty.

"My lady," he said softly.

She was very light, almost flaxen blond, and her eyes were as blue as a cloudless sky. Those eyes widened like moons as she heard his voice and she paused, her fair flesh blooming into the color of a rose as she realized that she was not alone.

"Sir James," she murmured nervously.

She was afraid of him, openly so, without guile or wiles, though she showed no intent of flight.

"You will be accompanying us, you know."

"Yes," she said simply. She looked like a little sparrow. He could see the pulse at her throat.

"Actually, it wasn't our intent. But the lady of the house seems determined that we will not escape without her."

Lauren nodded again, lowering her head. "I am to assure her good behavior, I believe."

"Hm, as it stands, yes. But that, of course, is because it seems there is no one here who will admit to your being anything other than a good friend of the family."

"I'm a very good friend of the family," she said. Her flush deepened. She was obviously very uncomfortable, and hedging the truth seemed to be a great effort for her. She was as soft spoken as she was regal, as mild and honest as Christina was wild and deceitful. Tempting. Sweet. Very sweet. And yet . . .

It crossed his mind that oddly, there was something he liked about the very wildness that was tormenting him so. The lady was a chameleon. A challenge.

He didn't need a challenge right now. He needed the supplies they had come to receive as tribute to the King of the Scots.

"Perhaps you should suggest to your very good friend, Lady Christina, that you would both be far safer, remaining here."

"I cannot."

"Because you underestimate your danger?"

"Because she would not listen, nor could she."

"Why?"

"Christina would impale herself on a sword rather than allow the English to believe she gave no resistance to the Scots."

"Ah."

Jamie smiled pleasantly, walking to Lauren, and around her. He was startled by the sudden sense of anguish and nostalgia that swept through him. She reminded him too closely of someone he had known so well, so many years ago now.

"I . . . I should hurry this to Christina," she said nervously. "I've heard that Crystal has returned, and that you are wanting to be on the road."

The Lady Christina. The current bane of his existence! He would be leaving behind more cows than he was taking if she started up with her dramatics once again.

He was startled as a vision of a long gone memory, painful beyond comprehension, stirred within him, and he wondered that it should do so now. Why should the desperate antics of this strange enemy cause him to suddenly relive the agony of the past?

Impatience stirred him. He didn't understand the desperation, but Robert Bruce, with so many of his household still incarcerated, never minded an abundance of prisoners of his own for ransom.

He took the gown from the woman's arms.

"I'll see that it reaches your very good friend," he told her, and turning with long, firm strides, he started up the stairs.

CHAPTER 4

There was a tapping on the door. Christina, who had taken the minutes of respite to sink back in the deep metal hip bath, reflecting upon her total despair, dared do so no longer.

"Lauren!" she said with relief, half rising in the tub to sluice the last of the soap from her body. "Come in, come in!" She heard the doorknob turn and continued. "Naturally, the Scots would send a wretched, arrogant ass on such a pathetic journey as this, but since I've irritated the ogre already, I'm eager to make sure that he doesn't determine to leave without me." She stood, dripping in the light of day, still shivering but for the warmth that came from the low fire burning in the hearth. "If you'd be so good as to hand me the towel?"

The towel landed on her head, and though the linen was not heavy, she was blinded for a minute, stumbled within the small metal tub, and nearly lost her balance, and the towel. "Lauren," she murmured.

She was caught and steadied, and naturally, at the feel of the hands upon her, she knew that it was not Lauren who had come. She attempted to turn with instinctive alarm, but was firmly twisted back, the towel wrapped around her.

"Stand still, my lady, before you bring us both pitching face forward into your tub of water and shed mud."

She couldn't stand still. It was quite impossible with him standing at her back, adjusting the linen around her shoulders. Panic seized her too easily as she tried to remember, word for word, just what she had said. With all her strength she twisted to free herself from the restraining hands, and did so just as he moved. With an extreme lack of dignity, she entangled her feet and fell back into the water with a hard plop upon her rear, dragging the towel with her.

He had managed to step back.

"My lady, you are the first young woman I have met to be such a hazard to yourself!" he informed her. "And you wonder that I am loath to bring you riding with me anywhere, much less into situations with the propensity for danger."

Soaked again, tangled in the towel, humiliated beyond reason, she had little choice but to face him, aware that she had flushed to every extremity of her body. And he was two feet beyond the tub, not soaked in the least; it seemed he had even escaped what droplets of water had flown from the tub upon her heavy downfall.

"Christina," he said impatiently, arms crossed over his chest, "This arrogant, ogre-ass of a Scotsman will indeed leave you if you are not ready to ride in five minutes."

"If you'd be kind enough to give me privacy to pre-pare . . ." she managed to say.

"Arrogant asses are never kind, be they Scots or other men. Get up, now."

"I can hardly rise with you standing there."

"As you wish."

He turned with such a heedless dismissal that she was afraid he meant to leave the manor at that second. She would be reduced to running after them in nothing but a soaked towel.

"Wait!" she said, all but strangling out the single word. She fought to free her hands from the linen wrapped around her to get a grip on the edge of the tub. The linen towel was caught beneath her. She meant to leap up so quickly, to be the most dutiful of all creatures in the world at that moment, but rather than make a swift, elegant, and disdainful rise despite her lack of dress, she managed only to struggle more and more desperately, like a wounded animal in a trap. "No, don't go! Please, don't go, I am . . . hurrying."

But, of course, when he turned again she was still trying to get her balance, her words were almost breathless, and she was tangled in both the towel and the sodden mane of her hair. She could barely see him as he took a step toward her, caught her firmly by both shoulders, stood her up, and lifted her from the tub. She arrived safely upon her feet on the rug before the fire. The towel, of course, was quite useless.

Between wet strands of hair, she could see that he was back no more than a few feet, staring at her. She felt his eyes, as if they touched the length of her. A shiver swept over her, sensations of both hot and cold. She was caught in the sudden fear that he would sweep her up, snatch away the towel, and from there . . . imagination fled in a great wave of dread and burning anxiety.

"What . . . ?" she said, yet could summon no more words.

"The rug," he said.

"The rug?"

"Persian, I believe. A handsome piece."

Anger, of course, was absurd. And yet, she could not help

but feel it. She stood trembling in the anticipation of sudden violence, and all he stared at was a rug.

"The rug! Yes, of course, let me get off it before the value is lessened by the wetness of my feet!" And so she moved forward, off the rug, hurrying across the room to the bed, where he had dropped her clothing. Ignoring his presence, she dropped the towel with all speed, thinking to slip into her shift more quickly without an effort at modesty. But she was wet and slick still, and found herself fighting then to get the shift down her body. To her great alarm, she found him at her side, and once again, she felt the size and scope of his presence, muscle, bone, scent, and being, and fear touched by that strange fire rippled through her. But his effort was all at getting her dressed; his hands were practiced as he tugged at the linen, righting it down the length of her, though his manner was nothing short of impatient. "Another towel might have been procured," he told her, and to add great insult to injury, it seemed he was amused.

"Not quickly," she said, "and speed, of course, is of the essence here."

He paid her little heed, having the fresh gown in his hands, ready to be drawn over her head. She stood still, accepting the assistance then, and wishing that she could stop the shaking that had seized hold of her. The gown went on. He turned her about to lace up the ties, impatiently thrusting wet strands of hair away from her back. Even with such a hindrance, his movements were sure and quick, a sure sign that he was familiar with either the dressing or undressing of women. She was certain that his skill was mostly with the latter, though she was apparently not one of those women he might choose to disrobe. He was all too impatient to see that she was duly clad.

"Shoes, hose?" he said impatiently.

"Really, I can manage," she murmured.

"Are you quite certain?" he inquired.

"You may trust, sir, that I am now as eager to quit this room as you are."

"Then here it is, my lady. You must come with us, yet you are like bringing along a plague. Lauren will accompany us, since you are so determined that we, who seek no ill upon your people other than the sum agreed to be paid, insist that there must be hostages. Therefore, you will swear on what honor you may have that—"

"And Sir Alfred!" she said suddenly.

"What?"

"Sir Alfred! You must take him. Oh, he is harmless, I swear it! But you must bring him as well, or else he will be left . . . to suffer what consequences there may be."

"How can you be so afraid of your own king?" he demanded irritably.

She was quiet for a moment. "Please," she said very softly, eyes downcast. "I have handled this quite badly—"

"Oh, lady! You have handled it badly? I can't think of the words in any known language to express just how badly!"

"I beg you, and I swear I shall be the most humble and obedient hostage you could possibly imagine."

He was silent. She was ready to cast all dignity to the wind—why not, she had none left—and fall to her knees at his feet, hating herself all the while. But before she could come to that last desperate moment, he sighed softly. "Fine, we shall bring you, Lauren, and Sir Alfred, though I don't believe that humility is really one of those virtues with which you are truly blessed. But you will travel separately, and if you should create the least disturbance among the riders, you will be escorted far from the party, and the fate of both Lauren and Sir Alfred will indeed be in jeopardy. Do you understand this, my lady? Do you truly understand what any infraction on your part will bring upon the others?''

''I do,'' she said.

''Then find your shoes, for I am most impatient now to be under way.''

She met his eyes at last.

''And may I suggest a brush?'' he said.

He didn't await a reply. Long strides brought him to the door, and out of the room.

Crystal had returned, she learned.

After insisting that Sir Alfred accompany them as well, Christina slid into hose and shoes quickly, ready to find her dear old friend and explain that she feared to leave him behind. She wondered if he would fear Scottish imprisonment more, but she believed he would know her intent immediately—he was a renowned and respected knight of old. She had to admit that Robert Bruce had been incredibly lenient with many who had sinned against him and it was most unlikely he would do harm against an aging man who had spent his military career in France rather than Scotland.

Sir Alfred would also be one less mouth to feed with so much taken from the manor.

Yet someone must be left in charge, and that left Henry, the steward, so she was eager to reach him as well.

She'd packed nothing, having had no time to do so, yet, of course, true prisoners were seldom given such a luxury. She hesitated, then took the few minutes to put extra shifts and hose into a large brocade travel bag. At the bottom, she shoved what few coins and pieces of jewelry she had remaining, thinking there might be some point at which she would need the valuables.

They were hardly enough to bribe anyone of standing,

but the time might come when a poor man in need of any small substance could render assistance. The room remained in shambles when she was done, but that mattered little. With her small task quickly complete, she raced down the stairs.

The hall was empty, and she was certain that they had all adjourned to the yard in the rear, ready to travel.

Either that, or she had been left behind.

No, she had heard the sounds of the horses' trappings and the men's shouts and calls when she was upstairs. She hurried out and found what she expected, a multitude of horses and cows, men moving hurriedly about, taking position, packing the last of the goods. As she walked into the midst of the men and beasts, she saw that one of the Scotsmen had come hurrying out behind her with the last of Sir Jamie's treasures—the Persian rug from her room.

She stood, not recognizing even those men who had come in to dinner. Then, at a distance, she saw that Sir Alfred and Lauren were both already seated upon their mounts. They were in the company of the man she knew to be Liam, big and Irish, and apparently accustomed to command on his own. She made her way through horses and baggage to their position and looked up at Sir Alfred, ignoring the Irishman who had apparently chosen to fight for the Scots.

"Sir Alfred, I beg your pardon, for it was my suggestion you accompany us."

The old knight smiled down at her. "Aye, my lady. And my thanks," he said very softly.

"Lauren?" she murmured uneasily.

"I'm quite fine, Christina."

Liam was watching, listening to her every word. She ignored him. "Everyone has disappeared. There's not a servant about. I had meant to speak with Henry."

"Matters have been seen to," Liam said, speaking to her.

She stiffened without replying. The Irishman ignored her lack of courtesy.

"Sir James has spoken with your man. And that, lass, will suffice," he said.

She gritted her teeth. *Lass.* She was suddenly a captive bereft of title and position. But then again, she was an *unwanted* captive. She was certain these men felt they were unwilling escorts for an asp in their midst.

"I'm quite sure that everything shall be left in the utmost perfection and order," she said. "Of course, Henry will not be overburdened with goods and stock to care for, shall he?" She didn't expect an answer and so continued. "Is there a certain horse I am to ride? Lauren and Sir Alfred are here, but I don't see another mount." She prayed suddenly that didn't mean that she was to walk or run behind the party. She wouldn't make it far. She didn't doubt that they might cast such a humiliation upon her, except that it would slow down their movement.

"Here comes Sir James now," Liam said.

Christina turned. She was startled to see that he was leading Crystal toward her. He walked the horse to her position and said irritably, "My lady! You've managed to arrive. Come, mount up. We were about to leave without you."

She didn't argue but accepted his assistance into the saddle, at which point she realized that a lead had been attached to Crystal's bridle. That was turned over to Liam, who was apparently aware of his duty already, for he accepted the lead with a grim nod. "That's not at all necessary, Sir James, since it is my choice to ride with you," she said stiffly.

"Yes, but you will ride where I choose," he said, turning then to Sir Alfred and Lauren. "The two of you will be so kind as to take a position toward the front of the party," he informed them. He turned, heading back for his own great war steed.

"You will follow," Liam said to Christina.

Lauren offered Christina a quick reassuring smile, and urged her mount forward as she had been bidden. Christina found herself chafing as most of the party wound before them. All who would come behind were a few of the men leading the stolen cattle and horses, and those who would follow farther behind to see that none were lost upon the road.

The party began its ride, being of a size now where it was some time before Liam even urged his horse forward.

As they left, Christina turned back. None of the household appeared as they departed. Hamstead Heath might have been entirely deserted. And yet, in the end, as she twisted entirely around in the saddle, she saw at last that Henry and several others had come to the old Roman wall at the front. Henry lifted a hand to her in farewell as they crossed the expanse of the valley and entered through the rough trail in the woods.

There were places they traversed where it was impossible for two to ride at once, but Liam never surrendered his lead, pressing forward and leaving her to follow closely behind. He didn't speak, and neither did she. Hours passed in which she rode in silence, hearing the talk and laughter of men before them, and men behind. She couldn't see Sir Alfred or Lauren, for they rode far to the front. Their movement was slow, with such a great caravan of goods to be brought on roads that were at best little more than trails. As the hours passed, Christina felt her muscles growing stiff, weariness taking hold. But these were men accustomed to very long marches, and often, she was certain, without food or rest. They did not mind their pace, nor the long hours.

They did not break at midday, yet when at last the light

began to fail, she found that shouts were being relayed down
the length of the group, and the men began to break ranks,
some moving forward, and some to the rear, seeing that the
cattle and horses were secured in the midst of the forested
valley where they chose to halt for the evening. Liam, who
in all those hours still had not spoken a single word to her,
at last broke his silence.

"Come, quickly, for I've business now greater than the
guarding of a cunning girl," he said irritably. He nudged
his horse's flanks, bringing them both forward at a sudden
speed that caused her to grip Crystal hard, lest she fall and
be trampled beneath. She wondered wryly if that might not
be Liam's attempt. But he looked back, realizing his sudden
burst of speed after so many hours of a gait that had been
little more than a plod. His face reflected either a quick
moment of relief, or perhaps even admiration.

She was eager to see Lauren and Sir Alfred, yet when
she was led to the center of the clearing, she saw neither.
Liam dismounted from his horse, and reached for her with
no ceremony, bearing her down to the ground as well. She
didn't remember a time when she had ever ridden so long,
and she was afraid that her legs would not hold her when
she stood. Fortunately, they were all moving about with a
brisk speed, heedless of her grasp on her saddle to steady
herself.

She was left standing, watching while men dismounted,
tethered their mounts, and went about the work of fashioning
a paddock in the glen for the horses and cattle. At last, one
of the men she had met briefly in the hall went by, and she
stopped him. "Please, where might Lauren and Sir Alfred
be?"

"They are tended to, lady," was his only reply.

She shook her head, feeling an irrational rise of temper,
since no ill had been done to her, she had simply been

ignored. She was afraid as well. Lauren was stunningly beautiful, and she didn't trust men who were so battle hardened, no matter their king's determinations on leniency. Robert Bruce's battle was not over, she knew well. There were pockets of English resistance, castles still held by his enemies. And she knew that when battle was engaged, many brutalities were overlooked, since they had been practiced so many years, by both sides.

Another man came by for Crystal, pleasant enough with his explanation that she would be tended for the night. And still, Christina stood in the center of the activity, with no direction for herself.

At last, as she fumed, Sir Jamie appeared, striding from a thicket of trees. "So, my lady, you've enjoyed the day's ride. Clear as a bell throughout the hours, don't you agree?"

"Lovely. Absolutely lovely. May I see Sir Alfred and the La—and Lauren?"

"No."

"No?" She set her hands on her hips in rebellion and surprise. "But we are all your . . . hostages."

"Alas, actually, they are our guests, while you . . . quite frankly you are a thorn in the side, no more. Since your brow is so furrowed, however, I can assure you that both are well, they have dined, and they are settled for the night. We ride again with the break of dawn."

"I see. And I am to stand in the midst of the copse, like a true thorn?"

"Alas, no. I ask no evil task of my men I will not take on myself. Therefore, as Liam was responsible for you during the day, by night I have drawn the straw to be at your side."

"You don't want me with you—but you're afraid I will leave?"

"Such innocence! There are perhaps many points upon

this ride when you might wish to depart, knowing that you are close to an English garrison.''

''I could have remained at Hamstead Heath, and awaited the English.''

''Aye, the furious English, who would have branded you a weak traitor for not dying rather than give in to the Scots. Rather than the poor ravished hostage, taken by the enemy, only to escape under the most dire danger, to bring men at arms down upon those who would steal English goods!''

She turned away from him impatiently. ''You don't understand the situation at all,'' she informed him.

He caught her arm, drawing her back. ''I see, such treachery would not be within your heart or cunning little mind, while poisoning men in a clever charade seemed an easy accomplishment.''

She stared at his hand upon her arm. ''I don't know where you think I might go at this minute.''

''I think that you will come with me.''

She lowered her head. ''As you wish, of course.''

He led her across the clearing of the same copse. As he did so, she saw that they had planned their place of rest quite well; to their left there was another clearing, serving as the nighttime paddock for their ill gotten gains and their own mounts. Their own horses, however, remained bridled, though their saddles had been removed, and she saw, by the arrangements around the trees, that the saddles would serve as pillows for the men as they took their rest in shifts. She knew that they would be easily able, should the need arise, to desert the stolen cattle, horses, and goods, and take only their mounts for a quick escape. The Scots were infamous for their ability to disappear into the forests as if they had never been an army, formed en masse. This was their terrain, and they knew it well. They did not travel heavily by any means; they had set up no tents, and their preparation to depart in the morning would surely take them no more than a few minutes.

Apparently, however, they did not think their danger great that night, for fires had been lit in various places, and some of the men had taken out pans and kettles. The aromas coming from the cooking were seductive, especially considering the long day, and their lack of break during those hours for any morsel of food. They didn't approach any of the fires.

"You go days without eating, Sir James?" she inquired, as if the words were casual, with no real interest.

"I have dined—with Lauren and Sir Alfred. I thank you deeply for your concern."

She was well aware that he was laughing at her, awaiting her own request for food. She determined she would not give one.

"So, do we sit around a fire, and listen as your men boast of their exploits against the English?" she inquired.

"Alas, I'm afraid not. As I said, we ride with the dawn."

They had come to a tree. Crystal's saddle lay beside his larger one, with its sword sheath and other trappings. "There you are, my lady. Not the comfort of a manor, I'm afraid, but then they do say that we often choose our own bed in life, and therefore after, must lie upon it."

She ignored his words. He, had, luckily, chosen a spot where oak leaves lay heavily upon the ground, softening the hardness, though the earth was cold as she settled down. Her throat was parched, her stomach was gnawing, yet she kept her silence.

She no longer felt any alarm as he settled down beside her; his contempt for both her character and form had long been established. Yet she was curious and startled when he asked for her ankle. "You . . . don't intend to . . . to . . . ."

"Cripple you, to keep you from running? That would be quite brutal, don't you think?"

"Naturally, I would consider it so!" she grated.

"I intend a noose around your ankle, no more, Christina."

She silently allowed herself to be tied, then caught his arm when he would have tied the rope to himself. "Please, I . . . I desperately need a few moments of privacy." She had determined that she would not ask for food or water, but ignoring such other needs could cause a far greater embarrassment as the hours went on.

"I'm sorry, what was that you said?"

"Sir, I need a few moments of privacy."

"No, that other word."

She sighed wearily. "Please."

"My lady, we are truly not barbarians! All you need do is ask."

"Indeed."

"I am sorely aggrieved, my lady. What have you asked that we have not granted? We would happily have left without accosting a single human being. And yet, you would come, and so you are here. You wished for Sir Alfred to come, and he is along, already sleeping like a baby in the midst of yonder trees. Now, as for Lauren, she is a delight, and sleeps as well, though she was not the one insisting she accompany us. We left behind cattle we had intended to take, just so that your people would not face severe hunger. So, Christina, what is that we have done that has not been entirely by your own request?"

He rose, helping her to her feet, removing the rope. "Come along then."

"Where are we going"

"There is a small brook."

He had her by the hand; he led and she followed. They moved through trees that seemed devoid of life, and yet she knew that his men were dispersed among them. At last they broke through the trail and came upon a thin rivulet, a tiny brook. It gave off a soft, almost sweetly quiet, bubbling sound, and it was more than she could bear. He eased his hold, and she rushed forward, falling on her knees, made desperate then by the sound of the water itself. He stood back as she drank, then set an arm upon her shoulder.

"Not so quickly; you'll make yourself ill."

She paused. "How kind of you to care."

"Of course."

And still, she didn't wish cramps or worse upon herself, and so she took greater care with her speed, cupping the water more slowly, and relishing the cool freshness in her mouth, against her tongue, and down her throat. He waited quite patiently. She bathed her face and throat, shivering and yet delighted after the long and dusty day.

At last, she rose uncertainly, meeting his gaze. She then said, "I swear, most humbly, Sir James, that if you were to give me but two minutes by myself, I would not run to the English. At this moment, I assure you, I certainly have no idea of where to find them, were it my will."

"Two minutes, Christina. Two minutes. And if you don't believe that our efforts have been to kindness, you will quickly learn what life on the road can be when they are not."

She nodded, and left him, crawling through the trees a distance from him. When she had gone that distance, she found another delightful place by the water, tended to her needs, then dared a moment longer to doff her shoes and hose and wade into the water, shivering again, but delighting in its feel against her limbs as she washed the road dust from more of her person. She was somewhat drenched when she finished, and delighting in the water when she heard his voice from the embankment. "Two minutes have long passed, Christina."

"Aye," she said regretfully, and came from the water, the hem of her gown gripped tight in her hands, lest she soak herself completely in the coolness of the night.

"Don't take more time than you say, lady," he warned. "If you'd play in the stream, you will do so in my presence."

"I dutifully await your next command," she said.

"What is it in your voice that suggests anything but?" he murmured.

"There should be nothing; I mean exactly what I say," she told him.

The sound he made was something like a snort, after which he took her hand again, and they made their way back through the trees to his chosen position for the night. The rope was replaced around her foot, and tethered to his own.

He lay down a small distance from her, and it seemed that the way he lay, head straight back upon the saddle, arms crossed over his chest, would be an impossible position in which to sleep.

She tried her left side, her right side, her back, and once again, her left side, seeking to find some position in which both her makeshift pillow and the ground might become more comfortable. Nothing seemed to work.

Despite his position, she thought that he had fallen asleep, he had lain without moving so long, and without speaking. Yet when she had found a position in which she thought that she might at long last fall asleep from sheer exhaustion, he spoke. "Are you settled at last? You are more wretched than a bedbug."

Her back stiffened, the meager comfort she had found slipped away as if a cold breeze had come to rip away any thought of comfort. "I will try not to move again."

"Since you lie awake, you must tell me more about Hamstead Heath."

Startled, she rolled back to her side. The forest was filled with shadows, and yet she could see the line of his profile, features strongly arranged, the breadth of him so near, a formidable presence in the night.

"Hamstead Heath?" she murmured. "What is there to tell. Once upon a time it was a lovely manor in a valley surrounded by hills. Many people lived there in a self-sustaining world where the fields were verdant, ample food was grown, and livestock was raised well. Artisans came and went. Grain grew rich, the grass was sweet and good, and over many years, some of the finest horses in the world were bred and trained. Then the war came."

He let out a derisive sound. "You've no idea how long war has ravaged the lands just north of your own. Rich lands, beautiful lands, laid waste as English armies trampled over them time and again, as every last blade of grass was rendered useless. All due to the greed of one man."

She rose on an elbow. "You're quite wrong, you know. All that was not done by the greed of one man, and you have blinded yourself to the truth, if that is what you believe. Your own great barons have had a heavy hand in destroying Scotland. They war upon one another in constant blood feuds. Your Highlanders accept no laws but their own. Even now your king fights his own men as he fights the English, and can never really know which side his people support."

Even as she spoke, she realized that she sorely tested his temper. She thought herself a fool, even as the words escaped her lips, true as she felt them to be. She found herself inadvertently retreating, and thus straining the rope that bound her ankle to his.

He turned in the darkness, and she felt a surge of unease fill her, but he spoke impatiently. "Did you think that I would beat you senseless for such an observation, Christina? If so, you don't see the difference that separates us. There is no great hunger for bloody retaliation against everything and everyone English. As we have fought one another, we have understood that *our* great barons had loyalties to England for their lands held by England's king. Being born a Scot has not eased the hunger for riches, titles, and property among many men. Neither does any man's place of birth secure his position as noble, courageous, or virtuous in any manner. But Robert Bruce has no desire to seize the English crown. We are a sovereign people. And no matter what other loyalties might have once existed, the time has come when this country is united.''

"That is why you fear I may still run to the English?'' she said softly.

"The English remain in Scotland,'' he replied. "And while they do . . . then there will be a great deal to fear.''

"So, all Scots are now loyal?''

"You know that they are not. But soon, Robert Bruce will hold the entire country. And the English will be cast out. I was not, however, asking you about the land, property lines, or even the construction of your home. Your opinion of the Scots is evident. Heathens, barbarians, men with no real laws, and certainly, no morals. But you chose—rather, fought!—to accompany such men out of fear of retaliation for paying a ransom to our king for his peace. That is a rather sad state of affairs.''

She remained silent, glad of the darkness, as he awaited a reply.

"Well, Christina?''

"Yes, it is a sad state of affairs. But as you have noted, men are not guaranteed any status of morality due to their birth.''

"Edward the First was a ruthless and brutal man.''

"To the English, you surely understand, he was a strong king, fond of the law—"

"Within England."

"He loved learning, the arts, building—"

"Yes, I daresay. He built the Welsh right out of a country."

"He was a far better man than—"

"Than?"

"The king we have now," she finished softly.

"My lady! At last there is something upon which we agree. This new king has all the sense of vengeance, and no sense of politics whatsoever. But he is young, and apparently in the best of health, and so you will have him to honor for a very long time."

She lay silent in the darkness, very aware of the perceptions of the man at her side, and curious, despite the precarious status between them. He completely infuriated her; he found her beyond irritating, and far less than appealing in any sense of the word, but she was intrigued by his thoughts, his beliefs, and his view of their world.

"So, my lady," he said softly, "who is Lauren? No household servant, I assure you."

She was startled that his words not only chilled her, but offended as well. She had, perhaps even in the secret recesses of her heart, considered her actions somewhat noble. She'd been willing to throw herself into any danger—more than that, she'd been willing to literally throw herself at his feet—and to no avail, for it was Lauren who fascinated him, and she remained in great danger. Not of losing her life—this particular band of Scotsmen did not at all appear to be cold-blooded murderers. But this man apparently far preferred Lauren's delicate beauty and quiet, serene manner to every attempt she had made to draw his attention from her brother's fiancée.

"I asked you a question."

"She is a friend. A very good friend."

"Not a poor relation, living upon the estate?"

"Yes," she said quickly.

"You're a liar."

"She is a very dear friend. That is not a lie."

She was startled by his sudden movement in the darkness, turning toward her so that he was suddenly very close.

"I have a feeling that she is the one with the power and position."

"I assure you, I am the daughter of the old lord."

"And sister of the new one. That I believe. Your great King Edward might have been a lawgiver, but it's doubtful that he improved your position any at all. Your brother is the master of Hamstead Heath. By the very nature of English law, you are property to be bartered. Definitely a lady of privilege, and only certain men might vie for your hand, the rich association you bring, and surely, a dowry of excellent horses and cattle."

"Did you leave any horses?" she asked sharply.

He shrugged, not responding to the question. "Then there is Lauren, a beautiful, young, well-bred woman living upon the estate. Therefore, she is to be your brother's wife."

"She is a friend," Christina repeated stubbornly.

"And your brother is a man greatly blessed, for her manner is gracious in the extreme."

She held her temper, and her fear, silent for many minutes. Then she said, "I would do anything if you would leave her be."

"I didn't threaten her. Not did I ask for anything in return that I should not."

The darkness covered the deep flush that must have rooted at her feet, and filled the length of her.

She turned to her side, determined that she would not

carry on any more conversation with him. The truth of her situation was evident.

"Of course, if your brother were to die, you most certainly would be in a sorry position. The sniveling, spoiled man who is king of England would hold your fate in his hands. He is king, and could force the issue of your marriage, if he chose, without your brother's death, but since the civil war within England lies so fresh in the hearts of many men, he wouldn't take extreme action unless he were desperate. Or in a tantrum. Ah, but if Steven were lost, the King of England would have all say over you, a noblewoman. He could marry you off to a pretty friend who keeps a close position to him, and thus have some defense against his critics. Or again, one of his brutal war lords, and there are many who go far beyond the force necessary to wage battle."

She couldn't keep silent. She flung back in sudden fury. "And there are many among them who are fine and honorable men as well, doing their duty as they see it, keeping their loyalty to their country and their king."

She thought that he was smiling in the darkness, amused.

"Truly, I understand your sad plight. Indeed, you must pray nightly that your brother doesn't die."

She sat up, ready to risk violence against him, hands clenched into fists. "I pray nightly that my brother doesn't die because I love him. Twist that as you may. He is not just my blood, but my best friend as well, trusted and loved throughout all the years we were children. Perhaps it is you I should pity, if you have no concept of family loyalty."

"Did I suggest I had no such concept?"

"You are impossible. You are more. You are rude and arrogant, and think to judge everyone. You consider that you know so much! You are nothing more than a grasping man, one among a den of lions, scratching, tearing, devouring, in your desperate efforts to prey upon innocents, since you cannot, as yet, oust the military power of the English king, no matter how ineffective he may be.''

"Take care, Lady Christina, with your words. As yet, I've not preyed upon any innocents.''

"You've robbed us blind.''

"I've taken what was agreed.''

"And robbed us blind.''

"Would that thievery was all that had befallen Scotland,'' he said very softly.

"I did nothing to Scotland. In fact, were the entire country of barbarians and painted Highlanders to fall into the sea, it would please me greatly.''

"But you've done nothing to Scotland.''

"Perhaps God has deserted your country.''

"And perhaps he has at last looked down upon men willing to fight and die to the bitter end for her, and therefore has graced our new king, while damning yours.''

"A king is but the head of a great force and power.''

"Just what is it that your brother has done? Why was he not at Hamstead Heath, to follow up on his promises?''

"My brother has done nothing!''

He moved, leaning very close to her in the darkness. "Did he refuse to fight, to lead a great force of power in the king's name? Is he held for cowardice?''

What happened was not really her fault; he had moved too close, and attacked someone far too dear. She didn't think; she struck out, and did so with speed and fury, catching him across the line of his jaw with a sharp, open-handed blow. And even then she did not think, heedless when that hand was caught and she found herself back on the forest floor, pinned there with him above her, the heat of his temper wrapping her in the cool of the night. But she ignored her position, speaking angrily still. "Never, how dare you!'' she cried, tears stinging her eyes. "My brother is no coward, he will fight any man. He is intelligent, and caring, viewing all the lives dependent upon him, rather than his own. He is honest, and speaks his mind. He has integrity, and will not go back on a promise. He risks everything that others might not starve, that . . . that . . . oh, there is nothing to say to you! You ride on a great horse, with the trappings and arms of glory, and you are nothing more than a wounded beast, lashing out wherever you may strike. You would mock my brother! He is good, and merciful. He prefers learning, art, and music, to death and destruction, but he can handle a sword against any man alive. At a fair play of arms, he would best you in seconds, you would be upon the ground, pleading for your life, bleeding and vulnerable beneath him!''

She fell silent, at last realizing her own position, and the irony of her words. She couldn't have moved a finger against him at that moment. The full force of his length was against her, and every inch of that was sinew and muscle, hard as steel. The face she had struck was close above her own, and the quick pounding of his heart seemed to echo her own. She gritted her teeth, closed her eyes, and awaited some form of retaliation.

He stayed too long, just above her, not moving. The weight upon her was heavy and firm, and she felt every little leaf and pebble in the ground beneath her. She dragged in a sudden breath, unaware that she had ceased to breathe in her waiting. And her eyes opened.

He studied her still, so close that she could see his eyes, and read the emotion within them. Anger remained, but curiosity as well.

''I believe I mentioned before that I couldn't quite accept humility as one of your virtues, my lady.''

''Perhaps you could order an execution for the middle of the night.''

"I wouldn't have you killed, Christina. Merely escorted back to Hamstead Heath. After all, we do have Lauren."

A shivering seized her. She closed her eyes again. "Your pardon, Sir James! Truly, I beg your pardon."

"An apology would be in order."

"Did I imply that you were anything but the most magnificent and benevolent of men? That the Scots were anything less than the most chivalrous of men, the bravest of warriors?"

"The mere tone of your voice would be enough to make most men violent, Christina," he said quietly.

"I'm not trying to use any tone!"

"That's the point, perhaps. You don't need to *try.*" He rolled from her. The sudden force of his movement caused the rope that tethered them together to jerk, and she was drawn along in a sudden snap of movement, ending with her back solidly against his side, her head resting against his shoulder. She froze, fearful that he would hurl her away, equally fearful that he would not.

"May I suggest that you try to sleep, that you make no movement, no movement at all, and refrain from speaking a word more, and I do mean a single word!"

She held still in absolute silence, once again, scarcely daring to breathe. And she knew that she would never sleep as she lay, wretchedly aware of his every breath, the slightest shift of his body, the constant pulse of his heart.

CHAPTER 5

Christina had never known that she could be so grateful just for the morning light, to open her eyes and see that day had come.

And that she lay alone on the forest floor.

She rose very carefully, and indeed she was alone. A sense of panic seized her as she first thought that she had been deserted here, that they would go on with Lauren and Sir Alfred, that they had shed themselves of her—the great thorn in their side.

But even as she blinked away sleep, she realized that she could hear the sounds of men speaking, moving about, preparing to ride. She heard the little clangs and clatter as horses were saddled. She also became instantly and painfully aware of an aroma on the air; meat roasting over a fire.

She rolled, and stood carefully, balancing against the tree trunk by which Crystal's saddle still lay. Leaves clung to her hair and dress, and she had begun an attempt to dust them all from her person, to look up and discover that Sir James had returned. He stood steps away. His hair was damp, his mantle was cast over his shoulders, held in place by the large silver brooch which must boast his family crest.

"I beg your pardon. Am I not moving quickly enough?" she inquired.

"Actually, I was thinking that I rather prefer you in dishevelment. You wear leaves quite well, my lady. In silence, you're not entirely unappealing. You've a look of an ancient forest sprite, or such."

"How kind," she returned irritably, then winced, remembering that she meant to remain a part of this party. His growing interest in Lauren was quite alarming. She lowered her head quickly, lest he should read any emotion in her eyes. She had to keep them apart, a difficult task when he'd come upon her in the bath, and registered nothing more than disdain.

"I am doing my best to hurry," she murmured. "You should have awakened me."

"Indeed. I considered it a kindness to let you sleep, since you endured such a rough night, tossing and turning throughout it."

"Again, you should have awakened me. I meant to remain absolutely still, as you—suggested."

"And risk more words tumbling so sweetly from your lips? Nay, I'd not have done so."

"Shall I ride with Liam again?"

"As I told you, I give my men no evil task I'm not willing to take upon myself."

"I am to ride with you?"

"For the first hours." He turned to leave, but hesitated, then impatiently, "You'd like a walk to the brook?"

"Yes," she admitted quietly.

"Then come along."

As they walked, they traveled this time through the center of the camp. His men acknowledged her with courteous and wary nods, and hailed him as they moved about. She thought it curious that there seemed to be a true camaraderie among them; they honored him, certainly, obeyed his every word, and yet there seemed to be a bond of tightly knit friendship among them all. She kept her silence, responding in kind to every nod that came her way, careful not to lose her moments by the small brook. As they passed one of the last fires, some called to Jamie, and he paused, accepting a large piece of meat skewered on a knife. Christina stood by; none was offered to her.

They walked again.

"I am assuming, due to the great benevolence of Robert Bruce, that Lauren and Sir Alfred are faring well, and have spent the night in safety?"

It took him a moment to answer. He was savoring a bite of the meat. The aroma was tantalizing, to say the least.

"But, of course," he murmured at last.

"Where are they?"

"Near the horses."

"Well, having spent a night in safety?"

"I've already assured you that it is so."

"Given water, and a chance for privacy, as well."

"Given whatever is in our power to give."

"Ah."

They continued through the trees. Christina tripped on a root, and his hand came out quickly to steady her. The meat was all but beneath her nose.

She pulled free quickly, murmuring a thank-you, and preceding him, for by the early light of the dawn, she could catch a glimpse of the water through the trees.

She came upon the embankment. He was directly behind her. "There is a log, Sir James, where I'm sure you could enjoy your meal in great comfort, and I swear I would move no more than a few feet down the water.''

''How courteous you are, my lady.''

''Unwanted hostages will do their best.''

''Ah. So this has been your best.''

''May I have my moments alone?''

''You've no care for a morsel of meat?''

''None was offered.''

''And, of course, you would not ask.''

''Should an unwanted hostage, attempting at the least to do her best, seek to take a sustaining morsel from a man who has the business of ravishing the countryside before him?''

''We're within Scottish borders, Christina, though there are pockets of the enemy all about, yes. But I don't believe I've any real pillaging before me today. You're most welcome to a piece of meat, all you need do is ask.''

She wanted the meat more than she could begin to say. But the arrogant amusement of his manner was far too much.

''I'll move on—but not far at all—to my place upon the water, sir. Enjoy your repast.''

She turned, somewhat proud of the dignity and indifference with which she managed to do so. But her determined exit into the surrounding growth was robbed of its elegance when she nearly tripped again, this time, upon a stray stone which gave beneath her foot. She managed to recover her balance, and since her back was to him, she could only imagine the entertainment her awkward departure allowed.

Yet moments later, she forgot her pride as she knelt by the water, savoring the coolness, and the feel against her flesh. She dared much, aware that he was not far away, and that he could certainly hear her splashing through the water. He knew exactly where she was; he could find her at will.

Yet as the water she drank settled, she felt again a cutting sensation in her stomach, and she wasn't at all sure if she was pleased or not with her ability to refuse to give in to his taunting, or if she was a fool, and should just insist that she be fed—since food seemed to be plentiful enough within their party. She could still feel and see the piece of meat, a thigh, she thought, from a large pheasant. Certainly, she could smell it no more, not from her distance. Yet it seemed that the scent was etched in her memory.

Shoes and hose on the bank, the skirt of her shift and gown wound high above her knees, she waded into the crisp water, and the chill against her flesh helped dispel all other sensation. She dipped to touch the water with her hands, bring its coolness to her face again. And when she rose, he was there, just feet away, waiting. She smoothed back damp tendrils of her hair, returning his stare.

"There is only so much time to tarry," he said impatiently. And so she returned to the embankment. He did not move. She found her hose and shoes, and at last managed a function without falling, sliding on her hose and shoes without staggering or falling. A fact for which she was grateful, since there was no easily accessible limb or rock upon which to lean or find support. And he offered no assistance. He didn't even wait until her second shoe was securely upon her foot, but started back through the trees ahead of her.

She followed.

By the time they returned, the fires were out, the horses were saddled, and she was relieved to see that Sir Alfred and Lauren were already mounted and ready to go. They saw her arrival as she saw them, and Lauren arched her brow just slightly, evidently as concerned as she was. Sir Alfred, the dear old man, spoke to the one called George, who was at his side, apparently doing his best to be indignant. George apparently said something reassuring, for Sir Alfred kept his peace, and offered Christina a smile.

She was left again amid the men and horses. Liam appeared with Crystal and helped her to mount. When she was upon her mare, Jamie reappeared, mounted as well on his great warhorse.

"Come then, Christina, we take the lead."

So he had meant what he had said. That which they considered their burden—she—was to be shared between him and those men closest to him.

"You speak, and I obey," she murmured, and his dry glance in her direction was a sure indication that she had gotten no better with her tone of voice.

He was impatient, not interested in conversation that morning. The lead remained on Crystal, but he did not take it up. He rode ahead of her, and she was aware that one of his men was but steps behind her. They left the forest, and she could hear, in their wake, the shouts of the men as they kept the cattle and horses in line, as if they had all been excellent herders in another life, and even on horseback at that. They came upon terrain that was beautiful and sweeping, great lowland hills and valleys, all rolling, excellent land for quick movement, the ground dry here. Sometimes, she knew, heavy snow and rains could make this very landscape a nightmare in which men and supplies bogged down, and it had often been the weather and the rugged terrain, rather than any lack of ardor, that had kept men from fighting.

Many times, in the open fields, men rode from the rear to the front, bearing words to Jamie. They moved well, they needed to slow the gait, they had lost a cow, they had recovered the beast.

They had ridden long hours when Sir James called a quick halt. They were in the open, with no place for his men and such a train of beasts to disperse into the trees, but evidently he sensed that there might be danger ahead. He called out swift orders for his men to fan out, and he commanded a young fellow named Ioin to come forward quickly, and take Christina to the rear. She hadn't heard or seen a thing herself, but just as Ioin arrived, taking her horse's lead, she saw a rider appear across the fields. A single rider, bearing a banner. The Scots needn't have taken their quick precaution, for the colors were those of Robert Bruce.

Jamie rode ahead to meet him.

Moments later, he rode back, calling to Ragnor, Liam, and a few others of their party to join him. She couldn't hear a word spoken for she had been led to the rear. She was still nowhere near Lauren and Sir Alfred, but at least could see the pair.

"What is happening?" she asked the young man at her side.

"We part ways," he told her, apparently assuming there was no harm in giving out what would soon be obvious information. He was a pleasant enough man, courteous in his escort, no more than twenty or so, with a head of beautiful long brown hair and very deep, dark eyes.

"Part ways?"

"Aye, the goods will go one way, while we travel by another path."

"Why? What has happened?"

"That I don't know, my lady."

And yet he knew what they were about, for the group around Jamie had split, and the men were dividing.

"Do I go with the cows?" she wondered aloud.

He glanced her way with a half-smile, and again said, "I'm sorry, my lady, I do not know." She could only assume that he had witnessed her wild ride from Hamstead Heath upon Crystal, and her ignoble return with Jamie upon his mount. But then, surely, most, if not all, of the men had seen her ... difficulties at Hamstead Heath. And thus, of course, were wary, and perhaps wondering if there might be any merit to having such a hostage. They all assumed, of course, that she must be worth something.

"Ioin!" Liam called, and the young man left her side. A moment later, Jamie rode to her position, and picked up the lead, saying nothing.

"Where are we going?" she asked. "What has happened?"

He ignored her, and his horse's gait quickened, and when she looked back, she saw that they were followed by most of the men. Only ten or so remained behind, veering toward the west with the cattle and horses.

They continued at a quick pace, leaving the open fields behind and taking a strange westerly course. She realized after a while that they were purposely avoiding villages and towns, and even large manor houses. Once again, it seemed that they rode very hard, and very long, and the sun was near down before they stopped at all, and that at the northwestern edge of another dense woods through which they had traveled. By then, Christina thought that she would fall from her horse; it had been all she could do for the last hours to keep herself upon her mare. Too often, the day seemed to be blackening before her eyes, and her stomach had ceased even to rumble.

She was dimly aware that the forest where they halted gave way to another sweeping plain of rolling hill and meadow. By then, shadows and fog had fallen, and she wasn't certain that she saw great walls in the distance, or that flickers of light shone through the mist and growing darkness. They were pausing just beyond some great fortress; they had traveled double the miles in that day than they had in the previous. She had lost track of their quick, but meandering course, and she knew only that they had headed toward the east, and it seemed that some matter of great import lay before them.

Jamie called a halt, and behind him the men reined in and dismounted, and there were shouts that there would be no fires, and cries of which men would take guard duty first. She heard it all without moving, for Jamie had dismounted and moved about in the small clearing almost immediately, calling to both Liam and Ragnor to join him at the edge of the wood. She was still seated upon the horse, numb, afraid to move, almost unaware of the passage of time, when he was suddenly before her again, gray-blue eyes like knives that pierced into her, faded before her, and seemed to observe her with the greatest disdain.

"Christina, come down," he said, and the impatience in his voice suggested that it was the second time he had spoken. He reached for her then, and she was dismayed to realize that she was all but helpless; her arms refused to either accept his assistance or push against him. He tried to set her upon her feet, but she could not stand, and the world continued to spin.

"Such an idiot," he said, his hands on her shoulders, and his eyes sharp upon hers again. "Would you kill yourself rather than say a simple please for a morsel of food when you'd no thought at all about begging to be brought along!"

She wanted to answer him, as disdainfully as possible, but she could not connect the right words together. He shook his head with tremendous impatience and went to move past her, but even the stir of air created then was more than she could balance against. She pitched forward, and the swiftness of his response kept her from tumbling to the earth. "Must I always be fetching you from collisions with the earth, my lady?" he muttered. She couldn't quite open her eyes, much less compose a fitting response. "Ioin!" he called.

"Sir Jamie!" the youth responded, rushing forward.

"Take her to the stream, allow her just sips of water, and see that she is fed, and that she eats—slowly! At least, for once, I can assure you she hasn't the strength to create trouble.''

Christina opened her eyes, but words still refused to come to her lips. ''At least,'' he said, ''no more than she has managed already through folly and pride.''

''I intended no trouble,'' she whispered.

''Curious, for it follows you whether you bid it do so or not.''

She was tossed to other arms, and truly hadn't the strength to protest. Her head fell against young Ioin's chest, and she rested there without care, for she was too worn and exhausted to have any.

Moments later she felt a cool cloth pressed against her face; she realized that she had been taken to another stream. Naturally, these men would know where to ride and find fresh water, and the depths of the trees to hide them until they were ready to appear. It was well known that most often, when the English failed against the Scots, when their numbers and arms were superior, they did not lose because they were outfought, but rather because they were outfoxed, with the Scots slipping away into such forests, refusing to fight face to face, allowing the English to bog down in the countryside, and then harry from the rear, striking quickly, stealing supplies, melting into the forests once again.

''Can you drink?''

She could. She was half-seated and half-leaned against a tree with a broad and ancient trunk. He was hunkered down before her, ready to catch her, should she veer to the left or to the right. She grasped the waterskin and drank thirstily, until he pulled it from her. ''Slow, ye've not eaten, lady. Here, start with bread, not even too hard, for we've not traveled so very long, though it may seem like eons.''

She knew that if she ate too quickly, and too much, she might become real trouble indeed, yet her hunger was such that she consumed the bread within seconds. Ioin had cheese as well, and a piece of dried meat. He spoke as she ate, his words gentle; with him she did not mind so much that her fingers trembled, and even holding the food she wanted so desperately was difficult. When she knew she must halt, she eased back against the tree, eyes closed, then slowly opened them, meeting those anxious dark eyes of the young man.

"I believe, from the way you speak, that you've traveled far longer, often, and with far less."

He shrugged. "We've gone days on the road with little enough food. But not of late, and the memories of the days of real terror fade on the one hand, and yet, are nearly all that I remember for a lifetime. This war has been waged many years."

"Once, though, for me, it was not so close."

"Always, for me, war has been life."

She found herself touching his hand. "I'm sorry. And . . ." she drew back awkwardly. "Thank you. For your kindness, and courtesy."

He lowered his head. "They are but commanded."

She shook her head. "Perhaps your Sir James can command you to feed me, but he cannot command such natural kindness. Thank you."

"Take care, my young friend!" she heard from a distance, and twisting saw that Jamie stood not ten feet away, leaning against one of the huge oaks flanking the water. "The lady of Hamstead Heath has a most dangerous way with words."

Ioin stood, "From the cradle, Sir Jamie, we live with wariness."

"Aye, my friend. Yet pleasant words may be taken as such, as long as they offer no chance of treachery. So, Christina, you appear far improved. May I suggest that unless starvation is one's only recourse, it not become the weapon of a stubborn will?"

"It was not intended as a weapon."

"I believe I will tend to my horse, Sir James," Ioin said uneasily.

"As you wish, Ioin Douglas, for it seems we've long days ahead," Jamie said with a nod. Ioin hurried past them, heading into the trees. Christina realized her position, and his height, and wanted to rise, but as she scrambled to come up against the tree, he strode the few feet toward her. "Sit, stay as you are. There is no rush to move from tree to tree."

"But you are obviously deep in the planning stages of some retribution, and I wouldn't draw upon your time," she told him. "I admit to being quite exhausted, worn, and still . . . far from myself. I remain without the strength for any real trouble."

She was wary as he walked to her, hunkering down at her side and studying her. He moved a stray strand of hair from her face, and shook his head. "You're a curious woman, Christina. In truth, I don't believe that you've a real wish for bloodshed. Actually, given a knife and a hog-tied Scotsman, I don't think you'd want to do him in yourself. But what's so very frightening about you is the very fear that you have of the king of England—and maybe others around him. For your cause, whatever it may be exactly, you would risk life and limb to earn the favor of the English. And you'd send every man I have to the block or the gallows. You must be aware that you have erred greatly; had you made yourself truly ill, I'd have had no choice but to send you back—and alas, the advantages of keeping the Lady Lauren and Sir Alfred are becoming rather attractive."

"In the future," she assured him, "I will request every mouthful of food available."

He smiled, lashes lowering for a moment. "We'll see what tomorrow brings. Can you rise?"

"I believe."

He stood. "Take my hand."

She did so, and she was glad, for coming up was not so easy as she'd have wished. Yet once upon her feet, she could stand. He waited for her to find her balance, still watching her far too closely.

"Enjoy the walk back, because then I'm quite afraid it's another tree for the evening."

"A tree—and a rope?"

"A rope to a tree. We cannot risk your movement."

"I see. There are battle plans to be made," she said, a statement, not a question.

"The woods are full of Scotsmen tonight. And many who have suffered great and grievous loss at the hands of the English."

"And what of the English?"

"They are not in the woods."

"You're certain?" she asked him.

"Do you ask that question because you're considering gnawing through ropes or a tree trunk in order to search out the enemy? Well, hmm. One can never be completely certain of the enemy. That is to lose the battle before it has begun."

"You think that I'm capable of gnawing through rope."

She spoke lightly, because of course, the idea was quite absurd. Yet he was studying her gravely. "I don't need my position known tonight. Therefore, my lady, I take no chances. So, it is time to return. A new tree for the evening, I'm afraid."

His hand at her elbow, he escorted her back through the trees. He did not seek to drag her: the vise of his fingers seemed more to keep her upon her feet than to force her along.

They returned to a clearing where again, horses had been tethered and men were moving about in quiet efficiency to guard their holdings and their position. She found a place arranged again, a very small copse, somewhat away from the larger gathering, and she knew that the men intended to meet, to talk, to plan, and that she would be kept far from the place where Scottish plans would be laid. She found another of Sir Jamie's men waiting; not a fellow she knew. This one was a burly Highlander called Magnus, and he was leaning against a tree, long sword sheathed at his side. She had a feeling that he would not change his position once while he stood guard.

Jamie pointed out her saddle, her place to sleep, and when she was down, she found that tonight, her ankles would be tied one to the other, perhaps so that she gave the huge Magnus no cause for trouble or impatience. He did not appear to be a patient man.

She was amazed to discover that it didn't matter in the least. She was exhausted. When Jamie went to the inner circle where she knew the men would draw around him, she laid her head down. The ground was wretched, the saddle for a pillow more so. It didn't matter. She slept.

Robert Bruce himself was near. And a plan was afoot.

Few English strongholds remained in Scotland, but the king was determined that every last one would be regained.

There was Berwick. The very name of the town brought a taste of bitterness to the tongue of every Scotsman.

Jamie had never loathed the English, despite the very personal tragedies they had brought upon him. In his years he'd had the acquaintance of far too many men of English blood who were among the finest he had ever met. Every man was responsible to his own sense of loyalty and honor, and those who offered their lives and blood in a true sense of dedication to a liege lord and country were often admirable. He knew, however, that many had obeyed only that sense of duty, who had practiced restraint even in battle, and he knew as well that many had only obeyed the direct order of a ruthless king in many of their brutalities. There were men as well, and he knew they came in all nationalities, who delighted in carnage, in the freedom to rain down upon the fallen with savage force that ignored all tenets of decency. In the many years of bloodshed and war, the sorry truth was that the old king of England, and now the new, had found many men willing to practice every possible form of cruelty in order to further their own futures.

At Berwick, Edward I had been at his most ruthless, and the streets of the town had been red with blood. It was said that even some of the attackers went down themselves, sliding in the mire they had created. No one had been spared. Not the old, not a child, not a babe in arms. The devastation had stopped, it was said, only when the king saw a woman slain in the very act of giving birth, and the gore had become too much, even for his sense of rage.

Since that time, the English had held the town. But since that time, not even the English had been able to give it a rebirth of importance. Robert Bruce wanted Berwick back; every man wanted Berwick back. There was the bitterness. And a longing for revenge.

They had tried to take back Berwick, and nearly succeeded. They had fashioned ingenious rope ladders with hooks that were only more deeply set by the weight of a man, and with a construction as well that allowed each man to rise up the ladder nearly as easily as he might a flight of stairs.

At Berwick, the barking of a dog had warned of their approach. If not for the canine, they might well have been triumphant.

They had failed that night.

But they had learned a great deal as well.

The same strategy was to be put forth again.

Bruce was with an army just beyond the walls of Perth. They had attacked the walls and now camped outside them, just as if they were settling in for a siege. But the English knew that the Scots had the supplies and the number of men needed for a long, drawn-out siege. Robert Bruce intended to enter the forest himself, and, when the English were convinced they were gone, double back and take the ropes across the river on foot, scale the walls, and allow entry for their own troops.

Perth was of tremendous importance to the English. It was a crossroad into Scotland, easily supplied from the sea. It was in a perfect position for invading armies to garrison from the south. It was a danger to all of central Scotland.

So . . .

It was to Perth that they would travel.

His force, brought now to a mere thirty-nine men, would still be an asset to the gathering Scots. He rode with those who had scaled walls, fled through lakes and streams, learned dead quiet while melting into forests, and gained a steel-like hardness through enduring every deprivation war could bring. They had held dying comrades, they had learned to run with the wounded with the slightest chance of life and recovery. They were exactly the men to scale the walls of a town in silence if necessary, to battle face to face when called upon, to withdraw again for a better day, since a dead man could not fight again.

The head of Ioin's clan, known among the men as the Douglas, was now one of Robert Bruce's most ferocious defenders; he was in the forest, not far from their own position, and other forces were gathering. The plan to attack was coming together.

With his men gathered around him, Jamie drew in the dirt with a stick, showing them their position, and where the messenger had said that the Douglas had taken up his camp for the night. The Scots had used many ruses to gain back their castles, often by appearing as if they were to fight, disappearing into the trees, and waiting in ambush for the enemy to come in pursuit, at which point they would fall upon him. The English were wary already, aware that too often, their greater number and power had been decimated by speed and surprise. There could be small pockets of Englishmen in the woods—not those drawn out from the fortifications, but rather those attempting to reach Edward's defenders with arms and reinforcements.

The attack here must be swift and sure. Thus far, it was decided that the first men would ford the stream with rope ladders, scale the walls, and find entry. The greatest stealth would be necessary so that the Scots could enter, and open the gates to their fellows, at which point the battle could begin in earnest.

"We're all aware that even now, with our numbers, our arms, and supplies, a siege is a foolhardy business. The enemy will gather in strength outside the walls, and our men could be caught between the defenders within the walls and the English coming quickly to reinforce from without. We've no choice but swift movement, and there has never been a time when an outcome in our favor has been more possible. We strike, and we strike quickly."

Ioin, among them that evening, said quietly, "My great-uncle is a hard man. 'Tis sure he means a certain revenge."

Jamie reflected on his words. Wallace, who had become a greater hero to them all in death, had been known to retaliate with terrible violence. But he'd not been a man to cut down infants, women, and the aged. He had, upon occasion, responded to some of the terrible deeds done by his enemy with equally terrible force, and still, there would be no repeat of the carnage that had occurred at the town before.

"Aye, Ioin, your uncle is a hard man. A clever man, and a brave man as well. But the Bruce himself leads us here. All goods may be taken. As always, we will support our king and country's treasury, and each man improves his own lot as well. The fighting will be fierce, and as always, you fight for your lives. Those who fight for me take their swords against men-at-arms, and not children; there are many of our people within those walls. And the fiercest man out there knows the king's belief that Scotland must be united, that mercy, not madness, will best repair our country. We go in to fight, not to commit murder. We have fought many battles together, and know one another. It's true there will be revenge, and vengeance is stronger in some men than in others, but everyone who gathers here fights in the name of Robert Bruce. We are also men who will live with ourselves when the din of fighting dies. The outcome here hinges upon our ability to scale the walls, and open the gates; stealth will be the greatest weapon."

"If the walls are not scaled, we fall back?" George inquired.

Jamie nodded grimly. "If those who attempt the walls fail, then we withdraw. But we will not fail. It is our time to take back our country. There are many forces converging now; and the time has never been more right. Tonight, we get what rest we can, in shifts. Tomorrow the last of us will gather, positions will be drawn," he said. "Until then, we keep tight, lest our presence be known. Our numbers fill most of the forest; there is a Douglas camp approximately here, and a group with MacLeod is here, my cousin has brought forces from the west, and they are moving in, here. The king moves his army into the forest more deeply here." He drew lines in the earth as he spoke, and when he was done they were quickly scuffed out. If they should be set upon by a larger force of the English, they would not give away the positions of their fellows. "We're a small group, but for the assault, an important one. We've experience with the ladders," he said, looking around him at the grim faces surveying him in return. They had all been at Berwick.

"So we lead," George said.

"The king leads. The king himself," Jamie said. "We will be at his shoulder."

There was a soft shout of agreement at that. What man could fail to fight for a king who took every risk and danger upon himself?

"We're experienced, but a small force, and we lose a man to guard the hostages while we fight," Ragnor reminded him.

"Aye, and true we cannot afford it. But though we'd not intended taking hostages, they may now be of use."

"Buying back our own," Liam said quietly.

They were quiet for a minute. Men had often fought and died courageously, taking down many times their number before death, rather than be taken prisoner. Too often the death afforded at the hands of the enemy, when the word *traitor* was branded upon a man, was far worse than that which came in the heat of battle. And yet, when a man was not on the list of those most despised by the English, especially now as the Scots held more and more of the country, there was the chance of ransom or exchange. The sooner such an arrangement could be made, the better.

"There is no more, until tomorrow, when communications will pass through the woods again, and we will find out the king's plans for the time of attack. We must make use of what hours we have, because it will not be an easy undertaking."

"How do we know there won't be dogs at Perth as well?" Ioin asked. He had barely escaped an arrow during their hasty retreat at Berwick.

Jamie stared at him levelly. "We don't."

Ioin shrugged, then grinned slowly. "Well, we've experience at escape as well."

"We'll break through those walls," Jamie said softly. "This time, we will prevail. The king leads, and the treasure to be taken is great."

There were a number of assents, and they broke, those on guard stating their positions as they moved to take them.

Jamie circled to the lower left of their position, where George stood guard over Lauren and Sir Alfred. Both slept, and he knew the pace that they kept was a hardy one; not many men and certainly few women could ride so hard. He nodded to George, and moved back to the center of the clearing. There were no fires that night, but they had brought out their rations of bread, cheese, and dried meat, and he ate sparingly before walking through the darkness again to find his own position, relieving Magnus to find some rest while he lay down himself, just feet from his sleeping hostage.

He found himself observing the lady as she slept. Their days of travel had worn upon her, and she appeared very fragile at rest. Tendrils of hair swept about her shoulders like a cloak, trailing upon the forest floor. Her flesh was pale in the moonlight and stars that filtered through leaves and branches. Stunning at rest, lashes sweeping her cheeks, her features never more classic and perfect than when she lay vulnerable, wariness cast aside in sleep. He kept his distance, oddly compelled to offer some form of security and protection, to draw her against him and smooth back that cascade of fire-touched hair. A curious woman; he considered it imperative to remain austere. She reminded him of many men with whom he had fought; she was blindly dedicated to one pursuit, and in that dedication, too easily prone to mishap. He didn't doubt her courage in the least, but as to good common sense . . .

He lay still, looking at the stars, remembering his confidence when speaking with his men. They would take Perth, but it would not be an easy task; what they attempted might be madness in itself, but they had learned so much through the years. Still, in any pursuit, there was the chance that they would fail. Magnus would remain behind with the hostages. His great size, all of it toned muscle, would be a deterrent in fording the stream and scaling the wall. His sword arm might be valuable once the gates were open, but it they were to fail, he knew that Magnus would be the man to ensure that their hostages indeed reached Robert Bruce. They would be safe beneath the wing of the massive Highlander. He came from a fierce clan who did not honor a king when he was crowned, but only when he was proven. Magnus had taken Bruce's side, and he would die for his honor. He would guard the women and the old man against any who would harm them, including Scots, and their own countrymen.

Jamie closed his eyes, but did not sleep. He saw instead the lady at his side, not as she was, but as she had been. Rising from the water like the Venus of the ancient Romans. He was afraid he knew his hostage far too well, and sleeping at her side had become a torment far greater for him than her. He had no interest in seizing upon the vulnerabilities of his enemies; he would have ridden far from Hamstead Heath with no thought of force or harm against its inhabitants. Circumstances, and those inhabitants, had changed things. The longer they rode, the greater his intrigue, and at times, he admitted to a grim pleasure in watching her fears and frustration when she meant above all else to guard her brother's fiancée. She had intended his men great harm.

She had created a wealth of trouble. Naturally, it was amusing to cast subtle verbal taunts her way.

He had slept upon his back without moving more nights in a forest than he cared to remember; he could close his eyes, sleep, and wake at the slightest whisper.

Tonight, he couldn't sleep.

She lay too close.

He turned to his side that night, his back to her. War had been long. He had pushed the personal agonies he had suffered at the brutal hands of his enemies to a place deep in the hidden recesses of his heart. There had been nothing to do but go on, and learn restraint, until the time might come when the men who razed his village might be brought to justice themselves. He had learned, through Robert Bruce, that killing innocent men or women would not ease the pain suffered, but that fighting for the greater good of a dream could ease the restlessness.

And still, this hostage . . .

He was tempted to turn in the night and seize upon her. She had thrown herself into his keeping, even when he had fought to cast her aside. But she was like a nettle beneath his skin, far more tempting than he would ever allow. She was a seduction to the senses that was slow becoming a torment and agony, and yet not the woman to be used lightly, no matter what price she was willing to pay. She evoked too much anger, and more. She had a way about her. She was his hostage, a lady born and bred, daughter of the enemy. A pawn to be played. But not a quick acquaintance in a village, a knock upon the door of a willing maid, paid by night, forgotten by morn.

She was far too much like . . .

No! He would not compare her. She was the enemy.

In anger, he felt his muscles stiffen, felt the ground grow harder. She wasn't just trouble, she was a plague.

The battle would come quickly. And then, if they failed, Magnus would see her to the king. If they prevailed . . .

There were other men who would gladly bring such a hostage to the Bruce.

Damn her, he would sleep.

And yet . . . the forest was too quiet by night.

He could hear every breath, he thought, subtle and soft though it might be.

He could hear a pulse . . . that of her heart, a slow beat.

He thought, against the pine and oak, the rich verdant earth, he breathed in her scent.

The pulse, the beat, was within him, and suddenly far too much.

He let out a sudden oath, startling her. She sat up, eyes wide with alarm, the cloak of her hair trailing behind her. He stood quickly.

"What is it?" she whispered in the night.

"Nothing. I am taking guard duty, that is all. Go back to sleep."

He strode away from her. His hostage was going nowhere—among the other things he had learned, it was to tie an excellent knot. Liam would take his place long before she could begin to work against the rope that bound her ankles.

He strode away, thinking that however tight her bonds, they were no more constricting than the tangled chains she had somehow twisted around him that night.

CHAPTER 6

Christina woke slowly. She had slept as if dead for many hours, and then been startled from sleep by Jamie's movement in the night. Sleeping again had proven to be more difficult, yet she had gone back to sleep, and apparently, had slept many hours. When she opened her eyes, it was full day. And oddly beautiful. Little rays of light were striking the leaves and the forest floor; greens were rich and deep, blues were soft and light. The sun's rays were gold. She was rested, far more rested than she might have imagined. It wasn't until she moved that she realized again the hardness of her bed, the discomfort of the earth. The chill from the ground did seep into muscles and bones, and rising might not be so easy, even though she felt strangely well.

She rose to a sitting position, realized that the ropes that had bound her ankles were gone, though she had not felt the slightest touch at their removal. She stretched, and looked about. Ioin was again her guard; he whittled by a tree. When he saw that she had wakened, he smiled, but there was a certain gravity about him. "Good morning, my lady."

"Good morning."

The copse seemed strangely quiet; perhaps that was why she had felt the beauty and peace of the place.

She straightened where she sat, staring at him intensely. "The battle has begun?"

"Nay, lady."

"Then . . . ?" Fear struck her. She came to her feet. "Have they moved on, and left you behind to . . . to escort me home?"

He shook his head again. "They are near," he said quietly.

"And what of . . . Sir Alfred and Lauren?"

"There are near as well."

"Oh."

"Would you like to go to the stream? You may stay as long as you like. The day will be long."

Then she knew. He didn't need to tell her. The Scots would attack Berwick by night. They would hold this position until their plans brought about their movement.

She wondered about her status at that point. And she could not help but wonder as well what the reward might be if the English at Perth were warned of the attack. The king would have to order that her brother be released if a member of his household was to prevent the loss of an English stronghold.

She rose quickly, not wanting Ioin to read her thoughts. "I would be grateful for time by the stream."

When he escorted her that morning, she was able to figure their position well. The stream, she was certain, led to the river Tay, for Perth was right upon the river, a position that had once given the town a greatness for trade that had seldom been equaled. The English prized their possession of Perth—

no other outpost in Scotland had been so repeatedly strengthened and reinforced.

Ioin was a far gentler and courteous escort than Jamie, pointing out a position where he would await her, assuring her that he would guard her privacy. She thanked him with sincere gratitude.

Moments later, she had shed her clothing down to her linen shift and ventured out into the water. She tested the depth of the water, all in a pretext of bathing, found that the stream was deep, and the water moved quickly. They could not be a great distance from the point where the stream would join with the river. She paused, looking back to the place upon the embankment where Ioin would be waiting. She hadn't taken much time as yet. She could afford the time for a swim. She had no intention of disappearing then; she would never leave Lauren and Sir Alfred behind.

Grave thoughts played upon her mind as she moved carefully within the water. She had to admit that they had been treated with no cruelty or brutality. Even after her attempt to drug the men and make them captives, no one had been hauled to a rope, the women had miraculously been spared rape and abuse, and though the goods of Hamstead Heath had definitely been pillaged, the damage done could have been far worse. Livestock had even been left behind, allowing the manor a chance to survive the coming season.

The water was very cold; frigid. She wished no great ill upon the men who had come to Hamstead Heath, not even those such as Magnus, with his dour face, great size, and frightening appearance. Where once, when she had plotted and planned, they had been strangers, men to be taken quickly away, turned over for her brother's life, whatever their fate, she now had no will to hear that they were imprisoned, tortured, or hanged, or set upon the block. But she thought as well that her message to the English would be only that they must prepare for an attack; the numbers of Scots ranging in the woods would keep the defenders at Perth busy shoring up their own defenses—not heading out to find the enemy.

She treaded water hard against the current and the cold, trying to ascertain her exact position, the lay of the water, and that of the land. She came farther than she had planned, but with a good sense of her exact position, she was ready to begin moving back along the embankment. She was eager to return, to find Ioin, and thank him for the pleasure of a chance to really bathe. There had to be a way then to convince Ioin that she must have a chance to see Lauren and Sir Alfred.

She turned to swim, knowing that the return would be difficult against the current. But just minutes after she had begun, she reached out a hand and came against a startling barrier. Hard, immobile, vital. Muscle, bone . . . and flesh.

She gasped, nearly inhaled half the stream, and coughed and choked. Fingers twined in her hair, caught her by the nape. Her head was lifted above the surface, and she remained captive of that grasp. Many fears raced through her heart in those seconds. She had come upon another encampment of the Scotsmen, and found a man not so prone to mercy. She had stumbled upon highwaymen, English ruffians, or worse.

She had not.

She had stumbled upon Jamie, a rock, staunch where he stood against the current, his hold upon her preventing her from being moved by the water as well. Sleek and wet, she realized his bare chest, each wedge of muscle, skin bronzed from many such occasions as this, a slew of crisscrossed scars upon his shoulders and flesh. The sun on the water was reflected back at them both. His features were tight, jaw square and very hard.

As he stared down at her, she wished that she had come upon a highwayman.

"Going somewhere, my lady?"

"The current was strong. I'd not realized how far."

"You hadn't. How curious. You're usually ever so observant."

"I would hardly choose to disappear into a forest filled with Scotsmen bent upon attack."

"Ah, Christina, what a glib, quick tongue you have."

He turned slightly, since it seemed the current would have its way with her. Then, when the water rushed, it did nothing but throw her against him. Despite the absolute chill of the water, she felt a wealth of fire sweeping over her skin. She had come upon his own morning ritual, which seemed to include a real bath. She was grateful for her shift, and yet it might have been nothing at all. She could feel every nicety of his form, subtle and not so subtle, the coolness of his flesh in this water, the heat that lay beneath. Muscle, sinew, fire, and flesh, and in the water, each of her movements to hold her own seemed only to bring her legs tangling with his, her shift rising higher and higher, her position more tenuous. She was nearly flush against him, never more aware of him as a man, or for that matter, herself as a woman.

"The current is very strong," she informed him, and there was truth in that, for she was beginning to feel that she was welded to his form. And the discomfort of the situation was painfully obvious to both of them. Second by second, worse. Now that she was still, the water was not cool, but frigid; he seemed not to notice, indeed, he was like a pillar of fire, and she was shaking both from the increasing cold, and from the tension and heat that seemed to emanate from him. She was afraid to do so much as breathe, they were so close, and so much of him was so very evident. She was frightened and dizzy; she had thought herself so mature, so willing to do what must be done at every turn, and yet she had been terribly naive, so unaware of the true construction of a man. And now she knew. She stood not in defiance, but in a sudden sense of terror, and to her great confusion and distress, more than a little fascinated and intrigued. More so, it was disturbing to realize that the sensations were not simply because he was a man, but because of the man he was. His face was striking, strong, appealing. His voice touched not her ears, but something else inside. His hands were fine, long and large, the flesh calloused, the fingertips oddly capable of so gentle a brush. Yet, of course, it was not his face, nor even his hands, which held her so very still, so afraid to breathe, and so suddenly, acutely aware of their sexes. Sensation ripped into her, not dampened but enhanced by the icy chill of the water.

"The current is strong," he agreed harshly. His grip upon her remained so tight and intense for a minute that she thought she would not only learn the mysterious with which she was woefully unfamiliar, but blend completely into his flesh. Then something dark and very angry broke within him, and he spoke chillingly. "But the current did not bring you so far along the water. Only a fool would miss your intent, Christina, when every mercy was practiced upon you and your people. It will not be so again."

He released her and turned, leaving her in the water, long strides taking him toward the bank. Her freedom came so swift and suddenly that at first, she could not move; her limbs had frozen. He had been standing in the depths of the water; she had not. She somehow remained afloat for a moment, then went under, coming to suddenly enough to fight the water and kick her head above the surface again. But as she did so, she rose sputtering, flailing, having to remind herself that she could swim, had known how to do so since she'd been a child, knew well, moved well.

All too late, or perhaps she had simply grown too cold. Perhaps she had swallowed too much water when she first went down. She forced herself to think, reason, and move, making toward the shore. The current, as they had both agreed, was strong. With her failing strength, she found that it was carrying her away once again.

Arms came around her waist. She was dragged from the water, and dropped upon the soft grass of the embankment. She inhaled deeply, furious that she had let herself become so intensely wrapped in his physical being that she had forgotten herself, forgotten the cold, forgotten what she had known innately all her life. He was hunkered behind her head as she lay there, at first, grateful for every breath, and then aware again of his nudity, and his disdain and lack of care for his state of undress.

"Perhaps I should have let the stream take you," he said. "But one can only wonder when you are in true distress, and when you are playing the part you believe to be appropriate for the moment. You swim exceptionally well, so it appears, and yet, suddenly, you are gasping in the water. Were you looking for pity? A chance to make me forget your intent?"

She lay with her eyes closed, wet and shivering upon the embankment. Her lips, she thought, must truly be blue. "Sir, you must think whatever you wish."

"Ah, I see." His words were frighteningly soft. "You were not thinking that there was surely a way, once we had ridden off, to disarm your guard—since, surely, we could not afford to leave many men behind—rescue Sir Alfred and the Lady Lauren, and join with the English?"

"I repeat, sir, you must believe whatever you will."

He was still a very long time. She thought that he remained directly behind her, and she could not open her eyes. When she did she realized that he had moved, though she had not heard him do so. She turned to ascertain his position. He sat upon a log, several feet away. His clothing had apparently been there upon the bank, for naturally, he would not have allowed the current to draw him far. He was dressed again in hose, breeches, chemise, and tunic, and even as she turned, he was stepping into his boots. She had never felt his anger or disdain for her so greatly, though he was now that distance away. Just as she had felt, in the water, the sense of emanating heat, she now felt as if he emitted a simmering rage, and she was loath to move, though she knew that she could not cower long where she lay; she was far too cold.

"Get up." His words were terse, lacking any sense of courtesy or mercy. Nor did he intend to offer assistance.

She rose, still shaking, and therefore, none too gracefully. Upon her feet, she felt the wet linen of her shift as if it were plastered against her. She crossed her arms over her chest, hugging them against her, to fight the cold. Her hair was in tangled wet strands around her shoulders and neck, further rendering it difficult for her to move with any dignity.

A slow, curt sweep of his eyes registered again a deep contempt that chilled her worse than the coldness of the breeze. "Your clothing, lady, would be in that direction." He indicated with a nod that she precede him along the edge. She squared her shoulders to the best of her ability and did so.

It was unnerving to feel him so close at her back. His sudden anger had seemed so intense she wondered if she might feel a knife strike her back at any minute.

She came to the place where she had entered the water. Nervous, aware of his eyes every second, she found her belongings, wishing suddenly with all her heart for the warmth of her room at Hamstead Heath, the roar of the fire when she bathed, the softness of linen towels touched by the heat of that fire as well.

She was not at Hamstead Heath, but in the chill of the land by the river Tay, a place, though not so distant from her home, that seemed to offer a severe cold. She had not been foolish, she decided with a certain bid for dignity within her soul, for she was blessed to have a brother, and a bid for his freedom and his life was not a mistake. It was a mistake being caught, and being known far too well by a man she had met just days before.

He had acquired his mantle, and it was over his shoulders as he customarily wore it, brooch with his family insignia in place. She had left her cloak by her saddle, in the copse in the woods that had been her bed.

When she was dressed she stood, very tall and very straight, shoulders squared, chin determined. He let out an impatient oath then, reaching for the brooch, sweeping the mantle from his shoulders and around hers. "Foolish girl, you quiver like a bow, you're so cold," he muttered, coming forward quickly and throwing the garment around her.

"You need give me nothing of yours," she informed him, wishing again for the distance between them.

"A dead hostage will do me no good when this battle is over," he told her, the words far colder than the water had ever been. She was dismayed to feel the sudden, hot prick of tears at her eyes. The more she discovered that she did not loathe or despise him at all, the more, it seemed, he became the enemy, avidly contemptuous of her. "What is it, lady? You are too proud to wear the mantle of a Scot?"

"I would not be so ill-mannered a hostage as to die on you on the eve of being useful, Sir James. Therefore I will accept your mantle with thanks, until my own is procured."

"We shall do that now."

"Naturally. My only dismay is that you should feel the cold due to my lack of foresight."

He still stood close. Far too close.

"Turn, my lady."

"What?"

"Turn. It is time to return to the camp."

"Indeed."

As bidden, she turned. She wasn't certain she knew the path they had taken through the trees.

They returned to her young guard, Ioin, who showed signs of distress at his apparent loss of a hostage.

"Jamie—" he began, but Jamie raised a hand in dismissal.

"Bear in mind, Ioin, that she is like holding a tiger by the tail."

"Aye, Jamie."

"My lady?"

She was being given new escort, she realized. Ioin was surely angry as well; she had not made him appear at all capable before the man with whom he had chosen to fight. And still, he remained courteous, taking her arm in a gentle hold to keep her from tripping upon the roots and leaves that littered the forest floor.

She didn't look back.

She knew that Jamie's eyes followed her. And she was certain that they smoldered with a deeper hatred than she had ever known. She had the feeling that a very long day stretched before her.

For Jamie, the hours were far too few. They held their position in the forest, disappearing into the trees when the messenger arrived until they had ascertained for certain he was from the king. When Jamie was given a summons in the king's own hand, he responded instantly, returning with the messenger through the trees until they came at last to the position of the main army.

They were well within the deep growth of the forest, now upon their seventh night there, since the king was determined that the enemy must be lulled into believing they had left—indeed, they had left behind several siege locations, when convinced that they could not win the prize.

When Edward I had marched into Scotland with his great army, he had come with expensive war machines that could catapult great burning missiles of terrible destruction over the highest walls. His men outnumbered the Scots nearly three to one. They were well equipped, and well fed. Through the many years of war, most of Scotland had been ravaged; only the north of England had ever been touched. The men of Scotland had been called upon as long as they could remember; the King of England could draw on fresh resources from the south, and could pay for mercenary armies as well. The Scots had never had those advantages.

Edward II was not the man his father had been. And yet, his armies were no weaker. They rode into Scotland grandly. They were as well armed and armored as they had ever been.

If they were forced to, Jamie knew, he and his men would abandon their intent at Perth. They all knew that living to fight again was the greatest service they could give their country. They had lost far too many men to war—and to execution.

But the Scottish king was not in a weakened position himself. A royal tent had been set up in a copse, and like Jamie's far smaller party, his army had made good use of the wood. At Jamie's arrival, Robert Bruce came from the tent, clad in his colors, but not a man to be ostentatious in the midst of war. Perhaps he had spent too many years as a king without a real country. He had earned the crown he would wear upon his head, though this morning, the gleam of his dark hair was all that was touched by the sun.

"Jamie!" The king was not so tall a man, but respectable in height, and extremely sturdy in muscle. His face was intelligent, somewhat grooved by the years gone by, but still arresting. A clap on Jamie's back was a strong one, which, of course, he did not return.

"Robert, by the Grace of God, King of the Scots," Jamie said, inclining his head.

"Yes, yes, enough, enough," the king said. "Come into the tent. I'll show you where we've sounded the moat for depth. The men are even now constructing ladders for our stratagem. We'll wait one more night. Men lay siege here for more than six weeks; the enemy must believe that we have moved on. Tomorrow, the night will be all but pitch black. Then, we move."

Jamie followed the Bruce into the tent. A desk held maps and plans, a print of the castle, the river Tay, and the moat. "Here . . . here, a man may stand to his shoulders, and make his way through with the weight we must carry. All horses, all trappings, servants, and goods are left behind; we must move with assurance, determination, speed."

"I did have an interesting question from one of my men," Jamie said.

"And that is?'

"What if there are more barking dogs?"

"We'll hope that there are not."

Jamie nodded. "We're ready to follow you. To scale the walls, pitch the ladders. Come what may."

The king straightened then, walking to a small camp table, pouring wine from a flagon. "What of the south? Were your efforts smooth?"

"Aye, quite smooth. Cattle and horse, fine stock, are being moved to the north. In my company, however, are three prisoners."

"Oh? The inhabitants were not to be molested, not if the tribute was paid." Bruce was disturbed. His eyes were sharp.

"Actually, a rather interesting threesome. The lady of Hamstead Heath asked to be brought along."

The king arched his brows. "An Englishwoman asked to be hostage to a Scot? So she fears Edward."

Jamie shrugged, swallowing the warmth of a long draft of wine. "Many Englishmen fear Edward. Not because he is strong, but because he is a weak man with power. Vengeful, petulant. And smoldering with anger, no matter what agreement he has come to with his barons. He means to have his revenge. Eventually. At any rate, the lady did insist on accompanying us. And with her is another young woman. She is evidently of good family, though I don't know what name. She is surely affianced or perhaps even married to Steven—who is, I understand, a *guest* of Edward at some estate in northern England."

To Jamie's surprise, Robert Bruce nodded. "Lauren of Altisan, affianced to Steven Steel, Count of Hamstead Heath."

"You know the lady?" Jamie said.

"I wouldn't know her now; it has been years since I have seen her." The king shrugged. "You forget, for my lands in England, Edward the First was my liege lord. My wife is the child of an English noble, and I have spent many days in the English court. I know the Lady Christina of Hamstead Heath, and Lauren, daughter of the French count of Altisan. Who is your third hostage?"

"A man known as Sir Alfred."

"Ah, yes! Sir Alfred. I remember him well. Once upon a time he was a stalwart warrior. An injury rendered warfare more dangerous to him than to most men. There would be no way for him to quickly vacate a battlefield if a retreat was sounded. He was ordered to stand as guardian of the

home at Hamstead Heath. He is a fine and noble old gentleman.''

"Indeed, pleasant enough.''

"Did you wish them in the care of this company? Many
will be left behind to tend the horses and battle encampment.''

"I intended to leave Magnus behind to guard them; he
is the only Highlander I've ever met who cannot swim,
though he would ford the water with us, out of a sense of
duty. He is a hulk of a man, and were he to falter, I'm afraid
he'd bring us all down with him.''

"A solid warrior. So the gnarly fellow is still with you.
God is good. He has stood like a rock against the enemy
time and time again. We'll not take him into the water. He
will guard your captives, as you've said. Now here . . . here
we meet. The men will be divided, so many to storm the
fortifications once we have scaled the walls.'' They both
straightened, hearing hoofbeats. "Douglas has arrived,'' the
king said.

The king's company greeted one another. Among the
commanders was a French knight in the service of the Bruce.
He was fascinated by the ladders, and amazed that the king
would lead the assault. Several hours passed as the king
assured himself that the men understood the exact point of
entry, the division of troops, the silence that must be kept
if they were to be successful. At last, the men broke. Jamie
would keep his camp where it was, for he was actually closer
than the king's men to the great fortifications the English
had erected at Perth.

Jamie returned to his position in the woods, ready to alert
his men to the fact that they would be moving the following
day. When he reached his encampment, he found them busy
at work, sharpening swords and knives, repairing saddles
and trappings, preparing, as always, for what would come.

The news that they moved the following eve, by the deepest darkness of night, came as no surprise. They were ready.

After meeting with his closest advisers, he asked after his captives. He determined to leave his one hostage stewing all day and all night, he felt such a fierce anger against her. But he was intrigued now that he knew more about Sir Alfred and the Lady Lauren, and so visited their position, where Grayson, the blacksmith by trade, now his groom, was on guard duty.

Not so heavy a task with these captives, he decided. The gentle, flaxen-blond Lauren was seated beneath a tree, reading from a book of poetry, to Sir Alfred and Grayson. She stopped, stumbling awkwardly over her words, when she saw him in the small copse where she made use of the last of the winter daylight.

"A lovely poem, my lady," he said. "Sir Alfred, how are you faring? Is the ground too hard a bed?"

Sir Alfred stiffened with great dignity. "Young man, many a night have I spent on the ground. Though . . . ah, well, I do admit, 'tis harder on old bones than young ones!"

"Well, perhaps it will not be much longer before you have the comfort of a bed again. Lauren, will you accompany me, please? For a walk?"

Wariness instantly struck her eyes, but she didn't demur in the least. She offered her hand when he would help her to her feet. "You needn't fear for her safety," he assured Sir Alfred, who was attempting a dignified rise in protest. "I wish only to ask the lady a few questions, in private."

He escorted Lauren by the arm, walking through the trees as he had done earlier. The area near the river was beautiful, especially as the day slipped away, the sun seeming to melt into the horizon. "I know who you are," he told her. "Why did you lie?"

"I never actually lied," she protested softly.

"Fine, your soon-to-be sister-in-law lied vehemently."

"She's been trying to protect me." Lauren hesitated. "Both my worth—and my humiliation—would be of greater import to Edward. He needs my father's support."

"So why go to such extremes? I would have left you all unmolested in any way."

"That wouldn't have worked, you see," Lauren said. They had stopped walking. She rested against a tree and looked at him squarely. "You know, of course, that most marriages are arranged. And my engagement to Steven was arranged. But . . . we were often at court together when we were young. And I was often at Hamstead Heath. I am, indeed, a great and warm friend of the family. Steven and Christina are the family. Their mother died when they were young. Their father, you know, was a fierce knight."

"You need tell me nothing about their father." He couldn't help the tension in his voice. The old lord of Hamstead Heath had killed many a Scotsman.

"Steven and Christina are close, truly caring about one another. Steven would never seek to improve his own lot through his sister's misery. And Christina . . . she would lie down and die before allowing harm to come to Steven. If you can't forgive us, I hope that you can at least understand."

"The lady remains dangerous," he said softly. "She is always plotting and planning. This morning, in the most frigid water, she was looking for a way to swim to the castle and warn of our impending attack."

"Surely, she was not!"

"The cold is terrible in the water these days. It's difficult even to attempt to remove the dirt of the road, much less swim."

"I . . . don't believe she meant any real ill," Lauren protested.

"Perhaps it all depends on what one considers to be an

ill,'' he murmured. ''Why you have such a great fear of
Edward's reaction to a mercy granted the family, I still don't
understand. But you're safe, for the present. You'll soon be
handed over to the King of the Scots, who bears no malice to
his hostages, and will most probably keep you in comfort.''

He took her hand and started to walk back, aware that
the dusk was falling all around them.

He chose his path carefully.

''May I see Christina?'' Lauren asked. ''She must be so
terribly worried.''

''Yes, I'm sure she is.''

''So . . . you'll allow us to speak?''

''Certainly not. Christina of Hamstead Heath needs to be
worried; it is the only leverage one has over so reckless a
woman. But I bid you and Sir Alfred to take heart; you are
in no danger.''

''Thank you for that. But . . . it's good that we are all
with you. We certainly appear to have suffered for our stand
against the Scots.''

''Hm. We came for a tribute, and if none was forthcoming,
we should have razed the manor. Instead, it appears we have
done a favor for the English.''

''Not the English. Just one man who always thought that
Scotland should be left to the Scots,'' Lauren said.

''I'll try to bear that in mind.'' He paused, purposely, in
the middle of the copse where they stood. With full purpose,
he smoothed a strand of blond hair from her face. She
surveyed him steadily with her light eyes, and smiled slowly.
''I don't interest you in the least, sir.''

He shrugged. ''Ah, now that's not true. You're soft spoken,
gentle, aware of your weaknesses. And certainly lovely.''

''And uninteresting, most probably,'' she said.

''Truly in love with your intended,'' he said. ''And that

is something rare and noble I'd not touch. Come now; I'll return you to the side of your dear old watchdog, Sir Alfred.''

She smiled, gladly taking his hand again as he walked her back.

Christina was dead still.

The hours had gone by more slowly than any she could remember in all her days. Magnus was not a cruel man. Neither was he a gentle one. Rather . . . he was just there. Like a rock. Like a stone wall. He had little to say to her. He had given her boundaries where she might pace, and she was grateful not to have spent the entire day tied to a tree. He saw that she ate, that she had water, that she had a few minutes entirely alone—while he was close. Very close. She wouldn't have dreamed of leaving him. It would have been like running from an agile mountain.

Despite the decency of the day, it passed so slowly. Seconds seemed like forever. Hours stretched and stretched.

She felt as if she were going to explode. Tension gripped her. Fear, uncertainty.

And then the coming of night.

Dusk.

Near darkness.

And yet light enough . . .

She saw them walking, saw them pause. Saw the way he touched Lauren's hair, and how Lauren took his hand. What choice did Lauren have? They were hostages. Her own fault. She had insisted on being taken. And so Lauren had been taken. And she had no assurance that her brother was all right, other than the fact that . . .

She would know. If something had happened to Steven, she would know.

But now . . . what had she done? Steven loved Lauren

more than his own life. There had been no choice in any of this. She hadn't been able to risk his life. And he was alive, of course, and as long as he was alive . . .

She had thrown Lauren to the enemy.

She lowered her head, pacing, oblivious to Magnus, the stone, the tree, the rock. He watched, and did not talk. She gnawed upon a nail, wondering what she could do. Lauren and Steven had something very beautiful ahead for them. She had only gratitude that she was spared a lifetime with Rowan DeClabert. There had to be a way to seduce Jamie Graham from a conquest of Lauren to her. Except that he didn't like her very much. No . . . he disliked her. He hadn't found her appealing even at her most . . . revealing moments.

"What a pity such restless energy can't be put to a greater purpose!"

She stopped in her tracks and stood dead still. Magnus—the big and silent—had departed. Jamie was back, leaning very casually against an elm, as if he had been there for some time. Watching her pace. Surely certain that she had been so introspective because she was plotting anew.

"Sir James. What a surprise," she murmured. "I had thought you'd be off pillaging a town or two by now."

"You knew that I was back," he told her.

"Oh?"

"Yes, you watched me escorting your friend."

"Were you escorting Lauren somewhere?"

He smiled, coming toward her. "It's amazing that you can be such good friends—and so very different."

"It's amazing that someone as kind and gentle as your Ioin Douglas rides with such a man as you."

"Ah, yes, we've really brutalized you," he said. "So, why were you watching?"

She set her hands on her hips. "You must leave Lauren alone," she said simply.

"Must I?"

"Please?"

"Please? I wonder why we haven't thought of that word all these years. Please, King of England, don't ravish our daughters, trample our fields, kill our sons! Leave our Crown alone. I don't think the old Hammer of the Scots would have listened. And his son seems to hear nothing. Please. You asked to accompany us. And now . . . well, here we all are."

She lowered her head. "I've told you before, I'll do anything . . ."

"Once again, you offer prematurely. No one has actually been threatened. Are you so eager then?"

"No!"

He smiled grimly. "I need sleep. I intend to get it."

She held very still, wondering if that meant he would walk away from her.

And seek to sleep with Lauren. *No one has been threatened.* No, he didn't threaten. But she was certain as well that he did find amusement in the fact that he knew, had always known, that she was continually in a tempest regarding Lauren.

He didn't threaten. He taunted.

Never once, unless she had instigated trouble, had these men offered violence. She lay awake, aware of the many horrible things that had been done to these enemies by those who had subjugated them. Word had gone out across the land that Robert Bruce was not a king who would rule through retribution. And still, men who had seen their lives, homes, and families the victims of savage attacks could not always be ruled by a king's policy.

"I won't move a muscle," she vowed softly.

"No, you won't, will you?" he asked.

"No."

He took his position by the tree. She sat, waiting. The ground was cold. She shivered, aware of his eyes all the while.

"Anything?" he inquired on a whisper of air. At least he was amused by her at the moment, rather than angered.

"You're truly enjoying yourself at my expense, sir."

"Anything?" he persisted.

She lifted her chin. He could taunt all he wanted. She had meant all that she had said as well, from the beginning. "Yes."

"Then lie down. Without a rope. And when you swear not to move, mean it."

Christina lay down near him, her back to him, head upon her saddle. She felt defeated, but determined.

Anything . . .

And all that he asked was that she go to sleep and allow him to do the same.

She realized that she was wishing he would do something . . . awful. Just do it. Get it over with. Instead of letting the hours go on and on and on. But then, the hours wouldn't go on much longer. They were planning an attack. It would be soon. Very soon.

And then . . .

Then, life would hinge on the outcome. Whether the Scots won . . .

Or lost.

And if they were to lose . . . she was familiar with the fate that had befallen many of the men considered to be enemies above the others. There had been a time when even Edward I had said that he would make peace with the many barons who had gone against him. Yet there had been those he had sworn never to forgive.

Those men had suffered incredible torture before dying.

She lay awake, thinking of all that the men risked, no

matter how far their king had come in claiming his countryside. The death of Edward I had saved many a Scotsman.
And now, the internal troubles of his son kept him from
focusing his entire attention upon the defeat of his northern
enemy.

The man at her side lay very still, keeping to his word.
She wondered suddenly what she might have thought of
him, had circumstances been different. Had they not been
enemies.

In the fitful sleep that at last claimed her, she inched
against him in the darkness, seduced by his heat.

She was unaware that he allowed her that comfort, lying
awake himself, staring at the darkness of the sky.

The following night . . .

There would be no moon at all.

And he and his men would be right behind their king.
Robert Bruce, despite his prowess, could fall. Death could
claim them all. They had all seen it often enough; it was as
if they were as close as children to the Grim Reaper.

He always knew he risked his life. Risked imprisonment—and an agonizing death at the hands of an English
executioner. He knew what he faced, and he did so willingly.
For his country, now for a king he could respect, and for
revenge. He didn't want to die, but he wasn't afraid of the
fate that eventually awaited them all.

But now . . .

He felt the earth, the fragrance of it. The coolness of the
air around him. The scent of the boughs of the trees.

The warmth of the woman. He closed his eyes. In sleep,
she was supple and giving. In sleep, she curled into his arms,
no barbs on her tongue, no hatred or desperate cunning

betrayed by her eyes. In sleep, in darkness, it was possible
to imagine . . .

The past.

No. He would not do so.

He lay awake, not angered by her again, not wrenching
away. Feeling her warmth. He was a fool. What did it matter,
her station in life, her title, her worth? She was willing to
do anything to keep him from Lauren. And he was willing
to watch her suffer.

But that taunting he intended turned on him always.

He could die the next night. For that matter, the English
could become aware. They could be prowling the forest.

No. The Scots would not be caught in the forest. That he
knew. But tomorrow night, they risked a great deal.

Still . . .

The softness of her hair teased his cheeks, tickled his
nose. He smoothed it down. She was shivering still. He
pulled her closer, folding her in his arms. She came so
easily. So guilelessly. There were no sides, by night. No
nationalities. If he closed his eyes . . . he could even forget
bitterness.

He opened his eyes.

No. He could not forget bitterness.

CHAPTER 7

The appointed time came.

The king's wagons, horses, followers, laundresses, and grooms were left behind in the forest. The Scots had fought most of their battles with the majority of their number on foot, so running across great tracts of land was not a difficulty, though the ladders they had fashioned were, of necessity, heavy.

Jamie, bearing a length of the rope, wood, and steel himself, saw his breath before his face as they ran. They did so in unison, and across the soft grasses, there was a beat as the men's footsteps fell in a steady gait. Despite the weight the men bore, they were so accustomed to a hard course that they managed to cross the distance to the moat in an eerie silence, other than that soft sound of feet against the earth. They moved like ebony wraiths against the shadows of the deepest part of night.

The greatness that had rallied men around Robert the

Bruce was apparent that night, for he was the first to enter into the frigid water of the moat. and like the common man who had become a warrior, he shirked no duty; he carried a ladder along with the rest of them.

The water was cold. Bitterly cold. All his life, Jamie had known the cold of the northern waters, and still, that night, the water seemed to bite into their flesh, paralyze fingers and toes, and constrict their throats. They moved by rote, all of them knowing the cold of winter, the hardship of battle. Man after man entered. The water rose . . . higher and higher. They bore their weight, still keeping their silence.

At last, the first of them crossed the water.

The ladders, with their hooks. makeshift wooden *steps,* and rope were cast high, catching into the battlements. Men began to climb, the king in the first of their number. Dripping and frigid, they scaled the stone fortifications. They reached the battlements, and in silence struck the night guards, who were taken entirely by surprise. Within minutes, the battlements were teeming with Scotsmen, and as yet, no alarm had been raised.

Directing his forces in near silence, the king divided his troops, leaving some to guard the battlements, and ordering the others into the town.

The element of surprise remained complete.

As was his way, Robert Bruce had ordered that those surrendering not be slain. Prisoners would be taken, and all goods seized. Leading his group down the battlements and into the walled section of town, Jamie used hand signals to time their attacks and entries into the halls and homes. At the gateway to an arsenal, he, Liam, and Ragnor aligned themselves, counted a silent three, and kicked the door in. They caught every man asleep, and stormed in, only then shouting that those who surrendered would be spared.

There were still those who would fight. A wily lieutenant

in his nightshirt still had his sword near. He charged Jamie as others rallied and took up their arms. But the Scots had come prepared. The defenders were barely awake. The man charging Jamie came at him recklessly, and his blow was easily parried, his sword met again and again. Their fight brought them to the stone wall, where Jamie again offered life as their swords clashed and froze.

"Surrender, and you will be spared."

The man started to lower his weapon. He meant to take his opponent off guard, but Jamie was ready when he turned back, his sword freed, ready to use it as a skewer. Jamie deflected the blow, striking in return, and his opponent fell.

"Jamie!"

He turned.

Ragnor had been set upon by three men. Jamie entered the fray. More of the defenders had risen and taken up arms. With Ragnor at his side, he found that they were being backed against a wall. They had fought together many times before. They turned from one another, making one another's back the shield they needed, forcing the men to take them on from different positions. Men fell; the floor ran wet and slick with blood. And still, the fighting was grim, man after man taking the place of the other, determined to bring down a mere two of their attackers.

Perhaps they could have.

But a cry sounded from the doorway. Liam came rushing in, sword swinging. And behind, more and more of the attackers began to pour in. In a matter of minutes, it seemed, the ground was littered with the dead, and then, a cry of "Surrender, mercy!" went up, and the rest of the men, many with blood-soaked nightshirts, threw down their swords, willing to believe in the promise of life offered by Robert the Bruce.

By then, women were screaming in the streets, children

had wakened in terror, and old men were desperately trying to arm themselves. No matter how the attacking Scotsmen cried out that Robert Bruce intended mercy, there was a sense of panic. Bruce himself cried out that Perth was a Scottish town, though held by the English for so long. Scotland was meant to be healed.

Still, the years of war had created mistrust. Some men surrendered; some did not. Some began to cheer, crying out that Perth was free.

Throwing open a door, Jamie saw a young woman in a chair, eyes bright, frightened. She made a strange movement, inadvertently blinking, and he realized that she was there just to draw the eyes.

He turned in time to avert an attack by a frail, bearded, old man. He avoided the first blow, crying out, "Cast down the weapon; I've no wish to slay you."

The old fellow shook his head, hands winding around the blade again. He moved to strike, and once again, Jamie did nothing more than deflect the blow. "Throw it down!"

The girl leaped to her feet then. "Father, cast down your sword. Now!"

The old fellow did so. The girl rushed to him.

"My life is nothing; you will not take my daughter!" he whispered.

"Your daughter may be safe," Jamie said. "Gather what you will. Robert Bruce will raze the fortification, burn the town. Take what you need."

He waited; the two gathered their scant belongings. With a heavy cloak about her, the girl took her father's hand. They left the house.

The living were gathered together, the dead were abandoned as the attackers steadfastly continued their assault, entering into every door.

By the early hours of morning, great treasures had been

seized, the injured were being gathered, and only occasional bursts of fighting could be heard.

The Earl of Strathearn, who had chosen allegiance with the English, was captured by his own son, who had been fighting for Bruce.

The King of Scotland openly forgave the man, and returned his lands to him once the earl had sworn Robert Bruce a new allegiance. The king's great mercy was seen by all, yet nothing would save the fortification, or take the riches from the hands of the assaulting Scots. Robert Bruce didn't have the manpower to hold such a fortification while attempting to seize the last remaining English strongholds in Scotland. The place would be razed.

The town had been taken completely off guard. By daylight, Perth had fallen. Goods of any value were being taken. Robert Bruce had proclaimed that the men would keep most of what they seized, and that night, many a poor man became a rich one.

Jamie received his own reward, an earnest thank-you from his king, and a pocketful of gold taken from the English treasury. But as the sun rose and he looked around at the town, he felt a deep sorrow in his heart.

He'd been at it too many years. Fighting. Always believing that somewhere, the fighting would create a justice for the past. There was no justice in any inhumanity. He couldn't take pleasure in the downfall of Perth. It would be rebuilt; it would be Scottish now. But the people here would have to eke out new lives from the cinders and ashes that would be left behind. He had smelled the acrid scent of destructive fires too long.

They had triumphed.

He was covered in blood.

The shouts had died down. The dead lay in silence. The only sounds now were those of destruction.

*   *   *

They were not so far, not so deep in the forest, that the sounds of battle could not be heard. Not even the fact that she was at long last with Lauren and Sir Alfred could ease the tension Christina felt through the long night. They could hear so much. Through the cold night air, they could hear the shouting. The muted clang of steel. And the cries and screams . . .

She, Lauren, and Sir Alfred stood, huddled together, under the watchful eyes of Magnus. He listened as well. When the morning light came, the sounds from Perth muted and died down, and then the forest, in the sunlight, seemed quiet again.

"What has happened?" Christina asked Magnus.

The huge fellow looked down at her. "They have taken the town," he told her. "Soon enough, you'll see the fires."

"They'll burn it all down?" Christina said.

"Robert Bruce will leave no walls for his enemies to use against him." Magnus walked away from her, taking his seat before a tree. For such a big active man, Magnus had tremendous patience. He never took his eyes off his captives, yet while he watched them, he spent his hours whittling pieces of wood. Christina had watched him, admittedly awed by his talent. Throughout the night, he had been fashioning a horse. Delicate and beautiful. Streaks of mane were carved with such realism that she was almost convinced she would feel an animal rather than a piece of wood if she were to touch the object.

"So, they have triumphed," Sir Alfred murmured, shaking his head.

"Perhaps it's best," Lauren said, touching his arm.

Sir Alfred stared at her indignantly. "We are safe in the escort of this man, Sir Jamie. All of our enemies might not be so benign. Had the battle gone badly, and the woods been full of fleeing warriors pursued by the English, our lives might well have been at stake.''

Christina sat warily, at a distance from Magnus, but watching him still. She was almost irritated with Lauren. After greeting her with an all but deadly hug, she had anxiously asked after her health and been assured that she was fine; she and Alfred had been treated kindly and allowed the utmost dignity. She wasn't worried about her fate, and actually liked their captor very much. He was, after all, an unwilling captor. Polite, courteous. Well spoken. Lauren was convinced that he had received an excellent education somewhere.

As she watched Magnus, Lauren walked over to join her. She leaned against the tree as well, and closed her eyes. She shivered suddenly. "Is Steven well?" she asked Christina.

Christina lightly bit into her lip. After a moment, she said, ''I'm convinced that nothing really terrible has happened to him. I know that I would feel it if . . .''

"If he were gone," Lauren supplied softly.

Christina nodded. She and Steven shared a very strange form of communication, always aware when the other was hurt, or in danger. The only thing that made each day bearable was knowing that Steven still lived; that there was still a fight to be fought and won, though it was not a battle that could be waged with conventional weapons. She was certain that there was a way to twist King Edward's hand. Edward was bitter against many of his knights. If he could only be convinced that Steven didn't bring about the death of his favorite, then the tribute paid to the Scots might be overlooked—as it had been for others. While they remained *imprisoned* by the Scots, Edward would surely feel a certain sympathy for Steven, as much as he was able. And he would understand that they didn't easily give in to his enemies.

And not even Rowan DeClabert would dare cause harm to her brother without Edward's direct command.

She looked at Lauren. "Steven is safe. I'm certain of it. More certain than I am of your safety," she added.

"I don't think I'm in any danger," Lauren said. "If he was irritated by anything, it was surely the lies we told. He knows who I am. And we talked about Steven. Curious, I don't think it mattered to him what my position in life might be; he was more intrigued when I talked about our relationship. I think you judge the man too harshly."

"I don't judge him at all; he is simply the enemy. True— we cast ourselves beneath the enemy's feet, and for good reason. But it is rather like attempting to tame a wild animal. You never know when it will turn on you."

Lauren turned, staring toward the town of Perth. Fires were beginning to rise to the sky. "They will burn it all— everything?" she said.

Magnus apparently wasn't listening.

"I suppose so," Christina said.

"We were lucky," Lauren told her.

Yes, they had been lucky. Hamstead Heath still stood.

A little later, in daylight, Christina at last slept. Sir Alfred and Lauren had both fallen asleep as well, and when she later woke, she realized that the three of them were curled together on a bed of leaves, much like a litter of new puppies. Sir Alfred, of course, was a rather old puppy, but actually, lying in such a deep sleep, he was almost as appealing.

She wondered what had awakened her, and she realized that George had ridden back. He sat atop his warhorse in the clearing, talking to Magnus.

She rose, dusting off her coat of leaves, and approached the two. She was startled when George looked at her and actually smiled. "You needn't fear, Lady Christina. We didn't lose a man—from our immediate number."

She halted, wondering if she could have possibly appeared concerned for her captors.

"I'm glad to see you alive and unhurt, George," she told him quietly.

"Thank you. Of course, in the midst of all . . . there are many injuries. That is not your concern. But I'm to bring you in from the forest. Time must be taken to empty the town, divide the spoils, raze the walls. We'll be camping in the fields around a group of old farmhouses, distant from the fires. I'm come for you. With a warning, of course."

"A warning?" she said.

Magnus let out a strange sniff.

"Regarding your good behavior," George said.

She looked at him, refusing to blink. "Go on."

"You're to be moved separately. You come with me now. Magnus will later escort Sir Alfred and Lady Lauren."

"I see," she murmured. Yes, of course, as long as he kept her from those she loved, she would be a model of good behavior. And yet, what damage could she cause him now? Apparently, their surprise attack had been a total success.

George dismounted from his horse. "If you'll gather your things, my lady, we'll be on our way. I'll go for your horse."

She forgot any sense of irritation she'd felt for Lauren, embracing both her and Sir Alfred tightly. George brought Crystal to the copse, and Magnus set her atop the animal, as if he lifted no more than a squirrel. George then led her toward Perth.

Their journey was long and wide; he did not intend to lead her through the moat, though that was the way they had come. George had a certain enthusiasm about him as he spoke to her. "It was magnificent! Robert Bruce, at the head of his troops. A French knight so moved at the sight of a king working so for his hamlet, like a lost sheep, that he burst ahead of the king, daring the ropes first himself. And then we were all moving, one after another, man after man, scaling the ropes. Jamie and Liam all but took down the men of the arsenal themselves—it was a complete and glorious rout!'' He glanced at Christina and his smile faded. "I'm sorry, I—well, I'm not sorry! Perth is our town. Invaded, raped and pillaged by the English. It's our town again. I'm simply sorry because . . . well, you're English.''

"Yes,'' she said, returning his stare.

"But you were glad to see me alive, weren't you?''

"Yes,'' she said again.

He smiled, turning toward their course again. "There, see in the distant fields? The house. That's where we ride. There's a river crossing just a few miles down now. I wish that it weren't autumn. You should see these meadows by spring. They lie in gold and violet beneath the sun.''

She shivered slightly, for from their position now, she could see across to the walls of the town. There were prisoners huddled together in groups. There were piles of goods rising everywhere.

There were bodies lying on the ground below the battlements.

Christina turned her face toward the river. "I can see no glory in war,'' she murmured.

"There is no glory,'' George told her. "But there is always great relief in coming out of battle alive.''

They rode in silence then. At length, they passed the river.

Apparently, they had joined with the main body of Bruce's army, for tents—banners flying—were rising across the field. They were stopped as they crossed the bridge and came upon the Scotsmen. George identified himself, and they were allowed to pass. They rode through men-at-arms, cooking fires, and further battle preparations. Men stared at her as she passed through. A few inclined their heads, with both courtesy and contempt. She was startled by the fear that suddenly rested in her soul. She was more vulnerable than she had ever imagined. She had never felt it more fully.

At last, they passed by the large group of knights and warriors. They had nearly entered on another wood when they reached a small thatched-roof house. George dismounted, reaching for Christina, bringing her down before him. "Well, it's not a manor or a castle, but far better than the conditions being offered many another prisoner, I assure you," George said cheerfully.

"It's lovely," Christina told him. She glanced at him, then walked along the stone path leading to a wooden door. Hesitantly, she pushed it open. The place was clean, swept of debris, while clean rushes were scattered across the floor. A table for work and eating stood near a large hearth. There was a loft, and an extra room. Christina walked across to the doorway leading to the second room. Within, there was a rough-hewn dresser and a large rope bed with real down pillows at the head and a quilted comforter covering all of it.

"If you've any talent at all with a kettle and fire, there are sides of smoked pork and beef, and dried vegetables as well," George told her. "Of course, we can bring in one of the king's followers, since you're a lady born, and probably—"

"I am capable with a kettle and fire, George," she told him.

He nodded. "Then I will leave you."

She looked at him uneasily. "Well, no, of course, you are never really left," he admitted. "But I must return. And of course . . . well, if you leave this house, I'm afraid that the repercussions could be grave indeed."

He bowed to her and walked out the door. She hesitated, wondering just what he had meant by the warning. Were there guards beyond the door? Or was it the elation of the men of a triumphant army she must fear?

It didn't matter. She wasn't leaving. She had already been threatened with the welfare of Sir Alfred and Lauren.

And she had nowhere to go. Her return to Hamstead Heath could only further endanger her brother.

She looked around the little farmhouse, wondering what had happened to the inhabitants. Did they lie dead somewhere? Had they been spared? The Scots would not take poor farmers as prisoners—they'd have no value.

She walked to the hearth where a fire burned. Water boiled in the black kettle that hung over it. She wondered if the people who had lived here most recently had been Scots, or English. Scots, probably. The English who came to garrison the fortresses were soldiers. Sometimes their wives came, sometimes their servants. But they did not bring along farmers, at least, not often.

She prowled around the shelves. As George had said, there was food. She realized that she was starving. She found onions and herbs to add to the water, and a large side of pork. No salt and no pepper—the farmer surely could not afford such luxuries for the table. The meat had been smoked, not salted.

As the food simmered to a stew, she sat at the table, rested her arms on it, and laid her head on them. The day was drawing to a close. She was very tired. And nervous. They were no longer riding with a party of thirty-odd men she knew to be sane and decent. They had joined with a massive army.

She didn't hear the door open, yet became aware that there was a draft, and that she was not alone. She raised her head, looking toward the door. At first, it seemed that all she saw was a stranger, encrusted in dirt and blood.

A great deal of blood . . .

Jamie had come.

She leaped from the chair, backing away, astounded by the amount of blood. A cry left her throat as she stared at him.

"Alas, sorry to disappoint you, but it's not my own," he said lightly. He turned, closing the door behind him. "Is there water here?"

She started to shake her head. Then she murmured, "Perhaps . . . a pitcher in the bedroom. I . . . I . . . I'm not sure."

"No matter," he said. He turned back to the door and called out to someone. A boy of perhaps fourteen arrived. "Find me a tub, wood, metal—any kind."

"A tub?"

"Hip bath," Jamie said. He shook his head. "Lad, surely you bathe once a year?"

"In the river!" the boy said indignantly.

"Ah, lad, you've not spent enough of your days in the mud and muck of winter . . . or in blood of your enemies. Whatever the old wives tales about the devil stealing your soul if you bathe too frequently, that is nothing but total rot."

"Wouldn't want to wash too much skin from me body!" the boy said. "The river does me well enough."

"Well, the river is cold, and thank you, I've had a taste of it. Go to my man near the wall, Ragnor, and see that a tub is brought. They've had such things behind the walls, you see. Get what help you need." He gave the boy a coin. The boy stared at the coin, bit it, stared at him, and grinned as if he'd just seen a glimpse of heaven. "Aye, Sir Jamie! Right away. If there is no such tub as you say, I'll gouge out a tree m'self!"

Jamie closed the door behind the boy. He had not worn armor to this battle. He took off his cloak, and she saw the tears in his shirt. He had said that the blood wasn't his, but she knew he'd been injured before. She'd seen the scars on his back.

He sat, taking the chair at the table that she had so recently vacated. He pulled off a boot, then paused, staring at her. "Dear Lord. Is there a meal cooking in that pot?"

"There's food, yes."

"Amazing. You, my lady, have managed a meal?"

"Striving, of course, to be a worthy hostage."

"And I am certain that when you've set it in your mind that you'll do something well, it's done very well."

"I'm somewhat capable, yes."

"Then I'm in heaven," he murmured, pulling off a second boot. "Warm food, a bath, a bed." He looked her way again. "Not the quality to which you are accustomed, my lady, but quite a boon, don't you think? The lesser prisoners taken from the fortress will be sleeping in the open, while those of higher position might perhaps find a tent."

"Imagine. And you are granted this opulence! Are you that prized before your king that you are worthy of a house?" she asked, aware that she used the mocking tone he so despised, and aware as well that it was something she didn't seem able to stop.

"Yes," he said flatly, rising. He walked to the fire. "The Bruce is magnanimous even to his enemies. To his longtime supporters, he is more than generous. Whatever it is that you have created in that pot, I will take a bowl now."

Christina started at the command. He had seemed amused and almost lighthearted when he spoke with the boy, but then he had spoken to her as if she were the lowliest of serfs, born to his beck and call.

She always meant to be regal, as serene as Lauren, who, in her very cool obedience, seemed to radiate a dignity at all times.

She hadn't Lauren's temperament.

"Suit yourself, Sir Jamie," she said evenly, not moving from her place by the wall.

His eyes seemed a very chill shade of blue-gray at that moment, enhanced as they were by the dirt on his face.

"I meant, Christina, that you should get the bowl."

"Oh."

He smiled. "I can always bring another prisoner in here. It makes little difference to me. In a few days' time, you'll be turned over to the king, and no longer my concern in the least. As will the rest of your party."

A few days' time . . .

She had been certain the other night that he made his veiled threats simply because he enjoyed her reactions. He offered no threat to Lauren. And still, he had made it evident that he far preferred Lauren's manner to her own, and that he found Lauren to be a far more appealing hostage than she was herself.

Could she be so very certain of her enemy?

The intense time they had spent together made her feel as if she had known him much longer than that time would warrant. But did she dare test him too far?

"I would be delighted to get you a bowl of—whatever this is," she said, moving across the room. What pottery the farmer had owned was on a shelf near the table. She found a bowl, then walked to the fire, ladled out the stew, and realized that she was starving herself. He wouldn't be leaving for a while. She set the bowl before him with a sharp sound upon the table, and went for her own.

Either she was much hungrier than she had imagined, or her creation was actually moderately tasty. He said nothing to her, but ate, and with an appetite as well. Yet before he had finished, there was a knock at the door.

The lad had returned. With a number of his friends and

someone's elegantly carved hip bath. It was of Nordic design, Christina thought, and exceptionally fine.

Jamie seemed intrigued by it as well. "A handsome piece," he told the boy. "You've done well."

She wondered if the tub would travel along with them—like the rug he had so admired in her room at Hamstead Heath.

"Lads, good job!" he advised the boys. "Now—"

"There's kettles aplenty brewing the water for ye now, sir!" the lad assured Jamie.

He opened the door further. It was true. The boys had set to work. Fires burned in the yard, as they did around the whole of the fortress of Perth. Tonight, it didn't matter if their fires were seen. They were victorious. They were about the business only of taking all that they could, and razing the walls to the ground.

"Bring them in," Jamie advised.

They came, one after another, all of them farm boys, some younger, some older, and all terribly intrigued, and happy, apparently, to serve such a great knight. They didn't seem to have suffered in the taking of Perth. But then, it was a Scottish town, and reclaimed, and the people must be relishing the return of their own rather than ruing it, and it would be no matter that the walls of the fortress were battered down. They would rebuild.

Kettle after kettle came in until the bath was all but brimming before the hearth.

Steam emanated from it. Christina felt drawn herself.

The lad paused at the door when the last of the water had been brought. "Is there anything else, Sir James?"

"No, I thank you, though. You've far exceeded my expectations."

"May I take care of your horse?"

"I've a groom who attends to such matters, boy." He

hesitated, then shrugged. "My men will be camped nearby. Find Ragnor again, ask him to send you to Grayson. He'll find some work for you and your friends."

A smile lit the boy's face. He stared suddenly at Christina. "Is that your wife? She's very beautiful."

"She's not my wife," Jamie said sharply, certainly, speaking with an anger he had not meant to set loose upon the boy. He changed his tone, speaking evenly. "Find Grayson, and he'll give you work."

The boy nodded and left. Jamie closed the door in his wake. For a moment his back remained to her. Then he turned and strode back to the table. He stopped before taking his seat again, studying the shelves. He found what he was seeking, bringing down a skin, testing it, finding that it was filled with ale. He took his chair again.

"You may go first," he told her.

"What?"

"The water. Once I've been in, I'm afraid it will be quite filthy. I can't imagine you wanting to bathe in a pool of blood."

She felt her face grow pale. "I wouldn't dream of taking your bath."

"Yes, you would."

"No, I wouldn't."

"Yes, I think you would."

"Why on earth would you think that?" she demanded, aware that anger was rising in her voice.

He leaned toward her pleasantly. "Because you would do anything—*anything*—to please me. And it will please me if you will get in there, quickly, and get out while the steam is still rising high."

"I could please you far more by allowing you the full heat of the water," she said.

He sat back, a half smile on his lips. "There are no

surprises for either of us, Christina. And if you haven't realized it yet, I will gladly point out to you that I find you to be deceitful, volatile, and a dangerous little witch. You're entirely safe from me. Get in there, and hurry.''

He stood suddenly, and to her surprise, took the skin with him, leaving the little house. The door slammed in his wake.

She sat for a moment in stunned surprise.

Then she prayed that he wasn't going for Lauren. The woman he found to be pleasant and gentle.

He was not. He enjoyed tormenting her, that was all.

She didn't need to be afraid for Lauren tonight. They had just scored a victory. They were within the camp of the king of the Scots. There were many women about.

And still, she wasn't sure that she had the nerve to defy him. She leaped up, nervously casting off her garments, plunging into the bath. She would certainly hurry. He wanted heat and steam. He'd be back.

And he was, sooner than she'd imagined. But he barely glanced her way. Rather he threw down a set of worn linen towels, and threw a sliver of soap into the water. He passed by her, going into the bedroom.

The soap was French; perfumed. She inhaled the sweet scent, amazed to realize she could take the time for such a sensual pleasure. Then she scrubbed quickly, rinsed and rose. She wrapped herself in the linen towel, grabbed her clothing, and sprinted to the doorway. He was seated at the end of the bed, honing his sword. ''I've left a great deal of steam,'' she said. ''The stew still fills the kettle that was on the fire, but I'm sure I can find another somewhere if you wish to have more water. I believe that the lads who are so eager to serve you are just outside the door. I can call them, and see that more water is brought.''

''That won't be necessary,'' he told her. He set down the sword and passed her again, returning to the main room and the bath. Shivering, she dried quickly, startled to realize that the hot bath had been a kindness. She felt clean as she hadn't since they'd left Hamstead Heath. She had barely slipped back into her shift when she heard him call her name.

"A minute!" she cried.

"A minute? What good hostage takes time when commanded to appear?"

"I am hurrying."

"Now."

Gritting her teeth, she walked back into the main room, keeping her distance, and eyeing him warily.

"The soap."

"What?" Surely, he wasn't expecting her to bathe him.

He wasn't. "I dropped it on the floor. Would you be so good as to retrieve it?"

She let out a long breath. "Certainly. Of course. Anything to be of service, Sir James!"

As she neared the tub, she tried to keep her eyes averted. It didn't really matter. The water was already darkening. She picked up the soap. As she rose then, she saw a line of red across his chest that had not washed away.

"I thought you said that the blood was not yours!" she breathed.

"This? A scratch, nothing more. But thank you for your concern."

"I'm not concerned. Not in the least."

"Well, then, I retract my thanks," he said. He seemed to be laughing again. She hated him for it. She wanted to retaliate, and she was curiously drawn at the same time. She moved nearer the tub, startling him when she ran a finger lightly above the line of his new wound.

He caught her hand.

"You said you were not concerned."

"Concern would not be the word. I prefer that you remain

alive, since you appear to be far better, at the least, than many of your fellows.''

"You'll be with some of those fine Highland fellows in just a few days," he told her pleasantly.

"Under direct orders from Robert Bruce, the magnanimous, who will see that no harm befalls his prisoners while ransom is arranged."

The boys had made the water very hot. Steam was still rising. She felt it seeping into the material of her shift, and the sensation was very odd. He still held her wrist in a tight grip. She was suddenly sorry that she had decided to goad him. The linen seemed to be molding to her form. The scent of the soap seemed to tease her again. Breathing was not easy. She felt her heart beating and knew that a telltale throb was pulsing against her throat. ''What a surprisingly gently touch you have, Christina,'' he murmured.

"I wouldn't aggravate your injury. As I said, I would prefer that you live, for the time being, at least.''

"As I said, the injury is nothing more than a scratch.''

She wasn't sure if she had moved, or if he had pulled her closer. Her face was just inches from his. She was tempted to trace the lines of his bones. She tried to keep her eyes level with his. The water had grown dark; not dark enough. Her eyes flew open, wide. She knew that her heart was beating like a hummingbird's wings.

"You said that I was safe with you!'' she whispered.

She was startled by the speed with which he released her. ''As you are,'' he told her.

She almost fell. She collected her senses and her balance, and turned to flee, hurrying to the other room. She glanced at her gown cast down near the door. Then she noted his huge sword laid at the foot of the bed. She walked over to the weapon, bending down. She picked it up. A heavy piece. Well made. Quite lethal. She tested its weight.

"I thought you preferred that I should live—for the moment," Jamie said from the doorway.

She spun around. The linen towel was wrapped around his hips. All remnants of battle were washed away. His skin remained damp. Sleek.

She gripped his sword as she had been taught. "A bit too heavy for me, but . . . a fine sword."

He rested his hands upon his hips. "And you know how to use it?"

"Indeed, sir, I do."

"Oh?"

"I could slice that towel clean from your person, Sir James. In fact, I could slice many—things—cleanly from your torso."

"Prove it."

"I don't wish you any further harm."

"How intriguing. You were willing to drug me and my men, and see that we were delivered to the English. Surely, even you would have realized what end we would have faced then as prisoners to your king."

"That, Sir James, was before the situation changed."

"Now, of course, you would be loath to see me face such punishment?"

"I've never enjoyed the concept of any man's demise, take that as you will."

"What kindness and mercy you have in your soul, my lady! Or is merely that you are so talented with a sword as you seem to believe."

"I am talented. Very."

"Prove it."

She shook her head. "Sir, I have no wish to hurt you, so I wish that you would stop issuing such challenges. I am telling you, I'm quite capable of wielding a sword."

"Fine. Wield it against me. I am the enemy coming for you."

He started across the room with long strides. He was serious. She raised the sword, striking as Steven had long ago taught her, with more finesse than power.

And even as he walked, she made her move.

The towel was ripped from his waist. Startled, he stopped and stared at her. She kept her chin very high, praying that her eyes wouldn't fall.

"So, you are familiar with weapons."

"Yes—I informed you quite clearly that I was."

"Indeed, but what incredible confidence you have! Perhaps just a bit too much. You think that you could take me?"

"Shall I weigh the odds? You don't even have a weapon at the moment, so yes, I could definitely take you, Sir James. Perhaps you should back off. And be aware, forewarned, that you are playing with fire."

He inclined his head slightly. "Again, I urge you, prove your talent."

"You're wounded already."

"Forgive me if I feel that you need some advantage," he said.

"Fine!" she murmured, and stepped toward him, sword cutting through the air. He backed away in time to avoid a blow, moving across the room with speed and agility. He leaped atop the bed, his lack of attire a distraction she didn't need. She struck out smoothly with the blade again. He jumped, rising above it in the nick of time. A moment later, she simply surged forward. She was convinced the point could have gone right though his chest had she not drawn back. But by that time, he had pushed away from the wall with a flying leap. His impetus sent them both flying back against the bed. She tried hard to maintain her hold upon the sword, but the hilt slipped from her fingers. The weapon fell to the floor at the side of the bed.

"There, alas," he said, looking down at her.

"I had you!" she told him. "I could have killed you."

"No. You never had me."

"Easy for you to say. I never intended to take your life."

"You're not as good as you think."

"I'm very good. Your sword is a shade too heavy."

"You know something about swordplay, my lady, I grant you that. And I suppose I should be grateful that, in your initial attack, you went for the towel, and not other things that might have been sliced cleanly from my body."

Her breath caught. Her eyes were wide as she stared into his. She had never been so aware of his form. The scent and feel of his flesh. The pressure and ripple of muscle. And more. Not even in the water had she felt him as she felt him now. Her breath escaped her. She felt again the pulse beating at her throat. Felt his breath, warm against her cheek. The pressure of his body molded them down into the softness of the bed together. The length of his form seemed to fit against her, and every variation of his shape pressed upon some point of her own. She moistened her lips, trying to speak. She struggled to remember the topic at hand.

"Were I to have done you any injury, there are hundreds of men just beyond that door who would have gladly entered and avenged your death."

"True. But I don't believe that would have stopped you— had you really had the determination to slit my throat. You do have talent. I, however, have power."

Power. He indeed had it. A very strange power, one that haunted, and attracted. She couldn't think of further words of argument. She was far too aware of the pressure of his flesh against her own. Aware, as well, that she was far more than simply drawn to him as a man. She closed her eyes, determined not to see. But that was far worse, for she found herself reminded of the tone of his voice, of the arguments they had waged, and the times when what he had granted had been, in truth, pure mercy.

Her eyes flew open as he touched her face. "You are, I do admit, quite the tormenter. There are many things you should learn. With other men, take care that you don't draw a sword, unless you intend to use it. And don't make promises that you don't intend to keep."

"Promises . . . ?"

"Promises, bribes, assurances. Offers of *anything.*"

She met his eyes, afraid to breathe, aware again of the vital blanket of his body, constriction of muscle . . . and the odd contrast of gentleness where his fingers touched her face. She had forced him too far.

The time had come . . .

"You should learn to take care in the battles you wage, Christina. For one day, when you fail in your reckless pursuits, you will pay with far more than you ever meant to risk."

With that, he rose suddenly, striding out the main room.

Christina lay without moving, stunned that he was gone, aware that she should be feeling the deepest gratitude, incredible relief.

She heard him moving about, looking for something. She realized that the saddlebags against the wall held fresh clothing for him, and that he was dressing.

She lay upon the bed, on the quilt that covered it. In a moment, he would go out into the night. She would be lying to herself now if she rose to stop him, determined to keep him from Lauren. It was evident that he had no such intent, though he would leave to celebrate, certainly. They had just taken a city. There were many camp followers in this army of the king.

The room had grown dark, lit only by the fire that blazed in the hearth of the other room. In her damp shift, she was cold suddenly, and hearing an echo of his voice.

Beware, in your reckless pursuits, that you don't risk far more than you are willing to pay.

She was alone, he had left, and she should have known nothing but intense gratitude, and instead, what she felt was . . .

Bereft. Cold. Engulfed by a sudden loneliness and loss that was frightening and foolish, and yet a growing tempest within her that she couldn't swallow with pride.

To her amazement, she sprang from the bed, wondering at her sanity, at her total lack of sense, dignity and wisdom.

She hurried to the main room. He was just throwing his mantle over his shoulders, ready to depart into the night.

There was laughter beyond the walls; she could hear it now. Laughter, singing. Of course, there was surely a great deal of drinking going on out there as well. Of course. They were the conquering heroes.

He paused, staring at her as she looked at him. Again, no words came to her mouth. She moistened her lips.

And she managed to speak.

"Where are you going?"

"Out, my lady. To leave you to your sanctity."

"Don't—go," she whispered at last.

He sighed, lowering his head, shaking it slightly, then meeting her eyes again. "Christina, I'm not leaving to seek out Lauren."

"I know."

"We do fight a long war, and never know at just what

times we might be victorious—and at leisure with . . . with so many of our own in attendance.''

"I . . . I wish that you would not . . . leave.''

"You're asking me to stay—tonight?''

"I . . . yes.''

He shook his head, a frown creasing his brow as he stared at her. "Do you know, *do you really know,* what you're saying?''

She met his eyes, then nodded slowly.

And she was amazed herself. She did. She knew exactly what she was saying. She didn't know exactly why. Perhaps, because she didn't know what the future would bring. Bargains, trades, ransoms, contracts.

Never anything so real as this moment.

Never anything so fine as what she had felt, crushed beneath him.

She knew that he fascinated and intrigued her, that he was sleek and hard and powerful and could have a touch as gentle as a breeze as well. She loved the contours of his face, and the sharp blue-gray color of his eyes that could change so quickly, the length and breadth of his hands. Even the sound of his voice could touch her, in mockery, in anger, in his moments of simple weariness.

She had no idea of what this madness would create, when the night was over, and morning light had come. Indeed, to think of it would only be a nightmare, and that would be paying the price she was now such a fool to risk.

"I can still walk out that door,'' he told her quietly.

That which she had always been willing to give as a noble and necessary sacrifice was now suddenly something she craved with a hunger greater than any she had ever known.

"I know. But . . . I wish that you would not.''

He remained at the door another moment. Then the mantle

he had been about to pin at his shoulder went flying to the floor.

Long strides brought him before her. He cupped her chin in his hands, raising her face to his. He studied her eyes, and she wondered just what he searched for within them.

He found something. She suddenly found herself lifted, and carried the few steps back into the bedroom.

CHAPTER 8

War was long and hard. He didn't know how many nights they had gone without eating, or how often they had run, going without sleep. Oddly enough, however, war had never precluded women; there were those who were widows, needing a night's solace themselves. There were those who were intrigued by the men who fought, risking their lives. And there were those who followed knights and men-at-arms simply for business purposes, enterprising in their right. There had always been women.

But not like this one.

He should have left more quickly. He should have known, when he grappled her to the bed, when the sword fell to the floor. He should have known then that he had to get out, quickly. The scent of her flesh had been far too warm and sweet, alluring. The green of her eyes too vast. The feel of her beneath him, far too seductive and inviting, whether such an invitation had been intended or not. Flesh, muscle, bone, all had seemed to fit too smoothly against her.

He hadn't left in time.

Now, he felt the delicate bones of her face with his palm as he cradled her chin, testing her lips. Hot, damp, eager, unschooled, sweet . . . her mouth parting to the onslaught of his, her fingers all but tearing into his flesh as she clung to him. Fires knotted throughout his body as he forced the kiss to be long and seductive, finding the depths of her mouth, stroking with the length of his tongue, a heady touch that awakened as much as it intimated. He was tangled in the length of her hair, silken against him, crushed upon the length of her body, aware of breasts, slender waist, long legs, the apex between them. His own heart felt as if it pounded to a desperate beat, one that sent a mist of desire to his head, obscuring thought, reason, taking away every sensation except for the urgency of the moment. He struggled to retain his grasp on sanity, withdrawing from the kiss at last, staring down into the sea of her eyes. He was startled to find himself shaken and angry.

"You asked me here," he said fiercely.

She moistened her lips, though they appeared damp and swollen.

"Yes."

"I was not going after your friend, your brother's beloved."

"I know," she breathed.

He arched a brow. "This is not a savage attack by an enemy."

She shook her head. "No."

"If you were ever to say so, we'd both know you were a liar."

"I've no intention of lying."

For once, she seemed to be completely open and honest,

barely breathing, afraid to move, yet meeting his eyes with her own fully open.

"Why have you asked me to stay?"

"I don't know."

He started to move, not to leave, just to adjust his weight. Yet it seemed that she didn't know that.

"Because . . . I may never know anyone quite like you . . . again," she whispered.

Her reply startled him. And sent a surge of heat searing through him that seemed strangely to begin within his mind, then travel to those extremities already coursing with tension and desire. He traced her face once again with the brush of his knuckles. Smoothed back her hair, found her lips with his mouth and her breast with the stroke of his fingers, the palm of his hand. Her fingers threaded into his hair, trapping him close. He eased from her lips, teasing her nipple through the linen with the tip of his forefinger and thumb, then settling his mouth around it, damp and wet over the material. She surged against him, fingers tightening their grasp in his hair.

He moved down the length of her so, lips and tongue teasing over fabric, stroking ribs, delving in her navel, lower against her. A shocked, startled little cry escaped her when he stroked between her thighs with the tip of his tongue. He caught hold of the hem of her linen shift then, rolling it to her hips, and making love then to the bare flesh beneath.

She was still. Locked, dead still, fingers in her palms, muscles constricted as if one. She barely seemed to be breathing. And yet he could feel the fierce thunder of her pulse, rapid, racing, pounding through her flesh, apparent with the tiny gasps of breath that escaped her. Mist rose again, reason, sanity, thought, vanished into that silver elixir of hunger. Here, there could be no mercy granted, no quarter given.

He teased, stroked, parted, seduced. And awaited a total surrender.

And surrender came with a sharp, gasped cry, a violent shudder, a searing of liquid fire. She strained against him with tension, and he rose quickly, finding her lips again, delving into every crevice of her mouth, parting her thighs with the pressure of his knee. He drew an inch away from her, studying her face. Her arms wound around him; her eyes were closed, her lips remained parted, slightly swollen, damp, enticing. He ran his hand down the length of her body. Then he eased himself into her, aware again of that frantic pulse, a desperate beat, now raging inside his head, pulsing through his veins, filling the length of his sex.

If she cried out, the sound was crushed and muted against his chest. Once again, she was as taut as a bow; her fingers dug desperately into his flesh. He paused, gritting his teeth, fighting the strength and hunger of the pulse. He had known, certainly he had known, that the daughter of such a house as Hamstead Heath would be untouched. Guilt tugged at the corners of his heart.

Not hard enough.

She had chosen to be here. For whatever reason, she had chosen to be here.

He eased himself from her, wishing he could withdraw. He could not. He thrust more deeply, cradling her against him. She remained taut; he felt the tip of her teeth against his shoulder, the ragged draw of her breath. He cradled her face, finding her lips, forcing himself to a slow pace, burrowing a little more deeply, embraced, engulfed, erotically seduced by the constriction that seized her so tightly. Then, at last, she gasped again; her body gave, and the tautness moved, arching against him, catching him deeper still. Her fragrance surrounded him, warmth set him afire, pulse of her heart and whisper of her breath seizing on every hunger within him. He felt her fingers on his shoulder, down his back. There was no hesitance. She clung to him as if she clung to life. And still, she moved. A natural rhythm. Erotic as the first taste of forbidden fruit. In the end, he found that his head was bowed, he clasped her to him, hands formed her buttocks, shaken by the force of the expulsion and climax that seized him.

He lay half at her side, half atop her, growing lax inside her. He realized his weight, and eased from her quickly. He was sated, stunned, and somewhat angry with himself, though he wasn't sure why. He leaned on an elbow, curious, wanting something from her, seeking something, and just as he didn't understand his anger, he didn't know exactly what he wanted from her.

She didn't open her eyes.

He was tempted to shake her, to demand to know just what had caused her to take this path.

Had he been taken in by her yet once again? Had she lied again, used her constant deception, eager to say that she had been seized upon by a savage? Perhaps she was desperate to feel that she had indeed been sacrificed to the enemy, that she had met the same violence done to so many of those the English had fought, beaten, and subjugated.

Again, he was tempted to rage against her, demand a deeper explanation.

He refrained, suddenly determined that he wasn't going to speak at all.

He told himself that her reasons didn't matter, and this was just a night. A night on a battlefield, when they had been triumphant, and they had known the just rewards of victory denied them so many times in the years gone by.

He closed his eyes, resting his head back. It had been almost two days since he'd had sleep at all. And yet he felt so strangely at war with himself, anger simmering his soul, entangled with a pain that had long lain dormant. The screams and cries of those assaulted, injured, and bested lay hard within his heart—along with the acrid smell of smoke on the wind. He could remember what it had been to ride back to his home, his house . . . and find nothing but ash, and learn from the survivors just what had occurred in his absence. Since then, there had been nothing but the fight to free Scotland from the brutal hands of his enemies.

Nothing but fighting . . .

And in that, learning that a like revenge could do nothing to still the agony of what had been done to him and his countrymen. He had mistrusted Robert Bruce when he gained his crown, but learned from him as well that to heal their country, and themselves, they had to learn temperance. It had been a practice to which he had adhered religiously.

And now . . .

He decried the very comfort he felt. He felt an urge to hold to the woman at his side more tightly, and at the same time, a fervent urge to push her from him. His exhaustion was so great that he didn't think he could do either. And yet, surely, he would find no rest.

To his amazement, he fell almost instantly into a deep sleep. But just before the last vestiges of consciousness slipped from his mind, he reached out, pulling her against him, offering her the warmth and comfort of his flesh and form for the hours of the night.

Christina woke up alone. She shivered for a moment, realized she was uncovered, and lay back down, eager to get beneath the quilt. The small house was not so cold; a new fire burned in the hearth.

She lay very still for a moment, aware of the night gone past. She groaned softly, turning into her pillow, wondering what had seized hold of her. She hadn't been drinking. She hadn't been forced. She had invited the enemy to stay. And though the thought of her own behavior now chilled her with embarrassment, she realized that in the recesses of her heart she wasn't sorry; she was glad. She had spoken the simple truth. She might never come across someone like him again.

A knock at the door startled her. She heard it open, and she grabbed the covers tightly around herself, inching back in fear. She was in the midst of an enemy encampment, even if she was coming to know the enemy far too well.

"Christina?"

She knew the voice. She breathed a sigh of relief as Lauren came walking in.

Lauren paused in the doorway, staring at her, mouth gaping with horror. "I don't believe it!" she whispered. "Oh, you poor dear, I just didn't believe that he was . . . that he would . . . oh, Christina, you have given too much!"

Lauren flew across the room, ready to take her into her arms, give her comfort. Indeed, Christina was tenderly pulled into Lauren's arms, and her friend rocked with her, holding her there. "Steven will be freed, and when he is, you'll see, you will be avenged. He'd fight his way into Scotland and cut this wretched man's heart out!"

Christina had to shake her head at that, drawing away. "Lauren . . . no."

Lauren moved back, a deep frown furrowing her brow. "He will fight for your honor! You know that."

"Lauren, there is nothing for him to fight for," Christina said softly, and Lauren's frown grew even deeper. "I had no honor."

"I thought Jamie was noble, above such violence!" Lauren said heatedly.

"It wasn't he," Christina said then realized that she confused Lauren even further.

"Not he! What wretch did burst in here?"

Christina shook her head again. "Lauren . . . that's not what I meant."

"What on earth are you saying?" Lauren demanded, distressed. "This is all my fault. I should never have let you do any of this, from the beginning. Steven would be furious with me, with us both. With me . . . I'm older. I should have been protecting you. Our plans were foolhardy. We shouldn't have thought we could trick the Scots from the very beginning. And then . . . God! He let someone . . . he let someone else hurt you!"

"No!" Christina said emphatically. "Lauren, I haven't been hurt."

"But you have been! Oh, Lord, how could he have set his men loose on you!"

"Lauren! No one was set loose on me. It was he . . . I just meant that he . . . that it was completely my own doing."

"Your own doing?" Lauren was shocked.

Christina sighed softly. "He was leaving. I asked him to stay."

To her surprise, this time Lauren didn't have anything to say. She stared at Christina in confusion, then fell silent. She folded her hands in her lap, looking down at them. "Ah."

"Ah? That's all you have to say? Aren't you entirely ashamed of me?" Christina murmured.

Lauren looked at her then, a rueful smile upon her lips. "No."

"You're not?"

"He is an admirable man. And certainly, very attractive."

"And the enemy."

"Sometimes, it's rather hard to identify the enemy, on a face-to-face level."

"He is the enemy. I'll still maintain that as a truth."

"But you said that it was your own doing."

"Yes."

"Christina, do you think you're the first woman to fall in love with such a man?"

"I'm not at all in love with him," Christina protested, horrified.

"Fine. Then you were . . . ?"

Christina thought desperately for a sane answer. "I just . . . I just . . . I don't know," she said. Then she added, "I do know. I've thought many times that Rowan DeClabert whispers words of poison to Edward because we so quickly evaded his suggestion that he would ask for my hand in marriage. And I've thought that, perhaps the only way to see Steven freed is to give in to that suit. In fact, I was so determined to put myself into this position, and when I've thought about it, and the fact that Robert Bruce is now aware that we've been taken, and ransoms will be demanded . . . well, it's likely that DeClabert will arrange my ransom, and that will come with certain demands, surely. He'll valiantly see that I'm returned, and perhaps even swear that he'll defend Steven before King Edward, see that he is forgiven. And then I'd really be trapped, with no choice. And if I were to spend my life with such a man . . . oh, God! I just wanted something better first."

"Yes, of course," Lauren murmured.

"Does it make sense?" Christina whispered.

"More sense than I think you really know as yet," Lauren murmured.

"Steven's life is really everything."

"You can't marry DeClabert," Lauren said.

"Brave words. But would you rather see Steven dead? I

wouldn't. DeClabert would be a horrible man, a miserable husband. But life is far dearer even when it is wretched than to give it up entirely!''

Lauren stood suddenly. ''There's no sense in discussing this. Right now, we are prisoners of the Scottish king. The future remains to be seen. But you need to get up, wash, and dress. I've been advised that there are many wounded. Many Englishmen. I'm waiting to tend to them. We might hear some word about your brother.''

She collected the towel Christina had so deftly stolen from Jamie the night before and tossed it to Christina, who wrapped herself in the linen and bounded out of bed. ''There's wash water on the table in the main room,'' Lauren advised.

Christina nodded, starting out. ''Christina!'' Lauren called. She stopped.

''Don't be so . . . disturbed by what you've done. I should tell you . . . your brother and I . . . Well, long ago . . . he's a very attractive man as well, you know.''

Christina paused in the doorway, staring at her. ''There is a difference. You've been betrothed forever. You would have been married already, if circumstances had been different.''

''None of that really matters. I just wanted to be with him.''

''The day will come when you do marry Steven.''

''Not soon enough, I'm afraid. I love him so very much!'' Lauren said in a whisper, and added, ''Come on, hurry! We must see if we can find anyone who has seen Steven, or knows the king's mind!''

Christina hurried to the main room, quickly washed, and more quickly dressed. When she was ready, she discovered that Liam was awaiting them just outside the door, and would escort them to the vast field where the injured, dead, and dying had been brought.

The sight was chilling. Christina had heard about the war, and the devastation—on both sides. She had never seen it before.

There were so many people there, desperately in need of help.

So very, very many. Men who had fallen so covered in blood it was impossible to discern their mode of dress, or what side they might have fought on. Those burned beyond recognition.

And more. As they walked into the field of bodies, they heard the cries of those simply caught up in the conflict, a child who'd been trampled, a woman who had dodged a sword, none too successfully.

A woman walked up to them with buckets of water and rags. She had but one tooth, and smelled horribly of onions, but she had kind eyes and kinder words. "Scots and English alike, my fine ladies. Bathe away their blood, and if they can be saved, the barber or physician will come, and sew up their wounds. If they be dyin', help 'em go in peace— ye can give a cry to Father Mulligan." She started to turn away, then looked back at them. "And bless ye, bless ye both for dirtyin' yer fine ladies' hands, for a dying man is eager for all the solace he may have."

She walked away. Christina and Lauren stared at one another, then parted, kneeling down to the injured.

They had come to find word about her brother.

Within minutes, however, they found out the importance of their task.

One of King Robert's physicians, a Frenchman named D'Avignon, was in charge of the stretch of injured; he spoke with them both, giving instructions, then pausing. "You've not come to dispatch those who may be dying, have you?

Because, should I get the first suspicion that you have come to kill my injured, I will cut your throats out myself, whether my own head should hit the block for such an act or not!''

''There are enough dead here,'' Lauren said simply, indignantly returning his stare. He indicated a direction she should take.

As the day wore on, she and Lauren were allowed to move among the injured, bathing blood from flesh, binding wounds, suturing, and giving what herbal comfort the local chemists had within their coffers. There was more help for the wounded than might have been expected. Many of the women from Perth came forward, returning from the forests, where they had run. There were barbers, and chemists, and a few more physicians. Still, there were many wounds. Sword wounds, axe wounds, pike wounds. By the afternoon, she had discovered that her tedious hours learning needlework as a child were at last paying off; she made excellent, tiny stitches that would serve the wounded well, so D'Avignon informed her.

When she could, Christina spoke worriedly to the men who were among the troops of the English sent to guard Perth. She was dismayed to find none among their number who had been to England recently, who knew anything of the policy, conditions, or the current plight of her brother. As the day went on, though, she became so engrossed in doing what she could for the men that she was able to swallow her disappointment. She was horrified by the number of injuries, but D'Avignon was quite practical. ''They could have all been dead. The Scots didn't take their fury near as far as some of the savagery that has been practiced—by both sides in the past. These men are injured—not dead. Most will live.''

By nightfall, she was exhausted. D'Avignon came to her,

took her needle and horsehair sutures from her hands, and bade her rise. "Your escort is here, my lady."

She nodded, thanking him.

"My lady!" D'Avignon said, calling her back.

She turned.

"If you wish, I will suggest to King Robert that you should be set free for the generous service you have rendered here, to friend and foe alike."

She shook her head. "No, no! But—thank you."

She fled quickly. Young Ioin was waiting to take her back to the small farmhouse. Lauren, she discovered, had already been escorted back to the tent where she was staying. It was one belonging to the king himself.

In the farmhouse, she fell upon the bed and closed her eyes. That morning, she had awakened with a tangle of emotions, shame . . . and elation. The day had stripped away the memories that had thrilled and plagued her. She could see only blood, the wounds, still hear the cries. She didn't want to see or hear them any more within her mind. She rose, hurried to the main room, found the skin of ale, and drank deeply.

It was late afternoon before Jamie was able to meet with his kin, his cousin Eric, and many of the good friends and longtime companions with whom he had fought for almost as long as he could remember.

He'd known that Eric had been camped not far from his own position in the woods, but he and his men had been assigned the task of guarding the battlements while Jamie's force had been commanded to scatter throughout the town. He'd known that his cousin had survived the battle, just as he was certain Eric had been informed of his own safety. They had both followed Wallace, and then Bruce, and were well known among the king's company. They were alike in height and form; Jamie had the darker, redder hair while Eric had more of the lighter, Norse appearance. Eric's eyes were a crystal blue, where Jamie's tended toward gray. Still, they might have been brothers, and it was easy for the close friends of one to assure the close friends of another that they were well, walking and uninjured, after a battle, if they hadn't fought in close ranks together.

They shared a skin of ale, taking time to sit at the fire burning in the midst of Eric's camp to talk briefly as they drank. Angus, older brother of Magnus, had long ridden at Eric's side, and indeed, had a wife and child back at Langley, a fortification on Scottish soil wrested from the English when a plague had struck, killing most within its walls. Eric had lost a wife and child to the disease, but had later married the lady of the castle, and now had an infant son. Langley still stood, for it had been taken before Robert Bruce began his policy of dismantling every English stronghold. In the time since Eric had claimed the place, it had been strengthened; its defenses were some of the strongest in the land. When the summons came from the king to join in the attack, it was to Eric's fortification at Langley that Jamie had sent the livestock and goods gathered at Hamstead Heath.

Jamie's first questions were about Eric's wife, a lady he had come to know well, and for whom he bore a great affection. She was well, as was his son, named Wulfgar in honor of the family of their mutual maternal grandfather, a Norseman. "And what of Langley?" Jamie asked Eric.

"Strong, I'm glad to say. Allen still remains behind whenever we set forth to do battle," he explained. "We have acquired more defensive mechanisms for war, small catapults that sit upon the battlements, and can easily be fired in different directions." He grinned. "I understand that I'm receiving an excellent herd of cattle and some magnificent horses in the near future.''

"Aye. Though the pick go to the king, of course.''

Eric laughed. "Naturally.'' Then he frowned slightly. "I've heard as well that you acquired three hostages in your quest for the king's tribute as well. That's not like you, cousin. You prefer to ride unencumbered.''

"Aye, that I do. But there were strange circumstances. I'm not sure I completely understand them myself. The hostages insisted on joining us.''

"Hostages—who insisted on joining the enemy?''

Jamie grinned wryly and nodded. Then he sobered suddenly. "Their fates, of course, rest with the king. But if he's in agreement, when we ride now again, I'd like to have them sent to Langley.''

Eric raised a brow. "Hostages are dangerous, lest they're confined tightly to dungeons. They can betray you when you least expect it.''

Jamie hesitated, about to inform Eric that he'd be holding willing hostages. But then again, given an opportunity to prove some fierce loyalty to Edward, Christina might turn. He wouldn't bring his cousin's great fortress falling upon them all.

"They can be dangerous,'' he agreed.

Eric shrugged, watching him curiously. "If they go to Langley, they'll be confined, guarded, watched.''

"I'd expect no less.''

"Angus!'' he said, calling to their friend. "I imagine you'd enjoy a ride home.'' He looked at Jamie. "We'll let Magnus act as escort as well. There are three in your keeping, I've heard. Two stalwart Scots should be sufficient to guard them for the ride, don't you think?''

Jamie hesitated. "I believe we'll send Liam along as well.

Sir Alfred is old and frail, but proud. Lady Lauren is mild mannered and quite charming.''

"And the third?" Eric inquired.

Jamie hesitated. "Dangerous," he said flatly. "Lady Christina, of Hamstead Heath. She fears for her brother's life, and is reckless in the extreme. She is the one who must not be trusted.''

"I'll write to Igrainia and Allen. They'll see that she is kept from harm's way, and from causing harm.''

"Thank you." He rose suddenly. "Would you care to accompany me, cousin? We've a prisoner here, taken in the battle, who might shed more light on the situation.''

"Aye, then, I'll be most curious to come along with you.''

Jamie bid goodbye to the many men in his cousin's service, and explained something of the situation he had come upon at Hamstead Heath as they walked.

Ragnor had been with Robert the Bruce when they went through the roster of English noblemen and knights who had survived the fighting, and he had suggested to Jamie that he might be interested in talking to the man, Sir Ralph Miller.

A number of the prisoners had been herded into a section of the forest where natural boundaries, including a sheer rock wall and a fast running stream, would help their guards be assured that they remained in the copse.

The Englishman stood against a tree, a look of weary resignation in his eyes, and yet, not one of defeat. He had fought. He had lost, and he would accept the consequences. Having done everything that he could, he waited.

"You're Sir Ralph Miller, of Yorkshire?" Jamie asked him.

The man surveyed him long and hard, then gave the same scrutiny to Eric. "I am," he said quietly. If he feared he was about to pay for his transgressions with his life, he

showed no sign of fear. "Have I been selected for a noose?"
he inquired.

Jamie shook his head. "No one is being selected for a
noose. Many men will be taken for ransom, or exchange."

"To whom am I speaking?"

"I am Sir James Graham, and this is my cousin, Sir Eric."

"Ah."

"You sound as if you know us," Eric said.

"Of you and your clan—many who are under a death
warrant, according to the English crown." He gazed at Eric
again. "You—you escaped a death sentence once, I
believe." His gaze touched Jamie's once again. "And you
have ridden together, and with others of your kin. Though
Edward the son has ignored most of the requests of Edward
the father, still, when they come to the shedding of blood,
he doesn't hesitate so much. When it comes to the clever
pursuit of war and troop movements . . . well, the one is not
the other."

The man didn't speak with disloyalty; his words were
merely a worn statement of fact. Jamie liked the fellow, and
he felt a moment's sorrow. Often, the men he killed in battle
were those he might most admire. They didn't run from the
field, they fought to the end. And often, those with steadfast
loyalty to their country, no matter what the Crown, were
honest, ethical, and worthy of the greatest respect.

"I am honestly to live, and be held for ransom, then?"
he queried.

"Yes," Jamie told him.

"Robert Bruce does not murder knights indiscriminately,
Sir Ralph," Eric informed him.

The man's eyes assured them that his king was not so
careful. "I'm grateful for my life. I'm afraid I'm not worth
very much. My value has always been in my sword arm."

"No harm will come to you," Jamie said again. "Robert

Bruce sees enough bloodshed as he battles for our country. Many responsible for the deaths of his own kin have been spared.''

''I will rot in prison a very long time.''

''Not so cruel a prison, I imagine.''

''Having been so recently and directly beneath the glory of the king of England, I admit, I have been seeing a noose before my eyes. So, you've come to ask me what I know about the movements of the king's troops?''

Eric laughed softly. ''Nay, sir! We've not come to demand disloyalty. We usually know, far before they arrive, about the movements of the king's army.''

''My query is more personal,'' Jamie said. ''I want to know anything you could tell me about a man named Steven, lord of the manor at Hamstead Heath.''

Sir Ralph's eyes grew suddenly wary. ''You ask me about a friend, Sir James, and one in a precarious position, at best.''

''Explain that to me.''

''Sir, I don't feel at liberty to discuss such a matter with you. We are enemies, you're aware?''

''I have an interest.''

''I believe my cousin would help the situation, were he able,'' Eric advised.

Ralph thought about their words for long seconds, studied Jamie's eyes, and then shrugged. ''I suppose there is no harm in me telling you what I know. None of it is secret. Steven dared to speak honestly. He begged for troops to be dispersed so that properties such as his own could hold against invasion. He said that if he could not be helped by his own country, he had but little choice to pay Robert Bruce for the safety of his people. He told King Edward that he would gladly take part in laying down plans to defend the borders, now that Robert Bruce's men have turned the tide.

King Edward, in turn, invited him to speak about the matter. At that point he went into a fury. Steven was declared a traitor. At the king's 'invitation,' Steven would remain a prisoner at a castle not far from the great fortress at Yorkshire. In the meantime, the king would test the loyalty of Hamstead Heath.'' Ralph paused and shook his head. ''I'm telling you more than I need to, and wonder why I do. The good king of England may get his hands on me yet.''

''If he gets his hands on us, as you've said, we're already dead men, so you needn't worry what words you say to us,'' Eric told him quietly.

''As Eric has told you, if there is a way, I would help,'' Jamie said.

Sir Ralph hesitated again, his hands wound into fists at his sides. ''All right. As to Steven, a classic tale, I'm afraid. Edward the Second is known for his tantrums; indeed, he is known for many things, and few of them virtues. When he is angry, men shake, not so much in fear, but because he is king, and has the power to order idiocy. He does have great thunderous bursts of fury like those his father had . . . but screams and shrieks, more like a child, when his toy has been taken. He plays with lives, and gives in to his favorites. That is another matter altogether, of course. The world has heard of our king's exploits when it comes to power and his 'favorites.' God knows, England herself has been split and torn over his behavior—we've killed one another while battling the Scots. Oddly, though, the man who whispers into his ear regarding Steven of Hamstead Heath is not among that strange number of favorites. He is a northern baron, who pretends the greatest friendship and understanding with Steven. Rowan. He acts as Steven's friend, but is careful to allow no chance of escape at all. Rowan likes having Steven as his prisoner. Likes acting the farce that he is Steven's friend, and fights for his life.

Meanwhile, he encourages the king in his beliefs that Steven was an instigator in the murder of Piers Gaveston. Now there, King Edward can really have his tantrums. So Steven remains at Rowan's fortress, Thistle-on-Downs, near death at any minute. Which is a ridiculous pity, due only to the greed and avarice of men. For you see, what Rowan DeClabert really wants is an interest in Steven's land, the fine horses that are bred at Hamstead Heath—and mostly, Steven's sister, of course.''

Jamie arched a brow. ''If this Rowan DeClabert is a great northern baron, and might be enticed to free Steven, why hasn't he been promised Steven's sister?''

Ralph smiled with a curious twist of wistful affection. ''The Lady Christina? Steven would never be so cruel. She, of course, would have done anything to free her brother, but he had thus far convinced her that seducing Rowan into releasing him would not solve the problem of the king, who would remain, in his misguided fury, after Steven's blood.''

''You know them all?'' Eric inquired curiously.

''Indeed, I know the household well. I've told you, Steven is a good friend, and a good man.''

''I see. Hamstead Heath is a treasure valued by many, so the Lady Christina does have a tremendous import. And what about Lauren?'' Jamie asked.

''Steven's fiancée. Yes, of course. Her father is a man of great wealth and power. I speculate that the king, even in all his fury, hesitates to do any more harm to Steven, lest he bring on the wrath of the father. However, Edward is king, and will keep a captive as long as he desires. Especially when he is so encouraged by DeClabert, who is able to raise, train, and equip many, many men for war.'' He suddenly spat on the ground. ''DeClabert should have been here. He'd been ordered north by King Edward.''

"Perhaps he has gone on to one of the other strongholds still held by the English," Eric suggested.

"Perhaps. I rather imagine that he has sent men in his place."

"He is not a man talented at warfare?" Jamie asked.

"Oh, he knows his weapons well enough. But he prefers tournaments, and gambling. He considers this a barbaric country, that the Scots are savages, and know nothing of the true art of battle." Sir Ralph stopped speaking again, looking at him suspiciously, then at Eric. "What is your interest is all of this?"

"Let me just set one point, Sir Ralph," Jamie said. "Both Christina and Lauren would prove to be captives of rich consequence to the king of England?"

"Certainly." Sir Ralph suddenly appeared worried. "But Hamstead Heath is east of our position, and the ladies would not have been found at Perth."

"The ladies were found before we reached Perth," Jamie said.

He saw the tension that constricted Sir Ralph's throat. The man wanted to jump at him. Only a sense of his position and a yearning for survival kept him still. "Lauren has caused no evil to any Scotsman, that I can assure you. Nor has the Lady Christina. If they are in your keeping . . ." He looked ill, assuming the worst.

"Both women are in my custody, and are alive, and well," Jamie informed him. He could say no more. "I assure you again, I've asked for none of this information to use against them, Lord Steven, or you."

"Indeed, no harm is intended," Eric said, glancing at Jamie. "In fact, it would please us both if no one else knew we had this conversation."

Sir Ralph looked relieved. He had spoken too freely.

"It pleases me as well."

Eric shrugged, looking at Jamie. Jamie gave his cousin a nod, then thanked Sir Ralph. As they turned away, Jamie paused, looking back to assure the man. "You will not be a prisoner kept in poor conditions, Sir Ralph. And I can also promise you that you will not be held forever."

Sir Ralph nodded, and held silent. Jamie started to turn away.

"Wait!" Sir Ralph said.

Jamie turned back. Ralph was drawing something from his finger, and he handed it to Jamie. It was a ring. The crest of the family Steel.

He looked at Ralph. "I saw Steven, before I rode north. He was safe and well, and told me that if I were to make it by Hamstead Heath and saw Christina, I must give her this, and assure her of his health and welfare. Since she is with you . . . perhaps you will let her know that he is well, and spends his days thinking of his family. He isn't afraid, but determined."

Jamie curled his fingers around the ring. "Aye, Sir Ralph, I'll see that Christina receives her brother's ring."

With that, they left Sir Ralph. As they walked away, Eric eyed Jamie cautiously.

"There is much more to this than you're telling me, Jamie," Eric said.

"No, you have just heard what I know about the situation. Steven was not there to pay the tribute, because he's a prisoner himself. One described as a guest, I imagine, but a prisoner, nonetheless, and apparently, his life rests on the whim of a volatile king, and the cruelty of a man who commands Edward's attention." He hesitated. "Christina of Hamstead Heath is interested in saving her brother above all else. After we spoke, I didn't want you to be under obligation to hold my hostages unless you were aware of the situation."

Eric gave him a small shrug. "I've had some experience with reckless prisoners," he told him dryly, and Jamie knew that, of course, he had—his wife had once been his hostage, and a very unwilling one at that.

"Still, this is my responsibility."

"I believe you held the fortress for me time and time again, when your help was needed."

"Aye, well then," Jamie murmured softly.

"You've something else in mind."

"A growing plan, and maybe a foolhardy one."

"Think of the years we've gone through. The whole of them might be described as foolhardy," Eric reminded him. "When you need me, I'll be there."

"When the king gives leave, then, I will call upon you," he said, then grinned suddenly. "Your wife will not be pleased."

"My wife understands that I ride when I must."

"For Scotland," Jamie said softly. "I have a wish to cross the border."

Eric raised a brow.

"Cousin, I am deeply intrigued. You're planning a raid?"

Jamie nodded.

Eric grinned. "Igrainia has learned to live with the fact that I'll fight until Scotland has gained her independence from those who try to oppress her. And though my wife may be English, she is well aware of the fact that men come in good and evil, English, Scottish, or any other. Lay your case before the king. It may be some time before he gives you leave for such an undertaking. For the moment, don't fear for your hostages. Langley is a fine fortress. There are massive bolts on many doors."

"I'm not sure if I fear for my hostages, or your household."

"My household has grown strong; even the king, in his

determination to leave no fortresses for the English to attack and hold, agrees that Langley is firmly in our hands. It will withstand your hostages. And as to a raid into England . . . I do find the idea very intriguing.'' Eric grinned, shrugging. ''I remember you telling me once that should you go down, you would surely want to do so in a blaze of glory.''

''Yes, and you reminded me that we should *live* in a blaze of glory.''

''So—we shall go on intending to live.'' He clapped his hand on Jamie's back, bidding him farewell. Glad of his kin's assistance, Jamie suddenly decided that he would see the king then and there, while determination lay so passionately in his mind.

Why? He asked himself.

The English had damned themselves.

Why not?

To decimate a fortress such as Thistle-on-Downs would indeed make them all rise in a blaze of glory. And that, he assured himself, was his only intent.

CHAPTER 9

Jamie strode across the field. The acrid smell of smoke remained in the air. Among the tents, he sought the banners that signified Robert Bruce's chosen position on the field. They flew grandly. His tent was fine, as were the appointments, and the portable furniture and finery that now followed after him during his campaigns. Jamie could remember when Robert Bruce slept on the ground with the rest of them, sometimes with only a few supporters around him as guards.

Those days had passed. With each success, he proved himself a strategist, capable of military genius. And with each success, his people gathered around more closely, forgiving the past, looking to the future.

Some of the king's retainers stood outside the tent. They bowed to Jamie, acknowledging the long service he had given to the king, and went in to announce him. Jamie went in. Robert Bruce was at his field desk, Douglas at his side as they surveyed the terrain, deciding their next movements.

The Black Douglas greeted him with a grim nod. He was a tall, lean, dark-haired man given quickly to anger, and just as quickly given to remorse if he had wronged a friend. His daring exploits were the stuff of legend; casting his fate with Bruce had decidedly been a strong factor in the king gaining the power he presently held.

Jamie was glad that Douglas was there. He was a man to whom the idea of a stealthy attack was always appealing.

"Ah, Jamie! We'll move on from here, striking while we've the power. Here, here, and here . . . we've still got the English holding fortifications. My brother is here, in the southwest, doing his best to prevent supplies from reaching those fortifications, Dumfries, Buittle, Dalswinton, and Caerlaverock."

Jamie leaned on the desk. "I have an urge to attack an English castle."

Robert Bruce sat back. They had ranged into England, many times, bringing devastation to English soil, and resupplying themselves with the abundance to be found in a land not destroyed by so many years of warfare. In his day, William Wallace had taken revenge deep into the very heart of York.

Robert Bruce had demanded tributes from many English villages right on the border. But it had been some time since they had ventured farther south, bringing an actual assault against an English bastion.

Now, he carefully weighed the words put before him.

"I've nothing against you bringing warfare to the English, not if you've a sound plan and good reason, such as a rich bounty to be found in such a castle."

"There's a very rich bounty to be had, from what I understand. And more. It's come to my attention that an English lord is being held unfairly—at risk of death because of his determination to pay tribute to you.''

Douglas let out a derisive snort. ''Leave it to Edward to offer no support to his barons, and punish them when they have no chance.''

Robert Bruce was staring at him contemplatively. ''We all know that the war has been unfair. The lowlands of Scotland will not recover for years to come, and it's true of the borders in England as well. Many men have suffered. We've grave business in Scotland, before turning to concern for an English lord.''

''I believe that the castle is a rich one, and that the holder, Rowan DeClabert, is an adviser to Edward, a powerful man, glad of the breach between the king and many of his earls over the Piers Gaveston affair.''

''Then he is of help to us. While the English still squabble among themselves, they are less dangerous to us,'' Robert Bruce said.

''I know of this DeClabert,'' Douglas said, stroking his chin thoughtfully. ''He rides to war himself, but not if other interests hold his attention. He is a man more fond of the tournament than of battle itself—he has increased his fortune vastly through the years by his participation in such events. He has wealth and power, and is a vindictive man. It's said that many a minor man captured by the English paid with his life at DeClabert's suggestion.''

Robert Bruce was silent for a moment. ''I know DeClabert as well,'' he said. ''I have ridden with him. It's true that he is a man continually seeking power—and glory. He is no coward, and I can assure you, he is adept at arms. I know of his holding as well, Thistle-on-Downs. It is north of the great castle at York, close enough to the lowlands. It's possible that he may be in Scotland now. The English may be squabbling now, but if the king is able to raise English indignation against us and create a rallying cry of onward to Scotland to finish it all one way or the other, he will definitely ride north at Edward's side. An interesting man. Even when men are on the move, he enjoys a challenge among his own troops. He takes on eager young knights, betting against their lords that he can take them in any game of battle. He enriches himself further with his earnings.'' He studied Jamie for a moment. ''The man he holds is Steven of Hamstead Heath, as we both know.''

''Aye.''

''Whose sister is now our hostage.''

''Aye.''

''I therefore assume that all this is related,'' the king said.

''Related in that I believe an opportunity presents itself,'' Jamie said.

''Aye, and because he has in his keeping Count Steven Steel of Hamstead Heath.'' He held silent for a moment, then a rare glimpse of his bitterness and the rage with which he was forced to live day after day escaped him as he slammed a fist furiously on the camp desk and surveyed Jamie with brooding eyes. ''Do you know how many members of my own family are held still by the English?'' he demanded.

''Indeed, I do.''

''Including my wife. '

''Aye,'' Jamie said.

Bruce looked down, and Jamie knew that he was filled with impotent fury. The king's wife, his daughter Marjory, many more of his family and friends, were still held in various states of imprisonment by the English.

They were nowhere near the border.

And still, Robert Bruce held tightly to the reason that had stood him well since he had taken the crown, and learned that his country was divided, and that the only way to truly become the king was to act rationally and wisely in matters of politics, while attempting the most carefully thought-out daring in any military campaign.

"The father was a vicious man, who believed that the Scots were a breed of lesser human beings, and therefore might be slaughtered with little more thought than a farmer taking a knife to his swine." He exhaled on a long breath. "Steven, however, tended to be sympathetic to the cause of Scotland from the beginning. Even in the days when I rode with Edward the First and had not learned the true sense of nationalism, Steven was greatly disturbed by many of the methods used by the English here. A loyal Englishman to the core, but disturbed by his country's politics. And when we began to raid, he said that it was hard to begrudge a payment to a land so long decimated by others. Still . . . we cannot afford chivalry over good sense."

"I am well aware that the fight for our country takes precedence," Jamie said.

"There is more about which you must be well aware, Jamie. King Edward the Second carries with him the legacy of many of his father's hatreds. If you're taken in England, it's likely you'll face a death preceded by agonizing torture."

"And you know that I risk that death every time I ride against the English. You know as well that I'm not a fool, and that I'd not risk my life, or the lives of my men, without sound judgment."

"We'll look into the matter," the king said. "But first, we finish what we've begun here. Then you will have my blessing, and perhaps my arms and support as well. Tomorrow, we leave. Dumfries is about to be set upon, a siege laid. If my brother has been at all successful, the garrison there will be suffering already. They will be forced to surrender."

Jamie knew Robert Bruce well, and knew his logic. "As I have since you took the crown, I will stand at your side."

"And as you have done so, Jamie, I will support your actions—once I'm convinced that they're sound. Are we agreed?"

Jamie nodded. He wasn't sure himself that his sudden determination was sound at all. He did have the argument that Lord Steven of Hamstead Heath suffered for his opinions regarding the English conquests in Scotland, an argument with which Robert Bruce agreed. But the king was right, many men had suffered. Far too many had died.

And it might be natural as well that he would agree to an undertaking that might set an Englishman free while so many members of his own family were still firmly in the hands of his enemies.

But it was true as well that Robert Bruce enjoyed the idea of at least refilling the coffers of Scotland, so brutalized by the English raids, with the riches of his enemy. He was certain, though, that Rowan DeClabert's holdings were worthy of being taken. Both the king and Douglas were intrigued by the idea, and it was apparent now that Thistle-on-Downs was not too far from the Scottish border—and places of retreat where the inhabitants were loyal to the Scottish Crown. There was much more that he needed to learn.

There was the matter of time, as well. How long before DeClabert managed to make a real case against his guest, Steven of Hamstead Heath?

The king was watching him still. "Word will go out regarding our hostages, Jamie. The Lady Lauren's father will indeed pay whatever price is necessary. As to Christina ... DeClabert will offer, and force the family to become beholden, perhaps even force Edward's hand and the English king will care little."

"Aye," Jamie said stiffly.

"However, negotiations can take forever," Robert Bruce said. "The hostage remains yours, Jamie. No decisions will be made without you."

Jamie lowered his head and smiled slowly. "Thank you. If it meets with your approval, I'd intended for the three to be taken to Eric's holding at Langley."

"Aye, Jamie, that will do well. And as to the other—we fight first where I choose. Then we will consider a raiding party into enemy territory. It will be an assault designed and pursued by my angry men, of course—not ordered by the Crown. For the moment, I don't wish to push King Edward into a rage. His mass attack will come soon enough."

"Aye," Jamie agreed.

"It's a ride that I would relish myself," Douglas told him. Jamie nodded, looking at Douglas, grateful for the support.

Robert Bruce drummed his fingers on the map for a moment. "I ride at first light. See to the safety of your hostages then, Jamie, and meet with the main party by midnight, tomorrow."

"Aye," Jamie said. Bowing, he started to depart. Looking up, he saw that Douglas was still grinning. He remained intrigued. He nodded at Jamie, and Jamie nodded in turn, glad that the Black Douglas had been there. He was a man known for both his reckless maneuvers—and for his successes.

Leaving the king, Jamie started back across the field of tents, hailing those he knew, pausing to talk to those who had been friends for years. He neared the farmhouse, specifically granted to him for his use by Robert Bruce. As he walked, darkness was falling. When he heard footsteps behind him, he turned quickly, drawing his sword.

He was surprised to see the young woman whose aging father had attempted to slay him when they had taken the fortifications. She was, he noted, quite a beauty, well endowed, and eager to see that such a pair of virtues was not missed. Her hair was dark, long, rich, and thick. Her father, he thought wryly, had been defending an honor long since gone.

"Sir James," she said softly.

"Yes?"

"My name is Isolde. We met briefly, if one can call it a meeting in the midst of such a melee. I've come to thank you."

"You owe me no personal thanks. Robert Bruce is eager to mend his country. It is difficult to mend a country with dead men. I'm curious, however, that you are let to run free, and that you're not with the other prisoners."

She smiled. "We are Scots ourselves, Sir James. My father is truly aging, and afraid now of every man. So you see, your mercy was most kindly taken. And as to Robert Bruce's orders regarding the value of human life, I can assure you, all the men who serve him have not behaved with such decency."

"Many of the men here have seen their daughters seized, their sons slain, their parents butchered."

She nodded. "But that is why I'm so eager to . . . thank you."

He shook his head. "I appreciate the . . . offer. But I'm occupied, I'm afraid."

"Perhaps another time," she said softly.

"Goodnight."

He turned from her, thinking that at any other time, he would have found her entertaining and amusing. If he had not insisted on bringing his own prisoner here . . .

But he had.

He had no obligation to return to the house, he told himself. None. If he so chose, he could follow the ebony-haired, buxom beauty. He should.

He even turned, angry with himself, suddenly wondering at his own sanity, thinking that a forced-upon-him hostage was not going to determine his actions or his life. He shook his head, amazed that he had begun thinking of a way to free an Englishman.

An enemy.

Not an act of nobility—or kindness for his hostage. Attacking DeClabert's holding would be for the riches that could be obtained. If, in the process, they were able to free a man considered by all accounts to be decent and intelligent—and a supporter of Scottish nationalism—all the better.

Christina meant nothing to him. She had been a dangerous burden from the beginning. And yet . . .

He was not in the least interested in following Isolde. He was anxious to return to the farmhouse. Not because of any obligation—or affection. The days ahead would be long. And after her every attempt to weaken him and his men, their battles had at last become far more *intriguing* than he had ever imagined. She was stubborn, reckless, irritating, and a totally fascinating woman. He'd be a fool not to take advantage of the night.

Tomorrow, they would ride in different directions.

She had caused enough torment, so perhaps it was fair that he longed to be somewhat of a contention in return. Admittedly, he was curious as to how he would find her that evening. Anxious to pretend that nothing had happened? Embarrassed, now that the moment was past? Razor-tongued and ready to give fight? Quiet, remote, wary, food cooking at the hearth, her manner that of the humble captive, ready to sacrifice all for others?

Ioin sat guard outside the house. Jamie greeted him and

entered. The fire in the hearth burned, but nothing cooked in the kettle. She was not in the main room.

He strode to the bedroom. She was there, lying at the foot of the bed, inert. For a moment, his heart stopped.

She lay dead still.

He rushed to her side. She was warm, her pulse beat steadily. Her golden tresses were fanned beneath her. They covered something. He reached for it, and realized that she wasn't dead, she wasn't even ill. She had consumed nearly the whole of the skin of ale.

He stood above her, not certain if he was just relieved, or irritated.

She stirred. Just barely. He moved her hair, then sat, drawing her head and shoulders onto his lap. Her eyes opened, and she looked up at him, groaned, and closed her eyes again.

"My lady," he said with a sigh, "humble, obedient, all-giving hostages do not drink themselves into stupors. They see to it that their captors return to a hot meal, warmth, and comfort."

Her eyes opened again. She wasn't really looking at him. Her features were pale and tense. "Some men . . . no longer had arms," she murmured.

"Ah," he said. "So you did tend to the wounded?"

Her eyes still didn't meet his. He wasn't even sure that she knew he was there, or even who he was. "There were so many . . . with gaping wounds. Broken bones . . . and the blood. My God, there was so much blood."

"Aye, the results of steel against flesh are indeed sad."

"There were bodies . . . many of them. The injured with the dead, and even among the injured . . . so many will still die!" she whispered.

"Yes," he said. "I'm afraid they will."

She rolled slightly, her eyes meeting his at last. "And you do this . . . fight . . . and fight . . . and fight."

"Aye."

"You could die as well, you know."

"Yes, I'm aware of that."

"You go on . . ."

"I fight a war that must be won."

"If only I were able to fight a war that could be won," she murmured, and the sound of her whisper was miserable. He wished that he could assure her he could do something, and then he was newly irritated with himself. She was an Englishwoman of standing, and she would be returned. He'd be a fool to risk his life in any manner for problems among the English. He assured himself again that if he went after Thistle-on-Downs, it would be for the riches that might be obtained, and for the audacity of such an attack.

He rose carefully, laying her back on the bed. She stirred, frowning, trying to regain her senses, and caught his arm suddenly.

"Wait."

"For what?"

"I didn't mean . . . to drink so much."

"But you did."

"My head . . . spinning."

"So I see."

"I'm sorry. I can get up. I can actually even tend to your weapons, and your armor. I'm very . . . good with weapons. Food. A meal . . . I didn't start any kind of a meal . . . I can, I must . . . I . . . I can rise!"

"There's food at many fires, and I have a groom who sees to my armor. The lads about this place are proving to be quite talented as well."

She shook her head, fighting waves of misery—and ale.

"Where are you going?" she whispered, and the sound was desperate.

He longed to be angry. Dismissive. But she had never been more vulnerable.

"Now? To take off your shoes and hose . . . and this outer gown. And then, Lady Christina, I intend to let you sleep this off."

She shook her head, appearing ever more desperate, a betraying sheen of tears in her eyes, even as she struggled to form her words. "No, please. Don't leave."

He struggled with the ties of her outer gown. She was certainly no help. He managed at last to draw it over her head. Hair tumbled around her in every direction. He found her face, smoothing the hair back. "Under the covers. There is a true winter chill tonight."

"Don't leave!" she said again.

He pulled back the quilt and linen sheeting, finding it difficult once again to maneuver her. When she was at last in the bed, she caught his wrist. He thought that he'd never seen a green quite like her eyes as she stared up at him.

"Please . . . I can do better."

"I m aware of that."

"But you mustn't—you mustn't go after Lauren."

"Christina, I've told you. There is no chance of that."

She almost smiled. "You see, what they have is finer than . . . life itself. She and Steven . . . she and Steven . . . well, they love one another. I know that . . . you find her . . . and that you find me . . . less . . ."

"Christina, in one aspect, I've lied to you. You are not unappealing, not at all. In fact, I can say that the first time I saw you, you were incredibly regal, quite glorious with your head held so high, and your hair falling down your back in a golden blaze. I don't think that this will penetrate your mind at all at the moment, but though Lauren may be very lovely, genial, and offer many fine qualities, she hasn't the lure of your . . . fire. Nor have I ever had the urge to use force against a hostage, or any woman for that matter. You won't remember a word of this, will you? Christina, I'm not leaving you. Try to understand. You're simply far gone in ale, and I'd just as soon you not wind up throwing up on me. I'm going out to the main room. I'm going to send a lad for something to eat, because I am hungry. Then I'm coming back to bed, to sleep, because the days have been long, and I'm also weary.''

She wasn't really listening, or comprehending. She had tried to drown away the agony of really seeing the results of war. And now she was afraid that she was losing her own battle.

"I'm so sorry. Please . . . I can do better," she said again.

"Yes, and you will."

"I mean . . . I mean . . . I just don't really know what I'm doing. But it seems one can learn. You don't . . . have to leave."

He smiled slowly, realizing how serious she was, and just what she meant. He leaned close to her, whispering in her ear. "It's a miracle," he murmured, "but you do very, very well," he said.

Her eyes had closed again. At last, she seemed to have given in to sleep. He touched the sunlight of her hair, turned, and left her to rest.

He could well understand her desire to escape the horrors of war. There had been many times when he had tried to drink himself into oblivion.

The only fault with it was learning that no amount of ale could wash away the blood that he had witnessed.

CHAPTER 10

Christina woke to the light of day and wondered which was worse, her behavior on the first night in the little farmhouse, or that of the previous night. She was afraid to move, fearing that her head would spin.

She eased herself up slowly, grateful that she seemed to feel stable. There was no fierce pounding in her head. And, thankfully, there would be another day of destruction before she had to face Jamie again at nightfall.

She rolled, ready to plump the pillow and rest her head again for just a few minutes. But she didn't lay her head down. He was there, still in bed, watching her. She returned his stare warily.

"You're here," she murmured.

"Indeed."

She shook her head, moistening her lips slightly. "Aren't you called upon to serve the king by day, pillage more houses, tear down more stones?"

"Men will come to see that the castle is totally dismantled," he assured her. "And I've pillaged quite a good sum
already, so I'll leave the rest to my countrymen."

A noise from the main room caused her to jump and look
to the doorway. The door was closed. She stared back at
Jamie.

"Someone is out there."

"Yes, there is."

"Shouldn't you . . . do something?"

"When they're gone."

He seemed completely at ease, just watching her, so curiously. She lowered her lashes uneasily. His chest was bare.
She was in her shift only. She had lost her clothing somehow.
Apparently, he had helped her into bed. And done nothing
more. She had a dim memory of his return, and telling him
about the wounded. She was suddenly angry with herself.
Seeing so many injured was painful, but she'd done the
worst thing possible. She's probably made him think she
was too fragile—too well bred—to be of service.

"I . . . I admit, I've not seen such grievous injuries
before," she said. "But I'm quite capable of returning to
the wounded, and being of service."

"I'm sure you are."

"Then, I should rise—"

He caught her arm. "You're not needed."

"I must be needed."

"Some good sisters have arrived from a nearby convent.
They are quite adept at tending to wounds." He paused for
a moment, listening. "I believe they're gone," he said.

He rose, and she saw that he had slept naked. He padded
to the door, opened it, and looked out. "Ah, breakfast." He
moved out to the main room. She froze, wondering whether
to follow him or not. He reappeared in the doorway. "Surely,
you're hungry by now, having gone the night with nothing."

She nodded, slipping from the bed, following him. A platter of fish, fresh bread, and cheese were on the table. There were a number of skins there as well.

"Ale, wine, milk, water," he advised. She turned. The hip tub was back, filled with steaming water, and he was within it again.

She sank into one of the chairs after helping herself to a mouthful of food. She chose to wash her food down with water, then looked back at Jamie. He seemed very comfortable indeed, head eased back against the tub, steam rising around him. "It's . . . day," she said.

"So observant," he murmured.

"Really, there's no need to mock me."

His head rose. "Mock you my lady? A woman with such a gentle mode of speech herself? It's just that, yes, most certainly, it's day. We've established that fact."

She shook her head. "I don't understand. I've never seen you with nothing to do once the dawn has so much as appeared."

"It's a different day," he murmured softly, his eyes on her. The humor was gone. There was something more brooding in his gaze. "A very different day. Come over here. What? Are you suddenly so shy? Promises are easy to make in darkness, are they not? And yet, not so easy to keep by the light of day."

She was so surprised by his words that she stood, walking warily toward the tub. "I made a promise last night?"

He lowered his head slightly. She saw the new smile that slipped onto his lips. Then he looked up at her. " 'I can do better,' " he said.

She was puzzled for a moment, then realized that he was quoting her words. She felt as if the whole of her body turned the color of a beet. "I said such words?"

"Vehemently!" he assured her.

"I must have meant that I could . . . make a far better meal."

"No, that's not what you meant at all."

Her knees buckled. She found herself easing down by the tub. "And you . . . intend to take the day to let me make good on such words?" she said, not sure if she was awed or dismayed.

"Exactly."

"Isn't your king a very busy man, waiting to ride?"

"He has done so."

"And you aren't riding with him?"

"I'll catch up."

She couldn't quite raise her eyes to his. The water rippled and splattered as he lifted his hand, bringing a finger to her chin.

"Well?" The word was so soft, it was almost a caress.

She hesitated. "You have to realize that I . . . I am deeply embarrassed by many of my words . . . my actions," she murmured.

"Why?"

"They're not . . . right," she said. "Especially for a woman in my position."

"They're human," he said.

"I'm not sure that a father confessor would agree with you."

He shook his head, blue-gray eyes hard upon her. "I've come to realize that it's very hard to judge what is and isn't right in this world," he murmured. "And it's God himself that we'll all face in the end." He was amused again suddenly. "What, would you close the gate with the horse flown from the field?"

She flushed. He shook his head. "The decision is yours, you know. Lauren has never been in any danger of injury or rape. And neither have you."

"I know that now," she murmured.

"You do recall that you asked me to stay the other night?"
She nodded.

"Well, do I stay now?"

She realized suddenly that yes, she very much wanted
him to stay. She simply loathed having to admit it.

"Christina?"

"Yes."

"I'm sorry. Was that an answer to your name, or a reply
to my question?"

"Yes, I want you to stay," she managed.

He rose suddenly, the water sluicing from his body. "Your
turn," he murmured. "I ordered the tub specifically for you,
and half the men out there think I'm entirely crazy, that
we'll both die within a year for so much bathing. As for
myself, I've grown terribly fond of a chance for a hot bath;
we've spent years washing the blood from our clothing in
very cold streams. Pity it's not larger, but . . . it's not."

He stepped out. Reaching for the hem of her shift, he
pulled it over her head in a fluid motion. She was shaking,
despite the time gone by, despite her words, sincerely meant.
She ducked quickly into the tub herself, sinking into the
water. It was delicious. Hot. And smelling so slightly of that
subtle French soap, which she found beneath her buttocks.
She luxuriated in lathering with it, then closed her eyes,
letting the heat sink into her flesh, bones, muscles. When
she opened her eyes, he was by her side. He stood suddenly,
and reached for her. She rose, lifted cleanly from the tub.
He swept a towel around her, drawing her close. And he
kissed her.

Differently today. Slowly. Gently. So much so that she
found herself impatient, struggling to free her hands, draw
his head down, find the force of his lips. He allowed her to do
so, smiling when she broke from him, a light of knowledge in

his eyes that made her long to protest with indignation, and draw ever closer. He let the towel fall. They stood in the light of day, with the fire still burning so warmly behind them. Color glowed on his flesh, gold and orange, shadow and light. She moved closer, lowering her head, pressing her lips to the flesh of his shoulder, lower upon his chest. She sank slowly, slowly against him, fingers rippling down his back, curving over the hard muscles of his buttocks. She found herself kneeling upon the floor, amazed at how instinctual the act could be, and awed by the intoxicating feel that could come from making love, from knowing that her touch, her kiss, her caress, evoked such hunger, even as it caused it to rise within herself. She'd known him so short a time. But in that time, the hours and moments had been intense. She had noted all the little things first. The color and depth of his eyes. The shape of his face. The power of his stance. The length of his fingers, the callouses on his palms, the blunt clip of his nails. The texture of his hair. All these things had become admirable to her. And now she knew as well that she loved the stroke of his fingers, the tenor of his whisper, the feel of his arms around her. All these things she knew now . . .

And yet could avail her nothing. He would ride to the king. She'd be held for ransom. And though her actions might have proven the loyalty of Hamstead Heath, it was unlikely that they could buy her brother's freedom. These moments were all that she had, and they would pass all too quickly.

She crushed against him, desperate to hold on. He came down to her, drawing her up, into his arms, the tightness of his embrace. Her feet never touched the floor as they moved back to the bed, the softness of sheets and down and quilt. This time his lips were everywhere. Grazing slowly down the length of her back, arousing as a cool breeze with fire

beneath. Shoulders, arms, kneecaps, ribs, breasts . . . She
writhed beneath the touch, and cried out when it came where
the root of burning anticipation lay. Aggression seized her
with desire; she rose wrapping him with her form, and finding
herself guided atop him, given leave to take every initiative,
soaring with her own sense of wonder, excitement, and
power. Her hair swept around her, fell upon his chest, danced
with each of her movements. And again the moments came
when there was nothing in the world but the sensation and
the wanting . . . and the exploding into shards of sun-touched
glass and stars, the sweep of the feeling, and even the wonder
as she sank back to earth, to the feel of mattress and sheets
and pillows, and the damp heat of his body at her side. His
fingers moved into her hair, drew her against him. She felt
him breathing deeply as they both lay silent.

After a moment he murmured, "I'm not terribly sure you
could ever do better than that," he said softly, only a trace
of amusement in his voice.

She didn't reply for a while. Then she asked him, "Where
am I being sent?"

"A place called Langley—protected by some of the most
rugged and fierce Highlanders you'll ever know," he told
her quietly.

"When?"

"Today."

"I see."

"I join the siege against Dumfries this night," he said.

"Of course."

"Lauren's father will be sent the Bruce's demand for
ransom."

"He will certainly pay. And . . . if the king has sent
messages regarding my captivity, I'll certainly be bought as
well."

"It's not just a matter of money. The English hold hostages as we do. English are traded for Scots. A simple matter, usually involving rank, wealth, and importance.''

"Yes, of course.''

"No one will harm you. You have the Bruce's protection.''

"Until I am traded.''

"Until you are traded. However, that will probably take months. Negotiations are slow. If the weather grows rough, the roads will become impassable.''

She wasn't certain just what reassurance he was trying to give her. The sudden reality of the situation came to her. She would probably never see him again. He would go off to fight. She would be held until ransom was delivered. It might take time. King Edward would know that she had defied the Scots. Steven would be offered a greater measure of protection for that reason. Her own situation would become dire. Rowan DeClabert would offer a rich sum for her return, into his keeping, and with his influence over the king, he might well demand that he had earned the right to keep her.

She started to rise, afraid that the ridiculous tears forming in her eyes would spring to her lashes.

He drew her back.

"No.''

"You need to ride to your king,'' she murmured, a slight sarcasm in her voice that she couldn't quite control.

She knew that he loathed the tone, yet at that moment, he ignored it. "We're not done here yet. Tell me about Rowan DeClabert.''

She stared at him, startled. Then she shook her head. "Rowan? Why do you ask about him?''

"His name has come up several times recently. I'm curious.''

She shrugged. "He is one of Edward's great barons.''

"That should make him enticing to a young English-woman of family."

"Yes, I suppose, if one finds such power enticing."

"Most women—and their guardians—do."

"It depends upon how a man achieves his power," she murmured.

"And how did he achieve it?"

"Stealth, and trickery."

"Ah—tactics to which you would never resort yourself."

She fell silent, staring at him coolly.

He smiled. "Tell me more."

She shook her head. "There's nothing to tell. He is Edward's good friend, and a mighty knight." She hesitated. "He—likes hurting people. When there are no battles to be fought, he seeks out tournaments. When there are no tournaments, he challenges young knights. He has left many a promising youth crippled for life. He can fight, and fight well. He is never disturbed by such elements as fairness, or the rules of a game."

"He's old, young? Heavy, light, fat, bald?"

"Young enough. Well built, as any man who spends his every waking hour in the pursuit of improving his capacity to kill." She hesitated again, then said impatiently, "I don't understand your questions. Why does it matter to you?"

"The enemy always intrigues me."

"Why?"

"I may see him riding on Scottish soil."

"And it's equally possible that you may never face him in battle. You, or any other Scot. He may avoid Scotland."

"And he may not. I want to hear about him. Anything that you can tell me."

"Why? This makes no sense."

"It would please me to hear what you know about him. And you're willing to do anything to please me, remember?"

"All right! If you must know, I would say that he is evil—pure walking avarice and evil. He was born with wealth and power, and a way with the king. His father was an opportunist, marrying a widow with family, title, and wealth. She was not a young woman, and died when Rowan was born. Rowan has improved upon his lot from an early age, first proving to Edward the First that he was a sound adviser for his son, who listened too easily to those of whom he was extraordinarily fond. All these years, he has taken the greatest care with his association to the Crown. He is still not what we call ... one of the king's favorites— it's his very power and masculinity which make him so invaluable to Edward. He is not a man the nobles can protect as an adviser. He twists and turns everything to his desires and goals."

"And he is the man holding your brother."

"Yes," she said, frowning, as he seemed to have a true comprehension of the entire situation. She didn't think that she had ever mentioned Rowan's name to him. But perhaps Lauren or Sir Alfred had been talking.

"Perhaps there is something that can be done," he said.

She looked at him in surprise, then shook her head. "There is nothing to be done. The barons in England might still be at one another's throats, but there is still an acknowledgment of the Crown. Most men keep a wide berth of Rowan DeClabert. They are far too aware that they might get entangled in one of his traps. But there is hope for Steven. Now. DeClabert might well offer for me, and if so, I'm sure it will be a generous sum, one your king will be quite willing to accept. He'll pay the ransom, and yet be aware that if he is to keep me, he'll have to see that Steven is forgiven. He has that kind of power. And if Steven is set free, then I will gladly pay whatever price saves his life, for despite Lauren's father, Steven is in grave danger every day in Rowan's care.''

"I see," he said slowly.

"Do you?''

"I believe that was your intent all along. Force the Scots to take hostages, show king and country the loyalty of Hamstead Heath—then be the bargain that would set your brother free. Tell me, if what this man has wanted all along was your agreement to marriage, why didn't you simply accept his suit long ago?''

"I never knew how far he would go to get what he wanted.''

"But now you know, so you will play out your game, and gladly accede to his wishes.''

"I don't believe there will be much choice," she told him.

"Ah. Well, I am glad that I have been able to serve you before you cast yourself upon the spindle of martyrdom.''

"Why are you being cruel?'' she demanded, ready to wrench away, and wishing she hadn't spoken so truthfully, and given away so much that lay within her heart and soul.

His fingers wound tightly around her arm, keeping her still. "Actually, cruelty was not my intent. I had merely thought that you were far more of a fighter than that.''

"It's not so difficult to risk much for yourself," she told him. "You don't understand. You really don't. My brother is a man who cares for others.''

"I've heard about your brother. A great deal. And I don't think he'd be so willing to see you throw your life away.''

She was silent. No. Steven would be furious. He would vehemently oppose any trade that put her in his place.

But DeClabert would never suggest that *she* should go to the block for treason. He wanted her. Mainly, she was certain, because she didn't want him. He was a man who would find a way to take whatever toy in life appealed to him. And when he tired of her, she would still be his liaison to the amazing horses and riches of Hamstead Heath. The family holdings were at an ebb now, certainly—but thankfully, Jamie and his men had not destroyed and razed the manor and village. They had left cattle and horses behind, and the excellent breeding of warhorses and animals with the greatest speed and agility would continue. Hamstead Heath could return to its wealth and splendor.

There was more to make her an appealing acquisition to a man such as Rowan. Her father had been a fierce lord, honored by Edward I. Her family was an old and respected one. She provided exactly what he did not have himself.

"I'm just a pawn," she said. "You have a few more moves. You, at least, are a knight."

"All of us are pawns," he told her. "Even kings. Every man faces damages that he can't bear, and yet he must bear them."

"I will not accept the damage of my brother's death. Not if I can prevent it."

"Perhaps Steven is not in great danger at the moment. Many of Edward's barons are being called to serve their feudal duty. You say that I may never meet DeClabert in battle. That's certainly true—and if we were to meet, God knows, in the heat of a fight, we might never know it. But he could be in Scotland, even now. And it's possible that the king will grow impatient with having such a man as your brother a prisoner when he, too, owes a feudal duty and could be riding to war against the Scots."

"The king listens to Rowan. Whatever Steven's abilities, he will remain a prisoner. As to Rowan . . . yes, I suppose it's possible he has come to Scotland. I believe, however, that he was at his estate when you and your men arrived for the tribute. If he has come since then, he is with a great force. He likes to do battle, but is not fond of the odds being against him. Ever.'' She suddenly found herself growing angry, fighting down her bitterness. ''And I loathe Thistle-on-Downs! The place is cold, gray stone. The land is flat, and the moat about the place has a stench. It always seems that it is brown to me, even in summer. It's nothing like Hamstead Heath. Though we are farther north, the winters never seem so frigid. In spring and summer our lands roll with a sweep of the deepest green, there are flowers every-where, and the forests nearby are cool and sheltering. And the horses! Well, those that are left! In spring, they race across the valley, the foals are born, and they are as beautiful as the landscape.''

''But Christina, a young woman of family and position is always an asset to the household, to be married well to increase alliances, strength, wealth, power. You have certainly known all your life that you wouldn't grow old at Hamstead Heath.''

She lowered her lashes, looking away. ''My mother was supposed to be a witch,'' she murmured. She stared at him then. ''Not a crone, or evil in any way. Just a woman with a touch of magic. She could sense rain long before it came, and she knew if a winter would be mild, or fierce. She had a sense about her . . . some of it apparently came down to her children. Steven and I have had a way of knowing certain things without being told. I can sense when he's in danger. And when he is well. If he has been hurt . . . just as he can sense danger for me. And there were far too many tragedies of marriage we witnessed as children. He swore to me, at our father's death, that he would never use me as a token for gain. We lived in the belief that we were far more civilized than others, that we would live as we chose, and I would marry when I pleased. When Rowan began to hint of a liaison, Steven was quick to say that he didn't consider his sister as a possession he had to give any man, and he was certain that though I would be flattered and grateful, I had no intention of making any promises at the time. Soon after . . . the king sent for Steven.''

He was silent. She was certain that he was thinking, like most men, that her duty in life was to marry where she was told, and be grateful that a man of means and power had offered for her.

"You weren't promised from the cradle?'' he asked her.

"Actually, I was. To the son of the count of Alsace. But he died as a boy, and therefore, I was betrothed to no one.'' She fell silent, wishing she hadn't spoken so freely. She felt more vulnerable, more exposed now, than she had in any physical way. She realized that she knew nothing about him at all—except that he had heatedly informed the boys the other day that she was *not* his wife. For all she knew, he did have a wife, at home, somewhere. She didn't even know where *home* was to him.

He was still watching her. Seeing what, she didn't know.

She let out a sigh of impatience. "Are you done tormenting me? What can any of this mean to you? You're going to go off and assault castle after castle. I will be taken to this Langley, and locked away until others decide my fate. I don't care to talk about my life anymore!''

"You're right, of course. And time is slipping away,'' he said.

His fingers threaded into her hair, drawing her close. She suddenly wanted to protest. But his mouth covered hers, and the length of his body blanketed over her. She felt as if she melted, and she deplored her lack of strength. Then even that thought was swept from her mind, and an urgency seized her to hold on to the moments she had, to cherish the fire, the touch, the feel, the ecstasy of feeling cherished . . . if only briefly, and even if the feelings were a lie. She wanted it all. The memory of his scent, which would never leave her. The brush of his lips. The fever of his filling her, the force of his arms around her.

Something to hold . . .

To remember.

Time indeed slipped away. So quickly.

It seemed it had just been morning. The shadows of night began to fall.

They lay, spent, exhausted. The truth of it all coming closer and closer. He would leave. She would be locked away. She couldn't escape. Not while Steven remained a prisoner.

His knuckles brushed over her cheeks.

"Christina, you're plotting and planning, even now. Wondering if perhaps there will not be a way to escape the castle at Langley, and do some heroic deed that will make Edward long to honor your household."

She shook her head. She lay against his chest. He couldn't possibly see her face, or read her thoughts.

"What is there to plot, or plan?" she murmured.

"I warn you, you will not cause trouble at Langley."

There was something suddenly very deadly in his voice. She twisted against him, meeting his eyes. "Really? Should there be trouble, it's no longer your concern. I believe I'm Robert Bruce's responsibility now."

There was a glitter in his eyes, somehow heightened by the shadows of night. The arms around her suddenly seemed like bars of steel.

"You will not cause trouble at Langley," he repeated.

"In what way? It is a fortress, right? What could I do, bring the walls tumbling down? You give me great credit. Or is it such a great and well-fortified castle that your family is there? Do you have a wife who resides there?"

The sudden violence that seized him was terrifying to her.

He didn't strike out at her; he simply pushed her from him with such force that she was stunned. He rose, well muscled and imposing in the shadows, striding to the door. His hand slammed against the frame with such force that it seemed the entire farmhouse shuddered.

He stood there, locked in tension, and it was as if she stared at the back of Atlas. She lay where she had fallen upon the pillows, too startled and frozen to move or whisper a word, or even to let out her breath.

He turned suddenly and she eased against the headboard, certain that he meant to strike her, terrified, her heart seeming to beat a thousand pulses a second.

She couldn't see his eyes, only the set of his face, in the shadows.

He took a step toward her. She remained dead still, heart pulsing.

He didn't touch her, but swept the quilt from the bed, wrapping it around his waist. He turned, and walked out to the main room. She heard a scraping. The chair moving.

Long moments passed, and she still couldn't move. At last, she rose in fear, shaking. She pulled linen from the bed, catching it around herself, and trod as lightly as she could to the bedroom door.

He was seated before the fire, an ale skin in his hands, staring at the fire.

He couldn't possibly know that she was there. But he did. He rose suddenly, tossing down the skin, coming after her. She started to retreat, but he caught her shoulders, and her arms were enveloped in the linen. He pulled her with him to the chair before the fire, drawing her down upon his lap.

"There, my lady, is your answer," he said, his tone deep and bitter, more biting than she had ever heard. "My wife burned to death, my lady. She scratched the face of the English lord who had been given our holdings, and in his fury, he tied her to the stairway when he burned the house to the ground. There was nothing but ash left by the time we returned from the forests where we were forced to flee when Edward's great armies came after us. What I know came from the servants who escaped the blaze, and were forced to the forest as well, to avoid starvation. We live with bitter memories, and many hatreds that lie just beneath the surface.''

She sat, staring at the flames, aware of his hold on her, wondering if he would toss her into the hearth itself, longing now to escape the demon she had so inadvertently awakened. Seconds slipped by, and she was sorry, deeply sorry. She could feel the heat, and imagine the agony suffered. And she was afraid.

At last she managed to whisper, ''I'm sorry. So very sorry.''

To her amazement, his hold suddenly eased. She slipped away from him, shaking as she made her way back to the bedroom, eager to leave him to his brooding, his anger, and his pain.

She softly closed the door. Shivering, she realized that she was in nearly total darkness. She stumbled against the bed and sat upon it, drawing the sheet more closely around her shoulders, never having felt so trapped in her life, so alone, so afraid.

Suddenly, the door burst open again. He stood in the doorway, a shadow, a silhouette, in the darkness illuminated only by the flickers of the firelight.

''Come here,'' he said quietly.

Her heart thundered again. She didn't know what he intended, and she was shivering wildly. She longed to ignore the summons, and more, she longed to go to him, to touch him again, to somehow ease the tension within him, stroke away the agony.

"Come here," he repeated.

And she rose, stepping lightly to him, wanting to reach out, afraid to do so.

She didn't need to do so. As she stood before him, she was suddenly swept up. His touch was rough, forceful, as if he was angry with himself, but compelled, fevered, driven by a strange fury. He didn't hurt her; but neither did the storm of tension and passion leave him. She was desperate to protest, but the simple force of his arms, of his tempest, left no room. And in moments, she realized she had become a part of it, desperate, urgent, swept into the volatility of the fever that had seized him. Her fingers kneaded into the taut muscles of his back, she felt the crush of his body, the steel of his form, and then knew nothing but the sleek feel of hot, damp flesh, the pound of pulse and sinew and form, and spiraling wind that seemed to bring her soaring ever higher in a maelstrom that could only cast her down upon a rocky shore. But it didn't matter. She saw stars, light, and darkness, cries tore from her lips and were buried against his chest. And then, at last, she was seized by such a sweet and violent climax that the world itself turned into a burst of stars, and then an ebony honey that wracked its way through her body again and again. She closed her eyes, aware only of sensation, of the weight of the man, the arms still locked around her. And at last, the world returned, and she was glad of the darkness and the shadows. She was at a loss, torn between the longing for the night to never end, and the knowledge that it was over, and that, for a moment, he had been as vulnerable as she, and now, indeed, memory would haunt her forever.

Moments passed, one after another. She didn't move.

At last, he rose. Once again, he disappeared into the main room. She heard the slosh of water as he washed. He returned to the bedroom, and in the darkness, found his clothing and dressed. She lay still, aware that he was done, that he was staring down at her.

"My lady, I do apologize for my fit of temper. I mean that most sincerely. Magnus will be here soon; you'll ride a few hours by darkness tonight." He didn't wait for a reply, but walked out to the main room.

She realized that he was going to leave. At first she remained still, then, hating it that she still found herself shivering, rose. She was not quite so adept at finding her clothing in the darkness, but at last managed to do so.

She heard the front door opening, and closing.

Her heart flew to her throat, and she hurried out of the room, certain that the main house would be empty.

It was not. Grayson had come, bearing armor. He acknowledged her with a courteous nod of his head, but his attention was on the pads and mail he was fitting over Jamie's head and tunic. Jamie reached for his riding gauntlets, pulling them on his hands as he at last turned back and looked at her.

She was startled by the gentle tone of his voice when he spoke, and by his words.

"My lady, you will be safe. Remember that."

He offered her a deep bow. His eyes swept over her, and he turned, departing with Grayson behind him.

She stood at the door, a feeling of cold sweeping over her. He was riding away. The time had come. She had been a fool. He was a Scotsman himself, the Bruce's warrior all the way. She now knew something of his past, and through it, much of his future. He was the king's man all the way, his one goal in life his fight for his country. When and if the Bruce won his final freedom, Jamie would be richly rewarded. His lands would be returned, and when the time was right, he would also be granted the proper bride, one who would bring him more property and esteem. And in

the meantime . . . others. Such as she. Willing captives,
camp followers, serving wenches. She was nothing to him.
A thorn in his side. One who had alleviated the tedium
of life and battles in the shadows and the darkness. She
had no right to be bitter. She had demanded they be taken;
she had literally thrown herself into his arms. She couldn't
have changed any of her own actions, but now, all she
could feel . . .

Was the cold.

She held on to the doorframe to remain standing. It was
best that they had parted this way.

She was startled when the door opened again, when he
came striding back in, enormous in pads and mail, sword
swinging now at his side.

He had come only for a saddlebag left on the table. He
picked it up, then turned once again, but this time, toward
her.

"You'll cause no trouble at Langley, Christina," he said
softly, coming before her.

She was glad of the mail, of the whole regalia for battle.
She felt as if it made him a stranger.

"I bid you good journey," she said simply.

She was stunned when his hand, clad in the gauntlet,
reached for her chin, lifting her face. "Take care, English!"
he said softly. He paused then, bending, briefly brushing a
kiss against her lips, a breath, as gentle as a summer breeze.
His eyes touched hers. He waited for her to speak again.

"I bid you good journey," she repeated, a note of desperation rising in her voice.

"And that is all?"

She thought for something more to say.

"Be careful of swinging swords, axes, and such. All
Englishmen are not cowards."

"Indeed. Many have tremendous courage and great

strength. Even if English women may be reckless, foolhardy ... and yet very brave. Tread with care, my lady,'' he told her. Once again, he hesitated, watching her. He strode to her then, taking her hand, placing something in her palm, and curling her fingers around it.

"Your brother is alive and well, at this time, Christina," he said simply.

With that, he turned and strode across the room and out the door. And that time, she knew that he was gone.

The cold seemed to pervade her ever more deeply. So much so that it was long moments before she uncurled her fingers, looking at the object he had given her.

A ring.

Her heart leaped, as she wondered at the meaning.

Then she saw that what she held was her brother's signet ring. He had seen someone who had been to Thistle-on-Downs. A prisoner, certainly, from Dumfries, but someone who knew ...

Steven was alive and well.

She lowered her head, grateful for the ring.

And more afraid of the future than she had ever been.

CHAPTER 11

Magnus arrived with a fellow who was so exactly his own tremendous size and girth that she was certain they had to be related.

They were. He introduced her to Angus, his brother. She decided that Jamie had chosen the escort rather well, since the two men together all but created a prison themselves. Liam was coming along as well, and when she emerged from the little farmhouse, she found that Lauren and Sir Alfred were already mounted, ready to be on their way.

She wished that Ioin had come with them. He, at least, talked to her. Apparently, there had either been orders given that she was dangerous, no matter how she appeared, and that she should still be separated from Lauren and Sir Alfred, for she was told that she would ride between Angus, who led the way, and Magnus. Lauren rode directly behind him, with Sir Alfred behind her, while Liam brought up the rear.

It didn't matter much that night. She was extremely tired,

and desolate, and she hated herself for the feeling. She certainly couldn't have come to care for the man who was an enemy cast into her life in the most hostile fashion. She had made every move with one goal in mind, that being a quest for Steven's freedom. There was truly nothing she could have done differently.

Except, perhaps, avoiding the mention of the word *wife*.

Yet, that aside, the chill had stayed with her. She was far too listless to cause anyone any trouble as she rode that night. It was not the past, she told herself furiously. It was the future. And yet the future loomed so far away. There would be long months now to be spent in a horrid stone castle, probably much like Thistle-on-Downs.

She didn't know how the Scots maneuvered in the darkness so well, or seemed to know so easily just where they were going. Thankfully, Crystal was sure-footed, and willing enough to follow the lead horse. It seemed that they rode forever. It was probably no more than four or five hours. Still, in that time, they came far from Perth.

That night, when they camped, there was a fire. They were well supplied, and a meal was afforded them of fresh cooked fowl, soft bread, and a harder cheese. She was allowed then to be with Lauren and Sir Alfred, who were both polite to their escort. She didn't intend to be rude herself; she was simply too weary to make much of an effort. She was grateful, however, for the few minutes time that she had alone with Lauren and Sir Alfred, for she was at least able to show Lauren the ring, and take heart in Lauren's belief that it was an omen, meaning all would be well in the end.

Despite the cold earth beneath her, she slept well on the saddle blankets, knowing that Lauren and Sir Alfred were near, and that a giant of a man watched over them while they slept. She didn't feel the real discomfort until morning, and she realized, when she woke, feeling an even greater sense of loss, that she missed the arms of the man she had slept beside—not really so many nights, and yet, it seemed she couldn't really remember when she had not.

They spent three more days riding during which she was kept apart from Sir Alfred and Lauren.

On the fourth morning, she was surprised when Magnus spoke to her, his big, craggy, bearded face appearing odd when a smile lit his features. "Ah, my lady, don't be so downcast. Langley is a fine place; ye'll find comfort there."

"I'm certain it will be well, Magnus, thank you."

"There are many good folks there."

She nodded, gracefully accepting his help as he lifted her onto Crystal. Angus stopped by on his way to mount his own horse. "Langley is my home," he told her, as if adding an assurance. "A good place to be."

She nodded, smiling at him as well. It was amazing that these frightening giants could be so kind and soft spoken when they chose.

Only Liam, who had once offered her courtesy and a touch of kindness, still seemed to be wary of her. His eyes, when they touched her, were not so full of compassion. They remained careful, and suspicious.

On that fourth day of riding, the restrictions set upon them seemed to ease.

Perhaps they had realized that she wasn't really a fierce one-man army in herself.

She was allowed to ride at Lauren's side, while Sir Alfred seemed quite able to carry on conversation with the Scots. Lauren seemed not to mind the long hours in the saddle. As always, she was serene, and appeared to be at peace with herself.

She set a hand on Christina's hand as they rode, her wide

blue eyes gentle as she said, "Christina, you are breaking my heart! You appear as if we are riding toward our doom."

Christina smiled ruefully. "Well, we are, rather. How can you be so calm? My head seems to churn constantly as I worry about the future!"

Lauren shook her head. "It will be well."

"How can it be well?" She hesitated. "Lauren, I know that you love my brother. How can you not be worried?"

Lauren shrugged. "I'll know when to be worried."

"How?"

"Through you." She frowned suddenly, touching Steven's ring, which she had taken to wearing on the slender chain around her neck which had previously carried only her cross. "He is—all right? You haven't felt anything, and not told me?"

Christina shook her head fervently. "No. I feel that . . . whatever is happening, for the moment, he is in no pain or danger."

That night, Angus talked to her again as he deftly made a fire. "So, my lady, ye've a touch of the sight, as well?"

"A touch of the sight?"

"Couldn't help but hear—I was riding behind you. You know when something is wrong, and when it's right?"

"I wish!" she said, and couldn't help but smile, he was so earnest. She hesitated and told him, "It's just my brother. We were close as children. We always know when one or the other is hurt, or in danger."

Angus nodded knowingly. "We've a lad at Langley you'll like. He has the true sight. He can tell you many things."

"Really?"

"Can't hear, but he reads lips. A gentle lad. Quite good friends with my wife, who can speak for him, as well."

"So, you've a wife. And children, Angus?"

He smiled broadly. "One on the way."

"I'm very happy for you."

"You like little ones, then?"

"Of course."

Angus shook his head. "There are times when I'm glad that I've not a royal title, or anything of the like. The nobility send their sons and daughters off, while a poorer man, he gets to raise his children. To know them. See them grow."

She laughed. "Not all folk send their children away."

"Oh? Were you kept home?"

She hesitated, then shook her head. "Well, sometimes. We were sent to London, to different households, but came home often as well. My brother trained at the house of a different lord, and I spent a few seasons at court . . . but, if I have children, they won't be sent away."

"There's a good thing for you. That's how the lady of Langley feels as well. She has a beautiful boy. And another on the way, so we believe, but she's not said so yet, so take care, it's a secret."

She was glad that Angus chose to share a secret with her.

"I won't say a word."

"Lady Graham is a fine mother, she is, indeed."

Her heart seemed to stop at the mention of the name. She felt like a fool, in a whirl of confusion. Jamie had said that his wife was dead, that she had burned to death, and she had never seen such a whirlwind of emotion when he remembered the deed. Neither had he mentioned that Langley was his home.

"Lady—Graham?"

"Aye, 'tis a family stronghold we're going to."

"Jamie's—family stronghold."

"Certainly!"

"And so this lady is . . ."

She gritted her teeth, awaiting Angus's answer.

"English! Like yourself," he said cheerfully.

Angus suddenly leaped to his feet. Sir Alfred and Lauren, who had been resting against tall oaks nearby, also started. Liam came striding in from the direction of the road.

"Rider coming!" he said tensely.

Angus instantly crushed out the fire, drawing his great sword as he did so. He caught Christina's arm, pulling her toward the copse where Sir Alfred and Lauren waited. Magnus appeared from the roadway as well, motioning to Liam. The two slipped down from the forest slope to the rough dirt road below, silently taking a post on either side of the expanse, hidden within the brush.

Angus looked down at her. "Not a word, my lady."

She shook her head, wondering at the flutter of fear in her heart. She realized that she desperately didn't want to be rescued by the English.

She heard a bird cry in the night; it was answered, she thought, from the roadway. Angus's hold eased from her arm, and he smiled broadly, stepping from the trees. The rider became apparent on the roadway. She stood very still, feeling the breeze of the night, for the man on the horse was Jamie. Angus started walking toward him, and she found that she was doing the same, anxious to see him, to assure herself that no harm had come to him. She imagined that he had come because he'd had to see to her safety. She started running as she neared the horse, then stopped, for something was wrong.

The man dismounted from his horse. "Jamie?" she whispered.

He wore the same mantle; it had to be Jamie. But it was not. He lifted his helm from his head, greeting Angus and the others with a warm enthusiasm. He turned her way then, and though he was a great deal like Jamie, he was, of course, someone else. His hair was far lighter, the contours of his face a bit different. He was perhaps a year or two older.

"Not Jamie, my lady." He studied her with interest. "But you would be . . . Lauren, or Christina?"

"Christina," she murmured uneasily, wishing that she hadn't spoken. She could have kicked herself. She was still disturbed by Angus's words regarding the lady of Langley. Who was she? Perhaps Jamie had married again, for political reasons, and simply refused to acknowledge any other woman as his wife. But here was this man, so very like him, obviously a relative.

"And you, sir?" she said coolly.

"Eric. Sir Eric Graham."

"Eric?" she murmured, embarrassed. If it had been Jamie, she'd have been a fool to rush forward as she had.

"Aye, lady. Same clan."

"I see. Are there more of you?" she inquired stiffly.

"Dozens, maybe more. The clan has quite spread like wildfire since the days of David the First. But we're the only two who resemble one another so closely."

"You're not—brothers?"

"Cousins."

"Ah."

"Langley is a family holding. So, you see, in a way, you're to be my guest."

"Guest. Such a curious word to be so continually used, and meaning anything but."

"In this case, my lady, I use the word with all good intent. Though we've all been informed you're quite dangerous, it would be to my great sorrow to imprison anyone in a cruel manner. Tell me, are you so dangerous then?" He seemed amused, having a like gift for mockery as Jamie. But there was something more courteous in his words, and the smile he offered her was pleasant.

"Dangerous? I travel with Liam, and two monstrous men. Each could break my neck with the flick of a finger. I hardly think I could be dangerous under the circumstance,'' she said. She lowered her head for a moment, then looked at him again. ''But I've been warned to cause no trouble.''

''Well, yes. You see, Jamie wouldn't want to be responsible for causing any harm to Langley, for the responsibility for the fortress actually lies with me.''

''It's my understanding that Langley is a tremendous fortress. Quite seriously, sir, what harm could I cause?''

''I'm not quite sure, but I never underestimate anyone.'' He was looking past her. Liam had come forward, greeting the newcomer as an old friend. Sir Alfred and Lauren followed in his wake. Eric politely greeted the other two, informing them as well that they'd be guests at his fortress and that he hoped they would be comfortable for the duration of their stay.

She was certain that this man hadn't ridden here to welcome hostages as *guests* in his castle, but whatever his business was, he didn't seem to be in a rush. He helped get the fire going again, and as Angus had turned salted venison into a rich stew, he joined them at the campfire. Despite his courtesy, he made Christina uneasy—he reminded her too much of his cousin.

She wished that he would speak more regarding Langley. About his own family. She was dying to ask if the Lady Graham expecting a child was his wife, but she could not bring herself to do so. And yet, just as she watched him, eager for any small word he might give away regarding Langley, she realized that he studied her with equal curiosity as well, and she felt a greater sense of unease growing within her.

His conversation remained general, and yet, she was certain that he had not come casually at all. The certainty that he watched her continued, and at last, when the meal was done, and the others had moved away to clean their gear, she realized that he had come for specific information. "Messengers rode south yesterday; they left early in the morning. There's every likelihood that you'll not have a long, forced stay in England," he told her. It was information that she knew, other than the exact timing of when word had been sent.

She nodded, not responding.

"I understand that your brother is a guest at DeClabert's castle in the north."

"Well, it seems that the troubles and tedium of my life are well known among men to whom English problems must truly mean little," she murmured.

"There are many games men play within politics, my lady. Your brother is of interest to us, yes. Just as we regard the tremendous breach between King Edward and many of his nobles with interest, amusement, and relief."

"Though I can't at all see what my brother's situation could mean to the greater glory of the Scottish cause, I begin to fear that I'd be a traitor to my country to say more."

"To your country—or to an injustice? Tell me, are you certain that your brother is still being held by DeClabert at Thistle-on-Downs?"

"I'm not certain of anything," she said.

"Ah, ever cautious!"

"If you think me dangerous, then you can only imagine, sir, how you appear to me."

He smiled. "Tell me about the castle."

"What?" she said.

"Thistle-on-Downs. I've not ridden that way. I've seen the fortress at York . . . under savage circumstances, in years gone past. I understand that DeClabert's castle is north of the great fortress at York. I'd like to know more about it. Have you been there?"

"Yes."

"Then . . . ?"

She hesitated, then shrugged. "It's a fortress. Nothing so grand as York. But it is moated, and there are sheer stone walls. There are three towers, and a large courtyard. Most of the village lies beyond the walls. Thistle-on-Downs has not been in any danger since . . . the time of William the Conqueror, I imagine. Oddly enough, in the many times the Scots have raided into the north of England, they have had different goals in mind. Perhaps it wasn't a feasible target when there were either easier or more advantageous places open to assault—or, like York, offering a greater revenge, a greater glory. Still, the area has known great unrest for a very long time. Rowan has a large contingent of knights living beyond the boundaries in various manors, some of them little more than large houses, some of them grander. He is intensely fond of games, and has a large armory." She hesitated. "In the many times he has fought here, in the king's service, he has accrued many Scottish arms."

"What of the battlements?"

She frowned. "Unassailable."

"No battlements are unassailable."

"Believe me—they are unassailable. Strong. They are well shored. Sheer walls rise high. The towers are deadly, with many narrow arrow slits that offer the defenders every advantage."

"What about the gates, and the moat?"

She paused, watching him, thinking his line of questioning quite insane. Then she shrugged. "A drawbridge. When it is up, there is truly no entrance—unless a man were to scale a sheer wall. There is no way to bring a ram against the gates, for they are far too close to the water. And should men be trapped in the portcullis, there is an oil spill above. There are a number of books written about the defense of the castle. I believe it was little more than an earth fortress when the Normans came. They were the ones to build in stone. There is a very elegant book on a defense that occurred there when there was an uprising against William the Second. It's illustrated, with grim pictures of men caught in the portcullis, caught beneath the cauldron of spilling oil.''

"Not a place your brother could escape easily."

"No. But in truth, that matters little. If he escaped, to what avail? The king would order him seized again—or worse."

"Curious that he would choose to honor such a king."

She stared at him, frowning. "Edward the Second is legally the rightful king. And our home is in England."

He shrugged. "That, my lady, may one day be a matter of question. Borders won't be set until this war is ended."

She shook her head. "Perhaps your armies have done brave and magnificent deeds. It seems apparent that Robert Bruce is truly becoming the accepted ruler here, and aye, much of Scotland now rests in Scottish hands. But you're mistaken if you don't think that the English barons will come together and rise en masse, once a real challenge exists. There is a quarrel going on now, but the king's barons are like children. When England herself is at honor, they will band together. And when they do, Edward can call upon tremendous forces. He can draw from the south, pay mercenaries from France and elsewhere. He has command of a treasury that can afford to wage a terrible war."

"But he doesn't have the one weapon essential to winning a war."

"And what is that?"

"A fierce belief in living and dying for a land that is rightfully his. No matter what tricks Edward the First played upon the people, Scotland was never rightfully there for the king's taking. We're an ancient people, ruled by our kings for far too many centuries. Not that there aren't divisions!

Or that the Scots can't still feel their old tribal loyalties. The clans in the Highlands are powers unto themselves, but once they have rallied around a king, there are no men more dedicated. The old blood of the Norse berserkers still rises in many a Scot. I believe with my whole heart that Robert Bruce will prevail, and that Edward will be forced, in the end, to accept that he is the king of a sovereign nation.''

"It has been a long, long time that this war has gone on," she said softly.

He nodded, a subtle smile on his lips as he stared at the fire. Then he looked at her. "We have never been so close to victory."

She shook her head. "You shouldn't forget Falkirk."

"Believe me, I never do."

He rose suddenly, excusing himself. "It has been a pleasure to meet you, my lady. I'm afraid that I need a few words with the men, and must be on my way. Take care. And please, don't make trouble at Langley. I am in deepest sympathy with your plight, but I have a wife and child, and another on the way, and have lost far too much already. I have no desire to see you confined to dungeons—and we do have them."

She started to rise; he offered her a hand. She accepted his assistance cautiously. He tended to give the same warnings as his cousin, oddly managing a similar tone of voice, with only a touch more courtesy.

"You don't underestimate people, sir, but I am amazed that I can possibly seem to be so great a danger. Were I as skillful at deception and cunning as you seem to believe, I'd not be here now."

"Ah, well, many efforts fail. Some do succeed. Usually, it is the unwary who fall. We don't intend to be taken by surprise."

"Still, you give me more credit for a cunning ability at treachery than is due," she repeated.

He nodded, refusing to argue her words further, and certainly, refusing to trust her as well. She wondered just what accommodations she would find at Langley.

"Godspeed, take care, my lady," he told her. She was startled when he kissed her hand with an elegant manner that would have stood well in any court.

"To you, too, sir," she murmured, aware that she meant her words. She hoped that he would not be slain.

He walked from her, heading for his horse, and conferring with the other Scotsmen for some time. She remained at the fire, aware she would be led from their group if she came closer, wanting to hear their words.

When he had mounted his horse, she found herself walking forward again. She stood between the brothers, Angus and Magnus, as he bid them goodbye. She wanted to ask where he was going, if he, too, shouldn't be hurrying to raid another English fortification. She wanted to know if he was going to join the battle with his king, and his cousin.

She said nothing as she stood there. He reached into a saddlebag to hand a rolled parchment to Angus, asking him to see that it reached his wife.

He stared at her again. "God be with you, my lady."

"And you, sir."

"Is there any word you would have me take to the battlefront?" he asked.

She felt a flush cover her cheeks. No . . . in truth, she had no words. There was nothing that could be said.

"No," she murmured, shaking her head, feeling then as if every man there stared at her, and knew much more than he should.

Eric waited a minute, then lifted a hand to his fellows, kneed his horse, and turned back down the road.

She stood there, seeing the dust rise in his wake until she felt a hand on her shoulder. Liam, leading her back to the others. God knew, she could surely cause no trouble on the road. They didn't understand her at all. She wasn't in the least dangerous, at the moment. There was nothing she could do now to impress the liege of the English with her loyalty to the Crown. All she could do was wait, and pray, and trust in her belief that Steven was alive and well.

Two days later, they reached Langley. It was, indeed, magnificent. Looking far up the high walls, she could see the war machines upon the battlements, and she understood how this holding, in the hands of the Scots, had been kept as a fortress, rather than razed and dismantled.

The colors flown by Angus and the mantles they wore announced their arrival. They arrived at dusk, and the gates had been lowered to allow the farm animals, grazing in the surrounding fields by day, entry into the paddocks and barns where they would sleep by night.

Her cattle, she thought, and not without resentment.

Their small party rode into a central courtyard. The door to the inner keep opened as they arrived. A beautiful woman with long, dark hair came rushing out of the castle as they dismounted from their horses, followed by a priest.

"My lady!" Angus said with pleasure.

The lady of the house did not appear beholden to propriety. She hurried over, taking Angus by his bushy chin, and kissing his cheek. She stood back, oblivious to the others for a moment. "All goes well?" she asked anxiously.

"Aye, lady. Perth has fallen. The king's men have moved on."

"No injuries?" she asked.

Angus shook his head, assuring her that the men who had ridden from Langley had escaped so much as a scratch during the assault.

"Of course, I knew," the woman murmured. "And we had some hint that you would be arriving, though not the cause or reason."

Watching the exchange, Christina became aware of someone behind her, coming for her horse. A tall, thin man with brown hair stroked Crystal's neck, ready to take her reins. He offered Christina a smile that seemed oddly welcoming. He didn't speak; he gazed at Crystal, then looked her way again, and she was certain that he was admiring her horse.

She smiled in turn, certain that this was the deaf Gregory. She said the name aloud, making sure that she looked at him as she spoke. He nodded, apparently pleased that she had heard about him before arriving, and as if he had been quite aware that they would be coming. There was something pleasantly strange about him, perhaps in his very gentle manner, making her feel as if she were greeting an old friend rather than making a new acquaintance.

"Angus, m'love!"

A second woman, wiping her hands on an apron, emerged from the main door of the keep, her face lit with sheer pleasure and adoration. She didn't walk to their group with any semblance of composure, but raced straight toward the bear of a man, throwing herself into his arms. Angus swept her up, twirling around with her, and Christina glanced at Lauren, and neither could suppress a small grin, for it was most clearly evident that the woman was Angus's wife. When he at last set her down, Christina thought that she was extremely pretty, but had suffered some terrible assault, for a scar still marked the length of her cheek. She felt a little chill, wondering if it had been the gift of a careless English warrior. Whatever the past had been, however, the woman was most evidently happy now, as was the great Angus.

Christina caught a glimpse of the lady of the house, and saw her watching the two, happy for them, but there was something in her eyes that clearly announced she wished that she were having such a reunion herself. But the look was quickly gone; she greeted Magnus and Liam, just as well acquainted with the two, and then she looked to her unknown arrivals, eyes sweeping quickly over her, Lauren, and Sir Alfred.

"Welcome to Langley," she murmured, arching a questioning brow.

"Thank you," Lauren said.

"Indeed," Christina murmured.

Liam stepped forward. "Igrainia, we've English ... guests." There, that word again, Christina thought. The way it was said somehow explained the situation implicitly. "Lady Christina of Hamstead Heath, Lady Lauren, daughter of the Count of Altisan, and Sir Alfred. They'll be with us until ... other arrangements are made."

"I see," Igrainia murmured, studying the three of them. "Well, please, come in," she added, looking back at Liam again, a frown furrowing her brow. She was wondering, of course, just exactly what she was supposed to do with them.

Christina was certain that Eric's letter would have specific instructions. And naturally, a warning about her.

Igrainia turned and headed back into the keep. Liam indicated that they were to follow. Igrainia was the perfect hostess, calling to a servant to bring wine, and hot food. The hall was large, and quite magnificent with rich tapestries, fresh rushes, a huge dining table and fine carved oak chairs. The hearth was large, and the fire that burned within it very warm. A stairway led to a second level, but Igrainia directed them all to the great table in the hall, which could surely seat a good thirty people or so.

Angus presented her with the letter that Eric had entrusted to him, and she read it before the fire, while directing them to warm themselves and enjoy the wine. As she stood in front of the fire, the slight roundness in her stomach became apparent, and Christina found herself remembering the warning that Eric had given her, an echo of the words she had heard from Jamie. She was to cause no trouble at Langley.

"I see," she murmured, looking back at the table where her three *guests* were now seated. She was biting lightly at her lip.

Christina decided to end the discomfort for her. "We're hostages, of course," she said. "Awaiting ransom. And I'm afraid I'm considered to be quite a burden, though I can assure you, I wish no ill to you or your family."

The woman smiled suddenly, a strange light of amusement in her eyes as she looked at Angus. "Of course. Well, as you can see, we've ample quarters. But I'm afraid there are instructions that you are . . . to be guarded at all times."

"Naturally," Sir Alfred said with dignity.

Igrainia's smile deepened. "Actually, sir, you're to have the freedom of the grounds, as is the Lady Lauren."

Christina sat very stiffly. "And I?"

"A room, or an escort."

"I see."

"You mustn't worry. We'll do our best to assure your every comfort." She seemed to be incredibly sympathetic, and yet, of course, would do her duty, as she had been bidden. "You must be tired; a journey such as you've taken can be very exhausting. Magnus, will you see that their belongings are brought up from the stables? Gregory has taken the horses; he'll bring whatever our guests may have with them." She hesitated, then continued as if she were making arrangements for actual guests, calling to the tall, slender, older man who had served the wine. "Garth. I think the Lady Lauren and Sir Alfred will enjoy the second level rooms and Lady Christina . . . the lovely little tower room."

The lovely little tower room.

She was certain it was a gentle way of describing a room where there would be little difficulty in watching her.

She stood, no longer hungry. "You're incredibly gracious, my lady. And you're quite right, it has been a long journey. If Garth would be so kind, I'd deeply appreciate retiring to the tower room now."

"Certainly."

Garth came forward, bowing to her slightly. She rose and followed him, aware that Sir Alfred and Lauren were remaining behind, and that the men who had escorted them were certainly waiting for all three of their hostages to be settled before explaining everything to their hostess.

The tower room was up three levels. And it was exactly that. A round room, at the height of the tower keep. There was a bed, a rug before the hearth, tapestries around the wall, to warm the stone. It was certainly no dungeon. There was but one door. And as she had expected, it bolted from the outside.

She thanked Garth for his escort, and he promised to bring her few belongings soon. The door closed. The slender old man was careful not to slide the bolt too loudly as he left her.

Christina threw herself on the bed when he was gone, wishing she had indulged in much more wine before making her determined exit to her solitary confinement. She wanted to sleep. To close her eyes and sleep, and dream of a time before any of this had come to pass.

The ride was harder than she had imagined. She stared at the fire, and her eyelids closed.

She never heard the door open and close again, or see that it was the lady of the house herself who had come with her meager belongings, leaving them quietly just within the door.

CHAPTER 12

Seldom granted freedom from so much as his guest room, Steven had learned certain practices within his confinement to work studiously at maintaining his strength. He practiced arms with a pair of long boots, battled his own cloak, and worked arm and thigh muscles continuously against the floor. With little else to do, he was able to spend long hours maintaining his strength, and yet there were many times when the desolation of his position seized hold of his mind, and he wondered to what avail his efforts would prove if the king chose to have him walked to a scaffold.

Sometimes he wondered if he would have his neck stretched over a block or if he would be hanged. The block was actually reserved for those of a higher position than he—even greater nobles had found themselves hanged rather than beheaded in the war with the Scots. Such punishments had usually been reserved for the actual enemy, but Edward II, like his father, reserved his fiercest anger for those he considered traitors. In his heart he was often indignant; he knew he had done no more than many a noble of higher birth than himself. And often, the highest nobles on both sides had been forgiven by their separate monarchs—their sway over their own people and sections of the country was too important to be ignored.

His deeds, however, had nothing to do with his incarceration, and that was a fact Steven knew well. He had tried to look at his captivity in the same way he had viewed his position at all times, with the greatest of reason. He would certainly kill himself if trying to escape from such a fortress as Thistle-on-Downs. Actually, he believed that Rowan DeClabert would be delighted to see him attempt to escape. He could be easily killed in a pursuit to bring him back, and if he were dead, then Rowan would certainly, and entirely, have the ear and influence of the king.

Though Lauren's father was a Frenchman, he was a powerful man. She had grown up in England with her mother's family, but the king relied on the men-at-arms to be obtained from such a man as the count, Lauren's father. Steven's betrothal to Lauren was certainly one factor keeping him alive. Lauren's father had the ear of the French king who was important in the negotiations that continued between King Edward and those of his barons who had been responsible for the murder of Piers Gaveston, men with a power nearly as great as that of the king. Therefore, politics had kept him imprisoned. Politics also kept him alive.

In recent weeks, however, he had felt a growing sense of unease, and a fear regarding his sister and Lauren. Though he had never imagined that his visit to King Edward would result in his incarceration, he had spoken to both his sister and fiancée about survival in the event of an attack. If they surrendered to whatever power fell upon them, they would survive. In his last long night with Lauren before riding to his audience with the king, they had talked about the possibility of assault, and Lauren, in his arms, had steadfastly sworn that she would die rather than find herself the victim of their enemies. And he had fiercely informed her that death was not the option he would prefer—if she were to lie with a thousand enemies and live, he would love her still. Life was precious; they would somehow have years to grow old together, and she must never, never consider her honor of greater importance than her life. And she must never consider his honor, because he would love her for the rest of his days, and prayed only for her health and well-being, those things being more important than any. He would never rashly forfeit his own life; they would prevail. He wished that their wedding had taken place before he had ridden away; it had certainly been planned long enough. But though she had left London to live at Hamstead Heath where she would be his lady, a man's betrothed often came to his household years before a wedding. Girls were sometimes sent to the households of the men they would eventually marry. Lauren's father, occupied in France, expected to be present for the actual wedding. Therefore, the woman who should have been his wife by now was still his betrothed, and now he rued their restraint in honor of her father. As an unmarried woman, despite the sanctity of a betrothal, he felt that he had left her in a more precarious position.

Then, of course, there was the matter of his sister.

Christina, far too reckless, far too confident. And far too frightened for him. God knew what she would do in her quest to keep them all alive. And God knew what options remained, for warfare had torn them apart year after year—indeed, it was almost impossible to remember when there hadn't been the threat of the Scots finding retaliation for the assaults upon their country. Once, they had been so dominated by Edward I—and their king, John Balliol, so humiliated—that they were all but a defeated region of pagans and barbarians, never so finely sophisticated as the English. Then Wallace had risen, and rather than face a nation of well-trained men-at-arms, they were facing an entire people willing to die for their freedom. Wallace's execution had done nothing but force the contest between the Scots vying for the throne of Scotland—the murder of John Comyn, whether at the hands of Bruce or his followers, had left Robert Bruce as the only contender. His careful politics, his penitence on his knees for the death of his distant kinsmen, had begun to rally the country around him. Now, the Scots didn't just have a great warrior, a common man, rallying them to fight for their rights and freedom; they had a king, proving himself a greater knight, leader, and ruler with the passing of every day.

Edward I, despite the cruelty he could practice upon his enemies, had been a king with such a love of learning and law that he had been respected as an ultimate power within his own kingdom.

His son was not so loved.

But the very distaste in which he was often held made him as dangerous as a child trampling bugs in a field. He had seen his own best friend, his lover, slain by his enemies. He had little thought, therefore, of pursuing his royal status and ordering executions in return.

Finishing a task he had allotted himself—that of hefting the bed higher and higher each day, an attempt to keep his shoulder muscles finely tuned—he walked to the one narrow arrow slit that allowed him a view of the world beyond his prison. He flexed his arms and mused that he had maintained an excellent condition. Were he to walk to a scaffold, he would certainly appear powerful and proud as he did so.

He was going to lose his mind. Day after day, he did nothing but reason his position, the politics of the world, worry about his own safety, and more than that, agonize over the fate of his sister and his betrothed. Something had happened, of that he was certain. Yet he knew as well that if real harm had befallen Christina, he would know. And so he forced himself to believe that all was well.

As he stood by the window, a tap sounded at the door, and it was then opened by the old servant who did his laundry, brought his meals, and saw to the chamber.

Lambert carried a breakfast tray.

"Ah, good morning, Lambert," he said, forcing a sound of cheerfulness. "You're looking hale and well."

In truth, Lambert resembled a skeleton. Surely, no man could be more dour.

Lambert nodded glumly in acknowledgment of Steven's words.

"Should I expect a visit today from my host, Lord Rowan?"

Lambert set the tray down on the desk that stood at an angle before the fire. A worthless piece; Steven hadn't been granted any books or writing materials.

Though not at all a warm or effusive man, Lambert did his job well, accorded Steven his position in life, and never failed to respond to a direct question.

"No, my lord. The master has ridden north, as bidden by the king."

Steven was startled, and yet, shouldn't have been. Rowan DeClabert had mentioned, when Sir Ralph had come, that he, too, might soon be sent to Scotland. But Steven had assumed that Rowan would somehow shirk the duty—he disliked the Scots. They had a penchant for a kind of warfare that Rowan detested. They fought to win. When they needed to retreat to the forests, they did so. When it was expedient to attack suddenly in the night, to spring an ambush upon the enemy, they did so. Rowan preferred a battle with the lines drawn. War, with the chivalry expected by God and country. And a man of Rowan's means was able to finance enough warriors to take his place in any campaign.

"He's gone to fight the Scots?"

"Aye, Lord Steven."

So . . .

The master was gone from the castle.

Lambert paused, staring at Steven with an uncharacteristic empathy.

"What is it?" Steven inquired.

Lambert sighed deeply. "The Scots attacked Hamstead Heath. Your sister and the Lady Lauren and even Sir Alfred have been taken as hostages. But you need not fear the barbarians, my lord. My master, DeClabert will see that they are rescued from the hands of pagans!"

Steven felt as if his heart had dropped to the pit of his stomach. He stared at Lambert, and even that dour old fellow must have felt something for he quickly said, "They are in no great danger, my lord. The Scots are aware they hold prisoners of esteem. Their safety has been assured by no less than the king of the Scots himself, as they await ransom negotiations. The count of Altisan will be informed of his daughter's position, of course, and surely, the Scots tread as precariously with the French as any man, and your lady will be cared for with all due respect. And as to your sister, my lord, you know full well that my lord Rowan holds her in the highest regard, and therefore, he will forcefully see that all is well for her. You may rest assured, my lord. Indeed, perhaps once Lord Rowan has procured your sister's release, the king will see his way to forgiving you all your transgressions, and you, too, will be freed from this misery."

Steven stared at Lambert, no words coming to his lips.

"I'm sorry, my lord Steven, deeply sorry," Lambert murmured, and left him.

Steven sank to the foot of the bed, ignoring the tray of food.

He rose then, pacing furiously, slamming a hand against the stone walls of his prison. He rued the day he had ever spoken rashly about King Edward's inability to protect his borderlands. He slammed his hand impotently against the wall again and again, until the damage done the flesh of his palm at last caused him to stop.

He lowered his head, staring at the injury he had done himself, shaking his head. Reason. He had always prided himself on his ability to reason.

DeClabert was gone.

Thistle-on-Downs was an impregnable fortress, strong and powerful. Not to be assailed. No man could find his way in.

And yet, with DeClabert gone, perhaps a single man *could* find his way out. If he escaped, he would still be under dire sentence by the king.

And yet, how could that matter now, when so much had already been lost, when so very much lay at stake.

He walked suddenly to the bed, ripping linen from the sheet to wrap his hand. He noted his tray of food, and sat down to eat, more determined than ever to keep himself in top form.

As he ate, his mind worked.

Reason, think, there has to be a way.

There always was.

And he would find it.

Whatever instructions the lady of Langley had been given, she certainly intended no ill will toward the hostages in her keeping. Christina learned that from the first morning of her stay.

She had assumed she would spend her hours alone in the tower. Every comfort was afforded her there—a tub and hot water, fine food, candles, heat, a wealth of books. But she had barely bathed and eaten when she was visited by a priest, a man who called himself Father MacKinley, who courteously invited her to come to the hall.

"I'm invited down?" she inquired suspiciously.

He was a tall, handsome, and well-possessed man, though a priest. With a quick smile he told her, "The Lady Igrainia is loath to bring misery upon anyone, and certainly thinks you'd be far happier were you to join the others in the hall. May I, my lady?" he asked, and offered his arm as an escort.

Surprised, she agreed. And below the stairs, she discovered that it was a large, friendly, and industrious household. Igrainia was instructing her people regarding their various affairs and tasks; in winter, the preserving of meat, work on looms, sewing, and more.

Her son was a toddling young lad with her own big blue eyes and very dark hair, and a quick smile for his guests. Little more than a babe, he was polite and correct, and yet eager to crawl upon Father MacKinley's lap to hear a story.

Father MacKinley did not seem the customary priest. He did not regale the child with stories of great doom and warning. Rather, he appeared to enjoy tales of magic and the whimsical, which delighted the little boy no end. Lauren, already below, and apparently having already won the friendship of their hostess, was delighted to see Christina—she already sat, along with the woman Rowenna, working upon a tapestry, planned for the great hall, Igrainia of Langley was quick to explain.

Despite her own position, Christina heard her first question slip from her lips, and it was a defensive one. "May I ask after the welfare of Sir Alfred?"

"Of course!" Igrainia assured her, a subtle smile curling

her lips. "He is at the stables, since he is well familiar with so many of the horses from Hamstead Heath, and as you know, many of them are now stabled here."

"Yes, of course," she murmured. *Her* horses. No. No longer hers.

She felt a presence behind her. Watchful eyes.

Liam, of course, was in the hall. Though he had once been easier and kinder to her than many of the men, he now seemed to have taken on the heavy responsibility of being her main guard. He continued to be quiet in her presence, suspicious, his heavy gaze appearing to have acquired a new green light of wariness.

Since her hostess was so kind, Christina chose to ignore Liam. At one point, he apparently argued with Igrainia, and Christina knew that she was the subject of their discussion. He had work beyond the walls; she should not be in the hall if a man such as he was not there to assure that she wouldn't suddenly become rabid, seize up the poker from the hearth, and fight her way out of the house.

Igrainia won the argument. Liam left the hall, his gaze upon her with a grim hostility before falling upon Igrainia with a warning.

Glad for the freedom and company in the hall, Christina chose to be the very model of a perfect hostage—or guest. She worked upon the tapestry as well, and yet, later, when Father MacKinley seemed to have run out of stories and patience, she found herself drawn to the little boy, Wulfgar. Though she had lost her mother at a young age, she still remembered the marvelous tales she had told, and stories sung to the lute. After a hesitant question to her hostess, she was quickly supplied with a fine instrument, and as the others worked their needlecraft, she found that she had a willing audience in little Wulfgar, a truly charming child, despite his tender age. One day, Christina thought, the lad would break the heart of many a maid. She taught him a number of the songs, and was surprised to realize that she had gained the attention of the hall, that Angus had returned from whatever his business had been for the day, that he sat with his wife, and that the company in the hall all enjoyed the tales and songs she performed for the child, and were pleased as well to join in.

When supper was served that evening, the *guests* were all kindly invited to remain in the hall. And as the meal progressed, Christina felt oddly as if they might have been guests in fact, for the company at the table was charming and polite. Angus, Magnus, Liam, Father MacKinley, and a man called Allen, evidently steward of the fortress in the absence of its master, joined them at the great table, along with the woman Rowenna, and the silent young Gregory, though certainly his position as groom would not have allowed him a seat at such a table. But Igrainia of Langley apparently created her own proprieties, and in doing so, she had created a warm household, indeed. Sir Alfred during the day, had apparently discovered a way of communicating with Gregory, and the staunch old Englishman had no difficulty discussing horseflesh, the feeding of livestock, the care of arms, and other such matters with the men who were their enemies.

Lauren, as well, seemed to have quickly found a place of deep serenity. She had evidently learned that she had a great deal in common with their hostess in the time before Christina had come downstairs herself. But at the table that night, though Liam remained grim, Igrainia was effusive, telling Christina about their extremely fine library, and how she was certainly at liberty to enjoy any book she might find of interest.

At the meal's end, Angus played the pipes, and Christina was startled to find what she had previously thought to be a discordant instrument capable of the most beautiful lament. It was to be the end of the day; she was soon escorted back up the stairs by Father MacKinley. But when she had been left, she heard his voice in soft tones as he spoke to someone far more impatient. Liam, she assumed, angry, certainly, that he felt himself required to watch her door.

Each day improved. The weather held fair, and she and they were allowed out to the courtyard. Igrainia once suggested that she might enjoy a ride, but Liam was quick to persuade Igrainia that such an outing wouldn't be wise. He didn't openly defy; he pointed out the possibility that there might be danger in the nearby forests, and that Crystal was such an incredibly swift and fine mare that she might easily panic and carry Christina straight into a path of utmost peril.

She would not be riding beyond the gates.

But by day, she was allowed the courtyard. She enjoyed the air and the freedom, time in the stables, at least brushing her beloved horses, and learning that she could find an extraordinary peace in the presence of the silent Gregory.

Sundays, they were all allowed mass.

Time passed, and it did so with a strange ease.

They had been at the fortress of Langley perhaps three weeks and were at supper one evening, enjoying the last of the day in their usual company when the master returned to his holding. Igrainia, they had learned, had her own abilities with a lute and a beautiful voice. Christina had been surprised and touched just days before when Father MacKinley had presented her with a gift: her own lute to play, made by one of the exceptional craftsmen who lived within the walls of the castle. Often at night, Angus would bring out his pipes, and she and Igrainia would play different tunes upon their instruments to harmonize with him, and they would sometimes take turns teaching one another different ballads and laments they had learned over the years.

They were thus engaged when the doors to the great hall opened and they all looked up to see that Eric had returned.

Taken by his resemblance to Jamie, Christina had risen, her heart in her throat. But Igrainia's glad cry stilled her, and she sank back in her seat. Igrainia flew across the hall as if she walked on clouds, throwing herself into his arms, and he greeted her with an equal passion and affection, holding her close, bestowing a tender kiss upon her lips. They exchanged a look that promised the world to come later, and Christina was amazed to feel the tug at her heart their greeting caused her; she had seen the love shared by Lauren and Steven, and it was such that she would have done anything to defend it. But she had never seen them greet one another when they had been so divided by war.

With his arm around his wife, Eric came into his great hall, greeting his men, and then his guests, in turn.

"So all is safe and well at Langley?" he inquired.

"Aye," Liam said simply with a nod, though the fierce knotting of his brow betrayed that however it might appear in the hall, he was forever on guard.

"And with you, Eric?" Igrainia asked fearfully. "You haven't returned because of some injury? The king is well?"

"All is well," he assured her. "Dumfries still holds out, but we don't believe it will be long." He glanced at Christina and the others, apparently choosing to say no more in their company. "Sir Alfred! You appear hale and hearty."

"Indeed, sir," Alfred agreed. "Your household has afforded us every courtesy."

"My lady Lauren?" Eric asked.

"I'm quite well, thank you."

"I'm greatly relieved. Your father has been promised that you are offered the greatest care and comfort. And Christina . . . what about you, my lady? Is life here too cruel, or are you finding that our hospitality is not unbearable?"

She didn't have a chance to answer because Igrainia laughed slightly, almost as if in defiance. "Eric! The lady has been a blessing to our house, Wulfgar adores her, and she entertains us nightly with a musical ability far above and beyond any I have heard. We have been delighted to have her, and she is a most gracious guest!"

Eric stared at Christina, arching a brow. "Not a bit of trouble?"

"One could not cause trouble in such a wondrous place," she murmured.

Igrainia was pleased, but too elated to have her husband returned to give more attention to anyone other than he. "Are you hungry? You must be. Surely you've had a long ride. I'll call Garth and see that more food is brought quickly—"

"Nay, my love, I'm not hungry at all; we are the ones laying siege, and for once, we are well supplied ourselves." He glanced at Christina, and apparently could not avoid a slight taunt. "We have had some excellent beef to see us through." Then his attention returned to his wife, his eyes a soft fire as they lit upon her. "Warfare is, of course, exhausting. My will is to retire."

His wife's smile brought another tug to Christina's heart, so much so that she found herself staring downward, into her chalice, unwilling to see any more of what was private between them.

"Or course!" It was a whisper, barely breathed, by Igrainia.

The evening was over, for when the lord of the castle was joined by his wife, bidding them all good night, Liam stood as well, staring at Christina, and she knew it was time to return to her tower.

The following day, she saw neither the master nor the mistress of Langley throughout the morning, or much of the afternoon. She was in the hall herself, little Wulfgar on her lap, when Eric made an appearance. Despite what must be his nearly constant absence, Eric's son knew him well, and deserted her with a glad cry, ready to throw himself into his father's arms. Christina sat silently as Eric lifted his son, complimented him on how he had grown. Wulfgar spoke happily about the many new words he was learning, how Father MacKinley had him reading, and even added that Christina had come to sing him the most marvelous stories. Eric murmured that he'd be interested in hearing just what the stories were, then sent his son off to the kitchens to see that something was brought to him to eat. When the boy had gone he looked at Christina, hands on his hips, eyes speculative.

"You needn't fear. I haven't been singing any song about English right and valor," she murmured quickly.

A slight smile curled his lip. "You're aware, of course, that my wife is English?"

"I believe that Angus mentioned it once, yes."

"She has had her own sorrows and difficulties in this war," he informed her. "Therefore, she is loath to see that any cruelty befalls you. I know that you would not think to use such kindness and generosity against her. Liam, you see, has known you longer than I, and is still convinced that the day will come when you will have lulled us all into trust—and will then strike like a viper."

"To what end?" she asked.

"The fear is, that you might see a solution somewhere in time, and no longer be such a docile and charming companion."

"Your appearance here leads me to believe that your king's forces are pummeling English positions, so I can only assume that there is little for me to do but wait out my time." Her heart was hammering a little too quickly. She longed to ask lightly if Jamie were well, withstanding the rigors of war, but of course, she would not. If she hated anything about being here, it was the knowledge that she was kept within the power of his family.

More. It was the hours she spent in memory of the past, and fear of the future. And reason, of course. He had swept down upon Hamstead Heath, made a mockery of her life, and gone on to his own pursuits, leaving her to the care of others. His business with her was done; God knew what new entertainments he found in the long days of siege. She was forgotten, as he must be. But it wasn't easy here. Eric's son had a way with his smile, too much like his father—and uncle.

Eric, she realized, had made no comment.

"We are to wait out our time?" she repeated.

He nodded, and she was certain that he knew more regarding her position, but had no intention of speaking.

"Has something happened?" she inquired, too sharply.

"Negotiations are under way, that is all," he said.

"Already?" she murmured. "I had thought it would take far longer for word to reach London, for any replies to be made." She was dismayed at the dread that filled her; it was necessary that the negotiations be made. She should be elated. Her brother's freedom could come with an agreement. His life.

"Lauren's father has been in the north counties, as has the king of England," he said.

She had been seated by the fire. She rose restlessly, suddenly aware of just how easy life had been at Langley.

"Are we to leave soon then?" she asked.

"No, I'm afraid not. There are many possibilities of exchange being bandied about." He hesitated. "I believe the Lady Lauren will be released first," he told her.

She turned toward the fire, careful that he not see the

tumult in her eyes. If Lauren left, she would be so very alone. And yet, if Lauren were exchanged into her father's care, she would be safe. The Count of Altisan was fond of Steven, and a man who loved his daughter, and was aware that Lauren would want no other. Her freedom could help Steven as well.

"Nothing will happen for some time yet, however. The siege of Dumtries continues. Perhaps, when that fortress falls . . ."

She nodded. "Yes, of course. Well then, we will await our fate."

She turned back to the fire, warming her hands.

"I'm certain you'll be pleased to hear that those men you came to know are faring well. George, Ragnor, Grayson . . . the others. All are faring fine. You're glad to hear that, aren't you?"

"Of course, since it's painful to hear of the death of any man one knows."

He laughed softly, causing her to turn, startled. "A pity you were not born north of your border lands. You have a sincere respect for life, you're incredibly talented and well bred, and take such care, with such a nonchalant manner, with your words. And yet there is always that light in your eyes that proves that you would defy the very authority of God—at the right time, when you had a fair chance of winning. It's no wonder that Liam is so dour in his task of guardian!"

She let out an impatient sigh. "I'm planning nothing!"

"Not at the moment," he agreed. "You've not inquired about my cousin."

"Should I have done so?"

"With your tremendous respect for the lives of all men, of course."

"I'd certainly assumed that he, too, was faring fine. You'd

not have returned with such a presence of triumph and pleasure had any ill befallen your kin.''

"True,'' he agreed. "You're quite perceptive, as always. My cousin spends most of his days securing the surrounding countryside, attacking whatever parties might seek to resupply the fortress. Sieges do not sit well with the Scots; we end them as quickly as we are able. Dumfries will fall.''

"I'm sure it will. Edinburgh, the pride of Scotland, however, still rests in English hands,'' she reminded him politely.

"For now,'' he said, turning from her as Wulfgar came hurrying back into the room, followed by Garth, bearing a tray laden with the best the castle had to offer.

Roast beef.

Christina was surprised to find that the aroma of the roasting meat was irritating; she wanted to escape the hall. But Igrainia came running down the steps to the second level then, still alive with the delight that her husband was in the house. She insisted that Christina join them at the table as others, as well, arrived. Father MacKinley was gravely interested in the events occurring beyond the walls; Liam was eager to go back with Jamie and the other men. Sir Alfred even discussed methods of siege warfare, explaining some of the victories over different fortifications during his day, and Lauren was polite and interested in everything that Eric had to say. She didn't seem at all averse to asking after Jamie's welfare, and she was delighted to hear that her father had been contacted. She managed to learn more than Christina had. "We've heard that DeClabert has raised forces, though where he rides with them at the moment, we're not certain. But we have had word that Steven remains safely at Thistle-on-Downs, and that Edward has begun to consider his release.''

The unease in Christina's stomach became a knot. She rose suddenly, feeling pale and unwell.

"Christina, what is it?" Igrainia inquired, concerned.

"Nothing . . . just a fear for my brother, I suppose. No . . . relief."

Lauren appeared distressed as well. "DeClabert must have offered . . . must have made an offer to the king," she murmured.

Igrainia stood, coming around to Christina, calling to Berlinda for more wine. She pressed the chalice into Christina's fingers, urging her to take a sip. She did so. It seemed to steady her. "I will be anxious for any agreement that returns me to the graces of King Edward, and allows for my brother's freedom," she said firmly. Everyone in the room remained silent, staring at her. "It's a true cause for rejoicing," she added. "Angus, if you've finished, would you play? That one song you play with such a light sound?"

"Aye, Eric would enjoy the sound of the pipes, I'm certain," Angus agreed.

He began to play. She was encouraged to get her own lute, the gift so kindly given by Father MacKinley, and play with the Scotsman. She vowed that she would appear as determined as ever to return to England, dismissive of all things Scottish.

The night, however, seemed a terrible effort. She was glad by the time Liam saw her locked into her tower room.

In the morning, Eric was gone, returned to the field of battle.

Word had come that a supply train from the English base at Carlisle would be skirting the action at Dumfries, and heading toward the bastion of Dalswinton, certainly next on the list of fortifications to be fiercely attacked by Robert Bruce.

With the king's blessing, Jamie led a troop of ten hand-picked knights into the forest, where they backtracked first, found the trail the English supply train was taking, and then skirted ahead once again, finding the perfect area for an attack. There, the trail grew narrow, with heavy trees on either side, allowing for the attackers to swiftly take on the riders before they could amass in any number, or defend the supplies they carried.

He and Ragnor took to the oaks on either side at the precise point where they began the assault. The others were arrayed along the line at various advantage points. Once the attack had begun, they would rain down upon the English in quick unison.

They waited in learned patience. Then, they heard the first sounds of the caravan upon the trail. Jamie signaled to Ragnor, and they both prepared for the initial assault by stringing forest bows with slender arrows. When the first of the men appeared in the tight knot of the trail, Jamie let out a soft whistle. Before the English could begin to fathom what was happening, he and Ragnor let loose simultaneously with their arrows. Because the English were clad in full armor, their aim had to be perfect, catching their enemies high up on their throats.

The first two men fell without a whimper. Then, a cry of alarm rose, but it was short-lived, for arrows began to fly fast and furious from the trees. Once the English were aware of the attack, the Scotsmen began to fall from the trees, and in no time, the enemy scattered on the forest floor. Seven of their number cried out, begging for terms of surrender, and laying down their weapons. Jamie called out quickly that, in the name of Robert Bruce, all would then be spared.

He had commandeered a fine line of supplies. One wagon was filled with dried and salted pork and beef, another held a cache of extremely fine weapons, forged, apparently, by German masters. There were fine coats of mail, sheets of various body armor, and a treasure of gold coins as well. The men exalted in their find, stripped the surviving English of their armor and weaponry, and began the ride back to the king's position at Dumfries.

George, who had been going through the correspondence being sent on to the English strongholds and their commanders as they rode, told Jamie that he found a letter promising a second train of supplies, dated, and signed. He mulled the information, pleased to realize that they would most probably be able to seize upon those as well, since word could not get back to Carlisle in time to inform the leaders there that the first supplies had never arrived.

As he looked at another parchment, George grew silent. Frowning, Jamie asked him, ''What is it?''

''A large sum of gold is being offered for the safe return of Lady Christina of Hamstead Heath,'' he said. ''A messenger was to ride out from Dalswinton to find Robert Bruce, whatever his position, and tell him that the money reward, along with the exchange of our own Lord Henry Wharton, would be offered so that the lady might be given over to Lord Rowan DeClabert, at a place to be determined when the agreements are made.''

''Ah,'' Jamie murmured.

George was quiet for a moment.

''You can't mean to let it happen, Jamie.''

''Why not? I believe it's what she desires. The lady is an Englishwoman. Henry Wharton has always shown a fierce loyalty to Robert Bruce. The king will surely agree with these demands.''

''Of course,'' George said stiffly.

Jamie shook his head irritably. ''Her brother remains a prisoner. The king will not give anyone leave to attack anyone else anywhere until the four castles here fall, and

are razed to the ground. If these demands are not met, and
Steven is executed . . .''

"The king can stall the negotiations," George said firmly.

"The king is occupied with bringing all of Scotland under
his control—and preparing for the mass invasion he knows
Edward will lead when his victories threaten the last of
English power."

"The king will listen to you," George insisted.

Jamie glowered at him. "George, you're forgetting that
you're talking about a woman who planned to drug us all,
to see that we were turned over to English forces to face
execution. She would have betrayed us at Perth."

"Aye, well then, 'tis a pity she wasn't for our king, since
she's got such courage and resolve," George said.

Jamie urged his horse forward.

He had no intention of allowing a trade to take place so
quickly.

That night, at their campsite just beyond the reach of the
defenses at Dumfries, Robert Bruce was in an excellent
mood, delighted by the cache of money, food, and arms they
had procured. Jamie was somewhat loath to allow the king
to see the correspondence they had received, but by his
honor, he would not keep it from the king's view.

Robert Bruce read the many papers taken. Jamie remained
silent as he did so. When the king was finished, he looked
at Jamie. "Well?"

"Henry is a good man."

"A very good man. And I will have him returned. But
. . . he is in the care of an honorable man. We will wait on
these matters. After all, Jamie, I did leave the fate of the
hostages you took in your hands."

Jamie lowered his head, praying Bruce didn't see the
complete relief he was feeling.

He was startled when the king said, "I am loath to return a woman such as Christina to a bastard such as DeClabert!"

Jamie was aware, then, that the king was indeed on his side. And impatient with himself. Everything he had said to George was true. He was annoyed that her fate should mean anything to him; annoyed that he considered reckless action on her behalf. Irritated beyond belief that his brief days with her still haunted him, and had any bearing on his actions.

The king's camp outside Dumfries was large, filled with grooms, bearers, laundresses, and more. The young woman, Isolde, had followed in the wake of the army as well, and had determined that she would serve Jamie in all things. When he returned to his position that night, the woman was folding clean shirts for him in the small confines of his battle tent. Grayson was just outside, cleaning his armor, and the sounds of the camp, the business of repairing mail and armor, the talk of men, the songs of a few, the plaintive wail of once-outlawed pipes, filled the night.

"Sir James!" Isolde exclaimed, welcoming him with a warm smile. "The camp is alive with talk of how easily you fell upon the English, and slaughtered them all!"

An acrid taste filled his mouth. She seemed to relish the death of others.

"We slew none of those who surrendered," he said impatiently.

"But such a day's triumph! Surely, you are weary. I can see to your comfort."

She could. He had seldom seen a woman so suited to just that. He felt the temptation again to agree, simply to erase the memories of another, not suited at all to the distractions he wanted in life.

She sensed his hesitation, coming behind him, placing practiced fingers upon his shoulders and back. He hadn't known his own tension; the soreness that pervaded him. He allowed her to work her touch of magic.

Then he heard a voice beyond the tent—Eric, calling out to Grayson, and asking where he'd find his cousin.

Jamie pushed his way past Isolde, eager to see Eric. His cousin had just arrived on Loki, a great warhorse, bred from the same sire as his own Satan.

"All is well at Langley," Eric assured him in greeting.

Jamie nodded, relieved, determined that no hardship would come his cousin's way.

"And the captives?"

"Alive and well—obedient and models of deportment," Eric assured him. "Liam is in something of a temper, champing at the bit, since he believes he should be assailing the walls of the English, rather than looking after a slip of a girl."

"Igrainia?"

"Ah, well, you know my wife. She is in deepest sympathy with another Englishwoman held captive at Langley."

"As well she would be," Jamie murmured. He looked at Eric curiously. "Another communication was found today in a supply train headed for Dalswinton. DeClabert has offered money, and Edward's promise that Henry would be exchanged along with the gold, if the lady of Hamstead Heath was returned to him."

"Ah. So . . . what has the king decided he will do?"

"Nothing, as yet."

"I believe that he feels that the matter is in your hands."

"Perhaps. All right, yes, he has said so. The matter is in my hands. But perhaps the exchange should be made."

"Would you really consign any woman to such a life?" Eric asked.

"Women go where they are told, and marriages are seldom made for happiness. We owe the English nothing; our numbers were brutalized and decimated. Your first wife died by a disease brought on by your imprisonment by the English; mine died in unspeakable agony, and there was nothing left for us to do but sift the ashes. I'd have done anything rather than allow Fiona to die in that fire. I've been angry, thinking that Christina was dangerous wherever she might be, but I've felt a sense of sympathy, and the desire to keep her from returning. But since she so desperately desires to sacrifice herself to DeClabert for her brother's sake, then perhaps it is the best and kindest answer.''

"Still . . .'' Eric murmured. ''Perhaps there is more that I should tell you.''

"Is there news from England of which I'm not aware?''

"No, just a suspicion . . . and not from England, but information I believe you should know.''

Jamie frowned, listening as Eric continued to talk.

When he at last parted from his cousin, his temper was sorely frayed. He was angry with himself, as much as anyone else.

He'd known better than to become involved in any way with the enemy. He'd known that it was a woman of position he'd held, from the moment she'd tricked him into allowing her and her two friends to come along with him, as hostages.

He'd known and now, he didn't know why he felt a twinge of emotion within that was almost rage.

Returning to his tent, he realized that he wasn't alone. Isolde had cast aside her clothing, and awaited him on the pallet on the ground.

She was the last thing he wanted at the moment.

"My lord,'' she murmured huskily.

He shook his head, ignoring her state of seduction. "Isolde, there's a tremendous amount on my mind; I have to see the king again.''

"I'll wait.''

"No, Isolde."

"You're a fool. So much is offered to you, and you are pining after the enemy!" she spat out furiously.

"I pine for no one, Isolde. There is a lot on my mind. I need my solitude tonight. Be gone when I return."

He left his tent, still in a turmoil, deep in thought.

He had no idea of what an enemy he had created that night.

CHAPTER 13

The days at Langley continued to be pleasant, especially in the absence of her lord, though in the time that passed, Eric returned occasionally for a night or two, delighting his wife, and bringing the news that the siege continued, but would break soon, for no supplies were getting through to Dumfries. Christina wasn't sure exactly how it mattered; when Robert Bruce leveled Dumfries to the ground, he would merely move on to another position.

As it was, the situation in England remained tense.

Eventually, however, a great army would be raised once again. Edward II, though not the man his father had been, would order enough of the finest military men of his country to see that the Scots, so outnumbered, so much poorer in arms and supplies, were brought to their knees again. Such a time would come, she was certain. But in the meantime, the days passed.

There were days that were severely cold, and those that

were far more mild, and on the mild days, even Liam somewhat relaxed his guard, allowing Magnus or Angus to take on the task of watching her every minute.

The two were fond of being outdoors, and in the courtyard, and working with their young friends. She knew that the war had stretched on so long that those who had been babes when Edward I first set his eyes on the country were now men. Thus it was that every generation felt obliged to teach the next all it knew, whether the youth would grow up to be men-at-arms or musicians.

It was while she watched Magnus at work one day, training a young man at his defense with a sword, that she found herself suddenly becoming part of the action.

"Magnus!" she declared, drawing the attention of teacher and student. "Forgive me, please, but strange as you may think it . . . I've some knowledge of what you're about." Both Magnus and the young man stared at her, as if she had truly lost her mind. She smiled, approaching them. "You, dear Magnus, are a giant! Young Simon here is not. He is very slim, but lithe. A man of greater power, such as you, would eventually take him in such a contest. But where such a man as Simon can take on a stronger knight is in his very slimness and agility. May I?" She asked Simon for his sword. Simon looked at Magnus. The huge fellow certainly thought that she'd be no contest for him and grinned, warning her, "My Lady Christina, I'd be loath to harm you in any way!"

"You won't harm me," she assured him, and added earnestly, "Magnus, in my home, there were just my brother and I most often, and he didn't mind at all that I trained with him—like most men, he was amused by my efforts. At first. I swear, I can help young Simon."

"Lady, come at me then!" Magnus told her.

"No, you see, that is the crux of this matter. You must come at me."

Magnus sighed, then thought he would make a quick matter of it, disarming her. But as he brought his great hulk toward her, she eluded him, using his weight and size against him, escaping beneath the very sword arm he wielded with such power. The contest went on; she knew that she needed leverage each time she parried a blow from him, and she found it, wedging her own weapon against the ground, and springing around his size after each assault on his part. She was so intent on their contest that she was unaware that they had drawn a crowd. Young Simon was gleeful; there were many calling out words of encouragement to her, and many indignant that Magnus should be taking so long to make an end of it.

Magnus, of course, had no intention of really hurting her, and of course, she didn't intend to inflict so much as a scratch on the friendly giant. So the battle went on, each of them making a gain, giving to the other. There were cheers on her behalf and applause.

Determined to keep the admiration and respect of those watching, Christina threw herself wholeheartedly into the difficult task before her, and became unaware when the crowd grew silent.

Equally unaware of the riders who had come into the courtyard. There came a time when Magnus suddenly cried, "Enough, lady! One of us will begin to bear the scars of such an engagement!" She paused, handing the weapon to young Simon, and happily accepting the engulfment of her opponent's arms as Magnus swept her up in a hug. Then, he pulled back, and she realized that the crowd was silent. There were no cheers, no clapping, and the onlookers weren't even observing her. She glanced up, and saw the horseman, and thought at first that Eric had returned once again.

Then it seemed her knees would give way; a clammy chill swept over her, and she realized first that the horse was not Eric's—it was Jamie's Satan. And the man on the horse was not Eric, but Jamie, with Ragnor and George mounted and armed at his side, Grayson bringing up the rear. The sun was on his hair, catching the gleam of the red within it, and she felt the fool that she hadn't realized that it was he from the moment she had glanced up.

Magnus was not disturbed by the sight, but left her side with a cry of pleasure to greet the other two. They were quickly surrounded.

"Dumfries?" Magnus asked anxiously.

"Dumfries has fallen. The king's men now dismantle it, stone by stone," Jamie assured Magnus. "So, Magnus, you are teaching the Lady Christina the fine art of self-defense?"

Magnus let out a hearty roar. "Ah, Jamie, I'm afraid the lady has been teaching our slender friends the art of defense against a greater power. She's quite good, with an amazing talent for a slight woman."

"An amazing talent, I'm sure," Jamie said coolly.

Christina stood very still, saying nothing. She was aware that the fight had left her with loosened hair all about, and a fair amount of courtyard dust upon her person.

Jamie dismounted from Satan. "Come, Lady Christina, I find it quite fascinating that we should bring in an Englishwoman bred within the finest of families to teach the common man of Scotland how to survive. I'm humbled, and willing to learn more myself." He was not wearing a helm, but was clad in mail, enforced by plate. He strode toward her, taking the weapon from Simon, pressing it toward her. "Come, my lady, I'm an eager student as well."

He wasn't in the least an eager student. He was curbing his anger as best he could in a manner that was incredibly alarming.

"I wouldn't think to bring arms against you, Sir James,"
she murmured.

"Take the sword."

Rather than have her fingers broken, she did so.

"Show me what my men should learn, my lady."

She shook her head.

"I insist."

She felt a flare of her own temper. "They should learn,
first, not to accept a silly courtyard challenge from a man
in full armor while they wear no protection themselves."

"Indeed, remember that well, men. When upon a battlefield with an enemy clad in mail, be certain that he hasn't
the right to crush your country, because he is armored, and
you are not. But under the circumstances, if that is all that
stops you, Christina . . . Grayson, a hand here, please!"

And so, Grayson quickly dismounted as well, unbuckling
plate, and helping with the weight of the mail. A moment
later, Jamie stood in shirt and breeches, his own great sword
drawn, staring at her. "Well?"

"Who would ever think to teach you, or imagine that
your prowess could be improved, Sir James?" she inquired.

"I am ever willing to learn, my lady, anything about my
enemy. It's best at all times to be prepared, to know the
power coming against one. Only a fool thinks himself superior before he has tested the strengths, whatever they be, of
the enemy." His eyes narrowed. "Come at me, my lady. I
insist."

She remained still. He brought his sword against hers,
though she had it rested on the ground. She was off guard,
and therefore the strength of his attack brought the shudder
of steel throughout the length of her arms, and into her
shoulders. Infuriated, she stepped back with the weapon,
determined once again that she would show him a thing or
two.

When he drew back with his sword arm to send the force of the next blow shuddering through her, she was prepared. She side-stepped the blow, and left his weapon flailing the air. She was instantly at his back, ready to attack, yet once again, she let him take on the offensive. He was not a man of Magnus's great height and size; few men were, and she was certain that he was somewhat aware of her tactics, yet he let her move again, and again, and again.

And finally, she realized his intent. She was tiring.

They faced one another across a circle. "This, sir, is not a fair fight!" she called to him. "I've been engaged with a mighty opponent for some time preceding this farce you insist upon waging! I am weary due to the previous battle engaged!"

"Ah, there is an excellent tactic when meeting the English upon the field!" Jamie said. "Tell the man intent on your life that he is not being chivalrous, you've just spent long minutes engaged in a mortal battle with his countryman, now slain upon the field, and that he hasn't a right to take you to task when your sword arm is already weary!"

Laughter arose, newly arousing her temper, yet she did her best to contain it, far too aware that anger was often the greatest cause of a rash mistake. But whether such tactics would work upon a battlefield or not, he had her at an unfair advantage. She had met Magnus with no desire to hurt or injure the man; she had therefore fought long and strenuously to maintain her own health and welfare. When Jamie came at her next, she parried and fled, only to discover that he had feigned his blow, and was awaiting her movement, and her sword was caught to the earth by the force of his. His eyes caught hold of hers. A flick of his wrist brought the weapon from her grasp, and the force of that simple movement caused her to lose her footing. She slid to the ground, and was furious when she found that he had brought his weapon to her throat. She gazed at him, eyes glittering.

"But an incredible performance, my lady!" he said, drawing cheers from the onlookers.

She smiled. When he reached down to assist her, she pretended to accept his hand. Instead, she used the moment to send a handful of dirt into his eyes, then flew to her feet, and retrieved her weapon.

She wondered if his next move might not bring a sword right through her heart.

He blinked furiously, teeth gritting, as he circled her anew. "Leave it to a lady born and bred to fight in such a manner!" he taunted.

"Ah, Sir James! Would you tell the enemy upon the field that it isn't a fair way in which to fight, to cast dirt into the eyes when a life is at stake?" she returned.

He inclined his head, accepting the truth of her statement. But his next step forward was so powerful and swift that when she raised her weapon in defense, she found herself on her knees, barely deflecting the blow. And before she could gather the strength in her aching arms to attempt a countermove, the sword had been taken from her hand, and she was pulled to her feet.

"An excellent lesson from our guest!" Jamie cried, turning her to the crowd. "We must be grateful for all that we have learned!"

Christina felt an increasing uneasiness at his apparent delight as he presented her to the cheering men around her. She hadn't realized her own exhaustion, and felt his hold as if he were keeping her up, and she had suddenly become a great weight herself.

He moved her toward the tower keep, and she stumbled due to the length of his steps, but quickly regained her balance, determined not to falter. Once inside the keep, she found herself propelled straight toward the stairs, despite the company in the hall, including Igrainia who had risen with great pleasure to greet Jamie.

"Igrainia, forgive me, I'll return immediately, but it seems that the Lady Christina is sorely in need of a few moments rest—and a brush, as so often seems to be the case with her."

"Aye, Jamie, but Dumfries has fallen?"

"Indeed."

"And Eric . . . ?" she asked anxiously.

"Not far behind me," he assured her quickly.

Lauren, sewing in the hall as was her custom, looked up without a word. Jamie nodded a polite greeting to her, still heading for the stairs. Christina found herself pressed before him, her temper growing with every forced step. By the time they were on their way up the second flight of stairs, she jerked free, pulling away from him. "Enough! I can manage stairs with far greater speed and dexterity when not being so rudely shoved from behind."

"Then move, my lady, at that great speed and dexterity you promise."

She swung around, hurrying on with tremendous haste, heading for the tower room which had become quite comfortable, and somehow personal to her, during her stay.

She assumed that he would follow, ready to rip into her regarding her audacity in believing that there was anything she might teach his men, furious that she had taken up a sword, that any man had been fool enough to allow her a sword.

But to her amazement, he didn't follow her into the room. The door slammed once she had entered, and she heard the sound of the bolt.

* * *

Igrainia had cleared the hall by the time he reached the level there. She had sent for wine and food, and the fire had been poked and prodded until the hall offered the greatest level of comfort. She awaited whatever he could tell her.

"Dumfries fell on February seventh," he told her, shaking his head. "The commander there was Dugald Macdowall. Six years ago, Macdowall was in good part responsible for the execution of two of our king's brothers, and though we were all furious and waited to warn him that Macdowall will only turn against him again, the king chose to let him go free. He is so bent on healing the factions in this country that he has been generous beyond belief. Macdowall is a bitter man, determined on his own course. I believe he will do nothing but join again with the English, and had he been the one to win the battle, Bruce's head would be rolling as we speak."

Igrainia, seated in a chair before the fire, said softly, "But Dumfries has fallen. And Robert Bruce is in power. From all that has happened, and for the fight that he wages, you surely understand that by being merciful he may bring those within Scotland who are against him to recognize what he envisions as a free nation!"

Jamie remembered his frustration with the king. All of them had felt it; every one of his knights and barons had rued his mercy at the fall of Dumfries. The king had been determined, and so, Macdowall had ridden free.

"What now?" Igrainia asked.

"Onward, to Dalswinton, where already, men are harrowing the defenders. The king is determined that Buittle and Caerlaverock must fall as well, and quickly. Spring will come then, and an easier time of it for the English, for those who are not familiar with the countryside.''

"Eric is coming here now, though?'' she asked quietly.

"Aye, that he is,'' he assured her gently.

"What news of hostage negotiations?'' she asked.

"Little more than you know already, except that . . .'' He paused, shrugging. "Despite the fact that the king's very good friend Henry has been offered as part of a bargain, when Dumfries fell and we had the great argument over Macdowall, the king made certain concessions to all of us, saying that in a man's life there were certain moves that he felt he must make, right or wrong. He admitted he might be a fool in releasing Macdowall, and in turn, he laid the situation regarding Christina, Lauren, and Sir Alfred entirely at my feet.''

"So . . . what will you do?''

"I'm not certain. Is what your husband told me true?'' he demanded.

Igrainia hesitated. "I believe so, yes.''

"Has she said anything to you?''

"No.''

"So . . . the lady would totally ignore the situation, and take every risk upon herself.''

Igrainia rose suddenly, and he was startled to see a flicker of anger in her eyes. "And you, my fine cousin-in-law! You've no feeling in this matter for your own involvement?'' She shook her head. "Jamie, I remember a time when your kindness to me was all that seemed to make life bearable. And yet with you, that is a kindness that extends only to a woman you see as a sister. Can you truly be so dismissive when it comes to others? Did you feel that you were on a battlefield all alone, and that whatever course you took was of no matter, that hostages were but the bounty of war, to be used and discarded like a stolen horse?''

He stared at her, eyes narrowing. "Igrainia, you don't know the circumstances at all."

"No, I don't," she agreed.

"I certainly never attacked the woman."

"Strange, for she seems to feel no sense of lost love for you."

"She has but one thing on her mind, and that is her brother's freedom. And she would give up my blood, your blood, and her own to achieve that goal. Had I considered letting the negotiations go as she certainly longed? Yes, definitely. There is no way to fight against such a set mind, though with any young woman out there, being good King Robert's knight in every way, I would have shunned whatever great reward was offered out of simple kindness. She doesn't want it. But now . . . well, the negotiations will indeed wait."

"And you'll leave her here, and become angry any time any of us shows the least compassion?" she murmured.

"If you wish, I can see that she is removed."

"Jamie, you held this fortress at Eric's side through many a turbulent time; it is your family holding, until such a time when you and many others may reclaim the lands that are your right by birth. I simply think that . . . you are being unfair."

"Am I? We'll have the entire company for supper this evening, and throw out the offer of exchange. No matter what the circumstances, she'll eagerly accept. You'll see," he said dourly. He rose, walking around her chair and speaking gently from behind her, "As you should have seen her outside, battling Magnus."

"What?" Igrainia said with alarm. "Magnus would kill her!"

"No, that was not the case. Your fragile guest, madam, is far more adept at arms than even I had imagined, and I have seen her ability with a sword before. You mustn't ever let down your guard. Speak to her yourself if you would, and don't feel that she is a gentle creature, and that you can let her roam so freely as you would like.''

Christina was not in the least surprised when Garth saw to it that a number of servants brought a hip tub, cauldrons of hot water—and a brush.

She was angry enough to ignore the bath, but far too sore to allow herself to do so. She also felt herself incredibly torn between indignation and . . .

Longing.

But there was certainly no reason to believe that Jamie felt the least actual affection for her. The days they had spent together now seemed almost as much a part of another world as Hamstead Heath. He had been busy for weeks seeing to the destruction of Dumfries. Part of a large camp, filled with knights and men-at-arms, of course, but many other followers as well. With the extent of his bitterness, she was certain that no female form meant any more than any other. Her only value lay in what she could bring the Scots, and she had been informed, early on, that her cattle were certainly more important than she.

That didn't matter terribly. But suddenly, her appearance did. There was little else to salvage but pride, and so she first luxuriated in the steaming heat that seemed to ease some of the pain and cramps she had acquired while fighting, and then worked to clean her flesh and hair. When she emerged from the tub, she sat before the fire and loosened every snarl from her hair, brushing it to a high, clean shine.

She watched the door uneasily all the while, certain that he would reappear. He did not.

She was furious with herself that it mattered.

At length, what seemed like hours later, there was a tapping at the door. She pulled her dignity about her and bid her visitor enter.

It wasn't Jamie, but Father MacKinley, kind as always, ready to escort her below.

She accepted his arm, grateful that she was still allowed down, now that Jamie was in residence.

As they walked down the stairs, she became aware of the sound of the pipes, and the lute. When she and Father MacKinley arrived at the foot of the stairs, she saw that it was Jamie playing the lute, and she was amazed at the way his fingers moved over the instrument. He sat with Igrainia near the fire as the servants prepared the massive table in the great hall, and they sang together while playing, a silly light tune that was enhanced by Angus's talent with the pipes. Jamie's appearance startled her in many ways, for she had never seen him so at ease. His smile was quick and charming for Lauren; when Berlinda came to take Wulfgar to bed for the night, he was quick to laugh with the boy, throw him in the air, and catch him again, delighting the child. All this, until he saw that she had come in on Father MacKinley's arm, and then again, his eyes narrowed, and the look of distaste within him was such that she felt a terrible unease.

She took her place at the table between Liam and Magnus. As the meal began, Liam questioned Jamie endlessly, curious about every moment of the siege of Dumfries. He was eager to join with the men again when they moved on to the next assault, and Jamie assured him that he would be free to join in the fight.

She wondered if that meant a new guard would be found for her . . .

Or if a guard would no longer be necessary, since she would no longer be a burden.

Lauren brought the conversation to the point at hand, quietly asking Jamie if there had been any more word from her father.

"Aye, lady," he said gravely. "The count is making arrangements for your return. He has offered, as well, to see that arrangements are made for Sir Alfred, grateful that he has been at your side since Hamstead Heath."

Christina knew that he was purposely omitting any reference to her, forcing her to ask. Annoyed, she did so.

"And what of the last of your hostages, Sir James?" she inquired, her tone beyond a doubt hostile.

"Ah, yes, Lady Christina. As to you . . . well, you'll be delighted to hear, I'm certain, that you've proven to be of tremendous worth. Not only has Rowan DeClabert offered a substantial sum for your return, he has offered as well to exchange an English prisoner, a man near and dear to the heart of Robert Bruce. Imagine, my lady, that we hadn't even thought to take hostages at Hamstead Heath, and you have brought about such incredible largesse for our people."

His tone was as cool as her own. Christina forced herself to remain perfectly still, straight, pleased by the information given.

"And was there word regarding my brother?"

"None, I'm afraid, but surely, considering the eagerness of those in power for your safe return, your brother's circumstances will be part of any negotiation—among the English."

She fell silent, wishing she could leave the table and fly into the night.

"Thank God, then," she murmured, "that things are progressing so smoothly."

"Of course," Jamie said, "you are not just willing, but eager, to see that these negotiations continue with all speed?"

"Of course."

"DeClabert will be pleased."

She wished that she had never spoken to him about Rowan. She felt extremely ill, suddenly, once again wishing that she could simply rise, escape the hall, and run into the cleansing cold of the night.

But she could not, of course.

As the food was cleared away, she started to rise, ready to beg that she be brought back to her cage in the tower of the castle. But she was quickly disabused of such a thought when Jamie said to her, "Are you in such a hurry tonight, Lady Christina? It's my understanding that you spend your evenings in the hall with the others, and that indeed, you've exceptional talent with instruments, and that you've entertained everyone here night after night."

She forced a smile. "Ah, well, Sir James, now that you have returned, I will leave such matters to you."

"But I am pleased that you should stay. After all, you will be leaving us soon—that is your desire? Therefore, I may not have much chance remaining to marvel at the wonder of your talents."

"A pity, since I spent the afternoon displaying a talent at arms—nothing, of course, compared to the grandeur of such a knight as you, Sir James—but nonetheless, for a woman, quite exhausting. I would consider it an extreme kindness to be allowed to retire."

"I'm afraid I'm not feeling quite so benevolent this evening, my lady," Jamie said.

No one else was speaking. Every eye in the room seemed to pass from one to the other. She was aware that he didn't intend to let her win any battles that evening.

"As you wish then. I will be as delighted to stay this evening as I will be to return to my own people."

"You're incredibly gracious, Lady Christina."

"I still strive to be the best hostage possible."

''Do you?'' he inquired politely, and she found that a rush of blood was coloring her cheeks, as she wondered just what implication he heard in her words.

''If music will please you.''

''Music?''

Still, no one else spoke. Their eyes had all returned to her face once again, wondering what reply she would make to Jamie.

''Indeed, that's what you're asking, is it not?''

''Naturally. It's my understanding that a lute has been made specifically for your use. So, come, join me, we'll take the chairs at the hearth.''

He had risen as well. His hand was stretched out to her, and she had little choice but to accept it. He led her around the table and to the chairs. Angus had arranged for the instruments to be gathered once again. Jamie strummed the strings of his own instrument, watching her. ''I'm curious . . . do you know this one? It's a sad tune, written upon the death of one of our heroes, William Wallace. Of course, you were very young at his death. I wonder, were you in London at the time? You might have been in the crowd that watched and cheered as he was tortured, castrated, disemboweled, and finally beheaded.''

''No, I don't believe I was there at the time.''

''Ah, well, strum along, I'm sure you'll find the melody appealing—Angus gives it such a touch of pathos.''

He began to play. And again she was startled that such a man could have such a pleasing voice, and such an ability with something so lovely as the lute. The arch of his brow reminded her that he had requested that she play along, and she did so. The tune was lovely, and the words were not so graphic or cruel as those he had used to describe the song. It was a beautiful piece, and the sound of his voice was oddly gentle and hypnotic.

And yet, when they were done, there was something in his look that seemed hostile, even when she had so diligently followed his direction. And despite her yearning to end the night on a peaceful note and be left alone to rue the future in her tower room, she could never quite leave well enough alone. And so she found herself informing him that she knew a song about a king who had stumbled on his way to the throne. She began to sing, and was on her own. The name Robert Bruce was never mentioned, but the tale was one of betrayal and murder, leading to the acquisition of a crown. No one joined in, and the room was entirely silent, other than the soft gasp Lauren emitted in horror when she had finished.

"Perhaps it's time you do retire," Jamie said, eyeing her coldly.

"Certainly. As you wish. I do, as always, strive to please," she reminded him. She set down the instrument and started for the stairs. The room remained still.

She thought that no one had followed her. She heard nothing behind her on the stairs. But when she reached the room and thought to close herself within, the door refused to close, and she discovered that he was indeed behind her. He didn't seem to be using any force at all, yet the door sprang back despite her efforts to close it. She backed into the room, wary, not knowing his intent in the least, since the cool hostility that still settled about him like a cloak seemed to preclude any interest in her as a person.

"All right," she said, standing by the fire. "I admit, I'm at a loss. Perhaps the song was not a good choice in this hall, but then again, sir, we are, as you have reminded us, nothing more than hostages who have almost shockingly proven to be of value. And as to this afternoon . . . I was actually showing my own enemies an excellent means of defense. If there is anything more that I have done to offend you, I can say that I am sincerely sorry, since I've not the least idea of what it might be. And, sir, since it appears you would just as soon strangle me as look at me, I might beg your indulgence in leaving, since my person is suddenly valuable to someone.''

He strode into the room, causing her to leap back as he walked to the fire, idly warming his hands.

"I think I can refrain from strangling you."

"I don't understand—"

"Really?" he inquired, turning on her. "So . . . you are so eager for the exchange? Even under the circumstances?"

"Especially under the circumstances."

"DeClabert will probably intend marriage the minute you're in his power."

"I'm aware of that."

"And it will, of course, be convenient."

"If he lets Steven go, of course."

She was amazed at the way he looked at her, as if she were a disease.

"I don't understand you at all!" she cried. "Did you think that I would have become so enamored of your cause of the decency that admittedly takes place at Langley, and forget who I am, where I have come from, and what my own obligations must be?"

"Your own obligations . . ." he repeated, and she was startled when he suddenly had her by the shoulders. "You feel no obligation to yourself, or to me?"

She jerked away. "Should I? Have you felt the least obligation toward me, sir? I think not. You have one goal in mind, and that is to serve your king, to get the despised English out of your country. You're bitter toward me, and my people, and you will never forgive anyone who is English for what has been done to you!"

"You're mistaken," he told her. "No matter how dark

and dire the circumstances, I have never hated an entire race for the incredible brutality of a few men. Igrainia is English, for God's sake!''

She had done nothing but anger him further, and she remained at such a loss that she longed to climb the walls, escape in any way imaginable.

''I owe you nothing!'' she whispered.

''You owe me nothing?'' he repeated. ''Well, it's not a matter of debt, is it? Rather it is a situation of right and wrong, and blood.''

She was stunned when he turned away from her, starting to leave the room.

''What is the matter with you?'' she cried, coming after him. ''Did the siege turn into a fierce battle? Were you hit upon the helm with a battle-axe? I am supposed to owe you? Because . . . you didn't want hostages and I persisted to such a point that . . . you gave in? Sir James, you didn't bring me along with anything that resembled kindness or chivalry. And all you had to do was *think* that I might have been giving regard to my own countrymen, and you were ready to pull your chains ever tighter around me. One could hardly say that you were particularly cordial at any time, even though it's true that neither could one say you were particularly cruel. And again, as for you, it seems that you have nothing but anger and bitterness, so what you can expect from me, I cannot begin to imagine.''

He'd held at the door, then turned suddenly, and she was again alarmed and confused by his scathing assessment of her.

''Common decency,'' he said. ''But then, that means nothing in your pursuit of your brother's freedom. The pity of it is, that, were you allowed your way, you would probably suffer an ungodly misery within weeks, perhaps days. And your brother Steven might live, and do so in misery, furious that he hadn't the power to stop you when you sold your soul and your honor for his life.''

''Well, honor is something of which I don't seem to have much left,'' she murmured.

''Much?'' he inquired flatly. ''None would be a far truer assessment.''

She was amazed and appalled. ''Thankfully,'' she said smoothly, ''there are men of honor here. I am loath to remain any longer in a stronghold held by any member of your family or clan. There is surely someone who can go to Robert Bruce for me, let him know that I am throwing myself on his renowned mercy, and would happily bide my time in any wretched dungeon as long as it kept me from the derision of your scorn and mockery.''

He leaned hard against the door, folding his arms over his chest. ''Robert Bruce takes the point of mercy to foolhardiness. He has taken a chance on forgiving the very man responsible for the execution of two of his brothers, all in the hope of a united Scotland. Imagine, he had forgiven that man! But as to you, my lady. No. You will not be held in any fortress not being held by my kin, nor by any man not my relation, nor a friend knit even more tightly to me by the bond of warfare and the bloodshed we've witnessed. Goodnight, my lady.'' He started out the door, then paused.

The door closed; the bolt slid, and she was left shaking, still at the most incredible loss.

She paced before the fire, mulled his every word, and her own, and could think of nothing that would draw such a reaction from him. She sat at last before the fire, watching the flames, furious with herself because she had truly prayed that he not come in contact with an English battle-axe. And when she had seen him today . . .

She had come alive. She had been thrilled, no matter what words of derision and warning she had given herself. She had imagined that he would have burst into the tower room, and that he would have been nearly insane, as she felt herself, at the time that had passed since he had seen her.

At length, she shivered. Her muscles were sore from exertion; she felt strangely ill. She changed into her nightgown, slipped beneath the covers, and drew them as tightly about her as she could manage.

The night seemed very cold. And yet, she was determined that she would find warmth, and she would sleep, escape through her dreams.

Exhaustion embraced her. She tossed and turned, but at last, slept.

She was startled awake by a furtive tapping on the door, and then the creak of the bolt. Christina sat up, afraid, drawing the covers against her, aware that Jamie would never come in such a fashion.

She was amazed when she saw that it was Sir Alfred timidly entering the chamber. "Sir Alfred?"

"Yes, my lady! And shh!"

She fell silent, frowning, as Sir Alfred made his way into the room, nervously standing by the side of the bed. "They think I've long been asleep."

"There's no guard just outside my door?"

"No, not now, but they will be returning, so you must let me talk, quickly. I listened to a conversation between Lady Igrainia and Sir James . . . he has written already to accept DeClabert's offer."

"I see." She was horrified, but wouldn't give her true feelings away to Sir Alfred.

"You will be returned as per the agreement offered, and if—and only if—your brother is also vindicated of any wrongdoing with the Scots, since his sister would not have been James's hostage if Steven had been in league with the Scottish king."

She let out a long breath. ''Well, then,'' she said painfully, ''we have succeeded completely, and he has shown a greater kindness than I had imagined.''

Sir Alfred shook his head. ''There is more to the contract, my lady.''

She frowned. ''And what would that be?''

''You're not to be returned until a year and a day from January seventh last.''

''A year and a day?'' she echoed incredulously, trying to fathom what possible reasoning could be behind such a condition.

''Until the child is born, and weaned.''

''What child?''

''Yours, my lady.''

''But . . . there is no child!'' she said, astonished.

Sir Alfred was startled. ''You're certain?''

She stared at him, feeling as if blankets of ice suddenly swept around her. No, she wasn't certain that there *wasn't,* but neither had she thought, or so much as hinted, to any human being alive that there might be.

''I'm—I'm certain!'' she said, but faltered.

Sir Alfred, staring at her, apparently decided he had enough of an answer, and he was also nervously watching the door, terrified of being caught especially with Sir James at residence in the castle. ''I try very hard to listen, to know what is happening,'' he told her hurriedly. ''For you . . . because I always knew that you cared for me, forced them to take on an old man of little use, lest I be punished in some way. Perhaps it has seemed that I have been of no use to you, but I have tried to silently ingratiate myself, so that I can know, always, what is being said when our enemies think themselves alone!''

''Sir Alfred! You have never been useless, and will never be so!''

His dignity didn't demand assurances; his fear was driving him, and she was grateful. He had taken quite a chance, coming to her.

"I must go!" he said, and turning, he sprinted with amazing agility to the door, slipped outside it—and returned the bolt to its locked position.

Christina felt the firelight dapple the covers, and once again, she shivered. She waited, then rose, walking to the door, a fury settling over her as if a wick of fire burned blue within her. She tried to fight the anger, thinking it was usually so much better when tested cold. She warned herself that she couldn't give away the fact that Sir Alfred had come to her with the information.

She could keep from giving him away. She was adept at lying—so he had told her.

She came to the door, the bolted door to her tower prison, and gave no thought to the hour of the night. She began to pound against it with a vengeance, demanding that she be seen.

The door was opened.

And there was Jamie. Wet and dripping, down to nothing but a linen towel around the waist. She backed away almost instantly, astounded. Then she realized that he had come running up from below, when her tantrum threatened to wake the whole castle.

She could see the stairs. And see that a flow of white material disappeared along the lower hallway. *He had been with someone.*

Stunned, hurt, and furious, she stepped back in the room. He followed, closing the door behind him, eyes narrowed. "What is it that you're about now, my lady? As you're surely aware already, there are dungeons here, cells below within the crypts, and if you scream and rage there, no one

will be assaulted by the sounds in the night, for no one will
hear you there.''

"I've no intention of continuing to wake others," she
informed him. "I needed to see you for just a moment."

"And that is because . . . ?"

She took a step forward, furious.

"Because it was necessary to my sanity to inform you
about something regarding yourself."

"And that is?"

"You are, beyond a doubt, the biggest *ass* in all of Scotland!" she informed him. And because she was suddenly
very afraid of tears of sheer frustration, pain, and rage suddenly spilling from her eyes, she took a single step closer,
and with all speed, slapped him as hard as she could manage.

CHAPTER 14

No one took such action without expecting that there would be a price to pay.

And she was willing to pay it.

If he knocked her to the floor, broke her jaw, snapped her neck, it would not be too steep a price to pay for the satisfaction of saying what she felt, and seeing her handprint upon his cheek.

But as he stood there, not moving, not retaliating, the courage that had driven her began to fade. He stared at her, obviously placing an exceedingly tight rein on his temper.

Then, after a moment, he stepped into the room, silently closing the door behind him. He leaned against it, crossing his arms over his bare chest, unaware of the water running from his wet hair down his cheeks.

''If you ever, ever, feel so inclined to speak or act like that again, Christina, be aware that I won't hesitate to return such a blow with a force that will send you to your knees.

Be glad as well that you didn't see fit to perform so in front of my men, because I would have been obliged to respond without warning. I promise you, you can be hurt.''

She kept her distance, so filled with rage and misery that none of it seemed to matter. If he would hurt her, cause her physical pain, she might even be glad, for then she could find a place to plant the roots of hatred, and pray that they would grow strong.

''Well, of course, Sir James. You wouldn't miss a chance to prove your great strength and prowess—over a woman.''

''We've learned not to trust a man, woman, or even a child with inclinations toward the enemy, Christina, so spare yourself attempts to cast shame upon me. So tell me now, quickly, what this is all about. Or prepare what you will to take below the stairs.''

She felt her heart leap. He wasn't as furious as he was dismissive. He had ridden away, forgotten the very brief time they had spent together, and found whatever he might have desired elsewhere. Maybe in many places. She didn't matter to him at all. He was simply convinced that she was going to bear a child with Scottish blood. She would be free to leave, but the child would not. And, of course, he had been implying that a speedy return would be *convenient* for her because she could so quickly marry Rowan DeClabert that the man might not suspect he harbored another man's child.

''You may take me wherever you so desire, and I don't care in the least. But you seem to be gravely mistaken on a matter in which I intend to correct you immediately, and therefore, perhaps, alleviate you of another burden. There is no child. I don't know who on earth, or what, would have given you such an idea. Rest assured. It isn't true.''

He arched a brow, and she saw that Sir Alfred had been right—yes, of course, that was exactly what he had thought.

"Did you hear me, did you comprehend me? There is no child. And you have the most incredible audacity to assume that I would simply marry a man—even such a ripe bastard as DeClabert—and think to foist another man's offspring on him. I used to pray that you wouldn't be hit by an English sword—now I will make my supplications nightly that one falls your way as soon as is humanly possible!"

He still didn't speak. Her frustration grew. "Do you understand me?"

"I understand," he said softly, after a moment, "that you remain the most reprehensible liar I've ever come across."

"What?"

"You heard me. I'm not at all sure how you heard about the reply being sent regarding your ransom and exchange, but your lies won't change it."

"You have the most incredible opinion of yourself, assuming that if you touch someone, she will create a life in your image. It isn't true!"

"I'm afraid that I have it on the highest authority, my lady."

"The highest authority? What on earth is the matter with you? *I* am the highest authority. This is insane."

"The letter has gone out already, Christina. You can give this up now."

She stared at him, stunned. "You bastard! You idiot bastard!" she breathed. "They'll kill him, they'll kill Steven for certain in that time, with that kind of a taunt . . . Oh, dear God! How could you have done such a thing, when it is all a lie!" Once again, but now without thought or reason, she raised her fists against him, furiously pounding against his chest with the full force of her terror and rage.

This time, it was something that he wouldn't tolerate, and she found her arms caught, herself flung about, elbows pinned as she nearly flew across the room to land upon the bed. In a matter of seconds, even as she gasped for a breath with which to continue her maddened fight, he was on top of her, straddling her, forcing down her wrists before she could let fly with another blow.

"Don't be an idiot, Christina—"

"Don't be an idiot! How can you say such a thing to me!"

"The reason wasn't given; merely the timing."

"But surely—"

"The king's wife was held by the English for nearly eight years!" he reminded her.

"Robert Bruce's wife is English," she spat out.

"Oh, yes. The daughter of one of the most powerful barons in all England. And still, my lady, the wife of the Scottish king, and kept from his side those many years. His sister and others were incarcerated for many, many years as well—a few in cages, attached to castle walls, that they might be shown to the entire populace. Robert Bruce's daughter was a prisoner of the English as well—once again, my lady, *for years.* So you'll understand that to this day, despite his many instances of mercy and incredible generosity, Robert Bruce is not customarily a man in a terrible hurry to return any prisoner in his keeping, certainly not after what was done to him."

"It remains insane. Your behavior will be like a signature on a death warrant for Steven!"

"If you think that you will throw yourself on DeClabert as things stand, you are indeed mad."

She glared up at him, still incredulous, and beyond fury. "Don't you understand? It isn't true!"

She felt the pressure of his hands on her wrists. She closed her eyes and shook her head with a sudden impatience, and sense of failure, loss, and doom. "I am telling you the truth. If anyone should know such a thing, it would be I! You've done nothing but irreparable damage, and on top of that you are hurting me! And there's nothing I can say that gets through your thick stone skull, so please—I shall be an angel of silence. Get off me, go back to whatever your entertaining pursuits were for the evening, and leave me be. There is no child. There will be no child.''

Nothing that she could say seemed to break through to him. He stared down at her, shaking his head with his contempt. ''We've a serious situation here, haven't we?'' he murmured at last.

''No! What you won't see is that there isn't a situation at all! It's most apparent that I disturbed you while you were engaged in . . . while you were engaged. Believe me, I am deeply sorry that I disturbed you. If you'll just leave, I'll not make another sound through the night, I swear it.''

''Ah, but is there anything sacred enough to you that your word, your promise, could be good?''

Suddenly he was up, but if she had thought that he had decided to leave her at last, she was mistaken. She was drawn from the bed as well. She was startled when he looked around the room, saw her mantle on the chair by the fire, and swept it around her shoulders.

He was still in a towel.

He had been struck by a battle-axe, she determined. He had lost his sense completely, and it was frightening indeed to see the madness he seemed to suffer.

''What on earth are you attempting now?'' she pleaded.

''Attempting? I do not attempt—I do, my lady.''

''But . . . you do what?''

''You're coming with me. We'll find out just what is important to you.''

''I'm leaving the castle now, with a man wrapped in linen in the midst of winter?''

"You're coming with me, however, whenever, I choose," he informed her.

Apparently she was, for he dragged her across the room, out the door, and down the stairs. On the second level, they burst through a doorway that led to another chamber. His bath was in it; the water apparently had grown cold, for no steam emitted from it. The room was well appointed and large, with swords and standards upon the walls, wardrobes, trunks, and a steel stand for his coat of armor.

The room was empty. Whoever had been with him—the woman in the white flowing gown who had disappeared down the hallway—had evidently fled elsewhere. He left Christina standing, in her mantle but barefoot, in the center of the room. He didn't dress, other than to sweep up his own wool mantle and cast it around his shoulders.

There was nowhere, of course, for her to go. But as she stood there, untouched for long seconds, she wondered if it might be possible just to run.

"There is nowhere to go, I assure!" he said, as if reading her mind. Then his fingers were around her wrists again, and in another second they were out the door, and down the stairs.

In the great hall, a number of men slept before the fire; hounds stirred and flicked their tails as they passed through.

One man remained awake, on guard perhaps, seated at the table, whittling patiently, as seemed to be the way to pass the time for many of their number. He looked up at Jamie, but merely to acknowledge Jamie's passing nod. He noted Christina, but went back to his task. If Jamie saw fit to drag a hostage through the castle in the wee hours of the morning, so be it.

A moment later, they were out the door, and into the courtyard. There were men on the battlements, but Jamie called out to them, and they gave no further note. The great drawbridge to the castle was raised, and would not be lowered until first light.

His hand remained upon her wrist with a tight hold defying her protest. She found that they were moving across to the chapel. It was unlocked, and from the wall outside, he brought in one of the torches that kept the courtyard illuminated by night. Inside, he found a wall bracket, and continued with her to the altar, where she found herself forced to her knees.

"Do you believe in God, my lady?" he demanded, staring down at her.

"Do you?"

"I'm not the one at question here, am I?"

"What difference does it make what I say? I tell you the truth, and you don't listen!"

"You can swear to me, before your God, that beyond all certainty, you're not having a child?"

She closed her eyes, lowered her head. "I can swear to you, before God, that I . . . that such an idea never so much as occurred to me before tonight!"

He hunched down by her, taking her chin firmly in his hand, and forcing her eyes to his. "All right, Christina, let's put it this way. Before God, if you attempt any violence against yourself, or against this child, in any way whatsoever, I will find your brother and kill him myself, do you understand?"

She gasped, horrified by the threat. "I have never thought to throw myself from a window, or from the battlements! There has never been a time when you could have possibly believed that I meant to take my own life!"

"But there are things that women can do. And I swear, if you do any such thing, I will find Steven, and kill him. Do you understand now?"

She was freezing in the cold chapel. And very afraid. The

torch illuminated so very little. Christ on the crucifix looked down at her. The cold stone of the altar seemed to eclipse her. Marble angels stared at her.

"I understand that you are as cruel as any Englishman has ever been to an enemy," she told him, feeling as if the world reeled.

"You've been given fair warning. And I mean what I say."

"All right! I swear on my brother's life that I have no intention of taking my own. And if this ridiculous story were true, I swear that I would do nothing—*on my brother's life!* to a child, if ever I were to have one. There—so avowed. I understand completely. But there is nothing to understand!"

He released her, straightening. "Before God, Christina," he said quietly.

She shook her head helplessly. "Aye, before God."

He turned, starting back down the aisle, taking the torch from the bracket. Frozen on her knees, she didn't move, alert and wary of his next action.

"Let's go. It's very cold."

Cold, yes. She was frozen through. So much so that her limbs didn't function. He came back impatiently, taking her hand. Drawn up, she followed him out. In the courtyard, her bare feet crunched over patches of ice that had formed on the dirt. They returned to the hall, where once again, the hounds stirred, looked up, and laid their heads back down. They traversed the two levels of stairs without a word. The door to her tower room was pushed open and she ignored him then, walking ahead, going to the fire that burned in the hearth and coming close, trying to thaw the frost that seemed to permeate her.

He didn't leave. She knew that he was there, though she didn't hear the door close. A moment later, she was aware that he had taken the chair by the fire. She rose stiffly at last, only her feet still icy cold. She ignored him, walking by him. He hadn't shed his mantle; neither did she. She crawled up on the bed, her feet beneath her. He continued to stare into the flames, apparently oblivious to her.

At last, she eased her feet back beneath the covers, still so cold that she was glad of her mantle as well. She laid her head upon the pillow, and, after a few moments, closed her eyes. In time, she drifted, and dozed.

She awoke later, fighting the discomfort of some restriction. She started, alarmed, aware that someone was with her.

"Stop, Christina. I'm just trying to help you from your mantle before you strangle yourself."

She realized that he was next to her. The dying fire cast a soft golden glow on his shoulders and chest. His eyes were intent upon his task as he twisted her upward to bring the wool mantle from under her. She burrowed deep beneath the covers, still cold, still half asleep, and far too weary to fight. She shivered with the wool gone, and after a moment, cautiously opened her eyes again. He was at her side, his back to her. His mantle, and the length of towel, had been discarded at the side of the bed. Afraid to move, she lay stiff and straight in silence for a very long time, then, once again, exhaustion swept over her. And the cold. Instinctively, she moved closer and closer against the bastion of his back, drawing to herself the heat that it offered.

She didn't know how long she lay there then, drifting, waking, cold, warmed, when suddenly she was startled by an exclamation at her side, a curse, she was certain, though in what language, she wasn't sure at all. The force of his arms suddenly came around her, drawing her closer still. Her back fitted to the curve of his body and chest. His arm was around her waist. His chin rested atop her head. Even her feet at last seemed warmed against his legs.

"Stop shivering!" he commanded roughly.

"Believe it or not, I do not do so to annoy you!"

He pulled her closer still, hand splayed over her midriff. She tried very hard to remain perfectly still. Surely, now, warmed as she was, she could sleep.

But of course, she could not. She was furious, and elated, and still feeling that she must ridicule him to the highest degree, for no one had a right to any assumptions regarding her person. And yet . . . she had lain awake too many nights remembering the very few they had shared. She couldn't help but take pleasure in the warmth offered her then, while ruing him, and hating them both, certain that while she had but the one swift relationship of which to dream, he had a life filled with such encounters. He had promised to return her to another man—just as soon as the child he assumed she carried could be born and weaned. Surely, even a hostage had some pride to maintain.

And so she forced herself to remain still, and she prayed for sleep to release her from the tempest raging in her soul.

Again, time passed.

His hand was no longer at her waist. Arm around her, he cupped her breast. His fingers moved delicately over the fullness, and teased at the nipple. She bit hard on her lip, and in a few moments, felt herself pulled toward him. The fire had burned low. Still, it seemed to dance with a glow of flame, catching the color of his hair, playing on his shoulders, leaving only his face in shadow. She felt his lips against her own, and then on her throat, the tip of his tongue compellingly erotic over the linen of her nightgown, damp and wet, arousing as his mouth played where his touch had been, as cold fell from her as a doffed cloak. Memory stirred a rise of anticipation, an inner aching so swift and sweet that she nearly cried out, and still, when his lips moved over hers once again, she forced a stiffness that brought him to a halt.

"What has happened to the hostage, willing to do anything to please?"

"Gone, I'm afraid. For there is too much at stake now."

"And what is that?"

"Pride, for one."

"Where was your pride at Hamstead Heath? As we rode, and the nights at the farmhouse outside Perth?"

"The world was different then. I was different then."

"You're still a hostage."

"Oh, yes. But I have already been bartered back."

"Not for a year and a day."

"Yet not for any sane reason."

"There, my lady, we differ. '

"There is no child."

"I can tell you now that you're wrong."

"*You* can tell *me?*"

Even in the strange shadows, she could see the curl of his lips. "I can tell you, yes. For you've changed."

"Changed."

"There are subtle ways a man can tell."

"How on earth could a man such as you possibly remember one woman from another."

There was the slightest hesitation, then he murmured, "My lady, I'm guilty of constant warfare, which does not allow for the time you credit to me for such diversion."

"Someone else waits for you tonight."

"They do?"

"I saw . . . a gown. Someone below the stairs."

"You saw my cousin-in-law, catching me in the hallway, telling me that I wasn't to hurt you."

"Igrainia?" she said, and fell silent, afraid of what she would give away.

"I owe you no explanations, you know."

"I didn't suggest that you did."

"You are a hostage, forced upon me, you do recall, with a promise that you were willing to do anything, that you could please as no other."".

"I'm afraid that I've grown weary of being such an object for amusement, dismissal, and anger."

He leaned back, rested on an elbow at her side, watching her in the strange play of light and shadow. "Well, my lady, I'm afraid that you did provide amusement. And often, you have deserved anger. And as to dismissal . . . well, you are a hostage."

"As I said, a wary one."

"But not dismissed at this moment."

"You've threatened my brother's life."

"Have I? Only should you threaten life yourself."

"But I have told you again and again—"

"Christina, even I can tell you that you're wrong. Perhaps I'm more familiar with you than you are with yourself."

She closed her eyes, wincing, wondering if he—if whomever!—could be right. And if so, her denials certainly would ring false. And if so, she didn't know if the idea itself was entirely horrible, or if in a way, it didn't fill her with joy. And yet, it could not, for if so, she was meant only to fall in love with the life, for it to be taken away. And if she fought for the child, she would fight against everything else she held dear.

She was startled to feel his fingers against her cheek, a brush of tenderness she had not expected, a stroke so gentle it seemed a lie itself. But then his words were as soft, as curious, as he mused, "Perhaps you are far more naive than careless, ignorant rather than callous and detestable."

"Detestable!"

"Hm. If you meant to deceive another man, with a life that involves me, I would indeed deem such behavior as detestable."

"And maybe you remain mistaken!"

"Maybe, at this moment, I don't care anymore."

"And therefore, I should forget your words, far more razor sharp than any I ever spoke to you."

He thought about that for a minute, then said, "No. You should never forget them. For I always mean exactly what I say."

She cried out in aggravation, angry, wishing she dared to take a hand against him again. Yet even as he leaned over her, as his arms slipped beneath her, engulfing her form, the anger she felt seemed to simmer and boil over, and yet even as it did so, she felt his lips against her again, felt his touch, hands, fingers shifting upon the ties, the gown, the bareness of her flesh. She meant to touch him with resistance, but she merely found a power in which to hold; she wanted to twist from his mouth, from his touch, and yet it seemed that all she wanted to do was to writhe against him.

She couldn't have escaped him had she desperately wanted to. Her very force against him became a seduction, and the anger her indignity had fanned became but a source of fury and passion, and in minutes, she knew that her pride was as futile as any other defense. She had lost the battle waged against herself. She had dreamed far too often of his touch, of nights in his arms, of the heat that permeated her being, that set fires in places she had not known to feel the senses. Memory itself aroused, anticipation made her ache and arch, and longing made her reach out when she thought that she would not, hungry again for the feel of his heat beneath her fingers, eager for the power she could wield with her touch, with her caress, her knowledge of him. Once, Lauren had suggested that she had been in love with him; at the time, so ridiculous. She had not been, of course. She had been grateful perhaps, for the fascination created by the man, by strong features, sound teeth, exceptional form. She had admired, she had been glad that he hadn't been a horrible, wizened, brutal man . . . but surely, she hadn't been in love, in any way. Nor could she be so now. And yet, now, she had discovered that he had a power to hurt her in a way she had not imagined, and she had been sorely wounded with his return. These thoughts rose to her mind; fair warning struck her heart. A year and a day. She was English, he was not. The Scots were victorious now, as they had been at Stirling Bridge. But the might of the English could still sweep in, and he could become nothing more than a corpse ripped to shreds by the power of a mightier people.

Thought . . .

And reason . . .

Tempest in her heart, her mind, and along her flesh, tearing into her with such sensation, that each moment, every subtle nuance, rush of breath, pulse, touch, became unbearable, and necessary. She was desperate again that she might never know these things again, this wonder of scent, emotion, and sensation, and she rued herself for the urgency, the hunger, and yet knew that no logic could spell the simple fact of longing. Her hair swept his flesh, lips, teeth, tongue, devoured him, knew no bounds and no quarter, frenzied still by the spark of anger that remained. There was no absolute power as sure as his hold upon her. No heat as elusive or searing as that of his lips, the caress of his tongue, the movement of his thumb, fingers, lips . . . used so dexterously upon her. There again, a spiral of stars, darkness and light and the feel of being one with another, the shuddering wonder of his being so deeply a part of her, the pleasure in that moment of knowing someone else so completely a part of one . . . and the world, exploding into a pleasure that seemed impossible, sweet and volatile, where the feet did not touch the earth, and yet there was no time when the flesh was more attuned to every touch—linen, pillow, flash of a fire's heat, the dampness of sweat on arms still embracing her, the sheen in the firelight, the way he held her still, remained with her, everything easing; a room in mist, then dispelling, and at last, in the drifting, the wonder and the pain that he had been so intent upon leaving her here, in this tower prison, alone. That this exquisite feeling could exist, and he was the one with the power, and he had meant to stay away from her.

A year and a day. She had been bargained back. And she was an absolute fool, because he was far more than good teeth, fine auburn hair, strong features, and a warrior's toned physique. He was the flash of his eyes, the tone of his voice, his tolerance upon occasion, his anger upon others. His humanity at so many times, his temper and ferocity when he thought himself wronged. She knew that he was far more personable, and though her intentions had always been honorable, she had sacrificed nothing, for she had been compelled by him from the moment he had come to dinner, drunk her wine, from the morning she had awakened up in her own room at Hamstead Heath to find him there, watching her . . .

A man who never believed a word she said. Who doubted her ability for truth, and had no lack of faith in her penchant for treachery.

And yet, he held her against him. And she was startled when he murmured suddenly, "Whatever was I thinking, to stay away, when time is so brief?"

She didn't reply, but rested easily within his hold. There was no fight to be waged or won. Only time, which would pass all too quickly. A night in which she felt the power of his arms, and the warmth, and the sweet wonder she had learned all too briefly. There was more in which to luxuriate, and truly, only a fool would protest the hours that remained. She lay against him, the hair on his chest tickling her nose.

He held her shoulder, then his hand moved down her arm. His fingers laced with hers. The soft ripple of his breath moved over the hair on her head. His leg remained over hers.

She slept, deeply. And even in sleep, she knew that he was there.

When she woke in the morning, they were still entwined. He watched her. When she opened her mouth to speak, she was quickly silenced. Light slowly filled the room, spilled upon them, and made the world new again.

New again.

And light again, and nothing, of course, had really changed. Indeed, it hadn't, for at last, Jamie rose without a word. When he swept his mantle around his shoulders, then turned toward her again, she curled away. She felt his presence at her back as he sat upon the side of the bed again.

"What now, my lady hostage?"

"You, sir, owe me an apology."

"An apology, when you are either entirely wrong, or a liar?"

She sprang up, suddenly furious. "Because I am *wrong* or a *liar!* Because I would go to someone I loathe because I must, because there is no choice? This is easy for you, there is nothing over your head! You hold English prisoners. You have your king's permission to do what you will, and your king's permission to gain all that you can. Your prisoners will bring you nothing but reward. So there you are! Sir James, in his power! Aye, indeed. You! What of you! If this farce were real, you are the one with the most detestable behavior! What? A child of yours is a Scot, therefore, most obviously, not to be given to the English. The answer to you, therefore? Take it from its mother. A year and a day— as if, indeed, every life at Hamstead Heath did revolve around the breeding of exceptional animals! How very despicable of you, Sir James! How very, very detestable! So yes, indeed, you owe me an apology! And I don't know who thinks they know what God has not seen fit to make clear to me, but my motives have always been for the life of another, while yours all revolve around war—and gain!''

She saw the tension in his face, features taut as her own, eyes storm-cloud gray. And he said simply, ''You've the luxury of a life to save. I have only the memory of the scent of burning flesh. You'll forgive me.''

He rose, striding angrily to the door, where once again he paused, turning back. ''Don't forget, as to your return to the great power of the English, that has always been your most steadfast desire. Far be it from me, or any other barbarian, to suggest that you deserve anything less. Oh . . . and believe me, of course, I knew only what Igrainia believed to be truth, and what Gregory saw in his mind's strange eye before, but I can assure you now, there will be a child.''

''There will be *a* child, you're so convinced! I'm certain that at some time, even Gregory's prophecies have proven wrong. But, since you are so convinced, if so, Sir James, I can assure you—it will not be *a* child. It will be *mine.*''

''A year and a day, Christina,'' he said softly, opened the door, and left.

She sat up in a rage, throwing a pillow in his wake. Then, she felt as if fingers of fear wrapped around her heart, and for the first time through it all, felt a wave of desolation engulfing her.

It wasn't a matter of her own feelings, what might be true, what might not. Nor was it even a matter of his kindness, or cruelty—whichever was, in truth, being offered.

There was simply no way out of the final outcome, for her loyalties lay on both sides of a battle. In the end, only one side could win.

CHAPTER 15

The day began like almost every other. Berlinda arrived with water and a breakfast tray, cheerful in the extreme, grateful, for Eric had arrived with the morning light, and the men of Langley were all present, hale and hearty.

She chatted as she straightened the room—about horses, cows, chickens, the mildness of the winter day. "Spring will come soon," she told Christina cheerfully, and departed.

For a while, Christina paced around the room, and then decided that she would chance the door. The bolt had not been slid, nor did one of her warders sit just beyond on the landing. Hesitantly she stepped from the room, listened and heard nothing in the hallway, and so made her way down to the second level, and then to the first.

She found Lauren in one of the great chairs before the fire, studiously working on a tapestry. When she saw Christina, she smiled, spread out the work before her, and said, "It is for Hamstead Heath."

Christina saw that Lauren had fashioned a combined coat of arms, including her father's shield of Altisan with that of Christina's family. Her work was impeccable, her artistry beautiful. "Lovely," Christina murmured.

"Steven will like it, I think," Lauren murmured.

"Steven will admire it greatly, I'm certain," Christina assured her. She moved closer to the fire, warming her hands before the blaze. "It's quiet here. Berlinda said that Eric has returned as well. I'd have thought that the hall would be filled."

"Ah, well, there were many riches in English arms and armor taken when Dumfries fell. The men are in the stables, sorting through goods. They've seized fine cloth, weapons, household goods, and much more. So much has gone to the king, and Eric and Jamie will take what they choose, and so forth, down the line. There's a new guest at the castle as well."

"Another prisoner?"

"No, a real guest. A young Scottish woman who had been held by the English at Dumfries. She was freed after the fortress surrendered, and arrived here with Eric. She seems to know a great deal about the many trunks they pillaged from the English, so they're all at the stables, surveying the new gains. Judging the arms and armor. And then, of course, they'll make use of what they choose for themselves, and ride out again."

"Another castle to raze."

Lauren shrugged, then halted in her work. "As Steven has always said, people will fight against a power that is not their own." She smiled wryly. "I always thought the Scots would squabble so long and viciously among themselves that their nobles and leaders would kill one another without much help from the English. Now, it is the English

who squabble, and the Scottish king who has taken a direct
route in the direction he would go.''

Christina sat in a chair opposite Lauren. ''He will probably
be fighting all his life. He may have swayed many of his
nobles to his cause, but the way he seized the crown will
follow him until the day he dies.''

Lauren gave her attention to her stitches, then looked at
Christina with a wry smile. ''And you think that Edward
the Second, impetuous, quarrelsome, and unreasonable as
he is, will hold his kingdom together with the same fierce
pride and iron fist as his father?''

''His is an established crown.''

Lauren shook her head. ''Actually, I fear for the peace
and sanity of England now, as I never have before. And
your brother was always right—the best we could have done
was to stay out of it all.''

''My brother was right—but he is languishing in a castle.''

''He will survive,'' Lauren said firmly.

Christina rose, feeling suddenly impatient with Lauren's
perpetual belief that everything would work out. It wouldn't.

She walked uneasily to the main hall, and looked to the
door. On an impulse, she decided that she hadn't been
stopped thus far—she'd give in to curiosity and see what
was going on with the inhabitants of Langley.

In the courtyard, men and women were going about their
work. A squat fellow hurried past with a basket of fresh
eels still squirming in a wicker basket. A woman shooed
her children along a path, a silversmith worked beneath the
thatched overhang of the castle walls, patiently plying his
trade. Berries, dried meats, fresh breads, cheeses, wool and
more were bartered along the many stalls. Christina paused
to look up around the courtyard at the battlements; as always,
they were manned. The bridge lay open, shepherds moved
with their flocks to the fields beyond. She wondered what

would happen if she should simply join the sheep and scamper out in the world that lay outside the high stone walls of Langley.

Then, as she stared up at the battlements, she saw that Liam was leaning against the stone, just to the side of the bridge.

She waved to him, turned, and headed for the stables. It was frightening to feel the sudden sense of freedom that seemed to be hers this morning; sobering to see that guards remained, and noted even the movement of her eyes when she watched lowly sheep escaping the place.

She moved on toward the stables, built into another of the strategically arranged towers; the whole of the ground floor was given over to stables and armory. She heard voices from within and approached the outer doors. She blinked against the shadows of the interior, for outside, the day was bright.

A line of trunks stretched across most of the dirt and straw flooring. Eric and Igrainia leaned against one of the stalls, watching as the men went through the haul taken at Dumfries. Angus seemed particularly pleased, having found a coat of mail evidently made for a man of his own size. She was startled when she heard an unknown woman's voice, and when she turned slightly, she saw that Eric had returned, not just with goods, but with people as well—a number of servants, and a tiny, elegantly dressed lady with soft sable hair, ink-dark eyes, a heart-shaped face, and flawless skin. She was a few years older than she, Christina decided, sophisticated in manner and entirely at ease with her situation.

"Jamie, I tell you, I saw the mail in use when it arrived. Well, at a tournament played on the practice field. I have never seen so fine a mesh. The coat is light, but the links so very fine that blades cannot pierce them."

Jamie hunkered down at one of the trunks, removing the mail in question. Ragnor, at his side, made a sniffing noise, telling him that the workmanship was too delicate.

"Ragnor! Not everything that is strong must be the size of a mountain!" the woman said with soft laughter. "Jamie, slip it on. The lightness will astound you. As will the strength."

Jamie rose, accepting Ragnor's assistance as he slipped into the coat of mail, securing the buckles at his side.

"Now, have at him, Ragnor!" the woman said.

"Lady Elizabeth, we've the English to kill us, we needn't take up arms against one another!" Ragnor protested.

The young woman turned with laughter, looking at Igrainia. "They've never any faith in the words of a woman, even when such words come from the daughter of a Douglas!"

"Ah, look!" Jamie exclaimed suddenly. "We've an enemy among us!" He had caught sight of Christina just within the doorway. "Here we are, Elizabeth, the Lady Christina of Hamstead Heath. She'd be glad to take a sword against me, I assure you."

The dark-haired woman quickly assessed Christina, yet she seemed to do so with no malice. She smiled, walking forward. "My lady. Elizabeth Douglas, and for once, I'd be quite grateful to see anyone English take a sword against Jamie! Men!" she said with an aggravated shake of her head, and a smile.

"Indeed, come on Christina," Jamie said.

"Jamie," Igrainia murmured, frowning.

"Ah, Igrainia! You mustn't worry. Christina has a rare talent with arms. We have . . . practiced together before, and she's actually quite determined that she has the greater proficiency with arms. I'm sure she's eager for any chance to prove it."

"Really?" Elizabeth said, fascinated. "Dear Christina,

you've been challenged! You must take a sword against
Jamie!''

''I don't think it would be wise for me to take a sword
against Sir James,'' Christina said. ''I've too great a talent
as it stands for arousing his temper.''

''You may never get such a chance again, Christina!''
Elizabeth insisted.

''This is foolishness,'' Igrainia murmured unhappily.

''Christina must make her own choices,'' Jamie said.

He was goading her, Christina knew. But he was right.
She had already lost to him several times. Another loss
would mean little.

The chance to best him was immensely appealing.

She shrugged, stepping forward. Jamie drew his sword
from the sheath he had rebuckled at his side. ''My lady.''

''I don't care for your sword. It's far too heavy a weapon.''

''Well, forgive me. Someone . . . we need a finer, lighter
weapon for Christina.''

''There—the trunk there,'' Elizabeth directed. ''There are
some very fine, light swords, artistry from the south of Italy.
And wait! If this would be fair, the lady, too, should have
her coat of mail.'' Elizabeth threw open another trunk, well
aware, apparently, of all the goods taken. '' 'Tis light, but
heavy still . . . Magnus, give a hand here, please?''

Magnus pulled the coat of mail from the trunk, and Elizabeth urged Christina forward. Before she knew it, between
the two of them, they were dressing her in the mail. She
had never seen such a fine mesh, and though she had seldom
donned such a coat, when she had before, the weight had
been tremendous, almost more than her frame could carry.
As Elizabeth had said, these coats of mail were different.

''Jamie, remember that you go against a woman,'' Elizabeth cautioned. ''Christina, remember that a lady's only true

strength lies in a man's pride and his certainty that he must go lightly, that he can't be beaten!''

Christina couldn't help but smile, and lower her head. She didn't know exactly who this woman was, but evidently a good friend to the household here at Langley. A Douglas, part of a fierce clan. A guest here, now.

In the real sense of the word.

"Come, Christina," Jamie said, beckoning her to come forward for the attack.

She held for a moment, remembering all that she had learned from her brother, and his masters: Passion was good, if under control. Anger must be cold, and calculated. Strength lay in right, and the mind must always move more quickly than the body; instinct was a fine guide.

She moved into the center of the room, but made no move to attack. Growing impatient, Jamie made a light swipe at her, not going for her person but her sword. She refused to be goaded, and she knew that—*because she was woman, just as Elizabeth had said*—he would lose his patience and come after her.

He did. And she was able to parry him expertly with a series of quick movements across the floor that left her untouched—and him skewering his sword into the side of the stables. He quickly drew his weapon free, turning upon her. Eyes narrowed, and yet amused.

"Ah, Jamie, there's a lass could take you down!" Elizabeth cried delightedly. "God, that I might have learned so well!"

"Aye, a lass to bring one down," Jamie agreed, his eyes carefully upon his opponent then. "But we're not testing the mail at all, for the lady actually refuses to fight."

"There are different ways to fight," Christina assured him.

"Really?"

He came at her again, sword swinging. The speed and intensity of his blows forced her to swing harder and surer lest she find herself at the end of the sword point. She managed a blow that slashed across the center of his chest, and yet he didn't so much as pause, the blade was deflected so well. And backed across the room, she found herself caught off guard, and the point of his sword at her midriff, but even then, the blow was deflected; Jamie had paused rather than chance a move that might really cut through, and so she was able to spin, gaining the upper hand again and bringing him back across the room. They tested the mail, the armor, of course, and though it proved with every thrust of steel to be an impossible defense, Christina knew that Jamie had no intention of beating her to the ground.

She felt no such compulsion for fair play, and there came a point when he allowed her the lead, pressing him back through the hay, and straight to the rear wall. He would feint to the side, forcing her around, but she suddenly knew her advantage and couldn't help but take it. The mail allowed for protection at the throat and around the head, but left the soft flesh just beneath the chin vulnerable. And in a second's time, Christina brought the point of her blade against him there. She could have killed him then. And they both knew it. He stood still, his eyes sharp, a smile curving his lips. "You think that you couldn't be in like danger, had I chosen?"

"I think that *you* are in the danger now."

"I think that you should let the sword fall, quickly."

"Hm . . . I was informed this might be my only chance to take arms against my enemy."

He moved in a flash, his sword arm flying high with such a speed and fury that she was not prepared. Her blade was cast far from its mark. She forced herself to remain still, to make it appear that she had allowed the action.

"I hardly meant to kill you in truth," she said lightly.

She turned away from him, striding back across the stable. She offered her weapon hilt first to Angus, and asked Magnus to help her from the mail.

Elizabeth Douglas moved forward. "What a gift! I'm amazed. You've not just ability with the weapon, but the talent to move. How were you able to acquire such learning?"

"My brother was not averse to a sister learning all she might," Christina explained. "And you're right—that's the most incredible mail I've ever seen."

"Sicilian craftsmanship, so I was told," Elizabeth said. "Now, if these fools will simply take advantage of it . . ."

"The swords and armor all need care and cleaning," Jamie said. "Grayson, if you will see to it all." He ignored Christina for the moment, turning to Elizabeth Douglas. "There are boundaries here you should know; a ride beyond the walls might be in order, lest you find yourself in danger again at another time."

"A ride would be delightful. I hope you've a suitable mount."

Jamie turned, looked at Christina with a slight frown. "A suitable mount? We've recently acquired some of the finest horses to be found in all Europe. The best for a lady is Christina's Arab mare, and I'm sure she'll not mind you taking her mount."

She did mind; she minded terribly. Not because of Elizabeth Douglas, but because of him. She smiled at Elizabeth, however. "She is a wonderful mount. Not pure Arab, but the best of our native horses, and those we have so carefully kept pure in all the years of breeding. I think that you'll find her delightful, and I am sure that she needs the exercise."

With those words, she left the stables, wishing that she

had, at the least, taken a good chunk of skin from Jamie's chin.

Supper that evening was more wretched than she could have begun to imagine.

The hall had never seemed so full, nor had the Scots ever before seemed to be in such good humor.

Igrainia was her most gracious. Tray after tray of food was brought from the kitchens, despite the fact that winter still precluded so many dishes. Elizabeth Douglas was charming and amusing, telling tale after tale about her incarceration at Dumfries, and delighting in well-told stories that mocked her English captors. Elizabeth was delighted to meet Lauren and Sir Alfred, showing them every possible kindness. The new guest was, in fact, so sympathetic and enchanting that Christina thought she'd be ill if exposed to such charm too much longer.

But a sense of spirit and victory remained in the hall that evening, and it seemed there would be no escape. The head of the table was taken by Eric and Igrainia, Jamie and Elizabeth Douglas. As customary, Christina found herself between Magnus and Liam. The former insisted that she eat when she picked at her food, and the latter frowned, it seemed, each time she picked up her cup of ale. She needed it, however, because it seemed that she was going to be called upon to play the lute along with Angus's pipes, while old Highland dances were performed by the two reigning couples within the hall. She could, of course, throw the lute down—break it, even—and insist that she was a prisoner, with no obligation to entertain her enemies. Yet, she kept playing. And with Angus, sang the saddest laments she had learned from him, and did her best to ignore everything else but the instrument she played, and the great bear of a man at her side. Still, it was impossible to ignore the rest of the hall. Jamie was truly oblivious to her. At times, he was passionately interested in whatever words Elizabeth earnestly spoke at his side; sometimes he laughed, and the flash of his smile was captivating and full of genuine affection and good humor. When he danced with Igrainia, there was a warmth about him as well, and even when he drew the protesting Lauren to her feet, it was with a kindness and charm that was both endearing and infuriating. There came a time in the evening's festivities in which he played and sang himself with Igrainia, a song they sang together as if they had done so for years, and even though it was a lyrical ballad extolling the virtues of freedom, it was exceptionally beautiful because it attacked no other power, but simply spoke of the soul on the wind, and the beauty of the land.

The tune was the kind that enwrapped and warmed one, and left all in a moment's silence after the last notes. And yet Christina knew that she'd had quite enough, and must escape. Setting the lute down by the fire, as others rose, she skirted the men and headed for the stairway, one flight, and then the other, and then in the haven of the room that had once seemed like no more than a cell, she poked the fire to a greater blaze, crawled into her linen gown, sat in the chair before the hearth and watched the fire dance.

Hours passed. And in time, she knew he wasn't coming.

Elizabeth Douglas had arrived at Langley. And she was lively, charming to the extreme. Kin to one of the greatest warriors in all of Scotland.

Certainly, the perfect match for a knight such as Sir James.

She closed her eyes, thinking that she was going to have to learn to live with her rage, her indignation, her sense of injustice. This was the way of the world, as it had been, in England, as well as Scotland. Even Elizabeth Douglas knew the truth—that knights ruled, and the luckiest women were probably those born to service, for there was some sense of love and laughter in the farms and fields, and serving wenches might grow up to marry the groom they loved.

She was startled, but kept from moving when the door opened. So much time had passed; they were surely into the wee hours of the morning. He strode to the fire, leaned against the mantel, and studied her curiously. "You're still awake."

"Barely," she replied.

"But awake. And in a chair, not the bed."

"The fire is warm, comforting."

"I had thought to find you somewhat pleased this evening."

"Oh, and why is that?"

"You've been allotted a great deal more freedom—surely, you've noticed."

She forced a smile. "Surely you're aware that a cage remains a cage, no matter what its size."

"You prefer a smaller cage?"

"No."

"Ah . . . but you wouldn't think to thank a captor for any small magnanimity."

She meant to keep her temper, entirely, but could not. "Any small magnanimity? Such a gift was my horse. But you see saw fit today to see that Crystal was given to another."

"I see. So you heartily resent Elizabeth!"

"No. I find her to be intelligent and charming. It isn't my place to resent anyone."

"No, it's not."

He left her where she sat, moving around the room. She forced herself not to turn, and was therefore startled when she heard his voice coming from the bed. "If you sit so through the night, you'll be cramped and in pain come the morning.''

She turned at last. He had shed his clothing and climbed beneath the covers. Fingers laced behind his head, he seemed to reflect upon the ceiling.

''I'll stay, thank you.''

''No, you will not.''

She turned angrily. ''You're going to force me to move?''

''Yes, if you don't do so on your own.''

''I should have skewered you right through the throat when I had the chance.''

''I would never have allowed you to do so.''

''You would never have allowed me?'' She rose, skirting the foot of the bed to accost him indignantly. ''You couldn't have stopped it!''

''Ah, but I could have, and I did.''

''Sir James, that is surely the truth in your mind only. Elizabeth Douglas is certainly wise and right in many ways—a man's pride will one day be his great undoing,'' she assured him.

That brought a shrug. ''You're jealous, my lady.''

''Not in the least. I'm merely informing you that I did have an opportunity to kill you.''

''Then why make references to Elizabeth and the simple fact that she went for a ride?''

''She went for a ride on my horse, and then, since you insist, I'm simply wondering what you're doing here.''

''I'm here to be with the hostage sworn to please me in every way.''

''When you've such a proper young woman as Elizabeth Douglas in residence?''

He shrugged. ''For a Scot, indeed she's from the finest family. Other than that of the Bruce himself, of course.''

''Ah, well, then—I suppose that you are considering a

match, certainly, with the blessing of your king as well. A wondrous political move.''

"Yes, of course.''

She felt exceptionally tense, infuriated, and ill.

"Might I suggest then, that it might be considered the poorest of manners, Sir James, that you should be here?''

"You may suggest anything you like. But then, again, there's little reason for it. Elizabeth is sweet and charming, and certainly from the best possible family. I admire the Black Douglas tremendously. And she certainly has his spirit. But there is no betrothal at this moment.''

"Well, Sir James, I would imagine still that she is the kind of gentle soul to take you from the pain of earlier years, and move with you into the new glory you now see for your country. It appears that a betrothal might be forthcoming.''

"Possibly. It's true that she is aware of my past, and actually, knew Fiona well.''

"Perhaps, then, you should be attentive to her at all times.''

"I have spent the proper hours of the evening being attentive.''

She turned away from the bed, going for her mantle.

"Are you cold?''

"No, I'm leaving. To enjoy my new freedom in the hall below.''

"I'm afraid your freedom doesn't extend into the hours of night.''

"Oh? You were able to enter the room and draw the bolt from the outside as well?''

A smile played on his lips, and she realized that he considered himself nothing more than challenged. "Your freedom does not extend into the night, Christina. May I suggest that you cease this nonsense and come over here.''

"You may suggest what you will, but I don't care to come to you."

"Why ever not?" He sat up, staring at her. "Has your situation changed, Christina? I think not. No matter what course my life may be taking, your situation has not changed. You remain a hostage. The girl who threw herself at us, insisting she be taken prisoner by the Scots. The woman who assured me that me she could please me as no other."

She turned, heading for the door, desperate for a moment that he not see her expression.

But, of course, she had bought time, and nothing more, because he was up and at the door ahead of her, muscles gleaming in the firelight, eyes misty gray and taunting.

She stopped short, turning back to the fire.

"Christina! What on earth is your game?"

"If you touch me again, it can only be by force," she said quietly.

"Because of Elizabeth?" he inquired. "What a strange notion."

"Your sense of victory has apparently done strange things to your mind."

"My mind!" he protested. She knew that he remained against the door. "Christina, you might recall that you were the one offering all manner of ecstacy when *your* intent all the time was to be returned to your people—and certainly, you must have always known that you would pay the price of such a bargain through a marriage to Rowan DeClabert. And yet . . . you were willing then to seduce and . . . enjoy."

"You knew that my intent was to keep you from Lauren!" she accused him, spinning to see that he had indeed remained by the door, arms crossed firmly on his chest, as indomitable in nakedness as in his full array of arms and armor.

"As always, so self-sacrificing, Christina!"

"Sir James," she said, striding across the room to him,

but keeping a few feet of distance as well, "I am going to do my absolute best not to be baited into your little traps, because torturing me does seem to entertain you no end while the conditions of my life exceed that of being purely wretched. I beg you, leave. I mean what I say, if you touch me again, it will only be with force. If you wish to sleep in that bed, sir, you must do so—for Langley is your family's holding, and God knows, you respect one another no end. I can be perfectly content in a chair before the fire. Do what you will."

"You'd lie to yourself, and even to God, Christina, wouldn't you?"

"I haven't the least idea as to what you are on about now!"

He took a step toward her, slow, agile, almost a spring against the door. She backed toward the fire, wary of each ripple of his muscle.

"You see, I think that at this point, you might be known as my mistress rather than as just an ordinary hostage. You refuse to admit to the child, but then, count the days that you have been here. And in the care of the servants at Langley . . . well, certainly, your needs are noted. As well as all that is not required."

"Your insistence on this nonevent is rather foolish at the moment, don't you think?"

He shrugged, musing. "No, not really. Do you know that Robert Bruce fell quite desperately and madly in love with his wife, who is the daughter of a great English baron? Naturally, that—and the extent of his lands in England— had a great deal to do with his one-time adherence to the will of the English monarch. But then came the true promise of the crown, and the king of the Scots became just that, and in his fight, his wife was taken prisoner. She is not so cruelly kept as others of the Bruce's family and retinue, of course, due to her father's position, but she remains a prisoner still. And despite the years, Robert Bruce really does love her, with all his heart and soul. Still . . . the king has fathered a multitude of bastards. The years in which she has been held from him are long indeed.''

''Are you trying to tell me that Elizabeth Douglas wouldn't mind in the least that you had a mistress here and were—as you insist—going to have a child with that mistress?''

''The deed has been done; who could protest?'' he inquired lightly.

''The deed is done, but only in your mind,'' she informed him.

''But why should she mind? Your intent is to return to your people. As you've pointed out, were I ever to remarry, Elizabeth Douglas would certainly be the perfect woman.''

''You are aggravating beyond all sanity!'' she assured him. ''Certainly, you should marry where you choose. And a lovely woman with such a fine family—indeed, where could you go wrong? She even possesses extraordinarily fine teeth! I wish you every blessing, but plead that you cease to torment me.''

''I torment you? Because I lay it all out as it is? Tell me, Christina, if I were to come to you and tell you that the king has said that there is no need to offer you in exchange at all, what would your reaction be? Don't bother to answer— you would be horrified. Come the fires of all hell, you will be exchanged! God knows, you are the only salvation for your brother.''

She felt her fingers digging into her palms, her hands tensing into fists. ''Is it so wrong to be desperate for the life of a man who is one's blood brother, who has had the power to use one as a pawn, but has refrained—at peril to himself?''

"It's wrong to emasculate your brother, Christina. To doubt his abilities."

"I don't doubt his abilities! I merely know his circumstances. William Wallace was one of the strongest, most powerful men ever to draw a sword and rally a people—and in the end, executioners had their way with him. No man is an army unto himself! Steven is kept behind impregnable stone walls, and that is the simple truth of it. And does it . . . matter? I am not Scottish. And though I have seen and understand and truly rue many of the horrors your people have faced at the hands of my own, I am English, and I know as well that there are valiant, honorable, talented, brilliant Englishmen. And women. And I cannot loathe my entire people."

"Whoever suggested that they hated all the English, or abhorred everything about them?"

"Englishmen took everything from you. Perhaps you strive for wisdom, but you must loathe the English as a country, as a people."

"Sometimes," he admitted.

She was suddenly exhausted. So desperate in her heart to fight, not even knowing exactly what she railed against, and aware that there was no way to win.

She turned away again, her shoulders falling.

She felt his hands upon her, strangely gentle on her shoulders.

"Come to bed, Christina."

She turned back to him, firmly shaking her head. "No. I mean it, if you touch me tonight, it will be rape."

She was startled when he smiled. "And I am the one with the pride?" he inquired.

"What?"

"Well, of course, you were throwing yourself at my feet all along to save the lovely Lauren from a man's uncontrollable lust. Now, that was rather actually amusing, because she was never in any danger, which you simply couldn't fathom. And now, of course, were I to go berserk, Elizabeth is in residence . . . Once, you might recall, you weren't so certain of your absolute allure. Christina, you are quite safe in bed. You are not so seductive that one can't lie down at your side and sleep.''

She wasn't at all certain which was worse, fighting her own longing just to be near him, or feeling so utterly dismissed.

''I admit to having enjoyed long hours in the hall tonight, and probably too much ale. But our days at leisure are numbered—as you are so quick to point out, there are many more positions to be assailed, castles to pillage, and so on. I need some sleep.''

She cocked her head slightly, reminding him, ''You have impressive quarters below, Sir James, since you are an honored part of this family.''

''But you see, I haven't decided if I trust you yet or not.''

''Of course you have decided, Sir James. You don't trust me in the least.''

''But you wouldn't go against a vow, not upon your brother's life.''

''God knows, my brother could die any day.''

''But he isn't dead. Not yet. Come, Christina, I mean it. I would like to get some sleep.'' He neither taunted then, nor did he sound as if he would entertain any further argument. She turned, crawling beneath the covers on the far side of the bed. And there, she intended to remain.

She felt him move in beside her, keeping his distance as well. She was able to remain stiff and unyielding because of her anger, not jealousy, she assured herself. Elizabeth was taken for rides—on her horse. And she was merely here, to be told when and where she would be seen, what she would and would not do.

A great deal of time passed, and she still lay stiff, and awake, yet thought that he surely slept by then.

He didn't. He spoke softly and suddenly in the shadows of night.

"There's a possibility that Steven has escaped Thistle-on-Downs."

She sprang around as if she had been catapulted. She stared at him, face dark in the shadows. "What?" she whispered.

"There were a few messengers in and out of Dumfries before the fortress fell," he said. "She heard a number of the men talking. About the Scots, the situation . . . many of the English are furious that they have been left without Edward's resources, left to fight or die, when the English king has not come forward with his power to help them when they are in greatest danger of death and despair. She heard some of them talking about those who had paid ransoms to Robert Bruce, and suffered for their desperate acts. There was a rumor that Steven had somehow escaped Thistle-on-Downs. Whether true or not, I don't know. I wasn't sure whether to tell you or not . . . give you false hope. But from all I have heard, your brother is an intelligent and resourceful man, and therefore . . . well, it's possible."

Shaking, she eased back down. A moment later, she felt the tips of his fingers on her cheek, and she knew that they were damp. He let out a soft sigh, drawing her against him. She allowed him to hold her. "He is still in danger," she said after a while. "Perhaps in greater danger . . . should King Edward seize upon him."

"I imagine that he is heading far north of the border, if he is free."

"There are many English troops yet in Scotland."

"Give your brother his due, Christina."

She nodded. "I . . . try to, really," she murmured.

But after a moment, she could no longer bear the cold, the stiffness, and the restraint. She didn't know if she was relieved, hopeful, or more afraid. Her mind was in an ever greater tempest. She twisted, head against his chest, knuckles brushing his torso. She twisted more, and her fingertips fell against his flesh, until suddenly her hands were captured in his hold.

"Christina, please! I'm doing my very best to prevent any semblance of force here. I beg that you do the same!"

She snatched her fingers back quickly, retreating again to her side of the bed. But it didn't seem that she could stay. And when she turned restlessly again, she came up against his anatomy in such a way that she was certain he did not lie so easily and dismissively at her side.

He rose on an elbow, capturing her cheek with the spread of his fingers. "If you're turning to me in a twisted form of gratitude, don't. I don't know that my information is correct. I want no bribes, no thanks, no deceit, or not even what you might consider a due form of surrender. No temper come the morning, and certainly, no reneging ever, on any vow you've given. I have no will to force you into anything. Not tonight, not ever. But I am human. You've a simple choice and here it is—keep your distance and be still, or be willing."

She stared into his eyes, and suddenly knew that only a great distance between them would ever keep her from wanting him.

"You do have elsewhere to go, you know. Your own elegant chamber within this gracious hall."

"Ah, yes. It's true. But then, the same freedom couldn't be allowed you were not someone on guard."

"I see. Your being here is another great mercy."

"A kindness."

"I'm ever so grateful."

"Which is it, Christina?" The tension in his voice touched her, and knotted within her.

"Willing," she whispered.

And so the night progressed. From willing to eager. From the awakening of hunger . . . to an urgency of thirst . . . starvation.

Eager to anxious. Anxious to desperate . . . and so on . . . to . . . oblivion. And then a deep, deep sleep in a strange comfort that kept her from eating away at her own soul with fear for what the morning light could bring.

CHAPTER 16

It was late when Christina woke. Apparently, Berlinda or Garth had quietly slipped in, for she had been left fresh water and a tray with food. She ate ravenously, having not been hungry in the hall the night before. She dressed quickly, then and was startled to feel, as she went to test the door, that she was dizzy, almost ill. She paused, fighting the wave of nausea and weakness that washed over her, irritated that she should be so delayed. She closed her eyes, opened them, felt much better, and tentatively tried the door. It opened to her touch.

In the hall, she found that Igrainia was directing the packing of food, Grayson was repairing armor pads, and Lauren and Elizabeth were both busy with needles, Lauren repairing someone's torn mantle while Elizabeth worked on a banner.

"Good morning, Christina!" Elizabeth said cheerfully. "My family crest!" she continued, displaying the banner.

"A handsome banner," Christina said politely, and her

expression must have been somewhat puzzled because Elizabeth smiled.

"They ride to join the new siege tomorrow, at dawn," she explained.

"I see."

"Hence the noise from the courtyard! Many newly trained men will join the seasoned warriors."

Igrainia paused in her work, joining the two of them, studying Christina. "Are you well?"

"Very."

"Last night you left the hall early."

"I'm not certain that I belonged at such a celebration," she murmured.

Elizabeth laughed. "Then neither does Igrainia! But then, you see, all that is left of her family is her brother, and he now fights for Robert Bruce!"

Christina gazed sharply at her hostess and Igrainia shrugged. "We may all rue the day that Robert Bruce claimed the throne," she said. "The men are so elated now ... but I know the English. And the time will come when they settle their difficulties, cease their argument with Edward, and come riding north with more power than we've yet to see." She shook her head impatiently. "Frankly ... well, you come from a place that might well be considered the borders, Christina. English and Scottish, it's the people who have suffered woefully. There are great tracts of land which will not feed anyone for decades to come. God knows how long we even dare to hold here, should the day come when the English ride en masse. But as for now ... well, the Bruce is decimating stronghold after stronghold of his enemies. And though the Scots truly loathe a siege, I must admit, such warfare is safer on those I love, and so ... I must move on to the smokehouse, and see that the men of Langley are

well supplied when they ride out. They'll not be riding back
for some time, I'm afraid.''

Igrainia left them. Elizabeth followed her movement and
said softly, ''She's so afraid! But of course, she'll never
show it.'' She smiled at Christina. ''You cannot, of course,
be expected to help in any way, but . . . would you mind?
I'll never have this done, and I'd dearly love to send it back
as a gift to my cousin, the Black Douglas!''

Christina hesitated, then took a seat near Elizabeth. ''What
would you have me do?''

''I'm sewing on the motto . . . if you'd take a letter?''

Christina picked up a needle and thread. ''I sincerely
doubt if my sewing letters on a banner will change the course
of history,'' she murmured.

Elizabeth laughed delightedly, and Christina again noted
that there was nothing to dislike about this woman.

Elizabeth Douglas might have read her mind. ''I'm not
your enemy, you know.''

''We honor different countries,'' Christina reminded her.

Elizabeth sniffed. ''Few men truly honor your current
king, my lady, but be that the case, this is certainly one of
the most muddled wars ever fought, when you consider that
even the king of the Scots once rode with the king of the
English!'' She surveyed Christina for a minute, then added,
''I daresay that you've met our king—at your king's court!''

Christina looped thread through a needle and set to her
task. ''I have seen Robert Bruce, yes. Years ago, before
Edward the First died.''

''He knows you.''

''Does he?''

''Yes, he saw you as a child.''

Christina hesitated, then looked at Elizabeth and said anxiously, ''Jamie told me that you had heard word regarding
my brother.''

"I've heard gossip regarding your brother," she said gently. "Men in the fortress, angry at their lot! They fight—and the king takes his time, busy with his fury against his nobles. And of course, he is in mourning, still!" She sniffed. "But I believe it might well be good information I overheard, and that is that Rowan DeClabert left Thistle-on-Downs with a large contingent of men, ready to relieve an English stronghold somewhere. Which, I do not know. And that after he departed, Steven somehow disappeared from the fortress."

Christina glanced over to where Lauren, as usual, bent serenely to the matter at hand.

"She knows," Elizabeth said.

Lauren looked up, aware of Elizabeth's soft whisper. She smiled. "I have told you all along, Christina, that Steven would be well."

Christina shook her head. "We don't know that he's well!" she protested.

"We do."

"But—"

"You would know if he weren't!"

Elizabeth was watching her again. "You're something of a seer, I understand."

She shook her head. "I'm afraid not. I do share a strange sense with my brother, that is all. And Lauren is right. If he were dead, I would know. If he were in severe pain, I would know. But I admit, I'd no idea that he had fled Thistle-on-Downs."

Elizabeth smiled. "Perhaps he will come north. You know that Robert Bruce is well acquainted with him? Maybe your brother will throw his lot in with the Scots!"

"Steven? He is as English as the Tower!" Christina said. "Not to mention the fact that he adores Lauren, and must retain his position. The count of Altisan will not allow his daughter to marry a penniless exile.''

"My father is a Frenchman," Lauren reminded her. She rose suddenly, stretching, and for the first time, Christina saw that Lauren only barely managed to appear less restless and distressed than she had been the many weeks that had gone by. "I think this will suffice," she said, looking at her handiwork. "I'll find Ragnor, and see if I can be of any further use."

She walked from the hall. Christina had never been much good at needlework, but since this piece was for Elizabeth and her family, she was determined that her stitches would be small and neat. "I must apologize; I am not very talented with such work," she told Elizabeth.

"Ah, if I but had your talent with arms!" she exclaimed. "Perhaps, in the days to come, you'll teach me something of what you know."

"If you wish."

"You're quite amazing."

"I was allowed to work with my brother day after day. My parents have been dead some time, and even when they were alive, in their absence, Steven's word was law at Hamstead Heath. Though we'd not been attacked by the Scots, the threat was always there. I believe he thought that it could do no harm for a woman to be able to defend herself."

"I think I'd like your brother very much. Of course, I've a fine family myself. It's a pity, however, that my male kin didn't see fit for me to become as proficient with a sword and arms as you are—actually, a pity that men are the way they are. Too many times, what has happened here has been brutal. Not so often to women of powerful families, but . . . Still, enough have suffered. And if they were fated to fall under that kind of brutality, it's a pity that they weren't able to deliver some harm in turn. But we are supposed to be protected, of course, yet in the days gone by, what protection could the farmer in his field afford against a powerful baron given leave to seize property and all else? The law, of course, should protect every man and woman. But in war, there is no law."

Christina hesitated, then asked her, "As a prisoner at Dumfries . . . were you in grave danger?"

"Not a single man at Dumfries, not even that wretched MacDowall, would chance much against me. I'm kin to the Black Douglas, and he is known for his temper."

"I'm glad that you . . . were not hurt."

"Not ravished or molested in any way," Elizabeth said dryly. "And there are those who would say that I remain as impertinent as ever, with an attitude against the English that might one day be my undoing. However, I don't intend to be in such a position again. If an English army marches now, I'll head to the Highlands. And if all Scotland falls, I'll throw myself upon the mercy of some of our Norse kin. I will never again be a prisoner." She caught her breath, realizing what she had just said, and Christina's position here.

"They will never hurt you here, you know," she said softly.

Christina gave her attention to the letter she sewed. She had already been hurt more than she could ever explain. Elizabeth's very presence was an anguish she had to accept.

"How is this? Done well enough, do you think?" she asked.

"Quite well enough. My deepest thanks."

Though there was more to do, Elizabeth suddenly stood as well. "Sewing is a tedious task," she murmured. "There will be time to finish this later." She started for the door to the keep, hesitated, and turned back. "The sun is out. A strangely beautiful sky for a winter morning. Are you coming out?''

"I, yes . . . I suppose.''

Christina sprang to her feet to join Elizabeth.

Outside, there was tremendous activity. Some men practiced at arms while others worked hard at sharpening weapons. Smoke from the smiths billowed into the air as horses were shod, swords were repaired, and plate armor was tempered. Grooms worked with leather harnesses, and laundresses brought their work here and there.

Christina followed Elizabeth around to the stables, and saw that the packs were being prepared for the animals who would be laden with supplies as the men of Langley returned to the service of the king of Scots. Preparations were fully under way.

"I wish that I had been born a man!" Elizabeth said firmly. "I would give so much to be a part of all this activity.'' She turned suddenly, looking at Christina. "Women have ridden to war. I've always loved to read about Eleanor of Aquitaine! But then, of course, she had so much power in her own right.'' She shrugged. "Still, it's much better to be here than sent to the protective bosom of my own family.''

Christina had ceased to listen. She could see that a number of the horses taken from Hamstead Heath were being groomed for the coming ride. She walked across the stables. The huge gray stallion they had named Zeus was pawing the ground impatiently, as if he, too, was eager to be off. Christina stroked his nose, talking to him softly. "They had best take care of you!" she whispered. "If those Scots cause you any injury, well, I shall see that they answer for it!" she told the horse. Zeus rolled his dark eyes, snorted, and laid his head low against her. She stroked his forehead, and turned.

Jamie stood behind her. He was clad in the mail he had tested the day before, a tunic in his colors over it. She realized that he had been at work in the courtyard, teaching the youth who would become men-at-arms to battle straw enemies, and strike off ham-hock heads.

"He's among the finest in the lot, I believe," Jamie said, indicating Zeus.

"Yes. Very well trained. Steven worked him himself. I have worked with him," she added.

"Such a horse is incredibly valuable; you know that."

She nodded.

"Don't worry," he said. "I'll tend to him well."

"What about Satan?" she asked.

"He picked up a stone, and has acquired a slight limp. Nothing too serious, but since we do have other horses, I don't intend to take a chance with him. Satan and I have been together for a long time."

"I see."

"You must have known that we seized your horses to make use of them."

"Of course."

"Ah, but it still galls you to see them taken."

"I'm sorry," she said flatly. "You'll understand that in my mind, they are still *my* horses."

"Alas, dear Christina! Then you'll have to learn to share."

"I try—daily."

He laughed. "And just what else do you feel that you're sharing?"

"My entire household goods and fortune aren't enough?"

He didn't respond because Elizabeth Douglas suddenly came to join them, admiring Zeus. "He is enormous! And so sleek. Is he as fast as he is powerful?"

"Faster," Christina murmured. "And yet, Crystal is actually able to maintain a speed to compete with any of the stallions.''

"But Crystal couldn't carry the weight needed for war," Jamie told her.

"She can maneuver, as few stallions such as Zeus could manage."

"He's magnificent, Jamie. You'll be taking him?" Elizabeth said.

"Yes, I'm glad you approve."

She sighed. "Scots are actually still best at warfare on foot!" she told Christina. "All those years of practicing. Why, there are Highlanders and others among us almost as fast as the fleetest stallion."

"Not to doubt our prowess, but I don't believe we're quite so swift," Jamie said.

"Ah, but Sir James! I've seen you in action!" Elizabeth murmured.

Feeling acutely uncomfortable, Christina slipped down the length of the stables. She came upon Satan, stroked his sleek black neck, and whispered softly to him. She saw he favored his right foreleg, and came beside him to study the injury. As Jamie had said, not so bad, but there would be no sense in causing such a glorious beast further injury.

When she looked back, Elizabeth and Jamie were deep in conversation again. Elizabeth, long dark hair curling over her shoulders, leaned against the wall. Jamie was braced against the wall as well, his palm flat, and very near her head. It seemed a most intimate moment.

Christina turned away, feeling as if she intruded, and feeling a tempest beginning anew in the pit of her stomach. No temper, she had said last night. And she thought of all the things that he had said, and that yes, indeed, Elizabeth was certainly of the right family, and knew him, knew his past.

She quietly slipped from the stables. In the yard, she saw that a few mounted men were leaving, riding out the gates and across the bridge. She took note of the signal they gave to the men keeping guard at that position.

Then she hurried quickly back to the hall. The banner that Elizabeth had thrown down remained before the fire. Christina realized that she was tempted to throw it straight into the flames. She refrained, picked up the work, and continued on it herself.

As she sewed, she became aware that a strange sense of peace had settled over her, as if someone had suddenly assured her that everything would be all right. She stopped, staring into the fire. And she exhaled a long, soft, breath. She believed suddenly that Steven was safe; that he had, indeed, escaped from Thistle-on-Downs.

She turned her attention back to the banner, suddenly wanting that it should be done. By the time she finished, Garth and others were in the hall, beginning to prepare for the many men who would come in for the evening meal.

She set the banner down and fled up the stairs, eager for moments alone. She was there, standing before the fire, when a soft knock brought her turning around.

Once again, Sir Alfred had come to her. She smiled at him, asking him in. "You look very worried. Are you ill? Can I do something."

He shook his head, then sighed deeply. "My lady, I'm leaving."

"Leaving?" she said, startled, then frowned. "You don't mean that you are going to ride with the Scots?"

"I'm afraid I'd not be of much use riding with anyone. The countryside is currently rife with opposing forces. Lauren's father has sent knights to finish negotiations, and I will ride out to join them, though they have chosen not to move the lady from Langley at this time, since there is too much danger in the number of outlaw troops all about. No one, however, is going to prey upon an old man, so I will ride out and assure them of my lady Lauren's safety.''

''I see,'' Christina told him. She smiled, and walked to him, embracing him closely and with the deepest affection.

''I'm sorry to leave you,'' he told her.

''I'm fine. And I must admit that I'm glad Lauren isn't going, because Steven is now an outlaw himself, and perhaps, somehow, he will find his way to her here. You have been a dear, dear man, and I am grateful to you. Be careful; God go with you.''

''I'll find you again as well, one day, my lady. God be with you.'' He cleared his throat, held her face between his hands, then kissed her hands, and departed without looking at her again.

She turned back to the fire.

She was startled to feel another presence in the room and she turned quickly, ready to be defensive.

Jamie was there. He was clad in mail, with his colors visible on the tunic he wore over the mail. He was even in a helmet that hid everything of his face, other than his eyes. He was definitely impatient, and not in the mood for any argument.

''Where is your mantle?''

''There, on the chair by the fire. Why?'' she asked uneasily.

''A group of English knights await a rendezvous just beyond the gates.''

Her knees threatened to buckle. ''So . . . they have come for me as well.''

''They would be delighted to take you now, my lady.''

''And . . . you've decided that I should go?''

''Is that what you want?''

She meant for her voice to remain strong. It came from

her as a whisper. "You believe that Steven has escaped from Thistle-on-Downs."

"It's what we've heard." He strode across the room, took up her mantle, and threw it around her shoulders. "Come on."

She squared her shoulders, hating him fiercely then. She could recall the way he had spoken with Elizabeth Douglas. Apparently, he had decided that a betrothal with her would not be a bad political match at all.

Therefore, he must have decided that children were easily acquired, and that she was nothing more than an embarrassment and a burden.

She jerked the mantle from his fingers, wishing to precede him from the room. She hurried ahead of him down the stairs and through the hall to the courtyard.

A number of the men, in full armor, were mounted. Sir Alfred was among them.

Her own horse waited.

She walked straight for Crystal, almost blinded by the threat of tears. She had been right all along. She was nothing but a pawn. Her temptation might have been to scream and rant and rave, but she was well aware that it would be to no avail.

No one would care how she came from the castle.

By her own power, or bound and trussed like a boar, dragged out.

She didn't need assistance to leap into the saddle. And she sat stiffly for they were all apparently waiting for Jamie.

He came out, striding behind her. To add to her sense of rage and desolation, Zeus was saddled and clad in trappings of war, ready to carry Jamie to their rendezvous with the English knights.

A cry went up, and the bridge was lowered. Crystal followed the other horses. As she moved across the bridge, Jamie passed her, riding to the head of the men.

She could see the contingent of English waiting. Ten armed and armored knights. They rode forward, halting a good fifty feet from their position.

"Sir Alfred!" Jamie said, and the old knight joined him, and they rode forward.

Christina sat stiffly upon Crystal, awaiting the moment when she would be bidden forward. Jamie turned Zeus, coming toward her. When she would have nudged Crystal forward on her own, he reached over, taking the reins from her grasp.

His eyes fell upon her with sharp gray warning. He led Crystal forward, and yet halted again some distance from the men.

He spoke in fluid French then, asking that the knights take note that the Lady Christina Steel of Hamstead Heath was indeed his hostage, alive and in good health. Lauren, the daughter of the count of Altisan, was kept in equal comfort, awaiting further negotiation, but it should be apparent to all that no harm had befallen the women. As the English had seen fit to keep many of their hostages through many years of incarceration, they would in turn be expected to respect his determination that time would pass before the lady was returned.

The man who was apparently the leader of the messengers nodded gravely in turn.

Jamie pulled on Crystal's reins, and they turned their backs on the opposing party, riding ahead of the others, back to the gates of Langley.

At first, Christina shook with relief. Then fury filled her. He had never meant to hand her over. He could have told her so. He had not. He had let her ride forth, quaking.

And she would never forgive him for it.

She couldn't shake his firm grasp on Crystal's reins, but before the mare had even come to a halt in the courtyard, she started sliding from the saddle. She felt faint, very afraid that she was going to be sick, and absolutely determined to escape Jamie at all costs.

He didn't intend to let her do so. His hand, in a metal studded gauntlet, fell upon her shoulder when she would have fled.

She turned to him, rage in her eyes.

"Leave me be."

"Were you so eager to join them, then?"

"Am I ever a game to you, Sir James? Has it ever occurred to you that the tortures you inflict upon the mind are greater than those that can be done to the flesh?"

"A game? Torment?" He shook his head, only the icy mist in his eyes visible as yet. "Sir Alfred has been let go. That, you knew. Perhaps you saw. But you never so much as bothered to look around, to note that Lauren was with us as well."

She backed away a step, startled. She had not seen that Lauren had been mounted with their party. She had seen nothing but her own blind rage.

"It's all a matter of power to you, and you are loathsome in the extreme."

"You didn't protest the possibility of leaving."

"Protest? To what avail? You'll do what you choose— always!"

"It didn't occur to you to ask about the previous terms described to you. There was but one question you asked, and that regarding your brother."

"Obviously! If Steven is no longer at Thistle-on-Downs, there is no need for me to care about the demands of such a man as Rowan DeClabert!"

"And if Steven were still at Thistle-on-Downs, you would

run out like a puppy, heedless of yourself, or any other man?''

"What would you have me do?'' she cried.

He turned from her in disgust. She stood in the courtyard, miserably aware that the argument had been witnessed by half the inhabitants of Langley.

Her knees would give any second. She had to retreat.

She tore for the hall, and burst in upon Igrainia. Her face must have been far whiter than she had realized for Igrainia let out a little cry of concern. "Christina! Come, quickly, sit down. I'll send for wine. You look like a ghost . . .''

She shook her head strenuously. "No—no, I'm fine. I just—''

She fled up the stairs. In her tower room, she leaned heavily against the mantel, praying for the world to cease spinning.

She was startled when Igrainia burst in behind her. She opened her mouth to beg for her privacy, but when she did so, she felt her stomach protesting in a manner that couldn't be ignored.

Her hostess was instantly at her side, with a small wooden bucket. Apparently, Igrainia had seen the tumult in her face.

And she was sick. Sick, miserable, furious.

When the spasms had passed, she saw that Rowenna, too, had come up the stairs, and was prepared with cool damp cloths. She, however, took one look at Christina and decided to leave again.

"Perhaps you should lie down,'' Igrainia suggested.

She was too torn to accept the sympathy being offered. She pulled away from Igrainia, her eyes filled with reproach and anger.

"Don't! Kindness here is nothing but a jest. How could you do what you did to me?''

"What I did to you?''

"There is no child!" she cried.

Igrainia sat at the foot of the bed, staring at her, saying nothing.

"There is no child!" she repeated, and she knew the words were an attempt then to convince herself.

"How could you know . . . suspect? And if you did, how could you . . . how could you make such a report to Jamie? This is . . . my concern."

Igrainia hesitated, then said quietly, "Is it entirely your concern?"

"*I* didn't know. Didn't suspect. And who will ever believe me when you saw fit to make such announcements?" she whispered.

"Well, I even noted you, and the passage of time, but it's Gregory who always knows these things."

"If he knows these things, perhaps he'd be good enough to *know* where my brother is!"

"And perhaps you should put some faith in your brother."

"Oh!" she swore. "I am sick of hearing that! All men fall before an army of swords!"

"Yes, but would your brother be foolish enough to go against an army of swords?"

Christina covered her face with her hands, still raging with frustration, and yet aware that she was once again defeated.

Steven was not in DeClabert's keeping. And to the minds of those here, she had made it apparent that she had been willing to rush to an exchange, no matter what the circumstances.

"You should lie down for a while," Igrainia said, turning to leave. "Truly, I meant you no ill. I'm sorry if you feel that I have been against you. You should get some rest. For your health. And that of the child."

"There is no child," she said weakly.

Igrainia was silent. They both knew that she was speaking a wishful lie at that moment.

Her hostess silently went out. Christina fell upon the bed, grateful for the welcoming warmth and softness.

She suddenly wished that she could fall asleep.

Sleep . . . and sleep.

And live only in her dreams.

She must have fallen asleep, and deeply, for when she woke, she was aware that night had long fallen, and that the room was dark, no torches burned from the brackets, and only the flicker of gentle blaze from the fire offered any illumination.

When she stirred, adjusting to the light, she discovered that she had slept not just deeply, but like one dead, for she was no longer dressed in shift and tunic, hose and shoes, but wore a soft unbleached linen nightdress, not her own, at least not until now.

She half rose, and only then realized that she was not alone in the room, that a form was seated in the chair at the hearth. She knew him now, even in darkness, and realized that Jamie had sat silently with her, watching the blaze. Armor and helmet were gone, he was in shirt, breeches, tunic, and mantle. She saw his profile, head bowed, in the flickering light, and for a moment, observed him without his knowledge.

Then he turned, aware that she had wakened. Rising, he came to the bed, sat at her side, and brushed his knuckles against her forehead.

"Far cooler," he murmured, then asked, "you're feeling well?"

"I'm fine . . . I must have been very tired, far more weary than I had imagined."

"You had a fever, induced by too fiery a disposition, so says our finest physician."

"But . . . I am fine," she said, and she was startled that her words were as much a question as they were a statement, and that she felt an odd touch of fear along with the words. *Yes, there* was *a child, and she was suddenly, and fiercely, praying that she hadn't lost it. A just reward,* she thought dismally, *for her insistence upon denial.*

"It seems that you are fine," he said, "though I must say again, a hazard to yourself, more so than any woman I have ever known."

He rose then, moving back to the fireplace, standing at the hearth, staring into the flames. He turned back suddenly. "What was your eagerness to ride out today?"

"I wasn't eager to ride out. It seemed that you were eager to see me go."

"And why would that be—when I've told you about the negotiations that have thus far been tendered?"

"I simply thought that . . . you had changed your mind."

"I see."

He didn't see, not at all. "What would make you believe that?"

"The way you came . . . the words you spoke."

"How curious, Christina. And strange, to me. Granted, we've had our differences. Well, there is the important fact of being from two countries at war, but . . . do you know, my lady, the last thing I wanted was a hostage, and then certainly, I was not in the least eager to feel any fondness for a prisoner taken. No harm would have ever come to you. I thought that surely, when you reached out the way you did, it was because you saw something in me as a man that you could at least respect. Perhaps, even a semblance of honor. Yet how could you possibly see any such virtues in a man, and then doubt that his word was not worth keeping?"

She was startled by his speech, and found herself trembling, and loath that he should notice.

"I . . . simply thought that you had changed your mind. That perhaps you had decided that I was too much trouble. That I was an annoyance . . . in your way."

He contemplated the flames once again, then moved away, pausing at the foot of the bed.

"Well, frankly, you are an annoyance—fighting yourself when there is no one else with whom to do battle. And a burden I intend to keep. A year and a day, Christina. And that is a long time. There will be no exchange, under any circumstances."

She knew that he stared at her, seeking something. But in the dim firelight his features were hidden in shadow, and she had no words that she dared speak.

"Maybe in that time you'll see your own value," he said softly.

"I do see my own value!" she protested.

"Steven is free, somewhere," he reminded her. "But if he were not . . . there would be other ways to fight his battles."

"All else can be changed. But when a life is forfeit . . . it can't be brought back."

He was silent. A log sparked and fell in the fire.

"Get some rest, Christina," he said, and turned to leave.

She sat up, fearful, shaking her head, and suddenly determined that she must convince him of something, though she didn't know what.

"I have rested. I am neither weak, nor fragile."

"Well, thank God, or else, you'd surely have done yourself in by now."

"You're leaving tomorrow," she said.

"No. We'll wait and ride the next day."

"You're staying another day . . . because of me?"

"There are many factors involved."

"Of course."

He turned again. She lowered her head, biting her lip, willing herself not to speak.

"Jamie?"

"What?"

"You've . . . been at the fire for a while. Please . . . don't leave now."

"You had a fever. And you need to rest."

"Yes . . . but . . . please, would you just be with me?"

"Why?"

"Because . . . there are many admirable qualities about you. You didn't burn Hamstead Heath to the ground, you left behind food and livestock so that the people could make it through the winter, and build again come the spring. Because . . . you can taunt and torment, but I knew before that you wouldn't purposely cause harm to those who were weak and vulnerable. You might well have torn my home down around my ears, slain us for what we had attempted against you." He hadn't made a move toward her, and she was suddenly afraid of her own words. "Of course, you are arrogant, and convinced of your power, and you enjoy certain forms of tormenting others, but . . . please, stay here a while. I keep feeling that when you're gone, I can never be warm. Really warm." She lowered her lashes quickly, wincing, and feeling like a fool. She had given away so much more than she intended! And she had asked for a greater pain to come her way if he turned and left.

Or even if he went by his word, keeping her here for a year and a day . . .

And moving on with his own life.

There were questions she was too fragile to voice.

But then, he came back to her side. And he took her

gently in his arms, easing her over so that he could lie beside her.

He held her against him, and she felt the steady thud of his heart. She was warm, she was cradled.

And she rested easily.

CHAPTER 17

"Hamstead Heath!" Steven exclaimed, standing on the roll of land to the southwest of his home.

"The house is standing," commented the man at his side.

"That it is," Steven said softly. "Still . . . we'll have to be very careful," he warned his companion, looking at the man.

Who would have ever thought that the frail and ancient Lambert would become his champion and his friend? But when the man had discovered him trying to rappel down the sheer rock of the fortress of Thistle-on-Downs, to Steven's surprise, he had been far more upset than angry.

The sheets, bedding, and clothing Steven had fashioned into a rope hadn't begun to allow for the distance he had needed.

Desperate, however, he had taken the plunge into the moat rather than attempt a return to his room. He could swim, God knew—their father had been the fiercest of men, insisting that his son have skills that might one day be necessary to a fighting man. But the fall had been from a tremendous distance, and he had hit the water hard, only to become entangled in the plant growth that rioted in the moat.

He would have died if not for Lambert.

He still might have died, for it had been freezing, and the old man had left the castle with one old horse and his own cloak, which he had put around Steven before setting them both upon the poor old nag and taking them as far as he could from Thistle-on-Downs that very night. It had been two days before Steven had roused himself from a stupor of chills and fever, and realized that he had been rescued by the grouchy pile of bones he had always assumed Lambert to be.

And at first, old Lambert had remained cantankerous, insisting that he'd had no way of getting Steven back in, and that he was fearful of his own neck since his prisoner had found a way to depart. But as they traveled northward, Lambert had come to admit that he hadn't seen it in the justice of God that a man such as Steven should face execution, while such an evil soul as his old master, DeClabert, whispered lies into the ear of the king, and, like many of his friends, brought about dissension and set England on the road to civil war.

So now, strange as the world might be, Steven was a pauper in the company of another aged pauper, and they had taken on the robes of a pair of priests on pilgrimage— stolen, Steven was afraid, after inducing the good fathers to overimbibe in a poor wayside inn. He'd made a vow that night to make an endowment to the Church, were he ever in a position to do so again.

They had headed straight for Hamstead Heath, and though Steven approached his home warily, they had learned a great deal while passing through the countryside.

Aye, the Scots had come, demanding tribute.

Hostages had been taken, along with most of the livestock and household goods.

But, no, as yet, no knights were combing the countryside, aware that he—evil traitor that he might be, holder of a ravaged and raided homestead—might head straight home at the moment of his escape.

Still, with Lambert at his side, he surveyed the place carefully before approaching. His heart was heavy as he pondered the fate of his sister and the woman he loved, but he could not allow his sense of fury and bitterness to overwhelm the need for judgment.

And action.

He surveyed the landscape, observing the lack of burned-out ruins in the fields and surrounding village.

They had been spared much.

Their greatest resource had always been their prosperity. His father had been no more than a knight, until raised to his title by Edward I, elated by Adam Steel's relentless and ruthless ability to wage war.

And so, it was not that they had ever had the ability to raise a large army of well-trained men-at-arms. What they had offered to the war effort was a line of supply that was even more valuable.

A few sheep and cattle still roamed the fields. The manor sat nestled in the glen, beautiful in the morning light.

"Come then, Lambert." Steven said. "Let's take our chances. If the Scots have left any—and the English aren't there to demand my head instantly—we can, at the least, acquire a few good horses."

Lambert looked at him, blue eyes bright in the midst of his skeletal face.

"Count Steven," he said dourly, "once we have these good horses, what then?"

"We go after my sister and fiancée, of course."

Lambert's old blue eyes rolled.

"They've been taken by Scottish knights, my lord. Men who rode in with power, who hold your family hostage. They will be held far from the men such as you, who want them back. What possible force will you have to bring about a rescue?"

"I don't know, Lambert. I won't know until we've come much closer."

Lambert shook his head. "My lord, there is no help for you!"

"Oh, come, Lambert! I went diving to my death, and God provided for me."

Lambert looked at him skeptically. "I don't see the provision."

Steven laughed. "You, Lambert. You saved me from the icy claw of death and destruction! So have faith, man. We'll find a way. Come along. We'll dare so much as a night at the manor, and you'll feel far more prone to faith after a good meal. And since the house hasn't burned . . . well, my good fellow, we'll find the store of coins put away, and have a far easier journey of it." Steven's heart was far heavier than he would allow Lambert to see. It did seem that rescuing his sister and Lauren was an impossible task for an Englishman despised by his own king.

But then again, he was already a dead man.

It wouldn't matter much if he met his true demise in an insane but gallant quest, or at the end of a rope, or upon a block.

For the moment, it would be good just to set foot within his own house once again. From there, he would draw strength.

And, pray God, a sound plan as to where to go from there.

* * *

By day, Christina felt not only well, but embarrassed that she had fallen prey to any form of weakness or illness. Waking alone, she was aware that once again the courtyard and hall were filled with the sounds of many men busy at the multitude of tasks of preparing for war. From the narrow arrow slit in her tower room, she could see that no time was wasted among these men. In one corner, a group practiced with pikes, creating the Scottish *schiltron,* or formation of men so close together with their weapons so braced as to destroy an onslaught of English cavalry. Farther afield, they tilted with straw men, honing the deadly aim that mounted men might use against their English opponents. Others were engaged at slicing vegetable heads from stick figures, while still others practiced the art of death as delivered by direct swordplay, one man against another.

There were more weapons of destruction as well. Great maces to be swung by the likes of men such as Angus and Magnus; the power with which they could wield such a weapon was chilling.

Some preferred the feel of a battle-axe.

And she knew, through history's lessons, that the Scots had gone against armed and armored men with pitchforks and scythes alone. They were adept at using what weapons might be found at hand.

And still, she wondered if even the heart and determination of the fierce army forming at last under the king of Scots could withstand the sheer numbers that would ride hard against them.

In the hall, Christina found Lauren alone before the fire. She was reading from a fine parchment, and looked up, her face radiant, as Christina walked to her side.

"It's from my father!" she said jubilantly.

"He's managed to get a message to you?" Christina said.

"Aye . . . he's with a group of men at Carlisle. He has suggested that he'll come for me himself, but he's wanting to have a direct discussion with the Bruce. The king of France is at his wits' end over his son-in-law, and my father is indignant over Edward's fury with Steven. There will be hell to pay if any man thinks to execute your brother, Christina, even if that man is the king of England. Oh, but you know! Edward would buckle instantly to such a demand; he doesn't really hate Steven, he's just still so bitter over Gaveston's murder. It's Rowan who keeps the king believing that Steven is against him." The elation slipped from her features for a moment. "There's a very serious problem in the fact that no one knows where Steven is, including my father." She arched a brow. "Christina, do you think Steven might try to link up with the Scots? He was often at court when Robert Bruce was there; he served in his wife's household!"

"I don't know," Christina said. She realized that Lauren was very fearful that Steven might make such an attempt, no matter what it might mean regarding his future peace with the king of England. Lauren didn't seem concerned with the future of their property or holdings, only with Steven's life. She knew then exactly why she had always felt so protective of Lauren, even if she was now certain that truly, neither of them had ever really been threatened. Lauren had a purity of emotion that demanded such respect.

She joined Lauren at the fire. "It seems then that the world is good—for the moment."

Lauren, radiant once again, offered Christina her father's letter. She quickly read his greeting to his daughter. Though he had been deeply dismayed to hear about the sacking of Hamstead Heath, he was glad to have the assurance of the

Scots king himself that she was safe, comfortable, and in good hands. He would be meeting with Robert Bruce himself regarding her return, and mentioned that the sum for Sir Alfred's release had been paid, and that he was grateful to the old gentleman for his care. "As to the Lady Christina, I'm afraid it seems that some of the Bruce's bitterness at the continued incarceration of his family has spilled into the negotiations. Though great sums have been offered for her return, along with one of the Bruce's most beloved men, it has been firmly stated that she will not be returned immediately, as was DeClabert's demand. My deepest regards to Steven's sister, and my assurance that I will be using my power as a foreigner to both kings to render what assistance I can in speeding along the proceedings of her release."

She looked up at Lauren, somewhat alarmed, but Lauren quickly assured her, "I've sent a reply already, assuring Father that he must use his influence on securing a pardon for Steven, and that you are comfortable, well-tended, and safe."

"I just wonder what power he can wield," Christina said, "since it seems that not even the king of France has much influence over Edward."

Lauren shrugged. "I'm afraid that Edward may yet bring about his own downfall."

"We must hope that he does not cast Steven down before him," Christina said.

"I have a wonderful feeling, don't you?"

Christina shook her head slowly. "No. I have a feeling that DeClabert is out there, perhaps somewhere far too close. The English base at Carlisle is not very far."

Lauren smiled. "They don't have the power right now to reinforce their own strongholds. They have nothing to bring against a holding such as Langley."

"I hope that you're right."

"I know that I am," Lauren said, then was worried suddenly. "You don't have any . . . ill feelings regarding Steven now, do you?"

"No."

"Then . . . ?"

"Nothing," Christina said. But she was lying, and she didn't understand her unease. It seemed that, under the circumstances, the word was good, as she had said before. Gregory the young prophet had been saying too much regarding her own person, and she was beginning to feel that she was acquiring a greater gift for sensing the lay of the land. She wasn't at all sure why, but Lauren's father's letter didn't make her feel reassured at all.

Lauren suddenly touched her hand. "I know that he is near us, somehow. Steven, I mean. I know that he is coming . . . that he'll find us."

Christina nodded. Whether she'd had her sense of association with Steven or not, she would have agreed. If her brother had escaped Thistle-on-Downs, he would, indeed, be making his way to them.

She was simply very afraid of the path he would have to take.

Later that afternoon, when she had retired to her tower room before the hall would fill with the men for the evening meal, she was startled to hear a soft and timid knock at her door. Sir Alfred was gone, and Jamie would never knock in such a tentative manner.

She doubted he would ever knock at all.

She walked to the door, opening it curiously. It was Elizabeth Douglas who had come. "Interesting prison!" she mused, eyes wide as she walked around the confines of the tower room. "Good fire—far better than they managed at Dumfries, but . . . this is a truly exceptional walled fortification, with all the niceties of a manor as well."

"I understand that they have dungeons here as well."

"I've not seen them," Elizabeth said, then widened her eyes, "but, indeed, I hear that they do exist. Down by the crypts. Actually, both Igrainia and Eric have been kept in those dungeons, and they're not eager to force that kind of imprisonment on others. A lucky happenstance, for you, so it would seem. You are not so brutally held."

"I'm aware that matters could be far worse."

"Um . . . imagine when the king of England held Robert Bruce's sister and had an actual cage made for her! How very cruel. So . . . Well, I came to thank you."

"Pardon?"

"The banner. The banner I was making, to be sent to my kin as they ride to battle. Yesterday, I left it and ran off. You returned and finished it."

Christina inclined her head slightly. "I have but time on my hands."

"True." Elizabeth ran her hands over the stone mantel, then paused, staring straight at Christina. "The room, however, seems . . . somewhat barren. Where are Jamie's things?"

Christina felt the color drain from her cheeks. She shook her head. "Jamie has a room on the second landing."

Elizabeth laughed softly. "Ah, yes, well, of course, his permanent place. For the time being. But this fortress is actually Eric's holding. If and when the war ever really ends . . . Jamie will head home. His lands are near Stirling, just at the base to the Highlands, the gate as they say. Mountains, rivers, valleys . . . exquisite countryside. And, of course, near some of the bloodiest battle sites in a country that is richly stained with the blood of her sons. Once, though . . . Well, I admit my memories are not all that clear of a time before the bloodshed began. But I do remember Jamie before Fiona died. Perhaps he's not so very different. I've seen him be extremely kind to others, and of course, he has always turned to the lute. Now and then, his songs are light once again.'' Elizabeth looked at her. ''John Graham was an avid defender of Sir William Wallace, and died in his defense at Falkirk. Some of the clan have strayed, but for the most part, since that time, they have all turned to the point of the fight, suspicious of Bruce at first—as were many men, but now determined on his cause. They'll be rewarded in the end, so, of course . . .'' She moved along the mantel, pausing, offering Christina a wry smile. ''Once upon a time I was so in love with Jamie that nothing else in the world mattered. He and his clan were so dedicated to an ideal! So glorious on their battle horses, and so determined. But you see, I knew his wife. I was much younger, with a childish infatuation with him, and a bit of adoration for Fiona. Then she died. And I still thought that I adored Jamie, that one day . . . The thing of it is, you see, I am a Douglas. And we can vie with anyone when it comes to pride. I think I'm a great deal like you—though I haven't actually got someone quite as rational as your brother! I am talented, with all the proper skills, with something of an education. I speak French, English, and Gaelic. And though I don't care to sound too terribly boastful, I'm certainly attractive.'' She grinned suddenly. ''I'm selfish. Very selfish. And, as you might have noted, vain. And when I do marry someone, that someone is going to love me. Jamie does not. I believe my cousin let me come here, assuming that Jamie and I might naturally drift toward a betrothal. And I'm grateful. I rode here with Eric and his men, but Jamie would stand up for me were he asked to do so. I admire him greatly, and he is my very good friend, and if you should plan any evil against him, I swear, I'll come right for your heart, but . . . well, you should also know that I wish you only the best, in whatever may come.'' She left the fire, walking by Christina, who had still thought of no reply, nor had she moved. Elizabeth stopped before her, kissed her cheek, grinned, and moved on, pausing only when she had reached the door. "You will help me learn a great agility with a sword, won't you?"

"I . . ." Christina turned, seeing her at the door. "Yes. Of course. I will help you in any way that I can."

Elizabeth nodded, and walked out. The door closed softly after her.

That night, the hall came alive with a constant flow of food, wine, and ale. There was music throughout the meal as minstrels played and sang, and then, as the men finished with their food, they took up their pipes, their lutes, their dancing, and their songs.

Christina ate, making a point of being polite and charming to both Magnus and Liam, and while she laughed easily with Magnus and could truly say that she enjoyed the evening, Liam still surveyed her with the deepest suspicion.

When it came time to play, she did so willingly. She watched Angus dance with his wife, Rowenna, and saw when Rowenna whispered to her husband, apparently suggesting that he teach the steps to Christina. He pulled her to her feet; she demurred, but both Rowenna and Igrainia were there then, assuring her that she could quickly find the steps, and it was true, the steps were not so tricky as they appeared.

Father MacKinley came as well, helping her to further her lessons, and before she knew it, she was doing the reels about the room with many of the fine men she was coming to know so well. Ragnor, too, laughing as he told her that she was doing quite well, that actually, she had the movements down like a Highlander born. She wasn't at all sure that she agreed.

She paused to catch her breath, then discovered that Jamie was standing before her, mist-gray eyes as elusive as ever.

"Shall you attempt to accompany a true expert?" he inquired.

"A humble one?" she inquired, arching a brow.

"Humility has never stood us well," he said. His eyes were veiled. "You're feeling rested and well?"

"Incredibly so. I told you, I am neither weak nor fragile."

"I'm sure that's what old King Edward thought the day that he took to his horse to ride against the Scots—and but hastened his own death."

"I am very well. And though you may not believe it, I am never prey to illness."

"Ah. Only to sleeping drugs you would use against others—and the fever of your own temper."

"I am quite well."

"And one hopes, you'll strive to stay that way."

"Naturally."

"So the dance is not too much for you? No loss of breath, or thundering of your heart?"

"A Scotsman's dance will never be too much for me, Sir James," she assured him.

Apparently, he believed her.

The pipes began again, and they were off, and it felt as if she moved about the room on air. She saw that Lauren, too, was seeing the room through the eyes of the Scots, and in them, she somehow realized as well that every moment of life was to be lived, and every nuance of what a man, or woman, might be, must be appreciated.

The pipes wheezed to a halt. She was startled to feel herself whisked away suddenly by Angus, who asked to play a tune she had done with him before, but in the midst of the whine of the pipes, he paused, and began to tell a tale of a night when the Bruce had nearly been killed, but fought his way free with the help of two brothers, who had been at his side ever since.

Not to be outdone, Magnus rose to his feet, his robust voice filling the hall, and told of a night when the Scots had scaled a wall, and taken the day.

Christina strummed the lute as he spoke, adding a background of soft music, the somewhat harsh tones putting an emphasis on his tale. When she had finished, the large fellow walked to her side, insisting that they hear something in a more genteel voice.

She hesitated, debating, then decided on the story of a highwayman, stripped of his heritage unjustly, finding it again in the arms of the lady he accosted along the way. It was a ballad Lauren knew as well, and she came to Christine's side, harmonizing throughout the story, adding the touch of a soaring soprano that made it a lovely piece indeed, and yet, she realized, when she met Lauren's eyes, that her friend was thinking of Steven. And she knew that she had perhaps chosen the song in his honor, rather than rile the Scots with an ode to the English, or dishonor her own allegiance with a tune of a different culture.

They finished to rousing applause, and once again, the pipes began to play. Christina found that the lute was taken gently from her hands. Eric stood before her, politely bowing to take her to the floor. Igrainia was laughing with Ragnor, and Elizabeth Douglas was with Jamie.

"A beautiful song, well chosen," he told her.

She offered him a rueful smile. "I'd not have you and your men start the battle against me, here and now."

"Is that it? Or perhaps you've discovered that there is honor among the enemy?"

"I've never denied such a possibility."

"You have heard, of course, that many men think your

brother is free, and hiding in the forests until his name can be cleared.''

"Until his name can be cleared?'' she asked skeptically.

He shrugged. "Until he can be forgiven for good sense,'' Eric said.

"I've heard that he has escaped,'' she said. "And I believe it to be true. And, as I'm sure you know, Lauren received a letter from her father. He plans to fight for Steven as well.''

"Aye, I'm aware of the Frenchman's letter. And Lauren was eager that both Jamie and I see her reply. I hope that you realize you have actually wound up in the safest place you could possibly be. There is no reason that you should do anything but accept the hospitality here—that's true, isn't it?''

She hesitated, searching his eyes. "I suppose so,'' she said carefully.

"Your exchange can do no good at this moment. We have made our own response, in reply to the offer DeClabert has made.''

"A year and a day,'' she said.

Eric nodded. "Many things can happen in such time.''

"Many things.''

"Don't leave Langley, Christina. Ever, even for a minute.''

"Your wife has been extremely kind to me, sir. I can honestly swear to you that I would do nothing to cause her the least heartache or hardship.''

He nodded, apparently pleased and trusting in her words. And at that moment, the wail of the pipes suddenly rose high, and she was greeted by a new partner, for another reel. She was surprised to come to rest in front of Jamie as the discordant notes of the fast-paced music whined to a halt.

She inhaled greedily, steadying herself on Jamie's arm.

"Enough?" he asked softly.

She hesitated, never wanting to admit that she might be tired or worn. And yet, that night, she nodded, meeting his eyes.

He slipped his hand into the crook of her elbow, leading her from the floor. As they walked up the stairs, she could hear the revelry continue.

She entered the room, very aware of him behind her, of the sound of the pipes, distant now, far below. She walked to the fire, studying the flames and saying quietly, "I can honestly say, Sir James, that you ride with very fine men. And I will pray for them all."

"I'm sure that they will be grateful for your care. They've all acquired a certain fondness for you as well, Christina."

"And for my horses?" she asked lightly, turning to face him.

"Well, they are excellent horses."

"And I came with very fine beef as well."

"Very fine. An exceptional bounty, too, for men who often went hungry in years gone past."

He crossed the room to the mantel, not touching her, watching the flames.

"Does Liam get to ride back to battle yet? Poor fellow, he's chafed here terribly, when others have ridden off to fight the good fight."

"He's chosen to stay."

"Chosen? I don't believe that."

"Well, it's the truth. Ragnor meant to stay and guard the fortress, with Allen, Eric's man who has seen that it has become so impregnable. But Liam has chosen to stay. He knows the defenses here as few men do, and he has certainly come to know you. He greatly admires Igrainia as well, and, of course, my cousin, Eric. He isn't being forced to stay; he has chosen to do so."

"I see, though it's difficult to believe."

His hands came to her shoulders, drawing her near. "And what of you, my lady?"

"What of me?"

"Are you here now by force, or do you choose to stay?"

"You're forgetting my position."

"Not at all. I'm asking you a question."

"I believe that my brother has escaped. I'm afraid for him, of course. But as there's nothing that I can do . . . I am content to bide my time. A year and a day."

"And what about tonight?"

"Tonight?"

"Would you say that you are content to be with me? After all, I'd not want to take too much stock in the fact that you were eager for me to stay at your side last night. You were cold; I offered comfort. I'm thinking in our directions this evening. So—you are content?"

She mulled those words, then said a slow and careful, "No."

"No?"

"Not content. That's not the word at all."

"Then . . . glad, perhaps?"

"Glad?" she murmured, then shook her head again. "No . . . the word I'm searching for is more like . . ."

"Ecstatic?" he suggested.

"Truly, there's not a drop of humility in you, sir."

"Hm. I've told you, humility is of little avail."

Her lashes swept her cheeks. A small smile teased at her lips. "Ecstatic? Mm. Elated, perhaps . . . excited, pleased . . . willing. Eager. Very eager."

She looked up, and was startled by the raw emotion that lay naked in his gaze for an instant, one so swift it might not have been.

And it didn't matter, because in that instant, she was

crushed against him, and the force of his hold was tempered by the brush of his lips, a kiss like the flutter of a breeze falling upon her mouth, her pulse, her throat . . .

Then she was up, and in his arms, and aware every instant of the night that he would ride away again, and that seconds, not just moments, must be cherished.

She knew full well that night that she was very much in love with him. Far more in love with a man than she had ever been with the concept of a country, God help her. Or perhaps the man had given her something of his passion for the fight for his country. Maybe such a passion created a tie in which the country and a fight for freedom lived in a man, just as he found life in the dream of freedom.

There was nothing that he offered her, she knew. His past was an agony of fire, and his future was dedicated to that past. She knew him ever better through the words of a woman who had once loved him, and decided that what he could give was not enough.

She had no choice, for their lives had become interwoven. And in that braiding of time and fate, she had somehow given up her heart and soul. As the hours passed, she determined that she wouldn't dwell on the uncertainty of the future. She lived for the night, the flicker of fire from the hearth, and the way it played upon sleek naked flesh, rippled over muscle and sinew, created shadows in which to hide the depths of her emotion. The length of him seemed entwined in the length of her hair, touched to the color of fire by the blaze in the hearth as well. She strived to know him in darkness with the tips of her fingers, and by light and shadow, she consumed him with her eyes. She bound him to her mind with memories of scent and taste and feel, and closed her eyes again to know the fullness of his wholeness against her, the force of him within her, the stroke of tenderness that came ever after. And though, in the end, she lay against him still and silent, she did not sleep, for she couldn't let go of a moment, not while he remained.

The logs that had burned by night turned to ash as the first sweep of dawn rose with a pale pink glow in the heavens.

At her side, he stirred. He pulled her close, lips brushing, lingering, over her forehead.

He was about to rise.

She touched his cheek, stroked it with her knuckles. "Jamie."

"Aye."

"I lied, but I swear, with no intent. I didn't know. Perhaps . . . I simply didn't want to think. Or know. But now . . . I think it may be true. That we . . . that I . . ."

He laughed, catching her hand, brushing his lips against her fingers. "Aye, it's true, and I know. Keep well," he said.

He rose then, and too quickly, was gone.

Without another word said between them.

CHAPTER 18

Life at Langley took on a routine, one which was not
unpleasant. The days still had a strange sense, as if each
was spent in waiting, and yet, the waiting had no concept
of time. War had torn the country for nearly eighteen years.
God alone knew when, if ever, it would actually end.

Igrainia ran Langley with a smooth and practiced hand.
The household always seemed to be in readiness. Allen, a
master builder, saw to the defenses, the raising and lowering
of the great bridge each day. The battlements were always
lined with men, even if it had seemed that every able-bodied
man-at-arms had ridden to join with those laying siege to
the English fortifications.

Evening meals were far quieter than they had been.

There was time to read. There were days when Igrainia
brought forth some of the silks and linens pillaged from
English wagons, and they chose fabrics and patterns, and
worked on clothing. Candles were molded, soap was made,

meats were smoked, and they awaited the growing season of spring.

Christina had not imagined that she would find the company of Elizabeth Douglas to be the factor that kept her from simply losing her mind.

Elizabeth had action in mind, and was very serious about practicing with arms.

Apparently Igrainia, and even Liam, had decided that Christina was trustworthy. Though she knew she wasn't to go beyond the gates of the fortress, she was free to indulge in whatever tasks or interests she could find within the walls.

Elizabeth's interest was swordplay.

And the stables, though largely depleted by the mass forces that had left the walls, still contained trunks of stolen English bounty.

There were many swords remaining, most of them of the light variety the men did not find so appealing, but were perfect for the lessons Elizabeth found so intriguing.

Many coats of the lightweight mail remained as well, and Christina insisted that they wear it, frightened for herself should her pupil fail to comprehend the practice, rather than the pursuit of the lessons, and determined as well that she would not falter as a teacher, and bring harm to Elizabeth.

Liam and the other men were aware of their practice sessions, and often stopped to watch, and sometimes to join in.

Lauren was content to wait and seemed to have found a strange serenity, though Christina often wondered how, since it seemed that far too many days passed with no news being heard.

In mid-March, Christina and Elizabeth were in the courtyard. Though Liam forbid them to leave the castle walls, there was enough space within to ride, and practice with the straw dummies, as the men did before leaving for battle.

Christina had reclaimed her own horse, convincing Elizabeth that another mare among the horses from Hamstead Heath was an excellent choice; she was well trained, but in need of exercise and a rider who could form her to her own will and ways. She was silver gray like Crystal, and called Athena. Steven had named her as a filly; he had always had a penchant for the tales of Homer and the myths and legends the Greek gods and goddesses.

Elizabeth had just done an exceptional job demolishing a head of cabbage with her sword when Christina noted that the men had gathered at the front, near the giant wheel that controlled the mechanism of the gate. A moment later, Liam, Allen, and a number of the other men were descending the wooden steps from the battlements.

She whirled Crystal quickly, catching Liam on his way to the stables.

"What is it?" she asked him.

"An emissary, from Carlisle."

"A single emissary—or a party of men?"

He looked up at her. "A single rider, Christina."

"Should you be opening the gates?"

He stopped in his tracks, hands on his hips. "My lady, you may play well at arms, but Allen and I have guarded this place in the absence of the others many times. I know my business."

"I'm sorry," she murmured quickly.

"The bridge is down as it is, only the inner gates remain locked by day. But you will kindly take care that you stay within them."

"Of course," she murmured indignantly.

Igrainia had come out then, and Liam headed her way quickly. She was, after all, the lady here. And she, Christina reminded herself, was a hostage.

Five men rode out, Liam at their head, Allen remaining

behind. Apparently, there was no treachery intended, for a parchment was delivered and received, and the men returned. Elizabeth sat atop Athena at Christina's side, watching as Liam returned and headed for the door to the keep, where Igrainia waited.

She and Liam went into the hall.

She started to dismount and Elizabeth followed suit. "Christina, there is no reason to believe that the message has anything to do with you."

"It does," Christina said.

Elizabeth sighed. "Well, they're hardly likely to discuss it with you, at any rate."

Christina ignored her, leaving Crystal in the courtyard, aware that Gregory would come for her, and care for her.

She went into the hall. Igrainia sat at the great table, the parchment before her. Liam stood at her side.

Christina walked straight to her hostess. "It's from De-Clabert?"

Igrainia didn't lie. "It seems you're now worth double the sum, and three of Robert Bruce's prisoners."

"Oh?"

She had never imagined her value so high. She was certain that in truth she wasn't worth such a ransom. DeClabert was simply being denied something that he wanted.

"Father MacKinley will write the reply," Igrainia said. "The time stated is the time that must apply. The original agreement will stand. He'll explain that you are Sir James's prisoner, and that he isn't here, nor have we the king's assent to any further negotiation."

Christina shook her head. "Igrainia, he may not know that neither Eric nor James is in residence here."

"It's likely that our movements are well known," Liam said irritably.

"Likely that they are suspected. But DeClabert may have

written with such terms simply to find out how well the castle is manned. I know that I have no voice here, but I would still strongly suggest that you take grave care in the reply.''

From the chair where she so often sat by the fire, Lauren suddenly rose. "I think that Christina is right. They may suspect that most of the men have left, but not know it for sure.''

"And what would they do?'' Liam said. "We can fend off a small army here.''

"Unless the English are learning from Scots how to scale walls,'' Christina pointed out.

"We're very well armed, with fine defenses,'' Liam informed her.

Igrainia stared at her thoughtfully, then looked up at Liam and shrugged. "Christina may be right. And there's no harm in watching what we say. DeClabert will be informed only that for the time, the original agreement must stand.''

"Indeed, no harm,'' Liam said. He appraised Christina coolly, and she was certain that in his opinion, it would be more than a fair trade to receive a goodly sum of money and three stout-hearted Scotsmen in return for her.

"Thank you,'' she told Igrainia.

"Thank *you,*'' her hostess replied. "You're quite right; there's no cause to invite an assault. Especially when we *are* in a weakened condition.''

Christina looked at Liam. "You don't know DeClabert,'' she said simply, and turning, left the hall again.

When she returned to the courtyard, Elizabeth and the horses were gone. Walking to the stables, she found that Gregory had indeed come for the horses. He was engaged in studiously brushing Crystal. His movements were agitated.

She set a hand upon his arm. "It's all right, Gregory,''

she murmured, and was surprised that she should be trying to reassure anyone.

He shook his head, words formed on his lips and she tried to read them. She knew that he kept referring to her, and that she must not leave Langley.

"Gregory, I don't wish to leave Langley," she said. "I know that there is . . . far worse beyond the gates."

The way that he looked at her unnerved her. And she understood the next sentence he said perfectly, despite its silence.

You will want to go.

She shook her head. "I am . . . content here," she said, drawing on Jamie's word.

You must not go.

"I have no will to ride out, Gregory, honestly."

There was nothing more she could say or do. She turned and left him.

There were long days in the field as Scottish forces of Robert Bruce lay siege to the castles of Dalswinton, Buittle, and Caerlaverock.

English commanders held fast, some in fear, some due to national loyalty.

Any attempts by men at the stalwart English base at Carlisle to move supplies to the besieged fortifications were steadfastly thwarted by the Scots, determined that the enemy strongholds in the southwest would be captured and razed to the ground.

Because inactivity was hardest on many of the Bruce's loyal followers, the king was careful to see that his men were kept busy, harrying whatever troops might be carrying supplies. And because he and his company had spent so many years in lightning raids against the English, Jamie and his men were often sent to harass the men who left the bastion of Carlisle, leading others of the king's choosing that they may not grow too restless during the tedium of a siege.

Time and again they took to the roads, and time and again, they observed their enemy, position, strengths, and weaknesses, and prepared their assaults, always using the tactic of surprise, striking and taking prisoners and all supplies when they could, using lightning speed and destruction and retreat when the numbers and power against them were too strong.

Each time they returned to Robert Bruce, so that they might turn the weapons the English would have used against the Scots, upon the English instead.

One by one, the strongholds surrendered, starved into submission. Robert Bruce maintained his course of action, ordering that the fortifications be razed to the ground. He upheld his tenet for mercy as well, though word had come to them already that MacDowall, pardoned at Dumfries despite his earlier involvement in the death of Bruce's brothers, had barely escaped the long arm of the king to join again with the English.

By mid-March, Jamie and Eric were both outside the gates of Caerlaverock, where the king's troops remained just beyond the reach of the defenders' attempts to strike.

Robert Bruce was there, standing before the walls, surveying the fortification. Jamie, newly arrived from an assault upon a small English contingent, strode the distance to the king, pleased to inform him that they had taken more vital supplies, and that they had come across a fair quantity of English sterling as well.

Bruce nodded, not with indifference or a lack of appreciation, but because he had expected no less.

"There is a priest waiting in your tent to see you, Jamie."

"A priest?" He had an appreciation for God and the Church, and bowed his head before each battle when prayers were invoked, but he had scant time for a priest when he had returned from such a raid, weary and aware that though the castle they now assaulted would surrender, it had yet to do so.

"I've no time for a priest," he said impatiently.

"You will want to see this priest," Bruce assured him. "Jamie! The man has traveled long and hard, and risked a great deal to reach this position. He is exceedingly weary, but determined, and I have seen him myself, but it is you with whom he feels the greatest urgency to speak. The day is waning, and you're weary as well, I know, but take a few minutes. Speak with this man. I believe you'll find him an interesting guest."

Jamie doubted that, but Bruce was insistent, and preoccupied, apparently planning his next moves, once the fortress had fallen.

He made his way through the encampment that stretched far, outside the defenses of the fortress, and found his own quarters. He impatiently lifted the flap of his tent and found that there was, indeed, a man cloaked in the heavy black robes of an order with which he was not familiar.

"Father, I've no intention of rudeness, but I'm worn and weary, and have little patience at the moment. If you would state your business with me quickly, I'd be grateful."

The man rose from the camp chair where he'd been seated, turning to look at Jamie. He was near to his own height, with light green eyes and a strong but aesthetic face. Jamie was certain that he'd not met the man before, and yet there was something strangely familiar about him.

"I'll be quick as I can," the visitor said, assessing him equally. "So you're Sir James."

"Aye, that I am. Father, state your mind."

"Frankly, my urge, sir, is to spring for your neck and demand to know what you've done with my sister and fiancée. But since I am a vagabond traveler, lucky to have come so far and found myself to be in the good graces of your king, I'll refrain, and ask you as politely as possible about my family, whom you have taken."

"Steven of Hamstead Heath!" Jamie said.

"No, priest, I'm afraid. But any other man traveling these routes without a full army is likely to fall prey to one knight or another, or the simple bandits who harry the countryside, after whatever riches might be left behind."

Jamie stared at him another moment, walked to the camp desk, and took up a full skin of wine, drinking deeply. He turned and looked at Steven again. He and his sister resembled one another a great deal. If it hadn't been for the priestly garment, he might have recognized him immediately. "Your sister and Lauren are very well; Sir Alfred has been returned to his fold. The count of Altisan has contacted us regarding Lauren." He was quiet for a moment, still assessing the man. "DeClabert has offered highly for your sister."

There was a slight sheen on Steven's upper lip. "The king has assured me that she is safe, but in your keeping. You've—not made any agreements as of yet?"

"Frankly, we have negotiated. Your sister would have had it no other way."

"He is not coming for her?"

"He has been told that a trade might take place in a year and day. More than eleven months remain of that time."

Steven sank back into the chair. "I was certain that I would know if she were in serious danger," he murmured. Then he stood again suddenly. "I'm anxious to see them."

"They are at a family holding known as Langley Hall."

Steven shook his head. "Sir, you may have raided Hamstead Heath, and easily made off with hostages. I assure you, DeClabert is capable of doing the same.''

Jamie shook his head, still watching the man. "Langley is a great fortress," he told Steven. "I don't take hostages merely to have them snatched back. If you doubt my word on the description, the king will assure you that it's apt.''

Steven shook his head, a small smile on his lips. "There was no offense meant. I speak with a certain amount of fear for my ladies, for though they have faced danger at your hands, I fear that it is a far greater danger they may be offered by what one would assume to be friendly hands.''

"It certainly doesn't occur to a man that he's done his enemy a favor by taking his family hostage, sir. But once the deed was done, I learned a great deal about this English baron of whom I knew little or nothing before. But Christina was most willing to be traded to the man—in return for your life.''

"I would never allow such a barter, sir!''

"I don't think she intended for you to have a say in the matter. I'm merely explaining your sister's view of the situation.''

"She needs have no view whatsoever. I am not in DeClabert's hands. And he has no right to offer for her; I am her rightful guardian. Perhaps it's true that I haven't the same riches to offer in her stead—having no Scottish hostages of my own—but I will accrue what is necessary. You cannot give my sister over to the man.''

"Don't you remain in a perilous position yourself?''

"Aye, on the one hand. On the other, I can thank God that I knew Robert Bruce in earlier years—and that I did do my best, when allowed, to pay his tribute. My life, at least, seems safe enough for the moment, since Robert Bruce is in sympathy with me, and indeed, allowed me in here, to await your return. I am a man of honor, sir. I will find the price you ask for the return of my sister.''

Jamie nodded, viewing the wineskin. ''She goes nowhere for a year, sir. And at that time, there will be no price necessary. She will be allowed her freedom, no bargaining necessary.''

Steven viewed him suspiciously. ''I am aware that the Scottish view has been toward leniency—and restraint from murder. But even Robert Bruce is quick to take what goods and coins can be had in any transaction. And I'm of the understanding that you, sir, are living off much of the bounty and loot you have seized from the English, and that your own lands are in enemy hands at this time.''

''Indeed,'' Jamie agreed. As he stared at Steven then, a bowed and cloaked woman arrived with fresh linen, setting them at the foot of the pallet where he slept. Not taking his eyes off Steven, he moved a step forward to offer the camp follower a coin and a brief word of thanks.

When she was gone, he spoke again. ''Whatever my situation, sir, that is what will happen. I can assure you that your sister is far more a guest than a prisoner, and that she is far safer at Langley than she could be elsewhere. She is in excellent health—and will remain a guest for the time being. If she has suffered at all, it has been at her own insistence that every step taken be read as pure loyalty to the king of England—lest she make your position any more precarious. And . . .'' he hesitated. ''If she hurts day by day, it is because of fear for you. In fact, with or without your permission, I intend to see that a messenger is sent immediately to Langley that Christina and Lauren both may be assured that you are alive and well.''

Steven's eyes widened and a slow smile crept into his lips. ''You are sincere.''

''Completely.''

His guest lowered his head for a moment, and Jamie could see that the man was trembling. He looked up again. "Well, then, I am remiss. I owe you my thanks."

"Your thanks? Sir, I am the man who ravaged your home. And you're not getting back your horses; I am far too fond of most I have taken. And as to the cattle . . . most have been consumed."

"I noticed a most curious kindness on my way here," Steven said. "My house is still standing. And my sister, whatever reception she gave you, and whatever goods she offered, saw to it that no one found a certain space in the kitchen floor. Therefore, I had the means to come here, and still have a few coins at my disposal."

Jamie had to laugh. "So—there *were* coins hidden in the house. We never so much as suspected. And Christina convinced us that to burn the house and strip the place bare would only suffice to leave starving serfs, and lighten the king's haul on tribute for the year to come. I should inform you as well that she did everything in her power to see that Lauren was left behind, but that was a chance we didn't dare take at the time. Frankly, we had no desire to take hostages at all. She was afraid that, if she were left behind, it would not appear that she had done her best to fight Edward's enemies in your stead."

"God, that that fool DeClabert was able to issue such poison into the king's mind!" Steven said, showing a flash of impotent fury. "She can be reckless to a point of danger, and I can only say again that I am grateful she wasn't taken by a less honorable man."

"Hm," Jamie murmured dryly.

"I would prefer, however, that you not a send a messenger, sir. I am a man of my word, and my honor, and if I were not . . . well, I am the least likely man in the world to go to the English now. I would be heartily grateful if you would grant me a letter of safe passage, so that I may go to Langley myself.''

Again, Jamie hesitated, mulling the matter. There would certainly be no greater gift he could afford Christina and Lauren. But perhaps he hadn't been completely honest with Steven. The thought irritated him—he owed neither Steven nor any other man an explanation for his actions.

''If you go,'' he said, ''you will become a guest of Langley yourself, sir. I understand the Bruce's explanation to me that you've ridden very hard and through great peril to reach this point. You're a good three days ride from Langley, even moving with all speed. When you're ready to set out in the morning, I'll have an escort arranged and messages of my own.''

''I'll be grateful for the chance to deliver them.''

''Outside, you'll find my groom, Grayson. He'll see to it that you're given blankets, a place to sleep, something to eat.''

''The king has graciously seen to my needs—you see, at a different time, a different day, we rode together. But my thanks for your concern.''

Jamie shook his head. ''Actually, Count, I'm nearly as pleased to see you here as you are to have arrived. If you have any other needs, Grayson will see to them. Fresh clothing, a new mount.''

''My horse is from Hamstead Heath—one you chose to leave behind, but a fine mount nonetheless, and a night's rest will suit him as well. I ride with an old servant, and I believe that he and I will keep to our priestly garments, since they have stood us well thus far. I admit to total exhaustion, and will be glad of a night's sleep, but look forward to the morning as well.''

Jamie nodded, and Steven of Hamstead Heath slipped quietly from his tent. He sat at the chair before the desk, drank more deeply from the wineskin, and rubbed his chin. He'd had no sleep at all the night before but he wanted his correspondence done, and so set to the task of writing.

Grayson brought him food later, and though the Scots had taken to taunting the defenders of the castle by playing the pipes loudly at night and celebrating within earshot, he was too tired himself to join in. When he was done writing, he lay down, musing at the astounding fact that Steven had managed to find his way to them.

DeClabert held nothing over them now; nothing at all.

Christina came into the hall in the late afternoon in time to see Igrainia disappearing down a long winding staircase that led to the keep.

Curious, she followed her hostess. She was certain that the dungeons which had been mentioned lay deep in the bowels of the castle, and she couldn't fathom why Igrainia would be visiting such a place.

The steps seemed to lead down endlessly. The deeper she went, the greater the damp. The richer the scent of mildew and lichen on stone.

She hadn't thought to take a torch; only that which Igrainia held, walking some distance before her, afforded any light. She quickened her steps, wishing not to be left behind in the darkness.

The light disappeared. She nearly missed a step, found her balance, and continued. When she reached the ground, she could feel the cold permeate her clothing, but the light moved ahead of her, and so she followed quickly. The steps gave way to long halls.

The halls were filled with the dead.

They were ancient crypts. Shrouds covered little but decaying flesh and bone, and in places, bits and pieces of fine fabric. Cobwebs covered shrouds, and once, when the light danced ahead of her, she turned to her left and saw a slack-jawed skeletal face staring with empty eye sockets. She nearly screamed, but swallowed and hurried after the bobbing light ahead.

They had come to an area where ornate slabs covered the walls of the dead. Looking ahead, she saw that the stygian blackness broadened and continued beyond the bound of the light. The dungeons, she thought, were beyond the crypts, truly in the furthest, darkest, deepest, regions of the fortress. She shivered, wondering if anyone could be kept in so cruel a captivity.

The light stopped. She slowed her own pace, and kept moving forward. Igrainia was ahead of her, laying a few of the first wild flowers of spring before one of the chiseled monuments.

Igrainia apparently knew that she had been followed. She spoke without looking back. "A strange pursuit, perhaps, but I come at the first of every spring."

Christina came forward, reading the name on the tomb. Afton, Lord of Langley.

Igrainia looked at her. "My first husband."

"I'm sorry," Christina said softly. "Was he slain in the war?"

"He wanted no part of the war. He was a Scot with nationalist sympathies, but years ago, this region was held so firmly by Edward the First that only a madman would defy him. We had a sickness at the castle, and then no man wanted any part of it!"

"He died of the illness?"

"Yes."

Igrainia turned, illuminating another stone. *Margot, best and most beloved wife. Aileen. Precious child.*

"Eric's first family," she said softly.

"They died—here?" Christina said.

"The plague. They were all prisoners, you see. Eric as well. The men were to be executed. But no man has control over the plague. Some survived, and some did not." She fell silent, then turned back to Christina. "Did you come down to see if we might be keeping some poor fool in the dungeons?"

Christina flushed. "I'd heard they were here, yes." She hesitated. "And that you spent time in them yourself."

"I was angry, and determined. But I can promise you, they are not pleasant, as you may well have guessed by now. And there is no one kept down here."

Christina smiled. "I don't know why I followed you. I had no right."

"The days are long, that is why," Igrainia said. "Naturally tedious. And therefore . . . well, I knew you were behind me. I purposely hurried ahead to leave you in the dark. But you're not easily frightened, are you?"

"I nearly screamed like a child," Christina told her.

"But you didn't."

"Actually, I was probably more afraid of your seeing me, at the time. But . . . it doesn't frighten you to come here alone?"

Igrainia shook her head. "Afton was a gentle and good man; Eric's wife a beauty with a heart that carried nothing but kindness. And his daughter . . . well, a child is always the greatest loss. The dead here don't frighten me at all. And it's good to come here sometimes, and realize just what we have, despite our losses. And, of course, to remember that I don't ever want to see anyone kept in these dungeons again." She shivered suddenly. "We should go back up."

"What of Jamie's wife? Is she here as well?" Christina asked.

Igrainia shook her head. "She died when the house was

burned. The blaze was fierce. From what I understood, they weren't even able to gather her bones.''

"How horrible," Christina murmured.

"Others died as well. Every sheep and pig was slaughtered, every man captured or slain. The devastation was complete. I wasn't there; I only know what Eric has told me. It isn't something Jamie ever talks about."

Igrainia turned then, heading deeper along the hall. "A minute," she said.

Carrying the torch, she moved downward. Christina didn't think that she was supposed to follow. She did anyway.

They came to the dungeons. They were dark; certainly, she heard the rustle of rats moving about. The dankness seemed almost suffocating.

Igrainia was still moving forward. They came to what looked like a dead end wall, the very last of the dungeons. At the end of the hall, there was a great iron door with a heavy metal bar just before it. Igrainia suddenly turned back.

"Well, you've seen it all," she murmured, hurrying along. Christina followed with her gait every bit as quick. She had seen the dungeons, yes. And more.

The dead end had been walled. There was something behind it, and she was certain that she knew just what it was: An escape from the castle. Walled in, the area provided for an extra cell—should the dungeons need to house a number of prisoners.

But if danger threatened from an outside source . . . the back wall could be broken down. There was surely a passage that afforded an escape from Langley. She was certain that it would lead beneath the moat, and deep into a densely overgrown place within the forest.

If the wall were torn down or weakened, it might also allow for a dangerous entry into Langley, should someone know the way.

She quickened her pace because Igrainia was moving too far ahead. As she sped up, she couldn't help but wonder what it would be like to be left down here, without the glow of the torch.

They passed the dead, and came to the stairs. "Watch your step," Igrainia warned.

"Thank you."

They came back to the small landing and the short way back into the great hall. Igrainia turned and looked at her carefully.

"I'm very sorry for your losses," Christina said. "And glad, of course, that you and Eric were both here to comfort one another at the time."

"At the time?" Igrainia murmured. Then she laughed softly. "At the time, I loathed the very ground Eric walked on, and I wound up in my own dungeon because of him. But . . . ah, well, life throws very strange roads before one."

"But . . . you seem very happy."

"I am. Perhaps you should be just slightly forewarned. I was in that dungeon because of Eric. He and Jamie can be of like temperament."

Christina felt a slight burn of irritation, no matter how much she had come to like her hostess. "There is nothing for me to escape to, my lady. I don't believe that I've created any harm here, and it's amazing to be so mistrusted when it's more than evident that I am in a far better position here than I would be elsewhere."

"Yes, but that could change," Igrainia murmured. "Remember, you should always take care."

"I will remember," Christina assured her.

Igrainia shivered suddenly. "It's cold. I'll warm wine by the fire. The men will be in soon, and supper served."

"Warm wine would sit very well right now, thank you."

"Of course. Christina . . ."

"Yes?"

"Don't ever go to the dungeons again. Ever. Please."

"There's certainly no reason, my lady."

Igrainia observed her carefully again, then turned. "Ah, here they come now. Liam, what news? Has anyone come before our walls?"

"None but our own sheep, my lady!" Liam assured her.

The others began to file in and Christina moved to the fire. Igrainia was already calling for the wine.

Lauren sat there, sewing, her head bent upon her task.

Christina felt a sudden flare of warmth. The fire . . . she thought.

No, it was a sense, something pervading her. She was captured by the feeling, still and white, as it swept around her.

"What?" Lauren said uneasily, dropping her needle, thread, and garment, and leaping to her feet. "Something is wrong."

Christina shook her head. She wasn't experiencing a sense of pain or discomfort. She felt as if she had been infused with strength.

"Christina, are you well? Are you ill . . . please, tell me, what's wrong?"

"Nothing is wrong . . . something is right!" she said happily. She looked at Lauren, bewildered but elated by the feeling of well-being that had come over her. She was certain that her brother was not just well, but close. She was so certain that she hesitated only briefly before telling Lauren, "Steven is somewhere near. Somewhere very near, I'm almost certain. And he is well . . . Lauren, I believe he's coming to us!"

*   *   *

A battle encampment could offer wondrous comfort, Steven decided. He had been given one of Bruce's own tents—possibly taken from the English, of course, but strong against the night air. He lay on a pallet of blankets, with blankets around. He'd been served a supper of rich, fresh roast beef.

His own possibly, but it had been well cooked.

And the wine he'd been given . . . exceptionally fine. And not from Hamstead Heath.

He and Lambert had traveled with far greater speed and ease once they had procured horses at Hamstead Heath, but the ride to find the Scottish position had been harrowing. They had ridden in the darkness and through the thickest, densest forest trails, all to avoid possible detection by his enemies. They had slept on the rough ground with only their horse blankets for beds, with the chill air penetrating their clothing, with stones and roots beneath them most often. They had avoided villages, and eaten little but the few days' provisions they had brought from Hamstead Heath, and the few dried berries they had found along the way. He hadn't known what kind of a reception he would receive from Robert Bruce, but he was a man who had spoken of the good sense of paying tribute to the Scottish king, and word had apparently gone out that he had done so. He had known Robert Bruce.

And he had been heartily relieved that the Scottish king had been pleased to welcome him. It was true that Bruce paid heed to those who had supported him—even if he hadn't intended his support.

And so the night was sweet. He hadn't felt such a sense of elation in a very long time. Comfort, a full stomach, and the belief that the women who meant everything to him were alive and well, cared for, and protected when they might have been abused and cruelly incarcerated. He couldn't remember a time of such great and abiding relief.

He saw the silhouette of the woman against the side of the tent, molded there by the fire still burning just outside. He frowned, curious as she entered into his small domain.

"Count Steven?" she said softly.

"Aye?"

"I've come to see to your comfort. Is there anything you need?"

"Nothing. The provisions granted me have been generous in the extreme."

"Would you like company, sir?"

Steven grinned in the darkness. The King of Scots had even sent him a woman.

"Ah, well, though I'm sure you'd be the most delightful of companions, I am a man about to be married."

"Many men are to be married."

"But not many men are as enamored of their fiancées as I, dear woman. I have done little but dream of my lady, since we've parted. For me, there is no other."

"How remarkable, sir. I have seen your lady, at Perth. The king himself was her protector there. She was soft-spoken and kind, tending to the injured, and seeking information about you."

"Well, then, you see why I love her so."

"Aye, and your sister, too. A good soul—tending to the injured. Alas, though, not in the king's care."

Steven sat up. "What do you mean?"

"Nothing. If you're set for the evening, I'll leave you."

"No, wait!" He had yet to really see the woman's face. "Tell me about my sister."

"I . . . there is nothing to tell."

He reached out quickly, catching her arm. "Tell me about my sister!"

"Sire, there's nothing. Other than . . . well, of course. She was the lady of the manor conquered, so they say. Seized and taken . . . you must understand. So much was done to the Scots, it was natural that he should take the lady as he chose."

"Are you telling me that my sister was abused by her captor?"

"I'm telling you nothing!" she said. "I must go!" With a quick and sudden movement, she wrenched free from his hold.

It didn't matter. He'd heard enough.

Jamie woke suddenly, alert, aware that he'd heard something in the night, a sixth sense warning him of danger.

He was in the middle of an encampment of his own men, and yet . . .

There was someone just outside, seeking entry to the tent.

He silently reached for the sword at his side, and waited.

His night visitor didn't enter furtively. He was stunned when the flap was thrown aside and a man walked in, brandishing a sword, heading straight for him, ready to put the point of his blade against his throat.

He had his own weapon up and leaped to his feet even as the man entered, and in a flicker of firelight from beyond, he saw Steven Steel's tense and angry face.

"I'd have your life, sir!" he spat out. Despite his words, his tone was level, determined.

"I'd take care with such a suggestion," Jamie said, frowning, and staring at the man who evidently meant his words. "You are a guest here, and remain an Englishman in a Scottish encampment."

"Yes, I imagine that when the deed is done, I'll be strung

from the highest tree by your companions. But you will be dead. Fight, if you will. If not, stand there and die.''

Steven moved toward him. Jamie struck a defensive blow. ''What? Have you lost your mind?''

''No. My sanity has been stolen, along with my sister's honor! You speak of what might be done with her—when you attacked and molested her while she was in your care.''

''I never attacked your sister.''

''You lived with her, intimately, in a farmhouse after the assault of Perth!''

''I'll repeat for you once again—I never attacked your sister.''

Steven struck another blow.

The tent flap flew open. Ragnor was there, his sword drawn, a look of amazement on his face as he sought out the danger that caused such a cacophony in the night.

''Stand back!'' he ordered Steven.

Jamie shook his head. ''No, Ragnor! He is a man defending his sister's honor—which he believes was stolen. It's a personal matter.''

''It's not a personal matter; half the camp is waking,'' Ragnor said dryly.

''Still, a matter between the count and I,'' Jamie said.

''No man could live with himself, knowing that such an insult was forced upon his flesh and blood!'' Steven said. ''So now, I will die, but you, by the grace of God, will precede me unto death!''

Once again, he slashed out with his sword, his blow so forceful that when Jamie countered, his sword all but flew, taking down half the tent.

The three men stumbled as it fell, Steven ripping his weapon from the fabric as they all jumped free.

Fires still burned. The men on guard began to gather around; those who had slept began to waken. Jamie rued the foolishness, and knew that Steven had pushed this now into a brawl that far too many men witnessed.

"For Christina!" Steven said.

"If you insist on killing yourself, you will dishonor her fight for your life!" Jamie said furiously.

"She is my sister. I am her guardian!" Steven roared. "And you . . . I will kill you!"

"There was no insult!" Jamie insisted, his voice harsh as he went on the offensive, coming at the man with a succession of damning blows. He caught the man in the arm, and saw a streak of blood run across his shirt. Steven winced, but didn't even glance at the wound.

"You attacked her."

"You sister chose to be a hostage!"

"You, sir, made use of your hostage."

"Steven, I never attacked Christina. Drop the weapon, or you'll die for sheer stupidity and stubbornness. You'll break her heart, losing your life for a foolish reason."

"Our honor, sir, is foolish? Is it only a word without meaning when pertaining to the Scots?"

"It's a word with meaning only when you know the facts."

The man was far too incensed to listen. And he was an able fighter. He came forward with a sudden burst of energy, rapidly swinging down hard with a heady round of blows that kept them both moving rapidly in a broadening circle within the tents and campfires. He was lean and wiry, with the ability to bring down many a far heavier man, Jamie was certain.

But he had a weakness in a fight with Jamie.

Because Jamie knew how he would move. He had met and fought with the man's sister, his most apt pupil. And so he anticipated the leaps and dodges. And when Steven surged forward again, he avoided the lunge in the same way.

He brought the hilt of his sword down on Steven's head. The man crumpled into the dirt.

A cry of pleasure went up among the crowd.

Jamie shook his head. "Someone see to him; he should come to soon." He looked around. "He fought well and for what he believed was a noble reason. There will be no retaliation against this man. We here are all too familiar with the fury of losing what is ours by right. He came after me with courage and conviction. He might even make a good Scot one day."

He stepped over Steven, and headed for his tent.

His arm was sore. Count Steven Steel was indeed adept with his weapon. Edward II was a fool. He had thrown away a good man.

Count Steven Steel, Lord of Hamstead Heath. Like his sister, far too reckless in the defense of others.

Jamie returned to bed, only to lie there awake.

He owed no explanation for his actions to any man.

And he would not apologize to this one, even if he was her brother.

And even if it meant that they would meet at sword point once again.

CHAPTER 19

Christina woke in the middle of the night, aware of a sudden and sharp pain. In the muted firelight, she knew a strange confusion, thinking at first that she had actually been attacked, and then wondering if she hadn't slept in the midst of a strange dream of which she had no memory.

The unease with which she had awakened was so great that she couldn't go to back to sleep, and she rose in the night, pacing the confines of her chamber. She held still before the flames, trying to concentrate very hard on her brother, but she felt ill, certain that he had been hurt. Yet she maintained the same sense that he was near, and that she would see him. She tried to shake off the fear.

The next morning, there was an ominous foreboding in the hall.

Liam, Allen, and others were around the table, with Igrainia at the head of it, discussing the current situation.

"But has anyone come forward, toward the gates, in any

way? As if a messenger would approach, but hasn't done so?'' Igrainia asked, a frown furrowing her forehead.

"No. And nothing, nothing by day. But by night . . . there is something,'' Liam said.

"What is that you all have seen, exactly?'' Igrainia inquired.

"Shadows,'' Allen said flatly.

Peter, another of the men always at Langley, spoke up then. "Far past the fields, the roll of the hills. Into the forests. There are movements. I'm convinced that there are men out there, that they have taken to the trees.'' He was a tall, solid man, built like the others, but his love was not for arms, but rather for equipment. He saw to the maintenance of the great gears and wheels that worked the inner and outer gates, and day after day, saw that the small catapults set at various strategic angles upon the parapets remained in working order. She'd heard Igrainia murmur that if the castle had truly become impregnable, it was because of Peter's genius for defenses.

He leaned forward. "I believe that there are many men gathering in the forests, my lady. The forces at Carlisle have been far too preoccupied thus far, trying to save what English holdings they might, to be able to consider the number of men and the war machines needed to come after such a place as Langley, especially since this area now rests almost completely in Robert Bruce's realm of control. But there has been word from many of the prisoners taken that new men and supplies have been pouring into Carlisle now as well. And too late for there to be any attempt made to salvage the fortification razed to the ground by the Bruce. With an abundance of men available, they may well be gathering, watching our position, waiting for the gates to be opened as sheep or other animals are herded out to the pastures, now that so much of the snow is gone.''

"They could well be close enough to attempt an attack, if they believe themselves hidden in those forests, ready to strike when the gates are open and the bridge is lowered," Igrainia said.

"That's our belief," Liam told her.

"Then, as difficult as it may be, we must begin to see ourselves as being under siege conditions."

Liam noted that Christina had come into the hall. Seeing her, he scowled. "Frankly, I see our position as very dangerous, at this moment."

Igrainia was quiet. "So . . . you believe that any movement from the gate is duly noted?"

Liam nodded.

"A messenger sent out to find our men's position . . . would most probably be seen, stopped . . . and possibly slain."

Liam nodded grimly.

"A messenger must be sent," she mused.

She rose. "Peter, we'll need workmen. You know what must be done. And we can't falter with our vigilance from the walls, in any way." She smiled, a wealth of affection on her features. "I thank you, and thank God, that I have you. Tonight, I'd like to keep watch with you myself for a few hours. Today, we'll set to work. Liam . . . see that the men we have are prepared and ready for trouble. The cattle will remain within the walls, but the sheep will be led out, yet to no distance from the walls. If we're being watched, I don't want our enemies to realize that we know as yet."

"A good choice of action, I think," Liam said.

"The men out there are still gathering, so we believe," Peter said. "We'd be fools to go out and attempt an attack, so we've nothing to do but bide our time. Better that they don't realize that we have seen their movement by night."

"Peter, when the gates are open, you must be at the entry yourself," Igrainia said.

"I'd have it no other way," Peter assured her.

She rose; the meeting was at an end.

The men at the table stood as well, all acknowledging Christina as they departed on their various ways. Liam gave her no more than a curt nod, but Peter greeted her with a greater sense of friendship, as did many of the others.

Christina hadn't been duly escorted from the hall when she had chanced upon the grave discussion, but neither had anyone chosen to explain the situation—and certainly not their defenses and Igrainia's words regarding "what must be done."

She thought that she knew anyway, of course.

They were going to break through the tunnel entrance, allowing a messenger to depart from the castle through that pathway. Peter and Allen did not leave the keep through the main door, but she noted that they strode to the stairs leading to the crypts and dank prison cells.

When they were gone, she noted Igrainia's frown of concern, and her concentration as she crossed her arms, pacing before the fire. She had forgotten that Christina was there.

Christina walked forward saying, "Igrainia, if men have suddenly come from Carlisle, I think it's quite likely that Rowan DeClabert is among their number." She was silent for a moment, considering her words. "I've promised not to cause trouble here, but I believe that my being here is trouble in itself. If Langley is threatened . . . then you might save many lives by ridding yourself of the burden causing the trouble."

Igrainia stopped in her pacing, staring at Christina. "The time has come to an end, you know, when any of the Scots roll over in fear, and accept death and defeat. When we're threatened, we fight."

"There isn't a full fighting force left at Langley, and that's the truth of it."

"We are protected by a deep moat—deepened in the past years, since the Scots themselves have learned that moats can be crossed, and walls scaled. The walls are thick, since we're aware as well of the power of rams and catapults. If Robert Bruce had the least belief that we could not defend the fortification here, he would have ordered that it be razed to the ground. Langley can stand."

"And how many men will have to die so that she can do so?" Christina asked quietly.

"We're not under attack, as yet," she said. She studied Christina for a long moment. "And, frankly, if you so much as suggest again that we should surrender anything—or anyone—to be left at peace, you'll leave me no choice but to see that you're locked away again."

"I'm merely telling you, Igrainia, that I will understand if you should think the lives of your men—your child, yourself, and your unborn babe—are worth more than holding a useless hostage."

Igrainia smiled. "So far, they are now like outlaws sniffing around in the woods. We'll have word out by today. Robert Bruce has been laying siege, not preparing to meet a mighty host of the enemy. He can spare men to return, and fight, if need be. There is no need for you to feel that you will bring about death and destruction." She started to turn away, and then paused, looking back. "Believe me, Christina, you have earned a certain respect and affection from everyone here. But if you were to threaten my child in any way, inadvertently or other, I would throw you out those gates myself."

Glad of the honesty of her words, Christina smiled. "Thank you. I'm certain, however, that many of the people here would just as soon see me gone."

"I believe you're mistaken," Igrainia said, and moved toward the stairs to the crypts and tunnels below.

Christina knew that she was not to follow.

She turned, with a purpose of her own.

Hurrying to the stables, she found Gregory at work with a harness. Maybe he had sensed the men in the woods. He was still restless, watching her as she moved about.

But she did nothing she hadn't done before, handling the lighter swords, surveying the contents that remained in the trunks, and the mail that had been draped for cleaning. She visited Crystal in her stall, and saw to the other horses.

She waited until Gregory had left his work behind, called out to perform some function for one of the men.

Then she carefully surveyed the arms before her again, aware that she would have to make a number of trips to the stables and back again, and that she would have to be very wary in her actions. She didn't know exactly what would happen, or what the men milling in the woods truly portended, but she meant to be prepared.

Steven woke with a raging headache, but it wasn't enough to block out his memory of the night.

He was still furious. He had come to Sir James, and been more than impressed with his mercy, stance, and person. Only to discover that while the man had left his house standing, his benevolence hadn't been so great when it had come to his captive.

He groaned, trying to move his head, and was startled to see that his nemesis of the night before was seated at a fire just outside the tent. A chill swept over him. He had fallen in a fight, and his enemies had not taken swift action to see that he died on the spot. God knew, kings liked to make examples of men. Perhaps he'd now face some ignoble form of execution.

But had there been any other choice for him once he'd heard the words that were more than apparent truth? Could there be any life for him at all if he didn't have some semblance of true honor? A man could live without possessions, but could he do so if he had no respect for himself?

"I see you're stirring," the Scotsman said curtly.

"Aye, that I am."

"There is no real damage to your skull; the physicians have seen to you. If you'd get a good day's ride in, you should be ready within the hour."

Steven came carefully up on an elbow, willing the pounding in his head to stop. "You intend to let me go to Langley?"

"I never blame a man who thinks his cause is just. However, if you come at me again, I will do my best to kill you."

"What do you expect of me? You have dishonored my sister, my blood, my name."

"There was no dishonor done your sister."

"You locked her away with you, and yet insist that you forced nothing upon her."

"I swear, by God, by my own good name, I forced nothing upon her."

Steven exhaled on a soft sigh of relief. "So . . . the woman lied."

"What woman?" Sir James asked softly.

"I don't know . . . a laundress, a camp follower. She insisted that you two lay together, at Perth."

Sir James was silent.

Steven felt his irritation rising, despite his situation and condition.

"You just swore that there was nothing—"

"No. I swore that I forced nothing upon her."

"I see!" Steven said icily. "You're trying to tell me that my sister forced *you?*"

"Not at all. I'm trying to tell you that there was a relationship of mutual consent."

"That cannot be," Steven said with great dignity. He frowned. "Do you then have some kind of thought that you could marry my sister?"

"No," James said flatly, rising. "I don't intend to marry again."

"Then you've still done her a great dishonor! Seducing a young woman who was surely terrified."

"I don't believe your sister has ever been terrified, Lord Steven. Under any circumstance, she is looking for the best means to do battle. And if you aren't aware of that, then I have come to know the lady far better than you do yourself. I am sorry for this, because I can understand your rage and your feelings, but there is nothing for you to do—your sister is my hostage, and her fate rests in my hands, by the word of Robert Bruce himself. As I've told you, I intend to let the allotted time go by, and when it has, her future will be her choice. It would give me great sorrow to kill you, because I am well aware that would break her completely, as no other threat has done. Whatever your hatred and your honor, contain them. If you wish to continue on to Langley, arrangements have been made. My man will carry the letters which will assure your safety in Scottish territory, and see you into the fortress. They also bear letters of warning that you are distraught. I assure you, those who hold Langley in my cousin's absence are seasoned warriors, weary of bloodshed, yet aware when it must occur. With God's grace, this last fortress will fall any day now. And we will follow behind you."

Steven kept his eyes evenly upon Sir James. He came

carefully to his feet. "This is a matter not yet settled, Sir James," he replied.

"Then it will not be settled now. If you would ride out, prepare to do so. If you are hell-bent on my death, I'll have no choice but to defend myself."

"We will see that the matter is settled," Steven insisted. "At a later date."

"Indeed. Well, we'll pray that you are not repatriated with your own people intent on your death, and that I don't fall to an enemy's battle-axe. Then the time will come when we can settle this dispute."

Sir James rose and strode toward the horse that awaited him in all the battle trappings of his house, and that of the king, Robert Bruce.

Steven forced himself to his feet. The matter was not settled.

But for the time being then, they'd both live.

And he would get to Langley.

The mood at Langley became one of tension.

On the parapets, men watched, and waited.

On the second night, Christina was startled when it was Liam himself who saw her in the courtyard, standing straight, and alone, and came to her side. Maybe the fear that had been growing in every heart was apparent in her eyes, for he was again the more courteous soul who had given a kind word or two after the first night at Hamstead Heath.

"Come up; you can see the shadows of which we speak," he told her.

She looked at him with gratitude, and accepted the hand he offered to lead her up the wooden steps to the parapets. They stood behind the low walls of the battlements, with men silently at their posts around them.

At first, Christina could see nothing. And then, in the sliver of moonlight, she began to see the movement of form and shadow, deep into the forest.

"They are lighting no fires," she murmured.

"No. They may still believe that we haven't detected their presence."

"What kind of a force do you think is out there?" she asked.

He shrugged after a moment. "Cavalry, which means they'll have to show themselves soon enough; there will be only so long they can confine their mounts to the forests. Archers, perhaps. And certainly, foot soldiers. But I don't think they can have come through harsh trails to maintain such a close position with any siege machines." He was quiet for a moment. "Edward the First came once with a catapult that he'd named the 'Wolf'. Even after the garrison surrendered, he kept tearing it to shreds. He wanted to test his newest weapons of war. Such machines are deadly. They have the power and force to release huge missiles that crush anything in their path."

"But such a machine would be very large?"

"Yes."

"Still," she murmured, "with archers . . . and ever smaller catapults . . . they could wreak destruction, and if they couldn't breach the walls, they could force a surrender by burning down everything in sight."

Liam looked at her, and offered a wry smile. "They'll have to get close enough to do it first."

"But you haven't the men here to return the fire they may offer."

"We don't know what they're about yet," he said quietly.

Christina looked at him squarely. "A large body of men massing by stealth? Sir, I haven't your experience, but even I am certain that they plan to attack!"

"Time may be on our side," Liam murmured.

"And if not?"

"We know our business," he said. "And we fight well. We are very, very bitter, you see. We will truly go down before we accept defeat!" He smiled. "Come, I'll bring you down. There is nothing that will happen tonight."

"Has the messenger gotten out?" she asked worriedly.

He paused just a second before answering her. "Aye, he has. So, my lady, have faith. Langley will not fall."

She stared at him there, on the parapets. "Liam, I've been quite convinced for some time that you'd love to have me sent packing to the enemy."

"Well, you're wrong. I'd love to be able to trust you."

"I swear, sir, I wish none of you the least harm."

"I believe you."

"Then?"

"You're still too certain that you can wage your own wars. No man, or woman, can do so, my lady. And if you believe that I think ill of you, you're truly mistaken." He shrugged and grinned suddenly. "I actually admired you when you indignantly demanded your own horse at Hamstead Heath. But ... now I am responsible for you. And you are frightening."

"But I swear to you, I am not!" she protested.

"Then don't assume that you can cast yourself from these gates and leave others in peace. We haven't been at peace for years. And we will not be at peace until these many fights are won. Let us fight, and win the peace that only the final battle can bring."

"Maybe peace can come another way."

He shook his head. "Edward the First meant to exterminate every one of us until the last man surrendered or fell. Edward the Second hasn't his father's will, which was utterly ruthless, but neither has he any sense for diplomacy, and so the fight will continue—until it's won.''

"And you're so certain that it will be won in the end?''

"Aye. Because we've come this far. And we will die, rather than be subjugated. Bruce betrayed his own for many years. But he learned. And now we have a king such as the English themselves have never seen. And we will stand by him until there is victory, or death.''

"A fine way for a man to live, with his passions for justice,'' she murmured. "And yet, what does it leave for a woman?''

Again he was quiet. "My lady, we've seen our wives, sisters, lovers, and even children butchered as well. Forgive us if we desire to protect what is ours now that we are gaining the power to do so. If you would give to the effort, lady, give your faith.''

She stood silent. Give her faith. To what end? Would her eventual value be in gold and exchange, since the Scots might win their freedom, but they would never have the simple population and manpower to dominate the English? At some point, if the precious freedom was ever won, kings would have to bargain.

Freedom for the Scots might still be a long way off. And until then . . . ?

A year and a day. That, at the least.

But what of the years to come? She didn't know how these people had borne the many years of bloodshed, of never knowing where the next battle would be, of sleeping in the woods, of knowing how quickly life itself could end.

Liam started down the wooden steps, courteously taking her hand to lead her. She accepted his assistance though it wasn't necessary, and came down the steps.

* * *

On the afternoon after Steven's departure from Robert Bruce's camp, the fortress sent its emissary with an official offer of surrender.

That night, there were tremendous celebrations. The riches of the castle were distributed among the men, prisoners were taken, and by nightfall, dismantling had begun.

That night, a number of the barons and knights surrounded their king, hailing his name, and basking in the victory.

The king never allowed a victory to distract him too long when there was still too much of his kingdom to be secured. He knew men, and allowed them their moments of glory. They were well earned and hard won. But as the night waned, he spoke to various of his men, delineating his next plan of attack.

He called upon Jamie to remain with him after he had told his many followers that there was much more work to be done, and that they couldn't stop while they were hot on a trail to victory. They stood before the walls, watching fires burn within, and a host of refugees fleeing from the destruction. "One day," he murmured, "we will rebuild." He turned to Jamie. "Bothwell and Stirling remain in English hands," he said. "FitzGilbert is at Bothwell, keeping quiet as a mouse, as well he might, being surrounded as he is by Walter Stewart's lands. As to the castle at Stirling ... I intend to send my brother Edward to see that it is forced into submission. When I ride from here, I intend to take a large force and meet with Angus MacDonald of the Isles."

"Aye, then? Do I take my men to Stirling, or with you?"

Bruce hesitated, then turned to him. "Neither. You spoke before of making a raid into England. If you would pull off such a daring feat as leveling Thistle-on-Downs, now would be the time. I don't know yet when it's coming, but you can be certain that our successes will soon scratch beneath the skin of the English with such a fury that the king will be able to stop the squabbling among his barons to launch a major assault. The king of France is an interesting man— his letters to me address me as King of the Scots, while his correspondence with Edward, his son-in-law, never refers to me in such terms. The French king has a daughter on the English throne now, and therefore, he wants Edward's England stabilized. He may eventually force a truce between all those with whom Edward is still quarreling so fiercely. Once that happens, I daresay that the English will find our victories a terrible affront, and they will then get together like children tormented by those outside their family realms, and mount a serious attack. When that time comes, every available man in Scotland will be needed. But as for now . . . are you still so tempted then to ride south, and assail such a stronghold as that held by Rowan DeClabert?''

Jamie hesitated. DeClabert held nothing over him now; Steven had managed his escape, and was under Scottish protection.

But equally important was the fact that DeClabert was somewhere in Scotland himself, though exactly where, no man had seemed to know.

The concept, however, of leveling Thistle-on-Downs was still an appealing one.

''You've done exceptionally well in your raids against the English,'' Bruce pointed out. ''Enriching yourself, and bringing invaluable supplies so necessary for the battles we wage. And, of course, each time we bring our fury to English soil, we do increase the cries of the border lords, who grow weary of their lands continually being ravaged.''

''Are you ordering me now to Thistle-on-Downs?''

''No. I wouldn't order you to take such a risk. But I am

telling you that I wouldn't be averse to having you make such an attempt at this time. Still, I'd have you throw no lives away. We can't breed ourselves nearly as fast as the English have killed us. So—do you remain interested in such an undertaking?''

"Aye, I do."

"Take your men to Langley, then. Lay your plans well and carefully. See that you are armed and supplied. And when you are victorious, see that I am informed immediately. Take your men and leave tomorrow; your work here is done."

"Aye, then."

"We'll be joining again soon enough," the king said.

Jamie left him. The fire on the night air was acrid. Victory was sweet, but the destruction they had wrought was in their own country. It would be good to wage war on enemy territory again.

Better, still, to return to Langley, which he could do with the king's blessing. He was suddenly wishing for a warm bed.

And even the conflicts that awaited him.

The English in the woods had still made no daylight appearances, or sent out messengers or emissaries with either demands or warnings.

The waiting continued.

The tension increased.

On the fourth morning after the shadows had been seen in the trees. Christina woke to hear a sharp and piercing scream coming from somewhere within the castle.

She leaped up barefoot and in her nightdress, flew to her door, threw it open, and realized that the cry was coming

from the level below. She sped down the stairs, nearly collid-
ing with Igrainia at the landing.

"What is it?" she demanded quickly, for Igrainia appeared so preoccupied.

But her hostess quickly stopped, a smile flashing across
her features when she had been frowning over whatever
business lay at hand.

"Nothing terrible!" she quickly assured Christina. "Rowenna's baby is coming, that is all."

Shouts again arose from one of the rooms down the hall.
Jamie's room, Christina thought. Angus and Rowenna had
their own home, a little cottage built against the southern
wall.

"She was here with me, when the labor started," Igrainia
said. "Jamie would not begrudge his bed to a babe. He
hasn't used the room of late anyway." She laughed suddenly.
"Listen! She is swearing with fury at poor Angus! Thankfully, he's far away, and cannot hear."

"Why would she swear at Angus?"

Igrainia smiled deeply, shaking her head. "At this particular moment, she sees him as a terrible culprit—she's in
pain. Don't worry, she'll be delighted soon enough, wanting
Angus to ride back, and share her pride in their child. I must
get Berlinda . . . we need water. Come in, keep Rowenna
company . . . a woman needs help, talk, and the strength of
others at such a time."

Christina felt as if she would be intruding, but she still
found herself drawn to the room. Rowenna was on the bed
while a midwife struggled to straighten the sheets beneath
her twisting form. "It will ebb, it will ebb!" the midwife,
a crone with few teeth, cautioned. "Bite down on the wood
as I told you, and learn some restraint! You've hours yet to
go."

"Hours!" Rowenna wailed.

"So it appears!"

There had been no way to grow up at Hamstead Heath without having been present for the birth of endless foals. She was quite familiar with birth.

But horses didn't scream and swear and toss in pain, not in this manner.

Hesitantly, she walked to the bed, taking a seat at Rowenna's side.

She took the woman's hand. "It's Christina. Can I do anything for you?"

Before the scar had marred her face, Rowenna must have been a very beautiful woman. Even with the scar, she offered deep-set eyes, a wealth of lovely hair, and finely shaped features. She stared at Christina, winced, and fell silent. Then her fingers seemed to bite into Christina's hand with an ungodly power and she cried out again. "Aye! Find Angus, and take your sword against him!" she cried.

"Angus! He's far too dear."

"That he is not!" Rowenna said indignantly. "Ah, but he is, if only he were here . . . I didn't know . . . I should have known . . . Oh, dear God, but this hurts!"

"When it hurts so, bite the wood!" the midwife admonished.

"The wood . . . where is the wood . . ."

"Here," Christina told her.

Igrainia returned to the room with a chalice in her hands. "Come, Rowenna, have a sip," Igrainia urged her. Christina looked at her.

"A mixture of herbs, to help the labor along," Igrainia said.

A few moments later, Rowenna screamed as if she had been speared with a sword.

"Dear God! It's worse."

Christina looked at Igrainia. "A greater pain—a far briefer time in which to endure it," she assured her.

A bowl of water was on the stand by the bed. Christina dampened the linen cloth in it, and began to bathe Rowenna's head. She was startled by the look of gratitude the woman gave her. "That's cool ... so good."

"When it hurts so, bite the wood hard, and squeeze my hand all you like. I'm very tough," Christina assured her, eliciting another smile.

Not even Igrainia's herbs could rush the labor along too quickly. But evidently, the lady of Langley knew what she was about, for the midwife assured her soon that they were moving along far more swiftly.

In two more hours, the child's head crested, and they were helping Rowenna to push. In minutes, her baby all but popped into the world.

"A boy!" the midwife announced with pleasure. "A strapping young son!"

"Too strapping!" Rowenna said, and yet, in seconds it seemed that she had forgotten that she had suffered, and was reaching for the child. Igrainia cut the cord, and the midwife continued to work over her patient. Rowenna didn't notice in the least; she was cradling the babe against her, eyes filled with awe.

"Strapping, of course!" Igrainia said with a pleased laugh. "What would you expect? You married Angus."

"Ah, but yes, it took us some time to have him," Rowenna said delightedly. She looked at Christina, explaining quickly, "We lost one babe ... some time ago. Oh, Igrainia! He's beautiful, is he not?"

"He's a need to be bathed," the midwife said gruffly, and with her patient washed, her nightdress pulled low again, the old woman went for the child, taking him to a table where she washed him quickly, attending to his nose and throat, and making certain that he gave forth great and gusty wails.

Christina watched her with the child, and the old woman was an expert. In seconds he was clean and pink, whereas he had, at first, somewhat resembled a slippery pig in the midst of a sty. The midwife turned then and thrust the child at Christina. "A handsome babe, indeed," she muttered, and returned to her Rowenna, changing the linen towels beneath her, and bringing sips of water to her lips.

The little mass of life squirmed in Christina's arms. He had a head full of dark hair. Flailing, tiny, perfect fists. He was warm, and vital, so innocent, small, and vulnerable. And yet—what a set of lungs! She cradled him against her, crooning, and was surprised by the fierce need to soothe and protect that rose in her like a geyser. She held still, turning away from the others, holding the infant tenderly and tight to her. A strange trembling went through her. So this was . . . life. She had known, of course, that they had all been right, and that she was carrying a child herself. But in such early stages. There was no sense of movement inside her—just a nervous unease in her stomach at times. She hadn't actually denied it to herself any longer, but she hadn't envisioned it, or allowed herself to think much about the truth and reality of the situation either.

And now . . .

She wished that she hadn't been with Rowenna, and witnessed such a simple wonder. She didn't want to imagine what her child would look like, how it would come into the world, or realize even, that it would indeed be real.

"May I . . . have him?" Rowenna whispered.

"Oh, Lord, of course!" Christina said, hurrying the babe to her.

"He's beautiful. Beautiful!" Rowenna said. "Dear, dear Angus! He'll be so pleased. Won't he?"

"He's surely the most beautiful babe I've ever seen," Christina assured her, helping settle the infant in his mother's arms. "Angus will be very proud."

"Thank you," Rowenna said. "Thank you . . ."

She was paying Christina no more heed. Her attention was all for her son.

Christina slipped from the room, realized her own state then of complete dishevelment, and hurried up the stairs, washing and dressing with an urgent speed, since she didn't care at the least then to be alone in her own company.

Starting down to the hall, she heard a man's voice addressing Igrainia, and the sound of it was tense and urgent.

She hurried more quickly down the stairs, and found the hall empty. She burst out the door, seeing that Igrainia was then going up the wooden steps to the parapets.

Christina gathered her skirt and went racing after her. Liam, with Igrainia on the battlements then, looked down and saw her coming.

"No!" he said harshly.

Igrainia saw her, and something in the woman's look of pity and concern stirred hard in her heart. She ignored Liam's command, and hurried up the steps. The only way he could have stopped her would have been to hurl her back down.

She reached the parapets and looked down to the green fields and valley stretching before them.

Riders had come. Four of them. They had apparently come from the northeastern trail to the left of their position.

Two were garbed as priests. Two were garbed in tunics that bore the heraldic pattern of the Graham clan set next to the lion of the king.

She noted first that she was very familiar with the horse on which the one rode. And then, she realized that though the man was dressed as a priest, it was her brother.

"Steven!" she breathed. Elation filled her. She had been

right! He'd been near, and now he was coming, just as she had believed in her soul that he might.

The two at her side were silent, and she heard then the strange thunder she hadn't noted before.

She looked past the men.

Coming from the southeast were more riders.

Dozens of them.

They were clad in full plate and armor, bearing down, a cavalry that numbered a good fifty men or so.

Christina gasped.

She spun on Liam. "Open the gates, open the gates quickly!"

He stared back at her, and she knew, of course.

He couldn't open the gates. To do so would be to allow the enemy cavalry through, for they were so close behind her brother and his escort. God knew what more men-at-arms were just beyond the enemy horsemen.

" 'Tis Ioin as well," Liam muttered, in a voice filled with anguish.

The armor-clad cavalry moved hard upon its prey.

Christina screamed, sinking downward as she saw her brother struck from his horse.

CHAPTER 20

All four in Steven's party were thrown from their horses, and collected by the riders, just beyond the gates.

Liam hoarsely called out for action from the parapets, and arrows flew from the battlements of Langley.

Three of the enemy fell. It made little difference. Their numbers were great; they collected their prey, and their own fallen, and retreated to the woods.

"They're fighting like Scots!" Liam cried furiously, his anguish and rage a bellow that swept into them all.

"They've gone," Igrainia said. "But they'll be back. Allen, Peter, Thayer! Keep a sharp eye on them; watch for any messengers. The gates are not opened on any account unless we're certain that their numbers remain as far back as the forest shield."

She started down the steps. Liam gave Christina a gentle shake. "We've got to go down."

"They'll kill him!" she breathed. "They'll kill him.

They'll have legal backing now. Steven was a traitor for certain; he escaped the king's *hospitality* and went straight to the Scots!''

"Come down," Liam insisted firmly.

At that moment, she had no strength. She followed his lead.

In the hall, Igrainia was pacing. "They couldn't have known that Steven was coming here, they were just watching and waiting. And he happened along. With Ioin . . . and the other two. They may not know that they have your brother, Christina. They were there to attack the minute a small party came to the castle, and the gates were opened, the bridge down."

She sank into a chair at the table, shaking her head. "I tell you, it's DeClabert. And he will kill Steven."

"We can do nothing now but wait," Igrainia said firmly.

"He may ask that I be exchanged for my brother, and you must do it. Not just for Steven. For Ioin. He will kill them. He won't kill me."

Igrainia spun on her. "We will not negotiate with them, Igrainia. We will not. The agreements have been made."

Christina leaped to her feet. "You must!"

"We are waiting now, and that is it!"

"Igrainia, I know this man. And I do have an idea."

Igrainia walked furiously past her. "No, I don't want to hear any of your ideas. We wait."

Lauren came flying down the stairs with Elizabeth Douglas. "What has happened?" she cried.

No one wanted to answer her.

She stared from one face to the other. "They've attacked at last," she said.

"Yes," Igrainia told her quietly. "Apparently . . . Steven found Robert Bruce and the great force of Scots at the siege. He rode here with a small party."

Lauren started to crumple. Liam deftly moved to her side, catching her before she could fall, leading her to the chair before the fire. She stared at Christina. "Is he dead? Is he dead?" she cried out.

"No," Christina said, and stared at Igrainia. "Not yet."

"Elizabeth, please, take Lauren back upstairs," Igrainia said firmly.

"No, no . . . I must . . . I can't . . . oh, God."

She lowered her head and started to sob. Christina felt frozen in place. Elizabeth, with a look of the deepest sympathy and compassion, hurried to Lauren. "Come, Lauren, you can't make yourself ill. That will do nothing for Steven. Upstairs . . . I've some wine that you must drink. It will help you wait, as we all must wait."

Lauren seemed broken. Sobbing violently, she allowed Elizabeth to take her, and lead her up the stairs.

"You won't even listen to me!" Christina lashed out.

Liam spun on her that time. "No, we will not! And this has been our very rational fear with you, my lady, that the time would come when you would risk every life here and every battle waged here for the life of one man."

"Ioin is out there as well!"

"And he has long known the risks of this war."

"That is all you can say?"

Allen came bursting into the hall then, stopping short when he saw Christina. He drew his eyes from hers, looking at Igrainia again. "My lady, if you will?"

He turned back to the door, with Igrainia and Liam following quickly. Christina flew behind them. As they neared the steps, Liam swung on her. "Why are you doing this to yourself?" he demanded harshly.

"I must see!" she told him, and hurried up the steps before he could stop her.

She wished that she had not come as gall rose in her throat.

Four English knights had seen that their prisoners were tethered to their horses. They raced across the valley, dragging their victims over the earth.

"They are killing them!" Igrainia whispered in horror.

"No," Liam said bitterly. "Believe me, lady, it is just a form of torture. They are only half dead. This is just to warn us of their capabilities."

"A rider comes toward us," Peter said.

The single knight stopped some distance from the walls. He drew out a bow and arrow, attaching a parchment to the arrow.

"Down!" Liam commanded roughly.

The arrow flew true, flying over the battlements, and falling to the courtyard. There, one of Langley's men procured it, tearing the message from the arrow, and striding toward the parapets. Igrainia started down first, accepting the message with Liam at her heels.

She read it quickly.

"I must compose a reply," she murmured.

As she headed to the hall, Liam followed, calling out to the others to man the battlements, and heat the oil, and set the small catapults.

Again, Christina followed Igrainia back into the hall, pushing past Liam. "Tell me what it says!" she insisted.

Igrainia stared at Christina. "Aye, it's Rowan DeClabert. And he will return all four men, in their current state of health, if you are turned over to him."

"Send me out then!" she said furiously.

"What makes you think that this man will live up to such a bargain?" Igrainia demanded.

"He—he must!"

She had already turned to Liam. "I'll explain that I haven't the authority, that they must let one of our men through to the king's position.''

"He will not allow it.'

"It will buy us a little more time."

"He'll know that we're stalling."

"There is one way to make him wait," Christina persisted again. "I know DeClabert. If you will just let me—"

"Christina, I think you should retire upstairs as well," Igrainia said quietly.

"I—I . . . no, please! I can't," she said, and managed to speak softly. The two weren't going to listen to her at all—ever, she realized. She walked to the fire, listening as they discussed the exact wording that must be used.

She had no idea where her next inspiration came from, only that it came, that it was a risky and really desperate plan—and that she had no other.

Standing at the fire, she turned, as if listening intently.

"What?" Liam said, suddenly and sharply, noting the way she stood.

"There's something . . . I hear something. The passageway!" she gasped. She turned, glad that they were across the hall. She collected a torch as she passed the wall, then started down the steps to the crypts and dungeons with a flying, reckless speed. She desperately watched each step, knowing that if she fell, she was done. Her brother would die, as would the gentle and handsome young Ioin.

She didn't fall. And though Liam and Igrainia were close behind her, she kept her lead, running all the way to the end of the passage, and to the secret tunnel which had recently been opened so that the messenger could make his furtive escape from the castle.

"Here, here, at the wall!" she cried, still running. "There's a noise!"

And then, just outside the iron bars, she stopped. The wall

had already been reset with mortar and stone. But Liam, being a stalwart and certain commander, moved past her, followed by Igrainia.

Christina didn't hesitate a second.

She threw the iron bars of the dungeon cell into place, quickly sliding the heavy bolt into the lock.

And of course, they both turned back. Liam in a rage, bellowing and swearing instantly. Igrainia silent, staring at her with ice cold reproach and anger.

"I'm sorry!" she whispered. "I'm terribly, terribly sorry. You refuse to listen to me, and I know what to do."

She left them there, and raced back along the tunnel, and up the stairs to the hall. She found the quill and parchment where Igrainia intended to make her reply. She sat down and quickly wrote, then bounded up the stairs to Lauren's room.

Elizabeth still sat with Lauren, but she had evidently slipped something into the wine that had induced Lauren into a deep sleep.

Elizabeth, seeing Christina, rose. "It's all right. She'll sleep until evening, poor dear. She does love your brother. I'm so sorry, Christina."

"Enough to help me?" Christina breathed.

"What do you have in mind?" she asked. "I—can't help you kill yourself, or send the men out—they'd all be slaughtered. I would do anything I could though—Ioin is my kinsman," she said.

"DeClabert likes nothing more than a challenge at arms. I'm going out to fight him."

"He won't fight you!"

"I'm going to go out as Jamie."

"Igrainia will never let you."

"Igrainia can't stop me. But I can't pass as Igrainia. You can. I need you to slip on her mantle with the hood . . .

summon one of the men and see that the reply I've drafted is sent out. You can't let Allen, Peter, or any of the others realize that it is you. And when I go out . . . they'll know I'm not Jamie, but they'll have to believe I'm Liam."

"This is . . . foolhardy. Liam will never allow that! And what makes you think that DeClabert will agree to hand-to-hand combat, winner take all?"

"I know DeClabert."

"But, he will renege."

"The terms insist that he deliver our people to the gate, and back away. He knows that the gate will have to be opened, if they are to be retrieved."

"What will keep him from storming the gates?"

"The terms that I have set down." She hesitated. "The moment that I'm out, you must see that Peter does retrieve the men. And then . . . he must lock the gate, in case there is some treachery at hand."

"You know there will be treachery. And you're going out to fight a knight, Christina!"

"I've seen him wage his games of skill. Elizabeth! I understand that the others might doubt me, but you have seen my ability—you'd be a liar to say that you yourself haven't learned astonishing skill through me!"

"I can't help you in this—my own kin would rack me!" she said.

"Elizabeth, on my knees, I am begging you!"

Christina prayed, counting heavily on Elizabeth's own sense of worth and self-confidence. "I don't know if they'll believe I'm Igrainia, no matter how low I keep my head."

"They will, if you don't let them see your face. Please . . ." She offered the parchment. "Take this . . . and go now. Then you must hurry back and help me with the mail and plate. Once I'm fully clad, it won't matter who sees me. And . . . Jamie left Satan behind, so any men who have come across him in a previous battle of engagement will know his horse. Elizabeth, I am desperate! God! How can any of you let Ioin die so easily.''

"We've learned to save what lives we can," Elizabeth said. "Oh, give me the parchment! But remember this—if you're killed, they'll all be ready to slit my throat. I'll have to go and lock myself in the dungeons!''

"Bless you!" Christina said. She left Elizabeth and fled first to Jamie's room, needing breeches and a tunic. The new mother rested with her babe; both were sound asleep. She fervently envied Rowenna. She had given new life that day—and knew nothing of the death that waited beyond the walls.

Elizabeth returned, still clad in the hooded mantle, trembling almost as hard as Christina was herself. Christina was grateful, aware that she could never have managed the mail and plate on her own. She was in one of the lightweight coats with the very fine small links, and when they were done, she had sound protection at her throat, chest, thighs, and even smaller plates to add protection to her arms and legs. At last, she donned a helmet, and the tunic in the family colors standing boldly next to those of Robert the Bruce.

"Well?"

"Thank God you have some height," Elizabeth murmured.

"I'm going for Satan.''

Elizabeth moistened her lips and followed behind. When they reached the door to the keep, Elizabeth quickly ducked her head as she accepted the response. She turned away from the man-at-arms before telling Christina, "DeClabert has accepted the challenge. His captives will be delivered fifty feet from the wall; his men will remain at the trees. He earnestly awaits a chance to meet Sir James at a contest of speed and skill, a challenge fought . . .''

"A challenge fought . . . ?"

"To the death," Elizabeth said, looking at her.

Jamie and his men were a few hours still from Langley when he lifted his hand, calling a silent halt. He heard the thrashing through the foliage, and indicated that his men should retreat to the sides of the road.

Then, listening, he realized that it was a man, a single runner racing through the forest. He urged Zeus forward, then reined in when he saw the man, panting, exhausted, running still. It was Thayer, one of his cousin's most trusted retainers.

The man came with such impetus that he all but ran into Zeus, gasping, "Sir James! Thank God . . . I'd not have made it without a horse . . . had you still been at siege!"

"What is it, man?" Jamie demanded, catching the exhausted Thayer when he would have fallen, and calling quickly for someone to bring water.

He drank but a little, and pushed the skin away.

"Men . . . many of them. Well armed, from Carlisle . . . we think. In the forests . . ."

Jamie's heart thundered, but he forced Thayer to slow down, to take another sip of water, to get his breath.

And then to tell everything that he knew.

When he was done, a horse was brought quickly for him.

And they began to ride again, this time with all speed.

She rode out on Satan, fully covered in helm, armor, and colors, men from the castle believing that she was indeed Liam, and—she hoped—those before believing that she was Jamie.

She rode out the agreed distance, then reined in the great

stallion. As per the agreement, she saw that the English had retained their positions by the trees. A single mounted rider in full armor awaited her challenge in midfield.

She waited until she heard the last of the tramping noises as the men of Langley came for their fallen and beaten. She was tempted to turn, and race Satan back across the field. But, of course, she could not. There was the sound probability that the bridge could not be raised in time, and that the whole army of men before could come rushing in.

She heard the sound as the great bridge was raised. And then there was no choice but to ride forward.

She recognized DeClabert's colors and insignia on both the man and the beast before her. When she approached, they eyed one another warily, circling at a distance. She continued to hold her pace, her heart pounding. She wondered if the real James Graham would have pitched forward, full speed into the battle, ready to attack.

She knew that she could not.

And so she waited . . .

At last, her opponent wearied of the circling. She was aware the moment he subtly kneed his great battle horse, and aware of the movement of his sword arm. She kneed Satan, ruing the weight of the shield she carried, yet knowing it was necessary. Her opponent raced forward . . . and she veered. His sword thrust caught only the tip of her shield, and he nearly fell from his horse on the first thrust. The thunder of hooves bit the earth as he passed by, reined in, regained his balance, and turned his mount toward her again.

A bellow of rage escaped the man, but he wasn't a fool, and he wasn't going to make the same mistake again.

Christina had planned that he should not.

This time, when he furiously galloped his steed for her, she swung Satan around in an entirely different direction, and to her own surprise, the ruse worked perfectly. Her opponent had expected his weight to be needed to the other side, and he was completely off balance, crashing to the ground with a clash of steel and chain, a heavy fall.

That was when she knew she needed to move quickly, leaping from Satan while the man was still down. She spent a great deal of her own force, thrusting again and again as he tried to stumble to his feet.

She tried not to allow any fault to trip her up. She had to remember that she faced a man who would have gladly slain her brother, and would gladly make her life worse than a living death were he ever to have her in his power now. She tried not to let either rage or fear cloud her judgment, or forget that a new decision must be made every split second. She hadn't the weight or the muscle power of the man, and it must be the agility of her mind that kept her standing.

And she must find a weakness.

She hadn't expected that the fight would be easy.

Yet neither had she realized just how long, how wearying, such a fight would be. She'd kept him down for some time, trying to rain her blows upon his helm, and disconcert his mind. He had still made it to his feet, and come after her with calm, steadfast force that sent her back twenty to thirty feet. Yet when he came to slash down with what he assumed would be the breaking blow, she spun, and eluded the force completely.

His sword pitched into the earth with an awful violence.

Before she could seek the weakness in his mail, he had retrieved it, and once again, she was fighting for her life, being forced backward dozens of feet, and listening to the cheers of the English army at what did not seem a great enough distance.

She remembered, the next time his arm raised to deliver the coup de grâce, never to feint in the same direction. And she realized that if she did not weaken him then, her own failing strength would be her downfall.

She danced away from the blow, and this time, when his great, heavy sword caught in the earth, she brought her sword down in a ferocious blow against his shoulder, then his head. When he fell to his knees. she kicked him in the chest with all her strength. And then, for the split second when a line of flesh was visible between his helm and the mail at his throat, she struck a blow with her sword aimed dead down, at that thin line of weakness.

She hit flesh.

Gasping, the man instinctively reached for his helmet, desperate to take it away from his face so that he could breathe.

She saw two things then.

One, he wasn't dead. He was bleeding profusely, but it hadn't been a strong enough blow to pierce deeply and sever an artery.

And the second thing . . .

It was not Rowan DeClabert she had fought.

A rise of sound went up at the ridge of the forest. Horrified, she saw that the enemy had indeed intended to allow the game.

But no more.

The horses were now pounding against the field toward her.

For deadly seconds she could not afford, she saw the wave of cavalry pounding down upon her. She was dimly aware of some other sound . . . the clank and crank of the drawbridge being lowered. Dismay filled her along with terror as she forced herself to turn at last and race for Satan. She was so weighed down with the mail, and he was so much larger than Crystal, that she failed on her first attempt to mount.

Then, another sound split the air. The wail of a pipe.

And as at last she made it upon Satan's back and turned toward the castle of Langley, she saw that men-at-arms in the colors of the Graham family and those of Robert Bruce were now spilling out of the forest trail closest to the castle— just as they were speeding out of the gates of the castle itself.

And still . . .

She could all but feel the breath of the horses at her back. She could hear the earth flying before her, churned up by hooves belonging to horses other than her own. She saw that a man, swinging a mace, was at her side, even as the riders suddenly came together in a great clashing of steel and roar of men and horses.

She ducked the swinging mace, yet fell so low that she was hanging by Satan's side. She couldn't regain her balance. She screamed as she crashed down from the stallion's back, hitting the earth hard, yet rolling instinctively to avoid being trampled.

She lay a second, gasping, trying to get her breath. She rolled again, struggling to her feet. She looked before her. Another man was aimed dead at her, swinging a battle-axe.

A horse raced around. Its rider wielded a sword, catching the man with the battle-axe in the center of his chest, sending him into a backward spin from his mount. She screamed, a sound covered by the clash of battle, as his mount panicked, reared, and crushed him beneath its heavy feet.

Another armed enemy was bearing down.

The rider turned, urging her to come quickly.

"Up, man!" he demanded, reaching out his hand with its heavy gauntlet. She grabbed hold, and swung up beside him. The cavalryman who was racing in the wake of the man just defeated was feet away then, swinging a battle-axe, just as the first. He was nearly upon them. Jamie brandished his sword, kneeing Zeus, ready to do battle.

The man didn't reach him. An arrow flew from the battlements, piercing his armor—plate and mail. He went down.

Jamie turned Zeus. The melee in front of the castle had become terrible. Men and horses were down, mired in blood.

Then, there was the sound of the horn. and suddenly, the English were retreating. And in turn, the Scots were ripping up the earth as they tore back to the walls of the castle, thundering over the drawbridge.

They came into the courtyard, horses piling in one after the other, filling it. Christina was shaking so badly she could slide from the back of Zeus, even without Jamie's help. She stumbled to the wall of the keep, grabbing on to it for support, looking desperately about for the men who had been brought back.

She saw Elizabeth then, streaking through those who had returned. She pushed away from the wall, still stumbling beneath the weight of the armor and her own exhaustion. She caught up with her. "Steven . . . Ioin . . . the others?" she demanded anxiously.

"Alive, alive!" Elizabeth said, hugging her.

She had nearly brought them both down. Then she felt a hand settle on her shoulder. "It's not Liam!" That in Jamie's voice. He spun her around, his expression curious and proud at first. He saw her eyes; a frown began. He wrenched the helm from her head, causing her to stagger back again.

"You!" he cried out in a fury. "What in God's name were you doing? Who allowed this? Where is Igrainia— where is Liam?"

She might well have fallen if she hadn't backed into a man. Magnus. His great size behind her allowed her to remain standing.

She didn't get a chance to answer at first because Peter

had come forward, amazed and furious as well. "Igrainia made the arrangement with the English, and it was Liam to have gone out to fight the man-to-man combat!" he claimed.

Jamie was suddenly in front of her, shouting again. "You fool! You were nearly trampled beneath that horse, axed to death. Your brain might have spattered all over the earth from that mace. They intended to ride you down all the time . . . Where the hell is Liam?"

She was, by then, shaking so hard that no words would escape her lips.

"Where?" he raged again.

She couldn't answer, and he was in such a fury that he didn't seem to realize that the clasp of his hand, now at her throat, would simply further her inability to speak. Elizabeth raced up behind him then.

"In the dungeons. Jamie, in the dungeons!"

He released Christina, shoving her back toward Magnus.

"Get her out of my sight!" he said softly, and turned, heading for the keep.

Though she found herself up the stairs and in the tower with more speed than she had thought possible, she wasn't thrown down and left.

Nor did she actually walk. Despite her weight and size in the mail and armor, Magnus picked her up without difficulty, and when he set her down, he was already yelling for Berlinda. She was quickly shed of the mail, and only then did Magnus leave her, telling Berlinda that he'd see to it that Garth brought a tub of very hot water, because the lady might not realize it as yet, but she was going to be in severe pain.

When he was gone, Berlinda became a tyrant, tearing off clothing that Christina hadn't realized had torn and shredded in many places during the fight. She was shivering in a towel, forced to listen to Berlinda's list of her scratches and bruises, when the tub came.

She had to admit to sheer delight when she settled her worn and abused flesh into the steaming water. She was certain, too, that Magnus had cared only for her comfort—even if Jamie hadn't—because she knew her muscles would be knotted miserably if not for the steam and heat.

She eased her head back, sank beneath the water, came up again, glad just to sit and steam. She closed her eyes, aware of Jamie's almost insane fury, and yet nearly equally angry herself.

Her plan had worked. Steven, loin, and the others the English had swept up as vulnerable prey—and brutalized!— were safe in the castle. She was alive. It had worked, and surely, in war, that was what had to matter.

The door burst open with a thundering sound that was terrible. Christina pressed her fingers into the metal of the tub, bracing, certain it was Jamie.

But it was not.

Igrainia came striding toward her, eyes narrowed, features tense. For a moment, Christina thought that she would strike her.

She didn't. But the words that tumbled from her lips were almost as painful as a blow. "You have been welcomed here, treated like family, or a friend, and you locked me in my own dungeons! Well, Lady Christina, you can be assured that you will have a taste of them now yourself. You fool, you idiot—you were nearly killed out there!"

Christina gripped the tub hard, lashing back. "I stood my own!"

"And Liam could have fought that battle, or Peter, or any one of a number of men better suited to bring down such an enemy."

"You wouldn't listen to me!"

"You have no say here."

"Why are you so angry? I am alive, and they're alive, and—"

"And only because Jamie and his men reached the woods in time to give numbers to the men remaining at the castle! They've been right all along, you will do anything, defy anyone, to reach your own ends!"

With that she turned, leaving the room in a second sweep of fury. Shaking, Christina eased down into the tub.

When Jamie did come, it was not with a burst of thunder, or a speed like the wind. He walked into the room, eyes deadly as he came around to the mantel, staring at her with ice and fire in his gaze. "You are the biggest fool I have ever met. The most dangerous. And the most cunning, deceitful, reckless, ruthless, and careless."

She had already tried the argument that what she had done had worked. She looked down at the water, bit her lip, then said simply, "I did what I had to do."

He walked to the tub, hunkered down, and drew up her chin without so much as a hint of mercy or gentleness.

"Fine. Then you'll understand that I intend to do what I have to do as well."

That was all. He walked out of the room. The door slammed, and she heard the bolt slide.

Only Berlinda tended to her that night, but she, at least, was kind, and her touch was gentle. She was concerned with Christina, working a salve into her muscles, seeing that she ate, drank. Her concern for her health was almost overwhelming.

Christina was touched until Berlinda said, "Do you realize that you risked not only your own life, but that of your child?"

It seemed there was only one answer she could give that meant anything to anyone anymore.

"I did what I had to do," she repeated.

Berlinda sighed with deep regret. "More blankets, if you're cold. We'll bring another bath tomorrow. I know that you and Elizabeth have played with arms in the courtyard, but the men say you've never felt a pain such as you'll feel in the morning. You must be careful, very careful now. To bed with you, and stay down, no rising tonight, no pacing!"

Clean, railed against, and oddly pampered as well, she found herself in bed. And glad of the comfort.

And aware that Jamie was back at Langley but—he would not come that night.

It was doubtful that he would ever come again.

She closed her eyes. Steven slept somewhere in the castle. And Ioin was alive as well.

She had done what she had to do.

As Berlinda had promised, she spent the next morning soaking again, and she had to admit to being grateful, as she could barely lift her arms or turn her neck. The determined woman made her get back into bed again after the bath, and she was surprised to sleep again, and be startled when she found that the woman was at her side, waking her.

"You're to come down, allowed to see your brother for a moment, my lady," she was told.

She was glad of the woman's help to dress, for she wasn't certain she could have managed on her own. She was even grateful that Berlinda gave such care brushing her hair, for that, she certainly couldn't have done.

She wasn't even sure she could make the stairs, but she was determined.

Yet when she neared the landing to the hall, she froze, aware of the angry voice already thundering through the hall.

Steven's, first.

"I understand your anger; I am furious myself. But that doesn't begin to address the situation. You know that I'd never have approved my sister's rash actions! But now that I have arrived here—aye, in the sorry state I'm in!—I have found out that not only has she been dishonored at your hands, but is expecting your child as well. Sir! Have you the least honor, you will marry my sister!"

Then Jamie's.

And it was doubly hurtful, for she could see his face from where she stood, and the coldness that laced it. Steven sat at the table, while Jamie stood, pacing, but then he turned on his guest, striding toward Steven, and slamming his hand on the table.

"No, Steven, I will not. I have no intention of marrying. Your sister and the child will be cared for in every way, but I will not marry her, and that is that."

She stood, frozen and humiliated, wondering if she wanted to strangle the brother she had so longed to see first, or Jamie. She fought for her dignity, and her strength, and went sliding into the room as smoothly as she could.

"Steven!" She didn't run to him, as she longed to do. "My delight at seeing you is tempered only by my outrage. I have no desire, absolutely no desire, to ever—*ever!*—marry this man."

He rose, wincing, and though he was clad, she could see on his face and neck where the skin had been torn from his body in the punishment inflicted upon him so gleefully by the English cavalrymen under Rowan's command.

"We're not speaking about anyone's desire here, Christina, but about the situation!"

"I'm telling you—"

"For once in your life, Christina, you'll listen to me."

"She's incapable of listening to anyone," Jamie snapped.

Steven turned on her with anger as well. "After that foolish deed—"

"Foolish deed!" she cried incredulously, finding that her strength was failing her again, and sinking into one of the chairs. "Isn't there anyone here grateful to be alive?"

Steven held still for a moment, walked to her and said more gently, "Not at that kind of cost, Christina. You were nearly killed. You would have been killed . . . if help hadn't arrived on time."

"Forgive me for loathing the sight of seeing you and the others tortured."

Her brother touched her cheek. It had been too long. She came back to her feet, in his arms.

He hugged her, carefully, not too tightly, but warmly, tenderly. "Christina!" he whispered. Then he was suddenly settling her back in the chair. "Are you expecting this man's child?"

She didn't get a chance to answer. Jamie spoke harshly.

"We've established that she is. If she doesn't lose the babe after all she's done."

"Then you must—"

"Steven, stop!" she pleaded. "It's not what I wish. Steven, you're the one who taught me to have my own mind, and you were the one to make a vow to me that I could follow my own heart—my own inclination." She didn't look at Jamie. "I will never marry him."

"Then, what—?" Steven began.

She knew that Jamie was staring at her, with that same gray ice-and-fire fury with which he had looked at her the night before. She refused to look his way. "She'll spend the following months in the tower chamber. And as I have now assured you time and time again, when the months have gone by, she'll be free to do as she chooses.''

"This is outrageous,'' Steven said indignantly.

"May I remind you that you are a guest here, too, Lord Steven?'' Jamie said coolly.

"You may put me in the dungeons, but I will still insist on my sister's honor.''

"Steven! Leave my honor be!'' she cried desperately. And she stood—no matter how eager she had been to see him, she couldn't bear the hall a moment longer. Like Jamie, she slammed her hand against the table. "I will never, never marry him!''

She didn't need an escort back to her tower room. She flew up the stairs on her own, finding strength in the tumult that raged inside her.

Someone came behind her and she spun around, crying, "Isn't anyone at all just glad that it came out all right?'' she breathed.

She was stunned to see that the person was Lauren. "I am!'' she told Christina, and she reached out for her, and the two women held one another for a very long time.

The night passed. Neither Jamie, nor anyone else, came near her after Lauren at last left at her insistence that she go to Steven.

In the morning, she was still in bed when she heard the bolt slide, and the door open. Her heart fluttered wildly despite all reason.

But it wasn't Jamie who had come; it was Igrainia.

Christina looked at her, then looked away.

"I need to talk to you,'' Igrainia said.

Christina shook her head, still not facing the woman. "Igrainia, I've told you how very sorry I am. I swear to you, I saw no other alternative. And though everyone is furious with me, I can not be unhappy myself. I am glad to have Steven back, and that dear old Lambert, or Jamie's own very fine young man, Ioin.''

''That's not why I'm here.''

''Oh?''

She was startled when Igrainia came around and sat at the foot of the bed, watching her strangely. ''You believe that I'm happy, respected here, right?''

''It's most obvious.''

''Well, it wasn't always that way. And though I was not in your position . . . it was worse in many ways. Eric believed that I was in part responsible for his wife's death. He married me because he was ordered to do so—by the king, who was furious that the English refused to return his own wife and child.''

''Igrainia, you're not only cherished by the man, but truly respected! The men consult you before any movement is made in your husband's absence.''

''But it wasn't always that way.''

''This conversation makes no sense. Jamie has sworn that he'll never marry.''

''It was something he never intended, certainly. But I believe he could be convinced.''

''I've no desire to marry a man who needs to be convinced.''

''Then . . . what? Surely, you've no wish to be returned to DeClabert. And I can promise you, Jamie will never let that child out of Scotland.''

''Then perhaps I'll have to find a way to let the child go. Lauren's father has wealth, power, and a title that demands respect. I could go to France. Maybe there is someone there who is not so covered in blood that he can't remember what it's like not to fight. Someone without so much bitterness that he is capable of . . . marriage.''

"You really think you'll find a way to let your child go?''

"And if I don't? What would I do—live as a cast-off mistress in that strange place at the base of the Highlands that Jamie remembers as his home? This was your place, Igrainia. Your home, even it had been with the husband you lost. You knew the people here, you were certainly welcomed and loved. This isn't my home, and these aren't my people. And when you think about it, why should Jamie marry me? I have nothing to offer. Hamstead Heath is not worth an army for protection. I can't bring any man riches or property or the promise of a title.''

"You can bring something far greater.''

"And that is?''

"Yourself. Your strength. Your will, and determination. And your love, because you're lying, you know, if you say you don't love him.''

"That isn't enough. He doesn't love me. And I'm sure that he can have many sons, and I might well be carrying a daughter.''

"You are stubborn!'' Igrainia accused her.

"Maybe I am more like the Scots than I knew myself,'' she said. "I am weary of humiliation. I've been told that my fate is mine to choose when the time has gone by. I will simply wait, and make my decisions when I am ready.''

"It will be a long wait, in this tower room,'' Igrainia told her.

Christina was silent for a moment. "It might have been far longer. Thank you for not deciding that I should now be confined to the dungeouns.''

"I admit—I was ready to see you so incarcerated. I was dissuaded.''

"Oh?''

"Such dampness and cold could cost you your health—
and the child."

"Oh, yes. I see."

"I wish that this were all otherwise."

"So do I."

Igrainia left her then.

And she wondered how she would endure the long days
to come.

CHAPTER 21

The woman stood outside the grand tent of Robert Bruce, alive with excitement, and unable to believe that she had been summoned before the king himself.

Yet she waited as his men-at-arms came and went, as the plans were completed for his next stage of battle. Already, a number of the troops had ridden out. Many were headed to Stirling, she knew, while others would follow the king on a different quest.

As last, she was called in. She was adept at keeping her meager belongings in beautiful condition. Her hair was full and fine and she was aware of its beauty, and kept it well combed, refusing to cover it ever with any headdress. Her greatest asset, however, was her form, and a way she had learned of walking. She made full use of both as she at last appeared before the monarch.

She frowned immediately, for the king was busy folding maps, and he barely glanced up as she came in.

"You sent for me, Sire?"

"You're the woman they call Isolde?" he inquired, and he glanced up at last, looking at her, but showing no particular interest. If anything, he was impatient.

"Aye."

"You'll no longer follow this camp," he told her curtly.

"Your pardon, Sire? I've been making my way as a laundress, since my home was destroyed at Perth. I lived there with my father, an ill and aging man, who died soon after the attack." Her father had died, that was true. It hadn't been from illness. He had drunk far too much one night and the old fool had fallen into the river. Certainly, she thought, with a small pang, he had loved her, and even believed in her defense. But in truth, life was easier without him. Still, when she spoke to the king, there was a definite tone of deep sorrow and loss in her voice, along with reproach. If they had not burned and razed Perth, her father would still have a home, still be alive, and she would not be out, a young woman alone, desperate to make her way through life by following an army and taking in the men's laundry.

"You're no longer welcome to follow this army," the king repeated.

"But ... Sire? I've done nothing against your men! Against the Scots. I am loyal, deeply, to this cause!"

"Woman, it came to my attention that you purposely caused dissent in the camp, and brought two men to sword-point over your words."

She gasped. "I did not—"

"You were heard by several men, telling Count Steel about the abuse his sister had suffered, and thus he attacked Sir James Graham, and one of them, and more, might well have lain dead. I cannot afford to lose my men to such arguments. Therefore, you will leave the camp. You will neither follow my brother to his position, nor think to come behind me. I'll see that you are escorted to a village south, and I would suggest that you either settle somewhere and truly respect the freedom we seek, or cross the border, and find a home with the English. I know them well, and they can be a fine people, when not following a leader intent on bloodshed at any cost.''

He gathered his maps and started out, staring back at her for a moment. ''I mean what I say, woman. If you draw my attention again, ever, you'll rue the day, and find yourself banished to a place that is not of your own choosing.''

He was gone, impatiently calling out to one of his grooms.

Isolde stood in the tent and felt again an overwhelming fury, and a sense of rejection that instilled a deep and instant hatred in her heart.

If she had simply ignored the rebuff of the Scotsman, Sir James . . .

But that had touched her pride, and she'd been compelled to her revenge, when the opportunity had presented itself.

And now . . .

She had done well at the encampment. Sir James had not been the only strong knight.

She was now banished completely. She stood there and felt a loathing for the king of the Scots that was so keen, she was tempted to snatch up a dagger and end the war once and for all for Edward II.

She was far too fond of life.

And so she turned, her hatred for the king, and his man, Sir James, growing with every breath that she took.

They made good use of the tunnel in the days to come, keeping the bridge drawn and the gates locked at all times, though it had appeared that the English had suffered heavy losses and retreated. Among their own company, there had been no deaths, but seven injuries, from minor slashes that needed just a few stitches to broken bones that would take months to heal.

DeClabert's men, at the end, had deserted their dead. By the second morning, despite the cool spring temperatures, the air was growing rancid, and a stiff breeze would bring the stench straight over the castle walls. But the men who went out by the tunnel returned by the gate, assuring those at the walls that the enemy had indeed departed from the encampment in the forest. Therefore, they came out en masse to bury the dead, twenty-nine in number, a large part of the attacking party, Jamie was certain, despite the finery of their horses, trappings, and weaponry.

Eric and his men arrived just three days behind Jamie, and knew already what had taken place, since a messenger had been sent to inform him. At his return, the tunnel was once again resealed, the fortifications studiously gone over for any fault or weakness, and the men and the takings counted and assessed. Langley must not be left without sound defenses. DeClabert's attack could not have been successful, but it still gave the castle's holders pause, for it was apparent that Langley, like any other great fortress, without apparent weakness, could fall from within.

Jamie had not enjoyed much sleep since his return. He had not seen fit to turn the wife of one of his finest men and her newborn from his room at Langley, and his temper had been such that he'd been afraid of his own anger in returning to the tower room. Nor would he have been welcomed, he was certain. He'd taken to a small garret above the stables, and though he had spent many a night upon the ground with his men, he found that at Langley, he was irritated by the snores of the men quartered in the rooms around him.

Neither had his evenings been comfortable, for the hall

was filled with men, along with Igrainia, some of the wives of the other men, the Lady Lauren, and now, Count Steven. Christina was conspicuously absent, but Igrainia remained as angry as her husband, brother-in-law, and even Steven, though Steven was as uncomfortable as he under the circumstances. He had given leave for Christina to be visited in her tower at any time by her family, but her argument with her brother was apparently a continuing one, for though Lauren spent hours in the tower, Steven had a tendency not to stay as long. Jamie was aware as well that Christina remained indignant and furious herself that everyone else should be so steadfastly angry with her, convinced that her actions had saved the lives of others. She might have recognized that she had jeopardized the lives of everyone in the castle as well, not to mention her own, but if so, she didn't intend to say so.

There were times when Jamie himself wondered at the depths of his fury. He had found her skills and abilities somewhat amusing and even admirable at other times. He had not recognized, or believed, that she could actually meet a knight in full armor and bring him down. And she had done so. He was thankful that she had managed to do it, still, the risk had been too great. And he passed each day with a feeling of dread that someone would rush to him at any time and tell him that the Lady Christina was gravely ill, she had lost the child, and was in peril herself. As the days passed, and the hours were spent planning the attack he intended in all earnest against DeClabert's holding of Thistle-on-Downs, his temper began to wane, and he knew that he was most furious not because she had taken a risk with the fortress—that she hadn't foreseen—but that she must have known what a terrible chance she took with her own life, and that of the child.

Others went to the tower room during those days. He did not.

He and Eric spent long hours in heated discussion regarding the coming weeks; they both knew that Eric's ability with strategy, not to mention his individual power and prowess as a knight, would be invaluable in such an attack. But whether or not it was safe to leave Langley in any hands other than their own was a deeply nagging concern. The farther they came from the danger offered by DeClabert, the sounder sense it seemed to make for Eric to join the raid. And still, they both felt the unease.

Lauren, when he saw her, continued to be earnestly pleasant and polite. His relationship with Steven became polite, but curt, and he was certain that Christina's own words to Steven were all that kept him at bay from harping upon his sister's fate, brought about by his attack on Hamstead Heath. Apparently, however, Christina had found some words to convince her brother that whatever her relationship with Jamie, it had been on her terms.

Just as her future would remain on her terms.

He was startled then, when they had still been at Langley less than a week, Steven made a point of seeking him out alone one evening in the hall, when Eric had just departed, and before the place would fill for the evening repast.

It had seemed an especially long and tedious day, and Steven's appearance created an instant weariness in him. He warned him quickly, "I am not in a frame of mind, Lord Steven, to discuss your sister at this time."

"I am not in a frame of power, Sir James, to insist that you do," Steven told him.

Jamie nodded. "Then what is that you wish to speak about?"

"Two things. First, Lauren and I have been duly and legally betrothed for some time. Due to recent events, we are eager to wed here, as soon as possible. Father MacKinley has said that he would be pleased to perform the ceremony.''

"It was my understanding that you two delayed the ceremony so that her father could be present.''

"Her father will understand that we have chosen to wed without his presence. But, since, at the moment, she remains your hostage, as do I, I must seek your blessing.''

Jamie lifted his hands, shrugging. "You are more than welcome to wed in the chapel, with Father MacKinley presiding.''

Steven nodded. "I didn't think that you would object. Also ... and I admit, I've not spoken about this yet to Lauren or Christina, but, since I've not been in a tower room, and am neither deaf nor stupid, I'm aware that you intend to take a party raiding into England. Against DeClabert's fortification at Thistle-on-Downs.''

Jamie stared at him. "Aye.''

"I would ride with you.''

Jamie lifted a brow high with skepticism—and suspicion. "If you take part in a raid against such a castle, you will never be forgiven or pardoned by the king of England.''

"Well, that is a matter that might bear discussion. Edward the Second is a man who may change with the shift of the wind. If there were a reason to forgive me that fitted his personal intentions, then he would do so. But I agree that it is most unlikely.'' He watched Jamie as he spoke. "My own home will remain part of lands ravished by both parties for God knows how many years now. We're supposed to be loyal to England, but most men in the region are sympathetic toward the Scots. So the English ravage and raid the land from their garrisons as well. The King of England reprimands the commanders, but does nothing to stop them. Robert Bruce accepted me into his camp, and led me to you, without threat of violence or injury, or even a thought as to the fact that I was then a runaway, and that he could have returned me to the King of England with a suggestion for reward.''

"Robert Bruce has, upon occasion, pardoned a man— only to have the recipient of mercy turn against him once again.''

"I am not that kind of man. Nor have I turned my loyalty easily. Resentment, bitterness, and a tremendous urge for revenge do figure in. I'd not have been imprisoned if it had not been for DeClabert. He had sworn to me during my incarceration at his castle that he kept me there with the greatest regret—yet his subterfuge of friendship was quickly dropped when I was taken by him en route to Langley. His orders to his men were that I, Ioin, Lambert, and your man Thorne were to be cruelly dragged over the earth, but not killed, since we were suitable bait only while we still breathed. He was quick to assure me that I was going to die, and he would have both my sister, and my land. Therefore, I would ride against him with the greatest pleasure, offering you my sword—and it is good against most men, especially when I am in a rational frame of thought—and more. I know Thistle-on-Downs. Lambert will return with us as well— he's very bitter regarding the fact that his old master barely noted him, and relegated him to torture without a thought. What he knows about the countryside surrounding Thistle-on-Downs and the fortress itself is information that can be invaluable to you.''

"I will think about the matter,'' Jamie said.

"I would also—most humbly—suggest that you think about another matter.''

"And what is that?''

"Your own mortality, sir.''

"You don't think that every man here isn't resigned to his own death in any battle he faces?''

"Your own death; you accept it, as I have accepted the

possibility of mine at many times. That's why I'm most
anxious for my wedding, and mine is more a matter of pride.
Lauren has a father who is titled and wealthy. She might
well make a better match, were it not that we do dearly love
one another. Your father is dead; your kin are good people,
but no man cares for the fate of his offspring as himself. If
you're killed ... what then for my sister? Ah, the same
freedom you had offered her, certainly, your fellows would
see to that. But then ... what of your child? She would be
the one to care; she might well feel obliged to accept an
offer by the English king, or other nobleman or knight, in
order to see that she survived, as she'd then be responsible
for another life. If you're dead, sir, you'll have no power
whatsoever, really, over the fate of that child. Not as it
stands. But were that child to be your heir ... Whatever
rewards Robert Bruce should feel are rightfully yours would
come to your child, recognized as your legal issue."

Jamie was silent. It was a sound argument, and one which,
in his anger, he had not considered. Nor had he given much
thought to his own death in the many years gone by—after
Fiona's death, he'd been beholden to no one.

Steven apparently knew that he had spoken with reason.
"I swear again that I would be loyal to the deepest core,
and would gladly ride at your side to Thistle-on-Downs. I
can be of great service, and I know it. Please, consider my
words carefully. In fact, I beg you, as a man who would
now follow you loyally into battle, behave with the nobility
you would ask of others."

Steven inclined his head, and left the hall, not giving
Jamie a chance to respond with either anger or agreement.

Christina chafed in the confines of her room, desperate
to accept the fact that she could well face this kind of

imprisonment for a very long time, while trying to be grateful that she was not facing far worse.

And yet it wasn't less painful to realize that she was there than to accept the fact that she remained alone. She tried to tell herself that she should take heart that Steven was with them at Langley, but she was still at odds with her brother. He seemed to agree with the others that she'd had no right to risk her own life, even though his had been saved. And though she continued to insist that she had no desire to marry Jamie, she would have thought that a blind man would know that she only insisted because the man could no longer abide the sight of her.

Though others came to her, he did not.

She was aware as well that something was going on at Langley, though none of her visitors told her what. It was apparent that once again, they were preparing to ride.

Jamie and Eric were certainly going once again to serve the King of Scots. The country was far from secure. Her brother had been aware, in his captivity, of the determination of the King of France to force a peace between Edward and his barons, and certainly, once that was done, the English would raise an army to march into Scotland. It was important that Robert Bruce bring as much of the country under his control before such a time came.

So the men would ride away again. And they could be gone for months . . . years, or even forever. He might well ride away without ever seeing her again. Any man could die. But even as far as the fight went . . . once Jamie rode away, she was truly doomed to the walls of the tower. No one would ever trust her again, or offer her the least freedom. Not at Langley.

Another dusk came. She imagined the others gathered in the hall, saw Eric and Igrainia, he in golden splendor, she with her ebony hair and fair skin, and at her other side,

Jamie, the mantle with his colors over his shoulders, auburn hair gleaming in the firelight . . . serious at the next prospect of war, yet perhaps smiling, maybe even picking up his lute, entertaining the crowd with an ability to play and sing that seemed to be the only betrayal of any gentler human emotion within him. Elizabeth would be there, of course, and she could always make him smile, even though she believed that though he might feel tenderness toward her, he certainly didn't love her.

Christina was glad that Elizabeth had not suffered for her part in the affair. Jamie had suggested the dungeons for Elizabeth as well, and she had reminded him that she was kin to the Black Douglas—at which point, she had told Christina, Jamie had assured her that the Black Douglas would be among the first to hear that she was most severely reprimanded for agreeing to take part in any of Christina's plans.

"But you weren't locked away," Christina had told her, and Elizabeth had hesitated. "I'm not carrying his child."

"Perhaps . . . by the time he leaves, he will have softened somewhat in his anger," Christina had said.

"Perhaps," Elizabeth agreed.

"But you don't think so."

"He's very angry."

And so, she thought, she was doomed to find sanity within this room, at least for the long months that stretched ahead.

She was afraid that she never would. She wished that she could be in the hall.

When a tap came at her door with nightfall, she assumed it would be Berlinda or Garth, one of them bringing her solitary meal. But when she walked to the door, she was startled to find that her visitor was Ioin Douglas.

"Ioin!" she murmured. "It's good to see you!" She touched his face, carefully avoiding the line of scabs, just beginning to heal, along his left cheek, where he had been dragged through the dirt. "You're doing well?"

"Aye, well enough," he told her. "And that is why I've come."

"Aye?"

He smiled suddenly. "I'm grateful for my life. Though, of course—you should not have risked your own. And you must realize that the moment you chose your path, you did put the castle at risk. A man such as DeClabert is not going to abide by rules, even his own. Of course, as it was, the men returned in a timely fashion. If you had waited, they would have arrived as they did. And DeClabert would have been forced—"

"He might well have felt himself forced to kill the four of you before taking up his arms against the others," she said.

She was startled when someone pushed the door open from behind Ioin. The young man was propelled forward as Jamie walked in behind him.

"And he might have known that he needed their lives in order to come against us," Jamie said severely.

She backed farther into the room, wary of his presence, and trembling because of it. He was freshly bathed, smelling of soap, his auburn hair slightly damp, cheeks newly shaven. His eyes continued to hold the gray mist when he observed her.

"Might-have-beens can mean nothing now," Christina murmured. She turned to Ioin. "I'm delighted to see you, indeed, and grateful that you've acquired no more than a few scars. You've always shown me every courtesy, and I will always pray for your continued good health."

He reddened slightly. "My thanks, my lady." He glanced at Jamie. "I was sent to escort you to the hall, but it seems that my presence is no longer required. Jamie?"

"Aye, I'll see to the lady," Jamie said.

Ioin exited quickly. Jamie was watching the fire dance in the hearth. She waited for him to speak, but patience was not a virtue she had learned well.

"I'm being allowed to the hall tonight?"

"And beyond."

"For. . . what occasion?"

"Your brother's marriage."

"They are marrying tonight?"

"Aye. And they've asked that you be there."

"And you're allowing it? How extremely kind."

"So I thought."

She stood still, then realized that he was watching her as intently as he had watched the flames. "You're feeling well?"

"Exceedingly so. And you, Sir James?"

"Well, my lady. Tell me, do you feel any movement as yet?"

"Movement?" she murmured with a frown, then realized the direction of his conversation. She flushed as Ioin had done, despite herself. "No."

"No sense of illness?"

"It has passed. I feel very well, as I said."

"You're lucky that you did not lose the child, and bleed to death."

"Aye, that's right—had I done any such thing, you were avowed to kill Steven. And he is so conveniently here, beneath your power, to be killed now."

He turned away from her, heading for the door. "We should attend your brother's wedding before I find myself tempted to wind my fingers around your neck. My lady?"

She hesitated, almost afraid to pass by. She hurried to the steps, and down. The hall, however, was empty but for the servants busily arraying the table for dinner.

At the landing, Jamie took her elbow. "The chapel," he said.

He escorted her from the hall and the distance through the courtyard. Torches blazed in abundance around the chapel. It was filled, as was the surrounding courtyard. Everyone had come out, so it seemed, every shepherd, mason, laundress, artisan and farm wife within the protection of the castle. Spring flower petals were strewn everywhere. Jamie brought her through the crowd, greeting the people who called out to him as he did so. People made way for her, and she was startled when a cry of her own name went up. She turned around as a young girl called out, "Our warrior lady! God bless you, Christina!"

Startled, she inclined her head in greeting, and felt Jamie's fingers tighten on her arm. They walked down the aisle, leaving her to one side of the priest, and she realized that they were to stand as legal witnesses to the wedding. Steven, resplendent in silk and linen, awaited his bride, and Father MacKinley, in the finest of his sweeping black robes, was waiting with pleasure. Lauren came then, on the arm of Eric, who handed her over to Steven in lieu of her father, but with her father's known leave and blessing, to her betrothed, now to be her husband.

They knelt together. The solemnity of the vows began, and the mass was said. She had never seen anyone more radiant than Lauren, now her sister-in-law at last. Nor had she ever received such a hug as that given her first by Lauren, and then by her brother, who whispered that in truth, neither of them would have made it, were it not for her. Congratulations rang around the church, pipes began to play, and dancing began in the courtyard as the people awaited the newlyweds, glad of any celebration of happiness in days that had too often been filled with death and bloodshed.

She stood by her brother, suggesting that he should go

first, since so many revelers awaited him and Lauren with their garlands of flowers, and petals to be thrown.

"We're going nowhere yet, Christina," Jamie told her grimly.

She looked around and saw that many others had lingered in the chapel, Rowenna with her newborn and husband, Angus, Eric and Igrainia, Ragnor, Allen, Peter, Ioin, and many others. Elizabeth was at her side.

"What are we doing?"

"Your brother has sworn an oath of fealty to me, Christina, since, were it otherwise, we might well find ourselves at sword's length once again, and since we are battling now for the same cause, the loss of life would be foolish."

She stared at Steven in disbelief. "You're going to fight— for the Scots."

"Indeed, offer up my sword arm, my fiercest loyalty, and my greatest talents. So I believe, my wits."

"You will never again be accepted by the English peerage!" she warned him.

"I've made my choices, Christina. And I remain head of the family."

She turned around, staring at them all. "Is there to be some ceremony then? Do you avow yourself to the King of Scots, and swear to fight for Sir James here and now?"

"No, you see, Eric and his lady were kind enough to offer Lauren and me the wedding boon of our choice. He had made such an offer, and is the older of their clan. He gave the boon on his honor, and what I asked was the marriage of my sister, and to uphold his cousin's honor, naturally, and to secure the peace and loyalty between us. Sir James has agreed to his obligation. Christina, it is now your turn to take your vows."

She stared at Jamie, whose expression seemed to imply

the greatest distaste, but then, by God, the honor of *his* family would be upheld.

"Sir James and I have not discussed this!" she protested.

"There is nothing for you to discuss; I'm your guardian, and I have made the arrangements and signed the contracts," Steven said flatly.

Jamie stood in silence, his eyes and features dark, and though she had thought earlier that she would do anything rather than commit herself to the solitude and endless hours of her tower chambers, she suddenly understood exactly how Elizabeth Douglas had felt.

She felt desperate, cornered, and far too aware of their audience. She turned toward Steven, whispering furiously, "I can't marry him."

"You can, and you will. By everything holy, my lady, I will not have my sister bear a child out of wedlock."

"You don't understand at all. You've forced him into this, and he will despise me for it."

"You went willingly enough to the man, Christina. So you swore to me. And now your feelings no longer matter. There is the family honor, and another life, at stake."

Her eyes narrowed furiously. She wanted to argue that she had gone to him so eagerly because of Lauren's honor— and his life. But, of course, such an argument wouldn't have been entirely true, because she had never been required to do so.

And still . . .

It was true. At some time, he might have forgiven her for the fact that she had ridden out on the battlefield. He was never going to forgive her for this.

"You will take your place!" Steven said coldly.

Father MacKinley stepped up quickly, as if he could solve the matter by rushing through it all. "Who gives this woman, and by what right?"

Steven pulled her forward, announcing himself as her brother and guardian, and that he freely committed her into the keeping of the Scotsman, Sir James. She was pressed down to her knees, and the Latin invoked seemed nothing more than a charade. She was certain that she never spoke the words that would entangle her into a lifetime of misery but that didn't seem to matter in the least. Father MacKinley was speaking of the power invested in him by God and the Most Holy Father in Rome, and stating that they were now man and wife.

When the deed was done, Jamie, who had been at her side, was gone. There was no kiss to seal the vows. But what affection she might lack from the man to whom she was now legally bound came to her when she stepped from the chapel to the courtyard, and the cheers went up, and people came to her, catching her hands, kissing her fingertips, applauding her—congratulating her.

Before they entered the hall, she discovered that Jamie was back at her side. Propriety would be upheld. At the great table, she was at his side. His men gave speeches, wishing happiness to both sets of newlyweds; wine and ale flowed freely. He never looked at her. When the music began at the meal's end, he escorted her to the floor, but the flash of gray with which he beheld her remained as cold as a blade of ice and steel. He was glad to hand her over to Ioin when the young man asked if he might have a turn with the bride.

Eric and Igrainia appeared as doting parents, pleased with the night. Lauren and Steven could not have gazed upon one another with greater happiness. Christina discovered that she once again wanted nothing more than the solitude and confines of her tower room.

Indeed, it seemed that Jamie was intent on any pursuit other than speaking with her. He danced and laughed with

Elizabeth, Igrainia, and even Berlinda, sweeping the serving maid into a fleet-footed number that caused her to gasp and laugh along with the rest of the room. He drew into deep conversation with Eric, with Peter, with Allen. When the pipes played, he moved to the floor with Lauren.

At last, Christina decided that she was so certainly ignored that no one would notice if she made the escape to her room. Once there, she nervously sat by the fire, thinking of the nights when she had wished that he had come, no matter how unreasonable his anger.

The hour grew late. No one came to slide the bolt.

And neither did Jamie appear.

She wondered if he had asked about her state of health, ready to tell Steven there would be no reason for the wedding if she had, indeed, lost the child through her foolishness at going to battle against a knight in armor. A man.

At length, exhaustion overwhelmed her. He wasn't coming. She changed into a clean linen nightgown and curled into the bed, her eyes to the fire. The flames rose and fell in a sea of burning colors.

She slept.

And then . . . at last, she heard him arrive.

The door didn't exactly burst open, but it flew, banging against stone. It seemed to take him some time to close it after his entry.

She remained stiff and away, staring at the flames, a frown furrowing her brow as she listened. He moved to the fire, holding on to the stone mantel over the hearth for a moment. He needed to do so, she realized, to manage to release the brooch at his mantle.

He had been kilted that evening, a length of his family tartan wound around him in that manner which allowed for the garment to provide many things: clothing, warmth, and a blanket for a night spent on the field, along the road. The unwinding seemed to cause him some difficulty, as did the removal of his shoes and hose. She observed it all through narrowed eyes, feigning sleep, though to sleep through the racket would surely mean that one was, in truth, dead to the world.

She felt him crawl into the bed, and wished that she had eyes in the back of her head. She waited, thinking that at last, he must have fallen to sleep. She slowly, carefully turned, and was startled and alarmed to find him resting on an elbow, watching her.

"So, Christina . . . are you pleased?"

She inched away. "Am I pleased? Should I be? You and my brother made a contract without my participation or consent. Yet before carrying out the deed, you came to assure yourself that there was a reason for it. And now . . . after days of abuse and absence, you are suddenly here. Drunk. Am I pleased? Life could hardly have been more distasteful with DeClabert."

"Well, I had to be drunk, you know."

"To enter a room with so horrid a creature, now bound to you for life?"

"To enter a room where a woman would call herself my wife."

"No, have no fear. I will not call myself so."

"And now, you say, DeClabert holds a sudden appeal?"

She turned away from him, announcing coolly, "As I said, you're drunk."

He pulled her back. "Yes, I am. And in a very foul mood."

"You shouldn't feel obliged to be here, then. You have evidently found other sleeping arrangements, despite the fact that your own quarters have been occupied."

"Indeed, and there is the point. I have spent wretched

nights, but would not be so callous as to cast a babe in arms from his rest, and his mother's recovery. So . . . here I am.''

"Didn't Steven vacate a place tonight?"

"Steven slept with the other men upon his arrival."

"And imagine, you might have thrown him into the dungeons."

"Ah, but he's a man to be somewhat liked and admired, honest in his thoughts and emotions, whatever they might be."

"Where I am not, of course."

"Never."

"Well, then, let me be painfully honest this once. You and Steven forced this; I did not. And you are drunk, and I despise the fact that you are here, along with everything that has occurred. You are all so full of pride and yourself that you will never respect another's view, or the fact that a woman has as much right to thought and action as a man. So . . . Here you are. And I'd gladly sleep in the stables with your men, but then, I am consigned to this tower, without the authority or strength to insist that I leave it. I am tired, sober, and not in a mood to be ridiculed this evening. Perhaps you'll be so good as to let me sleep. Otherwise, you might well pass out in the middle of your own argument."

"You think that I would pass out—in the middle of anything?"

"I think that you are more argumentative and stubborn than ever, and that you are even angrier with me now for what you have done yourself. And again—drunk. A state I must admit I have not witnessed before. So . . . sleep it off, sir, as you once suggested to me."

She turned her back on him again, a mistake, for nothing was so guaranteed to goad him as an assumption that she had made her point, and won her argument.

This time, he drew her back, and the heat and weight of him lay over her, and she saw that though he might have had a great deal to drink indeed, he was not about to pass out. She was startled, as well, by the torment in his gaze, half buried by rage and heat.

"Ah, well, I didn't want a hostage, and yet I found myself with several. I certainly had no desire for a respectable mistress of good family, be that an English family. And I certainly had no desire in any way to call another woman my wife, but here I am, with a traitorous little beauty who will always cause far greater concern than happiness. But . . . here I am. And since this is the case, it suddenly dawned on me that it was pure foolishness on my case to sleep amid the snores of my men when there was no cause—I am, after all, now a married man. And then again . . . my *wife* is a creature of rare beauty, young and fair in face and form. Sharp of tongue, but women can be silenced."

"Jamie, stop."

"On our wedding night? Are you mad?"

"You had no difficulty sending me here and ignoring me before."

"Before you were my *wife?*"

"Jamie, you are *drunk.*"

"Forgive me. I still think that I can manage. Like my hostage, I believe that I can do my very best to please."

"I don't want to be pleased."

"But *I* do."

She wondered if a wedding vow, a contract on paper, could really change one. She knew that at that moment, she was in a rage, and determined to fight him, no matter what. She shoved against him with all her strength. To her amazement, he rolled, and she was able to slip from him, escaping from beneath the covers on her side of the bed.

He might have been inebriated, but he was capable of standing. He followed in her wake all too quickly.

She found herself flying across the floor, certain that the bolt couldn't be locked from the outside, not if Jamie was within.

To her amazement, they were both locked in the chamber.

"Did you think that tonight would suddenly make anyone trust you?" he asked softly, as she leaned against the secure bastion of wooden door.

"And did you think that it would make me *grateful,* or feel that I owed you in any way?"

"What you feel, my lady, doesn't matter in the least. Rage, pain—impotence. Emotions with which we are all too familiar."

He strode across the room, tall and dominant, bare flesh, muscle, and sinew, all gleaming wickedly in the firelight.

With nowhere to go, she remained straight against the wood until he reached her, leaned against it, a hand at the side of her head, strands of her hair caught beneath it. Perhaps he wasn't quite as far gone to drink as she had imagined. "Tell me, madam, can you really say that among those *feelings* you have harbored, *desire* is not one that remains?"

She returned his questioning stare, aware of the pounding of her heart, and equally, what just his nearness aroused in her blood, in the center of her being. She would always want him, she thought.

But once again, she made a valiant attempt at dignity. "Such feelings within me, sir, have been greatly damped by the cold wave of hatred that seems to wash over me each time you are near."

She pushed against the door, a hand on his chest, attempting not to throw him or use force, but merely to escape with her head high. She did so strongly, and gasped a second later.

He had not stopped her . . .

But his knee, against the door, catching her nightgown had done so. She heard the linen shredding, and felt both the coolness of the air sweeping around her, and the colorful dance of the flames of the fire.

"Sometimes, my lady, the very passions of hatred can be a powerful aphrodisiac."

She was startled when his arms came around her then with an amazing tenderness. Knuckles under her chin, he lifted her face. She felt the heat of his form, though the fullness of it remained inches away. She longed to throw herself against him—and rid the night entirely of words.

"So . . . can you tell me that desire does not remain among your *emotions,* maybe even flamed by hatred and anger?"

She met his eyes. They were like smoke, yet piercing. His presence was far too vital. She was aware of the bareness of her own flesh, and of his hand, touching her face, no more than a breath of air when it could be so powerful. His knuckles suddenly trailed down her throat, and his mouth covered hers in an overwhelming, open-mouthed kiss that both forced and seduced her own, and she felt his fingers then, forming slowly over the fullness of her breasts, cupping, stroking, streaking lower against her abdomen, and her inner thighs. She never meant to do such a thing, but she was weakened suddenly, and might have fallen, had her arms not curled around his neck.

The floor disappeared. She floated on air, in a sea of smoke gray and the passionate, fiery golds and crimsons of the flames that rose in the hearth. She never did give him an answer; she managed to rid the night of words.

And yet later, into the hours, into the colors of night and of dawn, she was glad of his persistence, for in the days gone by, she had known in her heart that there had been nothing that she had wanted more than Jamie slamming his way into the room, insisting that she be with him, no matter what the arguments of righteousness in her mind. She was glad, and anger was indeed an aphrodisiac, hate a form of the most intense passion. She could not have been more intimate with a man, more a part of him . . .

And yet so very far away.

For the words she had dispelled by night remained abandoned by the light of day. And at that time he lay some distance from her, but awake, and he knew that she lay awake as well.

And when he rose, dressed quickly and departed, he did so without speaking until he had come to the door, and tapped upon it that the bolt might be slid. And only then did he turn back.

"Your pardon, Christina. I seldom do imbibe to such excess."

CHAPTER 22

Later that morning, she was surprised to find that the door had not been bolted again after Jamie's departure.

Washed and dressed, Christina trod gingerly down the stairs. The castle was quiet. In the hall, she found Igrainia busy with an inventory, studiously making a count of goods. She saw Christina, and didn't seem alarmed or appalled that she had come down. "Good day, Christina."

"Good day." She moved toward Igrainia. "It seems very quiet in here."

"Aye, well, some of the men are still sleeping. I doubt we'll see your brother or Lauren until nightfall, if then. Those who are awake are preparing to ride again tomorrow, except, of course, for the men who will stay."

Igrainia looked far too complacent, even for a woman whose husband spent most of his days riding to war.

"Eric is staying behind, isn't he?" she asked softly.

"Aye, he is."

"And the King of Scots will allow it?"

Igrainia hesitated. "The King rides one way, his brother another. Forces are split, at the moment."

Christina walked around her, frowning. "So Jamie will ride out . . . to join Robert Bruce, or his brother?"

"Neither."

"Where is he going?"

Igrainia looked at her a long moment. "To the southeast."

"More raids into England? No . . ." she said, watching Igrainia. "Not just raids. He's leading a large-scale attack."

"Perhaps you should discuss his plans with him," Igrainia murmured, looking back at the book, a cool note in her voice, a reminder that she hadn't forgiven Christina for the hours she had spent in the dungeons.

No guard remained to keep Christina in the hall, and so she left, noting that the mid-April day was exceptionally fine and beautiful. Men and women, busy at daily tasks, moved across the courtyard. She could hear the blacksmith's hammer, and as she walked, chickens squawked and fluttered before her.

When she reached the stables, she saw that Jamie was seeing to Satan's hoof. Others were there as well, securing personal packs, making their arrangements. She walked across the hay-strewn floor to Jamie. He was aware that she had come, but he said nothing.

"Where are you riding?" she asked.

She thought he was going to ignore her at first, but he answered at last, stroking Satan's neck, and still paying her no real heed.

"England."

"So I've heard. Where in England?"

His hands landed on his hips then and his eyes met hers. "What does it matter to you?"

"Why don't you answer me?" she asked.

"We're going to take Thistle-on-Downs."

She gasped. "That's pure idiocy! The place is surrounded by sheer walls. It's moated. DeClabert has troops there at all times, men-at-arms, well trained. There is no reason to go after Thistle-on-Downs."

"Christina, no one is asking for your military expertise, or even your opinion of the enterprise."

He walked past her, heading away from the stables. She hurried after him, catching his arm. "Jamie! You're so quick to upbraid me—what you're attempting would be suicide. And though many in the borders are weary of being torn about by both factions, that is no area where the people are sympathetic to the Scots. Many are fiercely loyal to the crown of England."

He stopped, looking down at her. "We don't make our plans foolishly, Christina. We don't attempt what we cannot win. Now, leave me be."

As he started walking again, Steven came from the castle, greeting Jamie. "Jamie! If you're taking Satan, I'd like to have Zeus, if I may. There is no horse that moves so well, and no animal I would rather ride."

"Aye, I'm riding Satan. He's fully healed, and eager to be out."

Christina listened to the exchange incredulously, then raced forward between the men. "Steven, you are riding with him—*into England?*"

Steven looked at her, a quick flash of guilt touching his eyes. "Christina, I have sworn our fortunes with his."

She looked from one man to the other. "You are both insane. There is nothing to gain. What, do you think you can really tear down England? It will not happen. There will be battle after battle for you to wage right here. Steven, if you are caught making war against an English castle . . ."

"Thistle-on-Downs can be taken," Steven told her.

"Steven, do you know what you'll face if you're taken again?"

"Christina, it's none of your affair!" Jamie said angrily.

"It is my affair!" she cried. "How dare you go into such a rage over what I did—when you're planning on riding into England, just to attack Thistle-on-Downs. You two should be locked in the dungeons, cared for there, as any men with mental impairments!"

Jamie's gaze smoldered. "I warned you once, Christina. And I'll warn you again. You will not harp like a fishwife at me, and you will not, in any way, question my authority in front of those who serve me."

"Why not? When you intend to kill them all?" she whispered. She was ready to concede and withdraw, however, thinking that given time, she could think of some way to fight their folly.

Apparently, she did not do so fast enough.

A firm grasp fell upon her arm, belying the pleasant tone of Jamie's voice as he said, "You'll excuse me, Steven?"

It was really too much. Her brother and Jamie, suddenly the best of friends, and Steven not only willing to serve this man under a king he should never have been forced to honor, but to follow him on a death march.

"You can let go of me, I'm not a child," she murmured.

He did not release her.

She sighed. "I know where I am to go!"

And still, he held her tightly, led her. When they reached the tower room, she wanted to slam herself against him, beat against him in a rage.

Yet suddenly, to her own surprise, she changed her tactic.

When the door closed behind Jamie, she spoke softly. "Please! Please, Jamie, I am begging you! You must think again what you are doing. It is surely suicide, for all of you. As for Steven . . . please, Jamie."

"I have tried to dissuade your brother, Christina. But then, the man tortured him, and assured him that he intended to kill him—after he had secured you and the property. Steven has sworn an oath of loyalty. And I cannot stop him."

"Stop yourself!" she said. "What can you gain?"

"A great deal."

"At what cost?"

She was shaking, wishing badly that she could think of something to say or do to force him to change his mind. "Please! Good Lord, I don't want you to die!"

"The decision has been made," he said softly.

He turned and left. She started after him, but heard the bolt slide in the door.

He was gone, and she had created more trouble. She wouldn't be allowed to do so again.

The day was long, the same arguments Christina might have waged being spoken by the men, but with greater reasoning, and greater question.

In the great hall, Steven and the old man Lambert both began to prove their worth, giving them detailed insights into the workings of the castle. Steven, despite his incarceration, had spent his days listening, and watching all that he could from his prison.

Lambert knew every nook and cranny and room within the place.

Their force could not be too large, or they would risk giving away the element of surprise. There had to be enough men, so that they would not be overwhelmed by greater numbers.

The meetings in the hall did not pause for the meal; rather it was brought in the midst of their planning, consumed there as well. There was no thought of music as the hour grew late.

At last, they broke, all aware that they would leave by morning.

Jamie, still concentrating on all that he had learned, was deep in thought as he walked up the stairs to the tower. At the door he paused, for Ioin had fallen asleep in his chair by the bolted door. He woke the young man, sent him to his own bed, and still hesitated.

He could remember her eyes. Green fire, and passion, and pleading. And he wondered if what they attempted wasn't as mad as she said. But, of course, he thought bitterly, he was bringing her precious brother along, now, in truth, a traitor to the English king. Naturally, that was her fear.

He pushed open the door. She had fallen asleep on the rug before the fire. Her hair was fanned out in skeins of golden burnished glory. Shadow and light danced over the thin white linen of her nightgown, and she had never seemed more vulnerable, or more beautiful. He strode to stand over her, saw the moisture on her cheeks, in the sweep of her lashes.

He reached down for her, lifting her high into his arms. Her eyes lit upon his.

"Please," she whispered.

"It is the plan," he said firmly.

She laid her head against his chest. He meant to let her be. He was stunned when she turned to him, when his garments were doffed and cast aside, trembling as she pressed against him.

Wife.

He didn't want to think about it. She was like silk, sweeping over him. Each kiss, each dart of her tongue, an infusion. She moved with a grace and sensuality that caught the gold of the fire, and she was unbelievable in her passion . . .

And tempest.

And something more . . .

And still, it seemed that there weren't words that could be spoken between them. No matter what, the reproach lay between them, and the anger.

But in the morning, when he rose and dressed, and would have walked out without speaking, she called him back.

He hesitated. "Christina, there is nothing at all that you can say or do to change my purpose."

"It's not that . . ."

She rose, supremely naked and agile, hair a massive, golden cloak, and softly padded the distance to him, like a forest sprite.

And there was a look of the strangest awe on her face.

"It's moved!"

"What?"

"Feel . . . Jamie . . . feel . . ."

Subtle, but sure. His hand, laid upon her abdomen, was touched by the strangest, lightest, movement.

"It's . . . real!" she whispered.

"Surely you've known that!" he murmured, and a subtle smile teased his lips.

Then her eyes focused on his again. "Jamie, please . . ."

"Goodbye, my lady," he said firmly, and stepping back, closed the door behind him. And yet was still . . .

Because he thought he heard, once again, an echo of the soft sound of tears.

For her brother?

Or for a child she was certain might now be born not a bastard, but an orphan?

Or perhaps, for . . .

He walked down the steps, hurrying suddenly. The hour was late.

* * *

Waiting had never been such agony.

In the days that passed, she wasn't confined to the room. But Ioin had been left behind this time, and he was apparently given the stern duty of dogging her footsteps. She didn't mind; he was a good companion.

Her days were changed, however. She and Elizabeth did not wage mock battles in the courtyard or practice with arms. Neither of them ever suggested that they should.

The last blustering days of April gave way to May. Heavy rains fell, and the masons were kept busy, seeing that no damage came to the walls. On one particularly stormy night, Liam came into the hall, wanting to talk to Eric. He spoke to him quietly, he nodded, then rose. "We've visitors," he said.

They all stared at him, and he smiled, looking at Lauren.

"Raoul, Count of Altisan, has arrived," he said.

Lauren let out a glad cry. Despite the rain, they all rushed to the courtyard. Lauren's father, tall and lean, knightly and dignified, silver-haired and handsome. He greeted his daughter first, holding her gently, and was then as kind and eager to embrace Christina. He had come with a party of ten knights, fifteen foot soldiers, and servants. Garth saw to it that quarters were provided for them all as wine and a light repast were prepared for their distinguished visitor.

Christina forced herself to remain quiet and as unnoticeable as possible as Count Altisan, Eric, Igrainia, Lauren, Elizabeth, and a number of the men listened to the count's information regarding the outside world. Philip of France had been making every effort to create peace within England. "I assure you, he will make this work. He will demand that the barons who saw to the disposal of Gaveston offer a humble apology to their king. In turn, Edward will publicly forgive them, and embrace them back into his fold. It has not happened yet, and may still take some time, but it will come to be,'' the count assured them. He was still disturbed that Steven wasn't among them, but Lauren described the way that DeClabert had attacked on the very day that Steven had arrived—that he had brutally tortured the men he had set upon.

Then, haltingly, she described Christina's place in the events to follow, how Jamie and his men had made it back in time, and thus, Steven had lived. "DeClabert, however, is still alive and well. Though we don't know his whereabouts.''

"If he knows that men are racing across the countryside to attack his holdings, he is surely on his way to meet them. I can tell you this, he is not at the base at Carlisle. I'm a French nobleman, and no man at Carlisle would dare to waylay me, not when I have traveled with letters from the King of France. So I went through, and I can tell you, DeClabert is not there.''

His words were not reassuring. Christina felt that she would have had a far greater belief in the possibility of success for her brother and Jamie if DeClabert was not in residence.

He must have seen something like naked terror in his daughter's eyes, for he was quick to reassure her. "But you needn't fear. DeClabert, if he reaches his stronghold in time, will not have more men than he did here. Too many of the northern barons are still arguing with Edward. No men were spared from Carlisle.''

Eric continued to question Raoul on events in France and in London. Lauren took comfort. Christina did not. She was weary, and ached to get to bed.

Count Raoul of Altisan remained several days. He was riding to find the Scottish King's position, having messages for him from both Paris and London. Christina wasn't at all sure what Lauren had told him about her situation, but he took time to bid her a special farewell when he departed, assuring her that should she ever need him or his help, he considered himself like a father, and would indeed be there to help her, or welcome her into his home. He watched her anxiously, as if he would offer his protection then and there, taking her with him, whether she had wed a Scotsman or not. She was surprised to find herself telling him that she was glad to wait at Langley; it was where both her husband and her brother would come, when they returned.

If they returned.

She swallowed the thought; it would do her no good.

Just days after the count's departure, Igrainia went into labor. Unlike Rowenna, she was almost silent through it, and her daughter was born in a matter of hours. The child was another beauty who delighted her father no end. Christina held the newborn, marveling at the little life once again, and was the one who brought young Wulfgar to meet his baby sister, who was going to be called Anne in honor of Igrainia's mother. The midwife had a new assistant, a surprisingly beautiful young woman with dark eyes and hair who had come to Langley in the company of the Count of Altisan. She was wonderful with Igrainia during the labor. Her patterns of speech were lovely, and she read well, and was quick to entertain Wulfgar as well.

Intrigued, Christina asked her how and where she had learned to read and speak so well. "Ah, many places, you see. My father was once a landed man . . . then he earned our keep when the English seized our home by teaching many of the men-at-arms to understand the Gaelic language, and others of course, to comprehend the French of our courts. We were never wealthy . . . but landed at one time. I'd thought once that I would marry a knight and know a life of this kind of happiness myself. . . That's really little more than a memory, my lady. My position was not enough to keep me above the subjugation of our people. But then . . . you are English, aren't you?''

"Yes.''

"But given over now to the Scottish cause?''

"Given to the cause of peace,'' Christina told her.

"Ah . . . now, well, peace. Perhaps,'' Isolde said.

"I'm certain, in time . . . you will rise to the life you seek.''

Isolde smiled. "There is pleasure in helping a midwife—joy in life, when there has been so much death. When is your own child due?''

"October. Still some time away.''

"Oh, but time can pass quickly,'' Isolde said.

"Not here,'' Christina told her. "Not when you do nothing daily but wait.''

The ride through the countryside was a good two weeks, and that moving quickly, with what supplies were necessary, but no more.

Throughout the days when they moved—sixty strong, all mounted, trained, and well-armed men—certain of their numbers would scout the road before them each day, venture into farms and markets, and learn what they could about the mood of the country.

Most of the country folk were bitter. They could no longer care which power seized their homeland.

All they wanted was to be left to live. They had no lost love for Edward, or for the Scottish king either.

There was no hint that DeClabert might have returned to his holding. People were quick to assure the travelers that there was no need for DeClabert to rush to guard the fortress. It was impregnable.

Two weeks to the day from their departure from Langley, they hovered in the last great forest before Thistle-on-Downs that could shield them from the eyes of their enemies. They made camp, and surveyed the comings and goings from the castle on a daily basis. Lambert brought them to the top of a hill that encircled the valley where the castle lay, and pointed out the walls, the weapons of war, the places where the guards kept their watch.

By night, they discussed the best assault on the castle. And a division of men and arms was decided.

The night before they planned to attack, Jamie stood on the hillock and surveyed the castle and found himself wondering about DeClabert. He had known other men as intent upon their cause, as dedicated to a goal. Yet, he had to wonder about himself as well. He had first considered the plan because of Steven, a man he hadn't even known at the time. He had considered it because he had felt a cold fury at the way Steven was being held—and because of the many chances Christina had been willing to take for her brother's release.

He had not been at all surprised by DeClabert's attempts at trickery when he had arrived before the gates of Langley. He had seen men behave ignobly as well. He had to admit to finding it extreme that what DeClabert seemed to want was not the supremacy of the English; he did not ride to battle intent on the pursuit of a dream, like the Scots. He couldn't even ride with the blind desperation of his own countrymen, because DeClabert had never before suffered the loss of his property, and he had certainly not faced the murder of a loved one, as had many Scots.

He rode with a strange fanaticism. For a woman. He had betrayed a good man who might have remained loyal to the

English king, even while paying tribute to the Scots. He had dared a fortress such as Langley, and ruthlessly threatened the lives of many. For an obsession.

And yet . . .

Here Jamie was, standing on a hill deep in enemy territory, determined to tear down a stronghold.

For the same woman.

For his king, he argued.

And because, perhaps, unwittingly or no, he had made an enemy of this man, and he was certain that DeClabert would come after him, and what was rightfully his, until he was dead. Jamie still didn't even know the face of his enemy.

Still, he knew, the man must die. He had what Scotland held against the English, greater than arms and the number of men who could be sent to battle. He had been wounded, sliced to the heart. And he would never allow that kind of subjugation and brutality to be practiced upon him, or his household again. Never.

DeClabert was obsessed.

Jamie was more so. And he had the memories of the past to be his strength.

The walls of the fortress gleamed by moonlight. He turned away from them, silently treading over the damp ground. It was time to begin.

They didn't attack at the darkest hour of night, but rather by the break of dawn. Half their company crossed the moat with hooks and new-made ladders, Steven among them. Twenty-eight men silently crossed the moat at the gates, while Jamie, Ragnor, and six others delved beneath the hay in a new stolen cart, with George at the lead, crying out to the sentries that he had come across the richest feed they were likely to find that summer. The guards, seeing no more than a poor and shabby man with a rickety cart, let open the gates. When the wagon was partially through, he jumped from it, crying out, and slaying the guard who came at him in confusion. At that, the others jumped from the hay, and the men at the gates poured in, while those who had crossed the moat and scaled the walls attacked the would-be defenders upon the battlements.

DeClabert had kept a force greater than a hundred and fifty men guarding his impregnable castle.

By midmorning, with less than half that number, the attackers had seized control of the castle. A third of DeClabert's men had never had the chance to dress, or draw a weapon.

DeClabert, however, was not in residence, and his men, dourly gazing at old Lambert, were quick to point out to Jamie that he was a very powerful lord indeed, and roamed the land with cavalry, weapons, and exceptional prowess. Many then fell silent, wondering if the Scots would question them—and then slay them all.

They had no such intent. Dozens of their number had been killed in the assault, but once the garrison surrendered, the men had been ordered to throw down their weapons, and promised their lives. Steven felt a great bitterness against the place, but even he was willing to abide by the policies of Robert Bruce. Prisoners were herded from the fortification. All items of the greatest value were stripped and pillaged from the place. Men, women, children, and men-at-arms were removed, and fires were set that would gut anything standing within the walls, and hopefully weaken them. They didn't have a score of masons to dismantle the stone. And they did not dare remain long.

Since it was well into spring, the guards were stripped of their clothing and arms, but left with their lives, and the Scots quickly began their way to the northwest.

The cattle and livestock stolen were quickly delivered to

those in the lowlands who had so frequently been raided by both armies alike.

As they returned to lands that were, at least, likely to have inhabitants sympathetic to the Scottish cause, Steven shook his head as they rode, looking at Jamie. "I am astounded. The fight was far too . . . easy," he said at last. "Could it be a trap of some kind?"

"Not on DeClabert's part," Jamie assured him. "To have such a place burned to the ground? The plate, silver and gold we have relieved him of are worth quite a great sum. No man would allow such pillage on purpose."

Steven shook his head. "Aye, so . . . we've destroyed Thistle-on-Downs. But not DeClabert. And I wonder if that is why I still feel such uneasiness!"

"We'll need to be alert as we ride. Word can travel with amazing speed. If he roams the countryside . . . he may quickly hear of the devastation at Thistle-on-Downs."

Thirteen days later, they were nearly upon Langley.

It was Jamie who stopped then, a curious unease of his own seizing him. He drew the men to a halt.

"What is it?" Magnus asked, riding up to him. "George and I skirted the way from Carlisle; there are no troops."

"A feeling, Magnus. I think we should call a halt, and take a few men for a walk around the circumference of the valley."

Magnus frowned. "We're so near to home!"

"Aye, so near. Near enough that we take our time, and grave care," Jamie said. "Call George and Ragnor; we've good experience running through the trees."

Christina had thought the woman Isolde to be kind, gentle, and soft-spoken. She had liked her. So had Igrainia, who trusted her often with Wulfgar, and the new baby.

But one night, Christina grew restless in the hall, and with Liam as her ever-present guard, she wandered out in the night, glad to feel the fullness of spring coming on the air. As she stood in the yard, she noted the woman on the battlements, talking and laughing with Liam. She couldn't begin to understand why the sight disturbed her, but it did. Liam was handsome, and capable of being very charming. He was an impressive man, a seasoned knight. Perhaps Isolde was on the way to securing her own future.

That night, however, Gregory took ill. Rowenna told Christina about it, in great distress. He had been upset, certain that something was wrong at the castle. But he hadn't told her what; he had fallen into a fever.

Igrainia had a talent with herbs, and Christina helped her tend the sick man to the best of their ability. Christina heard her speaking to Eric, upset that Gregory was so ill, and that he could no longer communicate the fears he was feeling.

"It's as if he's been . . . poisoned," Igrainia said. "But we'll bring him within the keep. And let no one near him whom we don't know and trust . . . completely."

Christina was bitter to realize that she was considered among those numbers herself.

Gregory was strong; he clung to life.

And the days passed uneasily. No sign of English invaders was seen. The gates were opened by day, and the flocks were allowed to graze and feed on the fresh roots and thick grasses of the valley.

Despite Gregory's illness, it seemed that no trouble loomed on the immediate horizon. The gates opened and closed. Animals, peddlers, merchants, traveling pilgrims, came and went, allowed careful entry only by the word of Eric himself, Liam, Peter, or Allen.

The weeks passed, and Christina began to pray vehemently each night.

The time had passed . . .

The time it would take for the horsemen to reach Thistle-on-Downs.

And the time it would take to ride back into safer territory.

And soon, they would return.

If they hadn't been killed.

Almost a full four weeks had passed since the departure of the men. Christina waited by the fire in the great hall until it was very late. She had no ill feelings regarding her brother. That meant that he was well. And it had to mean that he was, indeed, on his way back to Langley.

At last she gave up the worry and waiting, and started up the stairs to her tower room. She entered, and heard the door close and bolt in her wake, and knew that Ioin would sleep just beyond the door.

As he did every night—on a few occasions, she had tapped on the door again, anxious to see that he was comfortable enough, and offer a blanket if necessary.

She walked across the room with little thought, once again pausing before the fire at her own hearth.

May had come. And now, she felt the little flutterings on almost a daily basis. She realized that her child was becoming as real to her as those two who had been born at Langley so recently, Rowenna's boy, Igrainia's little girl. The emotions Igrainia had suggested were finding a place deep in her soul. She would have never let her child go. Now, she would not have to. She had married the babe's father—a certain place was assured to her.

But at what price?

"Good evening, Christina."

She knew the voice, but she couldn't have heard it. Not here . . . not in the tower room at Langley.

She spun around. And indeed, she had heard that voice. Rowan DeClabert was there.

CHAPTER 23

Jamie, hunched low, raced back to the position where his own men waited, Ragnor at his heels, calling out to Steven.

"They're there, and there's someone within the walls, certainly unknown to Eric," he said quickly. "They've something up tonight; they're mounted and prepared to ride, once the gates are opened."

"We've got to stop them from opening the gates!" Steven said.

Ragnor straightened at Jamie's side. Jamie glanced quickly at him. "George has made it into the tunnel?"

"Aye."

"So George can get to the battlements, and stop whatever they've planned," Steven said.

"No," Jamie told him grimly. "This must end. Here, tonight. The gates will be opened, just as they plan."

* * *

She could not believe what she heard. or even what she saw.

But it was the truth. Rowan DeClabert was there, in her tower room.

He stood by the door. She could think only that he had been behind it when she had entered, and yet . . .

His mustache and beard were perfectly trimmed; his hair was sleek and shining, and every bit as neat. However, his cloak was not of his usual finery; no colors announced the honor and glory of his family. He was in a dull, mustard brown coarse wool, but it was hooded, and in such a posture and dress, he might easily pass for tinker, peddler, farmer, or smith, off about his business.

That, of course, had been the way he had entered Langley.

"Rowan," she said simply.

"Rowan? That is all. My dear lady! Though your brother might be a traitor, I had expected more from you! I've risked life and limb to rescue you, Christina."

"Then you've taken a terrible risk for nothing, my lord. I am well aware that you threatened my brother's life. I saw what you did to him, and innocent men, taken at the gates."

"Your brother is not an innocent man, Christina. He is now a flagrant traitor. And all Scotsmen are in rebellion against their rightful lord, and therefore, worthy of the most horrible death. You are too soft-hearted, Christina, and refuse to see the truth about your enemies."

"I'm afraid that I've seen the truth about those who would claim to be my countrymen and friends," Christina said. "I could never, ever, forgive you the brutality you practiced against Steven, a cruelty I witnessed myself."

"Yes, you witnessed it all! And, of course, Sir James did not—since he was supposed to be on the field of battle, waging hand-to-hand combat, but miraculously rode in from the forest. I'm well aware that it must have been you to topple Sir Thomas of Northumbria.''

"It was supposed to be you on the field against me, wasn't it, Rowan?''

"Ah, but you see, I suspected some treachery.''

"You practiced the treachery,'' Christina said. She shook her head suddenly. "None of this matters. You can kill me, you know, which would give you great satisfaction, I'm certain. But I will scream, there is a guard behind the door, and you will never leave alive.''

"Imagine!'' he said, as if it hurt and stunned. "And all I had wanted to do in truth was honor you as my wife!''

"You wanted me simply because I had no desire to be that wife,'' Christina said. "You bear no love for me.''

"But a wife must have certain virtues, Christina! Height, you see, agility, as well as beauty. And of course, a home where fine animals are bred, and of course, a dowry rich in the promise of many of those extraordinary beasts to come each year. No, I did not love you. A man does not need to love his wife. He doesn't even need to enjoy her, though I'm certain I would have found you entertaining indeed.''

"I would have loathed you from the beginning.''

"And I'd not have cared! There are far more intriguing creatures than a wife to be found who can provide all that a man needs—other than the proper stock to breed the most excellent heirs. You surely understand this, coming from Hamstead Heath.''

"I understand every second more and more just why I asked my brother never to approve a marriage with you— and why Steven agreed.''

"Well . . . my lady, alas! You were wrong to feel such

a quick loathing. I might have been generous. Patient. Even kind.''

She wondered if Ioin couldn't hear their voices from where he sat, just beyond the door.

''Rowan, I don't believe you begin to grasp the meaning of such words. I knew that I would never be more to you than a prize won, as if at a tournament. I would be what I could provide, and never someone in my own right. Indeed, you would marry, force your heirs upon a legal wife, and yes, take your real pleasure and amusement with dozens of other women. There might have been a proper young woman out there somewhere, Rowan, to provide all that you want. Your ridiculous sense of vengeance just because you were rebuffed will now rob you of everything, perhaps life itself.''

''My sense of vengeance . . .'' he murmured, then grew angry suddenly. ''My sense of humiliation, brought about by you, and your mewling, traitorous brother, who could take a stand against Edward, but not his own sister! Well, lady, now I will have you. And you will know a true sense of humiliation as well. And much more. Come, take up a cloak. It's time to leave.''

She shook her head incredulously. ''You are in the middle of a heavily fortified castle. There is a guard who sits just beyond that door.''

''Is there?''

Rowan opened the door.

It had not been bolted.

Ioin was there . . . laid across the floor.

And the woman Isolde was there as well. She smiled brilliantly at Rowan, and then at Christina. She carried something wrapped within her arms.

''We should leave, quickly,'' Isolde said.

Christina started to race to Ioin's side. DeClabert caught her by the hair at her neck, jerking her back hard.

"Now, my lady, Christina. We're leaving."

She opened her mouth, knowing that she could scream loudly enough to wake the dead.

His hand clamped hard over her mouth and he drew her back against him, hard. She struggled furiously until she heard his whisper at her ear, soft in warning.

"The woman Isolde carries a bundle precious to those of this house. She also carries a very long, very sharp, knife. If you don't fall silent instantly, the knife will slash instantly into the bundle, and you'll be very, very sorry, indeed."

Isolde lifted her arms, causing the swaddling of blankets in them to fall away. She exposed the sweetly sleeping infant who had been born just days before . . .

Anne. Eric and Igrainia's baby daughter.

Her eyes flashed quickly from the baby to Isolde.

Isolde produced her knife, and laid the flat edge against the baby's cheeks.

"I have no honor, no scruples, no morals at all, my lady," Isolde assured her.

"Come, Christina, I hate to leave bodies littering the path as we depart. I do believe that the Scots are like vermin, and should be exterminated, but . . . too many bodies lying about might hinder our escape. First . . . Isolde, if you will?"

The woman balanced her knife against the babe, and slipped her mantle from her shoulders. She had a black shawl as well, which Rowan arranged around Christina's own light tresses. Next, the garment that was easily recognized as Isolde's was draped around her shoulders.

"Now, my lady, unless you want the babe gutted here and now before your eyes . . ."

Christina wrenched free from his hold.

Isolde led. Christina followed her down the stairs, aware that DeClabert was at her back so close, she could feel the fetid heat of his breath against her nape.

Christina stopped on the second landing, turning back to Rowan. "You can still live. Slip away now. If you try to escape through the hall, you'll find that there are many men here at Langley. And they will not let you walk through the gates with me. I am ... still something of a prisoner here, and deeply mistrusted. If you would save your own life, go now."

"Keep going. And don't stop, no matter who is in the great hall. I am resigned to death, if need be. And you know that neither of us will hesitate to kill that mewling infant."

She kept walking. To her distress, the hall was empty. They went out by the main door. There were a few men in the courtyard, talking, despite the late hour. The drawbridge, however, was drawn, and the gates were closed. She didn't know how Rowan thought to escape, even by threatening Eric's newborn child.

"This is the boy?" Rowan said to Isolde.

"The daughter—the son is too old, too much of a risk," Isolde said.

Rowan stopped. "A girl is worthless! What man would die for his daughter, when he has a son and heir?"

Isolde's eyes flashed with anger. "Which of the men is it that you want? You have this babe, and you're surely blind if you haven't realized that Christina carries the other's heir."

Rowan spun her around, and she knew that he had not realized.

"I've married him," she said. "There's nothing you can do to me."

"Ah, my lady, you're ever so wrong," he assured her. "Well, then ... this will do. Give her the babe, Isolde. Christina, do not let the child wake. See to the man at the gate and the bridge. Here is where you cannot fail."

Isolde nodded. Rowan urged Christina closer to the wall, against the gate. Isolde called out softly to Liam, and went scampering up the steps.

Then disappeared on the battlements.

Christina couldn't begin to understand how there were so few men in the courtyard, and on the battlements.

"You think that Liam will open the gates and lower the bridge?"

"No. I think that he will be dead, and Isolde will carry out the task."

Christina held the baby Anne, biting her lip, aware that Rowan held the blade just inches away. There were men visible in the courtyard. And of course, soon, Igrainia would realize that the woman had not returned with her babe, and . . .

To her horror, she heard the sound of the outer gates, and the lowering of the bridge.

"What, ho, what goes on?" One of the men in the court-yard yelled.

"Go!" Rowan insisted, shoving her.

She started to move, hearing the clanking sound, yet knowing the bridge would take time. She held dead still, aware of his hold. She felt the slightest slackening, and decided she had no choice but to move. If Rowan made good their escape, there was no doubt he would kill the child.

She tore furiously toward one of the men in the courtyard, shouting desperately. Aware that Rowan had now drawn a sword and that the bridge had fallen, and that his men were probably out there, somewhere in the night, she thrust the babe into the arms of one of the men. "Call Eric! Get the gates closed!" she cried desperately.

The man's hood fell back. She saw that it was Eric. She gasped.

A hand landed on her arm, and the blade of Rowan's sword fell against her neck. Eric quickly handed the babe to the man behind him, drawing his sword. But Rowan pressed his own blade with a greater force against her, crying out, "A foot toward me, and she dies this instant!"

She saw Eric's rage—and the fact that he had no choice but to halt as she was dragged backward, while the night came alive.

Eric shouted for his horse.

On the bridge, she could hear the thunder of hoofbeats, and knew that Rowan had ordered his men into the forest again, and that he had known as well that the fortress could only fall from inside.

And somewhere along the line, he had found the woman Isolde.

Or she had found him.

Horses were coming from everywhere . . .

Those ridden by DeClabert's men, and amazingly, those ridden by the defenders, and more. They met in the courtyard, on the bridge, and beyond, in the valley.

Men were crawling up and down from the battlements. That was all she saw, for Isolde's cloak was brought low over her eyes, and she felt herself plucked up, by someone. The horse she lay over reared, she heard shouting, and they were racing out to the grasses of the valley.

Once again, the horse reared. This time, she and the rider were unseated, and she found herself upon the green grasses in the darkness of the valley at night.

"There she is—get her, quickly! Into the forest!"

A number of Rowan's men had dismounted. They were armed and coming toward her. She turned to flee, running as fast as she could.

As she did so, she saw that the courtyard itself had come

alive with a burst of light and fire. There was fighting within the walls.

And there was fighting in the great clearing of the valley, as horsemen, scores of them, came clashing down on one another. And as she ran, she nearly came flying straight into Rowan, who was horsed now, and furious that his plan had somehow failed. He stared at his men, then stared down at Christina. He looked at her a long, cold moment while the sounds of battle rose to a screeching fever in the night, seeming to surround them.

"Kill her!" he said flatly, kneeing his horse and spinning the animal around.

Christina turned, as well. There were three of them on horseback, now determined to run her down. She started to run, aware that the horses could too quickly catch her. She increased her speed, listening as they nearly came up to her. Then she stopped dead.

The horses raced on by.

They would be back. She searched the ground, wincing as she saw the severed arm of a knight, fingers still clasped around a sword. She bent down, choking as she wrenched the weapon free. And just in time, for they had come upon her. She raised the weapon, protecting herself from the first blow that would come her way. A second man leaped down from his mount, ready to bring the battle to foot. He was nearly upon her when he stopped in his tracks; he stared at her, then fell.

There was an arrow in his back.

She gasped, backtracking again, aware that the riders were coming after her now with a determination to catch her between them, crush her, cut her to ribbons. She allowed them to nearly drive their horses into one another, then sprinted to the far left of the first, turning to slash at the leg of the man closest to her. He screamed in agony as her sword found its mark. The third man whirled his steed around, forcing the animal to rear time and again as he sought to catch her beneath its hooves.

She waited until the horse was high, and tore again to her left, desperately wrenching the injured man from his animal, and taking his place. She heard a crunch, and his scream of rage and agony, as his horse fell upon his body.

Mounted now, she leaned against the animal, racing for the gates of Langley. She had nearly reached the bridge when she was stunned to see a rope fly past her . . . and around her. She reined in the horse instantly, struggling to free herself from the rope, aware that the speed with which she moved and the force of the rope would have killed her had she been dragged to the ground thus. But she couldn't free herself, and she was dragged down, struggling desperately against the hold of the rope, and the man who sat his horse, holding it, pulling her toward him, bit by bit.

She had lost her sword in her mad dash for the castle. Men were still far too engaged in their own hand-to-hand battles to note her plight.

"Closer, closer, closer!" Rowan called. "And when you reach me, I will slit your throat, so help me. . ."

"DeClabert!" The cry was like thunder in the air, rising above the crash of warhorses, the clash of swords, the screams of the injured and dying.

The movement stopped for a moment. Rowan was staring across the field.

She saw that Jamie was there, atop his warhorse Satan, in his colors, his weapon, already dripping blood, in his hand.

DeClabert pulled at her harder.

Jamie bore down across the field.

In the end, Rowan relaxed his grip on her in time to come to his own defense. He drew his sword as Jamie thundered upon him, and they met with a deafening clash of steel, withdrew, met, withdrew, and met. Christina stumbled backward, aware that she was still on a field of battle, that her death had been ordered. She frantically searched the ground again for another sword, found one, and raised her head just in time to duck and strike back when a rider moved upon her.

She looked up; Rowan and Jamie had clashed once again, and the thunder of their meeting had sent them both down to the ground. They rose, and she had never seen such fury as the way which Jamie moved, clash after clash after clash . . .

Then she felt wind at her back, and found herself once again meeting the merciless blows of an armored, faceless man. She was down on her knees when someone rushed before her, bringing up his blade with a vicious twist, skewering her opponent to the ground.

"Christina!"

"Steven!"

Her brother drew her up. They turned to face more men on foot, but horses were pounding now all around them. Christina lashed out desperately, keeping her back to her brother. She forgot everything but the desperation to stay alive. Men went down.

Horses circled.

Sweat ran into her eyes.

And then she saw the man walking to her, saw his mail, his helm, his colors. She stopped, sword raised, poised.

"Christina."

She dropped the sword. Her arm ached with a fury. He

reached out for her, and she fell into his arms. A curse of fury sounded.

And there was Steven . . .

DeClabert was down. He was dead. But not to Steven. He thrust his weapon again and again, and Christina had to turn away.

The horsemen surrounding them were their own, she realized dimly. She tried to walk forward and stumbled.

And Jamie picked her up, and she let her head fall against his chest, and she couldn't even wonder how he had come to be there, she could only be glad that he was.

Someone came, leading Satan. He lifted her onto the saddle, and came up behind her. She looked into his eyes as he urged the horse toward the courtyard.

"I didn't . . . I had to go with him. He had the baby."

"It's all right now."

"How . . . how could you be there? How could you have known?"

He glanced down at her. "We returned, knowing that the men were deep in the forest again. And that—they couldn't possibly get in, unless there was a weakness. George made it to the tunnel, and though we made it appear that it had been fully walled from within, it was not. He was able to reach Eric . . . and Liam on the battlements."

"It was a woman who came in with Lauren's father," she said, frowning. "Isolde."

"I see."

"You know her?"

He looked down at her. She couldn't see his expression, for he still wore his helm.

"I knew her, yes. Like DeClabert, she wanted revenge because she had been rejected. He is dead; she will go to the king, and I can only pray he will find a place of deepest banishment for her. I have always fought for Scotland, and I have abhorred the things done by many of the English, but I have admired many as well, and understood their sense of loyalty to their own sovereign. This kind of hatred, that has nothing to do with a man's love of his country, loyalty, or honor . . . I can't understand it. But DeClabert is dead. If there was any chance that I had left him alive, Steven has seen to it that he will never draw another breath.''

''I didn't ride out fighting, you know. I picked up a sword to save my life,'' she said quietly.

''Thank God you knew how to use it,'' he said simply.

''Is it over?'' she asked.

''No,'' he said softly. ''It's not over . . . not for Scotland. But . . . as to such a menace and danger, yes. And with DeClabert's complete rout here tonight . . . well, I believe that Langley will not be a target for Edward's troops, not unless the whole of the country should fall.''

And that was all he could say at the time, for they rode over the bridge, and into the courtyard, and when he came to a halt, Igrainia, Lauren, and Elizabeth were there, ready to help her down as Jamie let her go. Eric, who had been riding among the fallen, calling his men to gather weapons, discard the dead, and see to the wounded, saw his cousin, and rode forth, and the two men dismounted to greet one another with respect and affection, then move to the matter of the aftermath of the battle together.

Igrainia held Christina's face between her hands and kissed her cheek.

''You may lock me in a dungeon any time, Christina. That monster's words were overheard! That a man would not die for his daughter! Oh, but he was mistaken. And thank God that he was such a vengeful fool, for his hatred was his downfall. Come in, come in to the hall, it will be a very long night, and your hands are frozen; we'll get you before the fire.''

She didn't wait in the hall the many hours it took the men to gather their own and the enemy wounded, dispose of the bodies, and regain complete order within the courtyard.

She was most grateful to learn that Ioin wasn't dead; Isolde had drugged him, nothing more. She had intended to seduce and stab Liam, but he had been warned, and thus her weapon had been taken from her, even as they opened the bridge—unaware that Rowan had actually been inside. Their plan had been to crush the English forces between the two factions of Langley men. It had served them well, and not even the baby Anne had been the victim Rowan had intended, because Christina had known his sense of blind cruelty, and known that he would dispatch the babe without a thought. Thus, not knowing, she had handed the baby back to her own father, who was aware and awaiting the action that was certain to come.

She was grateful as well that night for Garth and Berlinda both clucking around her as if she were the most precious person in the world. She couldn't bear the mud or the blood that spattered over her once again, and she still felt the presence of DeClabert around her. She wondered if she would ever really be able to wash the memories away.

She dried her hair before the fire, and it was while she was thus engaged that Jamie at last came up to the tower room.

He walked around behind her, taking the brush from her fingers. She was startled by the gentle touch, and his sure ability.

"Wherever I travel, among the spoils, I believe I will always be looking out for the finest brushes. It seems you are always in need," he said softly.

She didn't reply for a moment, then said, "I have ample supply now, of anything I could need."

"More ample than you know. We relieved Thistle-on-Downs of very large sums in plate and gold coin."

She shivered suddenly. "He probably never even knew that you destroyed his fortress."

"Probably not."

"You suffered no injury?"

"No," she said quickly. "And you?"

"No . . . well, a fall on the hill one night, but no one saw, and I certainly never let on. I limped to bed, and made sure I walked right come the morning."

She smiled, lowered her head, then leaped suddenly from the chair, throwing herself in his arms. His helm, plate, and armor were gone, and she felt the rough wool of his mantle against her cheek.

He held her, but drew away slightly, and she was afraid that she was receiving his kindness, rather than any explicit care.

"So now you're fighting me," she murmured softly.

He dropped the brush, and smoothed her hair from her face with both hands. "You've been fighting me, you know, from the minute we met. And the oddest thing was, of course, you could never know, but from that first instant I saw you . . . you were elegant, tall, stunning . . . and so regal, and dignified. And then, of course, the next thing I know, you're demanding to be taken hostage, and then you're insisting that your horse is your own . . . throwing yourself at my feet—while still plotting and planning behind my back, every minute of the day."

"You know I had no choice. But I'm not fighting anymore

... and I'm grateful that my brother was so wretched and forced everything, and I'm so sorry about your past, so glad that you're here . . . . so grateful that you arrived! And I'll ... do what you wish, go, stay, be here ... not be here. You don't need to fight me, when you're still taking on all of England!''

"I'm not fighting you. What I've been fighting is . . .''

He shrugged, and hesitated, then left her standing there as he walked to the mantel, looking for the right words. "I spent years after Fiona's death wondering what would have happened if she hadn't fought against Lord Andrews. The house would have been looted and razed, and the livestock slaughtered, but *she* might have lived. I had to live with the fact that she was killed because we were truly outlaws in those days, taken to the forests, following Wallace, with nothing but a dream, and Scotland herself torn over who her leader should rightfully be. The exact reason didn't really matter—the fact is that she died because of me. And still, if she hadn't fought ... she would have been assaulted, certainly, it was the nature of the man. But she might have lived.''

"You knew who attacked your home, then?'' she murmured.

"Oh, yes. I knew,'' he said. He glanced at her where she stood, and she felt a chill. "He's dead now.''

She didn't ask how the man had died; she was certain she knew.

He had died, as DeClabert had died.

He looked off into the distance for a moment, then back to where she stood. "Then you entered into my life—or I rode into yours. And right from the start, you waged such a battle. A strange one, since your sole purpose was to be taken prisoner, once your initial plan had failed. You were willing to swim across the Tay in the middle of winter to warn the English when you thought it might buy Steven's freedom. And then, you donned armor and went out to fight, when any man—or woman—in their right mind would have known that DeClabert would never keep a trust.''

She lowered her head, walking away from him, wondering why she felt she always had to make a point.

''But if a man would have ridden out, you wouldn't have been so furious. You all think that it's your right to risk your life for your dream, for your families, for the men with whom you have ridden for years. Jamie . . . I couldn't bear what I saw when the English seized Steven and the others. I knew that he would accept a challenge to hand-to-hand combat, though I didn't realize that he knew you weren't in residence, and meant to send his men against one of yours. Igrainia and Liam were so mistrustful of me, I couldn't even suggest a plan of action to them. Jamie, with my whole heart, I felt I had no choice. And . . . Jamie, don't you see, you'll fight to the bitter end, you'll die with Bruce if need be, and I understand that you feel you must, but . . . please . . . you can't condemn Fiona for the fight she waged, and . . .''

''I never condemned her. I simply couldn't bear the loss when it might have been otherwise. And I knew then that the war would be long, that we might well all perish. I didn't want to be the cause of another woman's death, nor did I ever want to feel such an agony again. And therefore, when you came into my life . . . I was determined to fight.''

She held still, staring at him. ''I swear, there is no battle here!'' she said. ''I will be whatever you want me to be. I will do whatever you want.''

''Really?'' He came back to her, reached for her, and

pulled her very gently into his arms. "I would have you be here, waiting for me, always. And ... of course, as that good hostage you once were, I would have you eager to please me. And as the wife I have now taken ... well, I would have you do nothing more than love me, as I have come to love you, no matter what war I waged with myself."

She thanked God that he held her, for his words were so surely and gently spoken that she would have fallen.

"Could you possibly love me, Christina?"

"Could I possibly?" she murmured. "I have done so for the longest time!" she whispered.

"Without the war being won. It will be long and hard as yet. I'll ride out again, and we'll both have to learn to live with the fear every time. And I won't have a real home to offer you, not until the English are expelled from Scotland at last, and we're truly free."

She shook her head. "You're so mistaken!" she said.

"Your pardon?"

"I don't care if it's in the forest, in a tent, beneath a tree, or in so fine a holding such as Langley. You have everything to offer, all that matters, Jamie. Home will be wherever it is that you come back to when you ride out, or wherever it may be that I come to meet you."

He smiled slowly, reflecting. "Well, wherever we go, come the future, we will get there on fine horses."

"The finest." She touched his cheek, still in wonder. "Daylight is coming," she murmured.

He swept her into his arms, and murmured, "No, Christina. The light came again into my life, when I met you."

Night or day ...

Exhaustion lifted away.

She was with him, and more.

She loved him, and was loved in return. And that, she

thought strangely, was a greater force than any power of arms.

With him, she knew, they had both found freedom.

And so, she was equally certain, his country would find its glory as well.

AUTHOR'S NOTE

Two kings waged war within their own realms.

In England, it was a power struggle between a furious king, and his powerful barons, convinced that their sovereign would destroy the great nation brought to glory by his father.

In Scotland, Robert Bruce continued to take every advantage of the situation in England, making war against any man who would seek to hold Scottish soil against his rule.

As so, by the summer of 1313, his forces had found a rallying success.

Roxburgh had been taken by the Black Douglas, and so Thomas Randolph, his good friend since his own capture by the man, when he had fought for the English, was determined on just so spectacular a feat. With a force of men accustomed to risk, he scaled the walls of Edinburgh Castle, and that great fortress, Scotland's pride, fell to her people.

The king rode with Angus MacDonald, bringing more of the land to his fold, but his brother, sent to lay siege to

Stirling, grew restless, and made a strange agreement of honor with the holder of that fortress, Sir Philip Mowbray. If the King of England did not resupply and reinforce him in a year, he would surrender the fortress without a single battle being fought. Robert Bruce returned from his triumphant ride to find that he could not break such a pact signed by his own brother.

And the defense of Stirling at last gave the real battle cry to the English.

Two kings knew that they must then wage a telling battle against one another.

Prince Louis, brother of King Philip of France, uncle to the queen, at last arranged a peace between Edward and his barons. They *humbly* apologized; he *graciously* forgave them.

A majority of the great, rich, and powerful peers of England answered to their king's feudal demands, sending troops to ride against the Scots, to finish them once and for all.

By spring of 1314, they had assembled.

As summer neared, they rode.

Not even in the days of the old king had such an army gathered to bring down a foe. At least two thousand five hundred heavy cavalry came, glorious in their power, array, and trappings. They came with squires, and more mounted men-at-arms, armed with swords, axes, lances, maces. There were Welsh archers, perhaps three thousand, renowned across the known world for their stunning ability with their weapons. To complete the mass army riding upon the forces of Robert Bruce, there were the common foot soldiers— fifteen thousand in number.

Robert Bruce had begun his slow rise to power with a fixed policy—never encounter the full weight and force of the English army head-on. The magnificent and daring raid of his commanders had been the strength behind his successes.

But the Scottish army waited in the forest of Torwood.

Robert Bruce's numbers nowhere compared with those of his enemies. With cavalry, foot soldiers, knights, and common men, he had gathered together five to six thousand men.

But every one of his men knew the king. Every one of them knew that he led men into battle; they knew his face, and his temper, his pride, all that he risked, and all that he had lost.

Still, Bruce must have wondered then if he should continue his policy: force his army to scatter, and disappear, and leave his enemies with no one to fight.

The English came across a beautiful green meadow on a summer day in June. And at the very start of the battle, Robert Bruce himself was seen by the Englishman Sir Henry de Bohun, wearing the finest armor, on a magnificent horse. Robert Bruce recognized the colors of the man, for it was to his family that many of the Bruce holdings had been given when stripped from him by both Edwards of England.

With de Bohun came a mighty, thunderous force, cavalry racing behind the leader, charging the Scottish ranks.

It was the king himself who rode forward to meet the challenge. And when he and de Bohun met on the field in their deadly rush it was the King of Scots who brought his axe down upon his opponent's head, and behind him, Highlanders, Lowlanders, and the whole of the great party began to roar with the glory of Robert Bruce, and they—like their king—rode into battle.

It was not a battle won in that simple clash of swords, but in two days' time, the English standard left the field. The fighting on June 23–24, 1314, became known as Bannockburn. There would be scattered fighting to come, but at long last, for the Scots, at last, the dream of freedom became a reality. Robert Bruce would spend much of his reign unifying his country, and there would be rough roads ahead, but from that time forward, Scotland belonged to her king, and to the Scottish people.

At last, as well, he had prisoners of such great import that he was able to demand the return of his wife, his daughter, his sister, and others who had been captured and held for eight long years.

In the years to come, there would be battles with the English; the old feuds among the nobility would rise anew, and true peace in the kingdom would be hard won.

But that the Scottish people were a free and separate nation was firmly established. The alliance between age-old enemies would come only through peace and politics hundreds of years later when James VI of Scotland became James I of England, and later still, when an Act of Unity was signed during the reign of his descendant, Anne, in 1715.

Robert Bruce would have many more battles to fight, both diplomatic, and upon the field. Edward II was doomed to die a horrible and gruesome death, with war waged against him by his own queen. Abdication did not save his life. He was captured, and plots were set to free him, once actually abetted by the Scottish king.

But he was captured again, and though it was done in a manner to hide the violence against him from the crowds who would see his body, he was horrendously murdered.

Robert Bruce died in June 1329, stricken with illness, surrounded by men who had followed him, fought for him, and who would carry his honor for the rest of their lives, even as they mourned their great king.

He had learned bitter lessons, fought desperately and with

power, and maintained a policy of mercy throughout his life.

But from June 1314, through his death the same month in 1329, he reigned and ruled. The great lion of Scotland, at last in his glory.

Chronology

c6000BC: Earliest peoples arrive from Europe (Stone Age): Some used stone axes to clear land.

c4500BC: Second wave of immigrants arrive (New Stone Age or Neolithic). "Grooved ware," simple forms of pottery found. They left behind important remains, perhaps most notably, their tombs and cairns.

c3500BC: Approximate date of the remarkable chambered tombs at Maes Howe, Orkney.

c3000BC: Carbon dating of the village at Skara Brae, also Orkney, showing houses built of stone, built-in beds, straw mattresses, skin spreads, kitchen utensils of bone and wood, and other more sophisticated tools.

c2500BC: "Beaker" people arrive, Neolithic people who will eventually move into the Bronze Age. Bronze Age to last until approximately 700BC.

c700BC: Iron Age begins—iron believed to have been brought by Hallstadt peoples from central Europe. Terms "Celts" now applied to these people, from the Greek *Keltoi;* they were considered by the Greeks and Romans to be barbarians. Two types of Celtic language, P-Celtic, and Q-Celtic.

c600–100BC: The earliest Celtic fortifications, including the broch, or large stone tower. Some offered fireplaces and freshwater wells. Crannogs, or island forts, were also built; these were structures often surrounded by spikes or walls of stakes. Souterrains were homes built into the earth, utilizing stone, some up to eighty feet long. The Celts become known for their warlike qualities as well as for their beautiful jewelry and colorful clothing; "trousers" are introduced by the Celts, perhaps learned from Middle Eastern societies. A rich variety of colors are used (perhaps forerunner to tartan designs) as well as long tunics, skirts, and cloaks to be held by the artistically wrought brooches.

55BC: Julius Caesar invades southern Britain.

56BC: Julius Caesar attacks again, but again, the assault does not reach Scotland.

AD43: The Roman Plautius attacks; by the late 70s AD, the Romans have come to Scottish land.

AD78–84: The Roman Agricola, newly appointed governor, born a Gaul, plans to attack the Celts. Beginning in AD80, he launches a two-pronged full-scale attack. There are no roads and he doesn't have time to build them as the Romans have done elsewhere in Britain. 30,000 Romans marched; they will be met by a like number of Caledonians. (Later to be called Picts for their custom of painting or tattooing their faces and bodies.) After the battle of Mons Grau-pius, the Roman historian Tacitus (son-in-law of Agricola) related that 10,000 Caledonians were killed, that they were defeated. However, the Romans retreat southward after orders to withdraw.

AD122:   Hadrian arrives in Britain and orders the construction of his famous wall.

AD142:   Antoninus Pius arrives with fresh troops due to continual trouble in Scotland. The Antonine Wall is built, and garrisoned for the following twenty years.

AD150–200:   The Romans suffer setbacks. An epidemic kills much of the population, and Marcus Aurelius dies, to be followed by a succession of poor rulers.

ADc208:   Severus comes to Britain and attacks in Scotland, dealing some cruel blows, but his will be the last major Roman invasion. He dies in York in AD211, and the Caledonians are then free from Roman intervention, though they will occasionally venture south to Roman holdings on raids.

AD350–400:   Saxon pirates raid from northwest Europe, forcing the Picts southward over the wall. Fierce invaders arrive from Ireland: the Scotti, a word meaning raiders. Eventually, the country will take its name from these people.

ADc400:   St. Ninian, a British Celtic bishop, builds a monastery church at Whithorn. It is known as Candida Casa. His missionaries might have pushed north as far as the Orkney islands; they were certainly responsible for bringing Christianity to much of the country.

ADc450: The Romans abandon Britain altogether. Powerful Picts invade lower Britain, and the Romanized people ask for help from Jutes, Angles, and Saxons. Scotland then basically divided among four peoples: Picts, Britons, Angles, and the Scotti of Dalriada. "Clan" life begins—the word *clann* meaning "children" in Gaelic. Family groups are kin with the most important, possibly strongest, man becoming chief of his family and extended family. As generations go by, the clans grow larger, and more powerful.

AD500–700: The Angles settle and form two kingdoms, Deira and Bernicia. Aethelfrith, king from AD593–617, wins a victory against the Scotia at Degsastan and severely crushes the Britons—who are left in a tight position between the Picts and Angles. He seizes the throne of King Edwin of Deira as well, causing bloodshed between the two kingdoms for the next fifty years, keeping the Angles busy and preventing warfare between them and their Pictish and Scottish neighbors. Fergus MacErc and his brothers, Angus and Lorne, c500, bring a fresh migration of Scotia from Ireland to Dalriada, and though the communities had been close (between Ireland and Scotland), they soon after begin to pull away. By the late 500s, St. Columba comes to Iona, creating a strong kingship there, and spreading Christianity even farther than St. Ninian. In AD685 at Nechtansmere, the Angles are severely defeated by the Picts; their king Ecgfrith is slain, and his army is half slaughtered. This prevents Scotland from becoming part of England at an early date.

AD787: The first Viking raid, according to the Anglo-Saxon chronicle. In 797, Lindisfarne is viciously attacked, and the monastery is destroyed. "From the Fury of the Northmen, deliver us, oh, Lord!" becomes a well-known cry.

AD843: Kenneth MacAlpian, son of a Scots king, who is also a descendant from Pictish kings through his maternal lineage, claims and wins the Pictish throne as well as his own. It is not an easy task as he sets forth to combine his two peoples into the country of Scotland. Soon after becoming king of the Picts and the Scotia, he moves his capital from Dunadd to Scone, and has the "Stone of Destiny" brought there, now known as the Stone of Scone. (And recently returned to Scotland.)

The savage Viking raids become one focus that will help to unite the Picts and the Scots. Despite the raids and the battles, by the tenth century, many of the Vikings are settling in Scotland. The Norse kings rule the Orkneys through powerful jarls, and they maintain various other holdings in the country, many in the Hebrides. The Vikings will become a fifth main people to make up the Scottish whole. Kenneth is followed by a number of kings that are his descendants, but not necessarily immediate heirs, nor is the Pictish system of accepting the maternal line utilized. It appears that a powerful member of the family, supported by other powerful members, comes to the throne.

AD878:   Alfred (the Great) of Wessex defeats the Danes. (They will take up residence in East Anglia and at times, rule various parts of England.)

AD1018:   Kenneth's descendent, Malcolm II, finally wins a victory over the Angles at Carham, bringing Lothian under Scottish rule. In this same year, the king of the Britons of Strathclyde dies without an heir. Duncan, Malcolm's heir, has a claim to the throne through his maternal ancestry.

AD1034:   Malcolm dies, and Duncan, his grandson, succeeds him as king of a Scotland that now includes the Pictish, Scottish, Anglo, and Briton lands, and pushes into English lands.

AD1040:   Duncan is killed by MacBeth, the Mormaer (or high official) of Moray, who claims the throne through his own ancestry, and that of his wife. Despite Shakespeare's version, he is suspected of having been a good king, and a good Christian— going on pilgrimage to Rome in AD1050.

AD1057:   MacBeth is killed by Malcolm III, Dun-
               can's son. (Malcolm had been raised in
               England.) Malcolm is known as Malcolm
               Canmore, or Ceann Mor, or Big Head.

AD1059:   Malcolm marries Ingibjorg, a Norse
               noblewoman, probably the daughter of
               Thorfinn the Mighty.

AD1066:   Harold, king of England, rushes to the
               north of his country to battle an invading
               Norse army. Harold wins the battle, only
               to rush back south, to Hastings, to meet
               another invading force.

AD1066:   William the Conqueror invades England
               and slays Harold, the Saxon king.

AD1069:   Malcolm III marries (as his second wife)
               Princess Margaret, sister to the deposed
               Edgar Atheling, the Saxon heir to the
               English throne. Soon after, he launches a
               series of raids into England, feeling justi-
               fied in that his brother-in-law has a very
               real claim to the English throne. England
               retaliates.

1071AD: Malcolm is forced to pay homage to Wil-
               liam the Conqueror at Abernathy. Despite
               the battles between them, Malcolm re-
               mains popular among the English.

AD1093:   While attacking Northumberland (some
               say to circumvent a Norman invasion),
               Malcolm is killed in ambush. Queen Mar-
               garet dies three days later. Scotland falls
               into turmoil. Malcolm's brother Donald
               Ban, raised in the Hebrides under Norse
               influence, seizes the throne and over-
               throws Norman policy for Viking.

AD1094:   William Rufus, son of William the Con-
             queror, sends Malcolm's oldest son, Dun-
             can, who has been a hostage in England,
             to overthrow his uncle, Donald. Duncan
             overthrows Donald, but is murdered him-
             self, and Donald returns to the throne.

AD1097:   Edgar, Duncan's half-brother, is sent to
             Scotland with an Anglo-Norman army,
             and Donald is chased out once again. He
             brings in many Norman knights and fami-
             lies, and makes peace with Magnus Bare-
             legs, the King of Norway, formally ceding
             to him lands in the Hebrides which has
             already been a holding for a very long
             time.

AD1107:   Edgar dies; his brother, Alexander, suc-
             ceeds him, but rules only the land between
             Forth and Spey; his younger brother,
             David, rules south of the Forth. Alexan-
             der's sister, Maud, had become the wife
             of Henry I of England, and Alexander has
             married Henry's daughter by a previous
             marriage, Sibylla. These matrimonial alli-
             ances make a very strong bond between
             the Scottish and English royal houses.

AD1124:   Alexander dies. David (also raised in Eng-
             land) inherits the throne for all Scotland.
             He is destined to rule for nearly thirty
             years, to be a powerful king who will cre-
             ate burghs, a stronger church, a number
             of towns, and introduce a sound system
             of justice. He will be a patron of arts and
             learning. Having married an heiress, he
             is also an English noble, being Earl of

Northampton and Huntington, and Prince of Cumbria. He brings feudalism to Scotland, and many friends, including de Brus, whose descendants will include Robert Bruce, fitzAllen, who will become High Steward—and, of course, a man named Sir William Graham.

AD1153: Death of David I. Malcolm IV, known as Malcolm the Maiden, becomes king. He is a boy of eleven.

AD1154: Henry Plantagenet (Henry II) becomes king in England. Forces Malcolm to return Northumbria to England.

AD1165: Malcolm dies and is succeeded by his brother, William the Lion. William forms what will be known as the Auld Alliance with France.

AD1174: William invades England. The Scots are heavily defeated; William is taken prisoner and must sign the Treaty of Falaise. Scotland falls under feudal subjugation to England.

AD1189: Richard Coeur de Lion (Plantagenet, Henry's son) now king of England, renounces his feudal superiority over Scotland for 10,000 marks.

AD1192: The Scottish Church is released from English supremacy by Pope Celestine III. More than a hundred years peace between England and Scotland begins.

AD1214: William the Lion dies. Succeeded by Alexander II, his son.

AD1238: As Alexander is currently without a son, a parliament allegedly declares Robert

Bruce (grandfather of the future king) nearest male relative and heir to the throne. The king, however, fathers a son. (Sets a legal precedent for the Bruces to claim the throne at the death of the Maid of Norway.)

AD1249: Death of Alexander II. Ascension of Alexander III, age seven, to the throne. (He will eventually marry Margaret, sister of the king of England, and during his lifetime, there will be peaceful relations with England.)

AD1263: Alexander III continues his father's pursuit of the Northern Isles, whose leaders give their loyalty to Norway. King Haakon raises a fleet against him. Alexander buys him off until October, when the fierce weather causes their fleet to fall apart at the Battle of Largs. Haakon's successor, Magnus, signs a treaty wherein the isles fall under the dominion of the Scottish king. The Orkneys and Shetlands remain under Norse rule for the time being.

ADc1270: William Wallace born.

AD1272: Edward I (Plantagenet) becomes king of England.

AD1277–1284: Edward pummels Wales. Prince Llywelyn is killed; his brother Dafyd is taken prisoner and suffers the fate of traitors. In 1284, the Statute of Wales is issued, transferring the principality to "our proper dominion," united and annexed to England.

AD1283: Alexander's daughter, Margaret, marries the King of Norway.

AD1284: Alexander obtains from his magnates an agreement to accept his granddaughter, Margaret the Maid of Norway as his heiress.

AD1286: Death of Alexander III. The Maid of Norway, a small child, is accepted as his heiress. Soon after the king's death, Edward of England suggests a marriage treaty between the Maid and his son, Edward.

AD1290: The Maid of Norway dies. With the number of Scottish claimants to the throne, the Bishop of St. Andrews writes to Edward, suggesting he help arbitrate among the contenders.

AD1291: Edward tells his council he has it in his mind to "bring under his dominion the king and the realm of Scotland."

AD1292: November. Edward chooses John Balliol as king of Scotland in the great hall at Berwick. Edward loses no time in making Scotland a vassal of England; King John, he claims, owes fealty to him.

AD1294: The Welsh, led by Madog ap Llywelyn, rise for a final time against Edward.

AD1295: Edward has put down the Welsh, and the principality is his.

AD1296: Not even King John can tolerate the English king's demands that Scotland help him finance his war against France (ancient ally of the Scots). John rises against Northern England; Edward retaliates with

brutal savagery at Berwick. King John is
forced to abdicate and is taken prisoner.
The king of England demands that the barons and landowners of Scotland sign an
oath of fealty to him; this becomes known
as the Ragman Roll. Among those who
sign are the Bruces, who, at this time, give
their loyalty to the king of England.

AD1297:   September 11. Wallace and de Moray
command the Battle of Stirling Bridge, a
spectacular victory against far more powerful forces. De Moray will soon die from
the mortal wounds he receives during the
battle. But for the moment, freedom is
won. Wallace is guardian of Scotland.

AD1297–1298:   Wallace is knighted. England is invaded,
the country of Northumberland is raided
of food and supplies for Scotland's population. For ten months Wallace governs
his country, his spies informing him of the
massive English army being formed by
King Edward.

AD1298:   July 22. The Battle of Falkirk. It is later
argued that the battle might have been won
if Comyn hadn't taken his troops from the
field. The Scots suffer a brutal loss: Sir
John Graham, longtime close friend and
supporter of Wallace, is slain. The eight
remaining years of Wallace's life, as later
recorded by the historian Blind Harry, are
full of both legend and myth. Knowing
that he hasn't the army he needs to defeat
the English, Wallace turns his talent in
other directions, seeking foreign recogni-

tion and aid. In this time period, he definitely travels to France (probably twice), receives the king's friendship. The French king's favor of Wallace is documented when later, before he is executed, letters from the French king commanding that Wallace be given safe passage to Italy to put his case before the Pope are found on him. More than one historian relates the tale that he did indeed come upon the pirate Thomas de Longueville and find pardon for him. During this period, the vacillation in Scotland continues, with certain barons bowing to Edward, while others desperately cling to their dream of freedom. Violence continues during Wallace's lifetime and though he has no army, he is believed to have participated in skirmishes after his return. During the winter of 1303–1304, Edward again invades Scotland, receiving little opposition. At that time, Wallace is in the area; and many men are charged with the job of apprehending him. Relatives urge he submit, but he refuses. King Edward, however, means to give no quarter. Robert Bruce, for one, was ordered to capture Wallace, yet there is speculation that later, when the king's men were close on Wallace, it was Robert Bruce who sent him a warning to flee. Robert Bruce has learned something important from Wallace: the loyalty of the common man is one of the greatest powers in the country.

AD1304:	Many men, including Comyn and Lamberton, come to the king's peace at Strathord. The king's terms are easy, probably because he intends to besiege Stirling Castle. The king offers terms to many men as a bribe to demand the capitulation of Wallace; to his credit, Comyn, sometimes accused of being a traitor at Falkirk, scorns such a demand.
AD1305:	March. King Edward suffers a seizure. More men rally around Wallace, but, according to Harry, Robert Bruce, in England at the time, arranges to leave London and meet with Wallace on Glasgow Moor on the first night of July. Bruce does not appear. On the eighth night, Wallace is betrayed by Sir John de Menteith and his nephew, Jack Short. His faithful friend, Kerby, is killed immediately. Wallace fights with his bare hands until he is told they are completely surrounded by English troops. He is taken, and only when his hands are tied does he find out that they are not English troops, and he has been betrayed by Menteith. He is turned over to King Edward's men. He is bound on his horse for the long trip to London, surely knowing he is doomed.
AD1305:	August 22. Wallace arrives in London. August 23. Wallace is tried at Westminster. He denies to the end that he is a traitor, for he has never sworn an oath to the king of England. He is brutally executed at Smithfield, being hanged, cut

down, disemboweled, castrated, and finally, beheaded and quartered. His head was placed on a spike and carried to London Bridge. The death of this great patriot creates a legend of mammoth proportions, and in the years to come, many brave men will rally to battle, shouting his name.

AD1306:   February 10. Robert Bruce and John Comyn meet at Greyfriars Church. Comyn is murdered. Controversy remains as to whether Bruce did the deed, or if he wounded Comyn and his men completed the task of killing him. As well as fighting the English, Bruce will now have the relatives of Comyn as his enemies.

March 25. Bruce is crowned King of Scots at the Abbey of Scone. Palm Sunday, forty-eight hours after his first coronation, he is crowned again so that the ancient rites of tradition may be carried out—Isabella, sister of the Earl of Fife, married to the Earl of Buchan, Edward's ally, has arrived. To assure his succession, Bruce goes through the ceremony again, in which the golden circlet was placed upon him by Isabella, representative of the family.

May 22. King Edward knights his son, and in turn, three hundred young men eligible for the honor are knighted by their future king.

June 18. Bruce, with the men he can muster, draws up before Perth, where the Earl of Pembroke has brought his forces. Unable to take the castle by traditional means,

Bruce challenges Pembroke to an old form of chivalric battle, and the earl promised to meet him the following day. But that night the English attack the camping Scottish forces. Bruce's troops are taken unaware, shattered, and Bruce is nearly captured himself. The battle of Methven is a tragic defeat. Bruce loses many loyal men to the English king's rage and revenge.

August. Legend has it that Bruce went to the shrine of St. Fillan of Glenlochart, and there, did penance and sought absolution for his part in the death of John Comyn.

August through September. For the safety of his wife and sisters, Bruce sends them away from him with his brother Nigel. At Kildrummy Castle, they discover that the Earl of Pembroke is at Aberdeen, waiting for the Prince of Wales to attack. The ladies push northward, but are seized by allies of John Comyn. Nigel valiantly defends Kildrummy, and is only bested from treachery within when a bribed blacksmith sets fire to supplies. Nigel is executed; the blacksmith had molten English gold poured down his throat for his reward. The Bruce women will suffer years of incarceration and humiliation at the hands of their captors.

Autumn. Bruce travels north and is given aid by Christiana, widow of Duncan of Mar, mistress of the lands of Arisaig, Moidart, and Knoydart, and many of the islands. In the highlands of western Scotland, he gathers support.

AD1307: January. Bruce has gathered enough men and supplies to return to Rathlin.

January 29. Edward sends out orders for a fleet to find Bruce in the islands.

January–February. Douglas, sent ahead, ambushes English soldiers and supplies at the Castle of Arran. His attack is fierce and victory is his. But on February 7, Bruce's brothers, Thomas and Alexander, who had been mustering forces in Ireland, are ambushed by the MacDowalls of Galloway, allies of King Edward, as they entered Loch Ryan. They are subsequently hanged, drawn, and quartered. Bruce himself, however, has been awaiting word at Arran, and as his ships arrive at the mainland, he is warned that fires lit at Turnberry Castle were those of Henry Percy, holding the castle. Bruce, trained to chivalric combat, knows that he hasn't the real strength to take the castle. He and his men set silently upon the troops camped before the castle. Henry Percy, behind the walls, certain he is being overrun, gives his men no aid. Almost all are killed, and the Scots go to the mountains of Carrick with a tremendous booty in arms and supplies. Soon after, Douglas lays waste to his hereditary castle where the English have been in residence and Bruce is victorious, with his small party of men, at the battle of Glen Trool and Loudoun Hill.

AD1307:   July 11. King Edward, who had grown so
             furious with his failing commanders that
             he had mounted a horse to lead his armies
             himself, dies at the little village of Burgh-
             on-Sands, just north of Carlisle. He orders
             his son to separate his bones from his flesh,
             and carry the bones with him at the head
             of the troops, and let them remain with
             him until Scotland is beaten.
             Edward II did not comply. Edward I's
             body is left at Waltham Abbey, while
             Edward II marches on to Cumnock, after
             awaiting the arrival of his banished favor-
             ite, Piers Gaveston.
             August 28. For want of provisions, Ed-
             ward II retreats to England.

AD1308   January. Isabella, daugter of King Philip
             of France, is married to Edward II. Edward
             II continues to prefer the company of his
             favorites, especially Piers Gaveston, creat-
             ing extreme disaffection with many of his
             nobles. Robert Bruce wisely uses this time,
             subduing his dissenters in Scotland, and
             slowly bringing those who oppose him
             either to his friendship, or their destruc-
             tion. He calls parliament, and corresponds
             with foreign powers. Though they don't
             offer him the title in their letters to the
             English king, leaders address him Robert,
             King of Scotland.

AD1309–1310 Skirmishes occur, but both kings remain
             occupied with their kingdoms, and there
             is a lull in the hostilities.

AD1310   Summoned to swear fealty to the French

king for his lands there, but aware that his wife had complained to her father about his relationship with Gaveston, Edward II demands that his feudal lords follow him into battle against Scotland. The king's great army approached Biggar, but Robert Bruce, warned of the advance, took all supplies and disappeared into the forest. Edward, again lacking provisions, is forced back to Berwick, harried all along by the Scots following his progress through the woods. Once the English had retired, the king of Scotland turned to harrying the borders, invading Lothian, inflicting damage, and acquiring great gain to his coffers as he sets in practice the collecting of tributes for leaving people at peace.

AD1311   Piers Gaveston flees to Flanders.

AD1312   Early in January, he returns. Edward II is so desperate for his favorite that he attempts a negotiation with the Scottish king. Bruce doesn't trust him.

May. Piers Gaveston is taken at Scarborough Castle by the Earl of Pemberton. The Earl of Warwick seizes him from Pemberton. By order of the Earl of Lancaster, he is executed on June 19.

Edward II joins with the Earl of Pemberton, whose promise not to execute Gaveston had been dishonored by Lancaster's actions. England is torn.

AD1313   Robert Bruce, taking full advantage, begins punitive raids into England, greatly enriching himself, and once again allowing for border lords to pay tribute for a peace. Throughout the year, he begins a steadfast plan of attacking and leveling the fortresses held by English garrisons within Scotland. He enjoys a great success, often through the brilliance and daring of his commanders.

Midsummer. Edward Bruce, the king's brother, signs a pact with Sir Philip Mowbray, Edward's commander at Stirling Castle. If the fortress wasn't rescued by the English king's troops within a year, the castle would freely surrender. Robert Bruce is furious, but cannot renege on his brother's word of honor.

The treaty is a challenge to the English.

Louis, brother of the king of France, arranges a truce between Edward and his barons.

AD1314   Roxburgh falls to the Black Douglas on February 27.

Edinburgh falls to Thomas Randolph soon after.

By summer, Edward II has assembled his great army, numbering, in total, over twenty thousand men.

June 23–June 24. The Battle of Bannockburn is fought, and won by the forces of Robert Bruce.

Against incredibly superior odds, the Scots decisively win their freedom.

They will remain a sovereign nation until the Act of Union joins them to their age-old enemy, the English, under Anne, direct descendant of James VI of Scotland who came to England as James I at the death of Elizabeth I.

To this day, the blood of Robert Bruce runs through the British royal family.

For a sneak preview of Shannon Drake's
next historical novel, *The Queen's Lady,*
coming from Zebra Books in
January 2004 . . . just turn the page.

PROLOGUE
BEFORE THE FIRE

Gwenyth heard the sounds of footsteps and then the clang of metal that meant the guards were on their way, closing in on her cell.

Her time had come.

Despite the knowledge she'd had since the beginning that she was doomed, and her stalwart determination that she was going to die defiant, scornful, and with complete dignity, she felt her blood grow cold, turn to ice, and congeal within her veins.

She was terrified.

Easy to be brave before the time.

Hard now to stomach the truth of what was to come.

She closed her eyes, seeking strength.

At least she could stand on her own two feet. She would not have to be dragged out like so many pathetic souls who had been "led" into confession. Those who had seen the light of their ways—through the gentle guide of the Maiden, or thumbscrews, the rack, or any of the other methods from encouraging the accused to confess. She had stood tall at the beginning, and she was certain that she had made a mockery of her judges through her ridiculous and sarcastic "confession." She had saved the Crown a great deal of money, since the monsters who utilized such devices to draw the "truth" from the accused must he paid for their heinous work. And she had saved herself the ignominy of being dragged, broken, bleeding, and disfigured, to the stake.

Another clank of metal; footsteps, drawing closer.

She had seen what they were capable of doing.

And still . . .

She stood as straight as a ramrod, not through pride, but because the length of her had grown so cold that she was made of ice. Not for long, though. The flames would quickly thaw that chill with their own deep and deadly caress. Those flames were not intended, for the sake of severe punishment, to add torture to the poor doomed and broken souls brought to their kiss, but rather to see that such a damned creature was destroyed completely, ash to ash, dust to dust. Before the fire could lick the body, the damned were usually strangled. Usually.

When the judges were infuriated, the flames could be lit too quickly, not allowing the executioner time to quicken the end, and lessen the agony.

And there were those who believed, of course, truly believed in the Devil, and believed that witchcraft was the source of all evil in the world. They believed that mankind was weak, that Satan could come in the night, that pacts were signed in blood, and curses and spells were then cast upon the innocent. They interpreted the word of the Lord as they saw fit, and in their hearts, thought that confession could save the eternal soul, and that excruciating torture and death were the only way back into the arms of the Almighty.

Indeed, there were many who so believed, for in Scotland now, as in most of Europe, the practice of witchcraft was a capital crime.

She was not guilty of witchcraft. Nor was the accusation cast against her on any real suspicion, as it might be against so many of the other poor unfortunates so grossly persecuted. Her crime was one of loyalty, of love for a queen who, with her reckless passions, had damned them all.

The cause did not matter. Nor the sham of a trial, or the cruelty of the judgment. She was about to die.

She had sworn she would not fear her own death. And she had not been afraid for herself, or even sorry that she had fought so vociferously for what she thought right.

And yet she was sorry. For she hadn't realized all that she had traded to fight the good fight, to adhere to the right that lay within her heart. For the pain of what and whom she was leaving behind had been like a ragged, bleeding wound, her heart torn open, salt poured upon the tender flesh. Nothing done to the body could be so heinous as that which tore at her soul.

For once she was gone . . .

What might happen to Daniel?

Nothing! Before God! No evil, for surely, this was being done to silence her, and her alone; Daniel was safe. He was with those who loved him, and surely his father would allow no harm to befall him. No matter what she had done or how she had defied him.

The footsteps came again. For a moment, it was as if she were blinded. The three men who came were in a haze.

Then, for a moment, her heart took flight.

He was among them.

And surely, he could not mean for her to come to this end! Despite his anger, his warnings, his threats. In a way, she was far too like the queen she had served. Rash in speaking her mind. Blind to the dangers that could arise. And still, surely, he could not he a part of this spectacle of political injustice and machination. He had held her in his arms, he had given her a brief and shimmering glimpse of why the heart could rule the mind, how passion could destroy sanity, how love could sweep away sense . . .

They shared too much! Far too much!

And yet . . .

Men were known to betray one another as quickly as the wind shifted. For their own lives, for the sake of position and wealth, property . . . and prosperity.

And still, surely she had been mistaken. He would not be a part of this travesty.

The haze lifted. Her vision cleared.

She had not been mistaken.

In all his height and prowess and grandeur, Rowan had come. He appeared almost as a great and glimmering god, wheaten hair almost gold in the flicker of the torchlights, noble in his attire, kilted in his colors, a sweeping, fur-trimmed cape cast over his shoulders as well, adding to the great breadth of a swordsman's shoulders. He stood before her at the iron gate, surrounded by her judge and executioner, strong chiseled features grim and condemning, eyes dark as coal, disdainful. The chill she had felt reached up, and like long fingers of ice, curled around her heart. He had come, yes. But not to help her. He was not immune to the political machinations of his day. Like so many of the nobility through so many years of bloodshed, he was adept at blowing with the wind, landing upon the winning side in a battle on the field, or in the great halls of government.

She stared at him without moving, not seeing the other men. She felt the filth and dishevelment of her own state— clothing torn, crusted with the damp and dirt and mold of the dungeon cell. She refused to allow herself to falter beneath his eyes. Despite the rags that clung to her now, she remained still and regal, determined she would end it all with grace. He watched her, eyes so scorched with condemnation they appeared like stygian pits of the hell to which she would find herself cast once she had breathed her last of this life, endured the final agony of the fire.

She returned the look with abject scorn, barely aware that her jailor was reading the accusation, and the sentence and informing her that the time had come.

"Burned at the stake until dead . . . ashes cast to the wind . . ."

She didn't move; didn't blink. She remained with her head held high. She saw that Rector Martin was behind him then. They had even sent their esteemed lapdog to try to force her into abject terror and a renewed confession, even at the stake. Naturally. If she were to assure the crowd that she was indeed the Devil's pawn, guilty of all manner of horrors, then the whispers that she was innocent, a pawn in the political machine, would not rise and become shouts that stirred resistance in the length and breadth of the country.

"Lady Gwyneth MacLeod, you must confess again before the crowds, and your death will go easy! Confess and pray now, for with your deepest repentance, our great Father in Heaven may well see fit to keep you from the very bowels of hell!"

She couldn't tear her eyes from those of Rowan, still so tall among the others, still watching her with such loathing. She prayed that her own scorn showed in her eyes.

"I stand condemned, and if I speak now before the crowd, I will say that I am guilty of nothing, and I will not confess such a lie before a crowd, for then my Father in Heaven would abandon me. I go to my death, and on to Heaven, I am assured, because God knows I am innocent, and that you are using His name to rid yourselves of a political enemy.''

''Blasphemy!''

She was stunned, for it was Rowan who shouted out the word. The bars were flung open then with a terrible violence. Before she knew it, he had seized hold of her, spinning her around. His fingers were threaded brutally through her hair; she was forced to stare up into his eyes, feel the touch of his hand against her cheek.

''She mustn't speak before any crowd; she knows her soul is bound for hell, and she will only try to drag others down into Satan's rancid hole along with her!'' Rowan said, his voice deep with hatred and conviction.

He hadn't come just to bear witness to her agony, but to be a part of it!

His hand, large, the fingers long, strangely aesthetic for their calloused state, and for the fact that he was so accustomed to wielding a sword with that hand. His hand, those fingers, that once had seized, only to stroke and touch with the greatest gentleness . . .

And his eyes!

That had gazed upon her with such humor and light, the greatest amusement at first, anger at times, such deep, shattering passion at others, touching her soul, inside her body, as she could never be touched in the flesh . . .

Now nothing but darkness, brutality.

And as he stared, he moved. There was something that he held. A small glass vial. And he held it to her lips. His mouth moved, no sound coming, but she could read the words. ''Drink this, now!''

She stared at him blankly, and his mouth moved again as the vial was forced against her lips.

''For the love of God, drink this now!''

She had no choice.

The liquid went into her throat.

In an instant, the room began to spin. And she realized that there had been some mercy in him, some memory of the sweeping passions that had been, for he had given her poison to spare her the searing agony of the flames lapping against her flesh, roaring until she was nothing but ash cast into the wind . . .

"Satan's bitch! She'll make a mockery of us all before the fire!" Rowan shouted aloud. And she felt his hands then, curled around her throat.

Darkness came and she sank against him. She was grateful that she would be dead before she was consumed by the fire.

And yet . . .

In those last moments . . .

She raged. Her heart raged. Inconceivable, unbelievable, that the man whom she had come to love and trust above life itself, the man with whom she had learned the most incredible ecstacy, known paradise, should be the one to cast her at last into the pits of hell.

She saw his eyes again, blue flame, and she wondered if those fiery beacons would follow her, even unto death.

Her lips moved. "Bastard!" she told him.

"I shall meet you in hell, lady," he replied, his words deep, yet a whisper, and like the fire in his eyes, they would surely follow her into eternity.

How could she have known? How could any of them known?

For it had all begun with such power and grandeur, with such beautiful and glorious dreams. Even as the light faded, it seemed it shone again, as once it had, so long ago.

For just a taste of Shannon Drake's next
contemporary novel, *The Awakening,*
coming from Zebra in the fall of 2003 . . .
just turn the page.

PROLOGUE
THE FOG

September

There had been rain the entire time Finn Douglas skirted New York City. The Jersey Turnpike, never the easiest driving on the East Coast, was slowed to a torturous crawl, and with drivers becoming more impatient, fender benders lined the way. After crossing the Hudson, he nearly missed the sign that led to all of New England. Maine was still a hell of a long way away, and he was already exhausted.

He'd figured he might have at least made the state line that night, but it wasn't going to happen. By the time he crossed through Connecticut he realized that he was becoming a hazard to himself and everyone else on the road. At twenty, he could have stayed awake a solid forty-eight hours and not felt a desperate need for sleep. That wasn't all that long ago, and he taunted himself that at the ripe old age of twenty-eight, he should still be in decent enough shape.

Strange. Once he crossed the line into Massachusetts, he didn't feel just tired—he felt as if he were being drawn to leave the road. By the time he neared the signs that told him he was coming to the city of Boston, the urge had become a compulsion. He had to stop.

It was stupid to stop in Boston. The city lived in a state of "under construction." The roads all went one way. The congestion was terrible, and the motels, hotels, and restaurants would be pricier here than anywhere north. But still . . .

Off. Get off now. It's imperative.

It was almost as if there were a voice inside his head. That of a state trooper, he thought wearily, warning him that he would kill himself, and someone else, if he didn't rest awhile.

He should have gotten off the highway in Connecticut.

There was an exit ahead. He was somewhere in the north of the city, near the old turnoff or the airport.

He didn't even know where he was when he followed a ramp and, naturally, found himself on a one-way street.

Boston. He'd never even find a parking space.

Ah, but Boston. A great city. Food.

A drink.

Those were of the essence. He had left Louisiana during the wee hours of the morning, and driven straight, allowing himself pit stops only when the car was nearly on empty. How the hell many hours had he been driving? He was simply a fool. An idiot for taking so long to come. After he had sat home so many nights, telling himself that she would come back, that he hadn't done anything wrong, Megan would know it, and come back to him.

But she hadn't done so.

And there had been a moment of startling clarity and panic when he had realized it didn't matter that he was right.

He had allowed certain perceptions to grow because of his pride, and since he had furiously refused to deny any of those perceptions, he'd given her little choice. He lay in their bedroom, feeling the breeze from the balcony, hearing a muffled version of the cacophony that never really left the streets of New Orleans, and noting every little thing that was a piece of Megan. The beige drapes that fluttered in the night, the headboard and canopy of the large bed, the antique dressers, not yet refinished. One of her drawers remained open, and a trail of something made of silk and lace streamed from a corner of it. He could swear that he smelled her perfume.

And if he were to rise, it would be to turn on the CD player, and listen to the sound of her voice.

He had almost called, but then, he hadn't. They had exchanged too many harsh words. He could see the fall of her long blond hair in a clear picture in his mind, the passion, and the tears, in the endless blue of her eyes. Calling wouldn't do it, not after the way he had shrugged when she warned that she needed to leave, go home . . .

He was parked, he realized. He squinted. He thought he was somewhere near Little Italy, and thanked God that he somewhat knew Boston, since he had played it, though he knew almost nothing of the surrounding area— he had flown in and out before. There was a neon light blinking almost in front him. It was like a flipping miracle—he had gotten a parking space in the city of Boston right in front of a restaurant. Or a bar. Or something.

He couldn't make out the name. It wasn't just his exhaustion. There was a fog sitting over the city.

He stumbled out of the car and straightened, blinking. Wherever he was, it didn't matter. He needed something to eat, and something to drink. And no matter how desperate he had become to reach Megan in person, he was going to get some sleep, somewhere very near. Even if he paid too much for a hotel room. He'd die on the road, for sure, and take someone else with him, if he didn't get some sleep.

But first . . . food.

And a cold beer.